Texas Lonesome

Other Books by Caroline Fyffe

McCutcheon Family Series

Montana Dawn
Texas Twilight
Mail-Order Brides of the West: Evie
Mail-Order Brides of the West: Heather
Moon Over Montana
Mail-Order Brides of the West: Kathryn
Montana Snowfall
Texas Lonesome

~~~*~~~

Prairie Hearts Series

Where the Wind Blows
Before the Larkspur Blooms
West Winds of Wyoming
Under a Falling Star

~~~*~~~

Stand Alone Western Historical

Sourdough Creek

Texas Lonesome

A McCutcheon Family Novel

Book Eight

Caroline Fyffe

Edited by Pam Berehulke – Bulletproof Editing
Edited by Linda Carroll-Bradd – Lustre Editing
Cover design by Kelli Ann Morgan
Interior book design by Bob Houston eBook Formatting

Proudly Published in the United States of America

ISBN# 978-0-9861-047-5-6

About the Book

Dustin McCutcheon gets the surprise of his life when he comes face-to-face with Sidney Calhoun, the spitfire offspring of his father's worst adversary. The whole of Texas knows that McCutcheons and Calhouns just don't mix. Period. Yet Dustin is drawn to Sidney. The stirrings of attraction she brings out leave him with a serious decision to make. Break the hearts of his family—or break his own. Neither choice is palatable . . .

Texas Lonesome, book eight of the McCutcheon Family Saga, continues the story of the brave and passionate men and women of Y Knot, Montana, and Rio Wells, Texas, by *USA TODAY* Best-selling Author Caroline Fyffe.

Dedicated to my dear friend, Kathy Harrell,
for all the love and laughter

Chapter One

San Antonio, Texas, November 1886

Dustin McCutcheon shifted his weight from one hip to the other, feeling his denim trousers pull snug around his thigh. He gazed at the three choices in the palm of his hand. Which flavor would the cowhands prefer? He lifted the rectangular Fry's Chocolate Cream bar to his nose and took a deep whiff.

Sweet. His mouth watered.

The store clerk loudly cleared her throat.

Turning from the mercantile's fifteen-foot front wall where the chocolate bars were kept away from pilfering hands, he gazed down the long maple countertop. "Sorry, ma'am. Just getting an idea of which to buy."

At that, he caught sight of a young woman standing in line behind a man holding a can of lamp oil. She waited for her turn with a small boxy item in her hands, a *V* pulled down between her delicate brows.

Dustin's heart thwacked against his rib cage, causing a small cough to escape through his lips. Embarrassed, he thumped his chest with a fist and felt a silly grin pull at the corners of his mouth.

"Excuse me," he quickly said, daring another fast glance at the young woman.

The portly clerk pierced him with her cranky gaze.

"Do you have a preference?" he asked, holding up the chocolate for the clerk to see. "A favorite flavor?"

"I don't eat candy, young man!"

The woman's disdain-filled voice was meant to slice him to the quick, but it only made his smile grow. She probably thought he meant to stick a few bars into his shirt pocket when her back was turned.

Again, he glanced past the clerk to the young woman, who was now looking in his direction. He smiled and lifted one shoulder.

A stain of rose started on her neck and then colored both her creamy peach cheeks. She quickly looked away. Her toe tapped on the scarred wooden floor.

She likes me.

His sisters, Madeline and Becky, were always chattering on about men and suitors and the like. How embarrassed they got when they couldn't control a blush from coming on under an attractive man's attention. Or how they caught themselves wringing their hands, tapping their toes, or God forbid, giggling.

The signs are all there.

The clerk finished with the man and he headed out the door.

Still looking at the candy in his palm, Dustin watched surreptitiously from the corner of his eye as the young woman stepped forward and placed her item on the counter. No sign of a wedding ring.

"Will there be anything else?"

"No, just this music box, please," she answered.

"Two dollars and ten cents."

Dustin tried to pull his attention back to the chore at hand, but he had little luck. The young woman looked pleased with her purchase. He wondered if she was buying it for herself or for someone else. He liked that idea—might be nice to have a sweetheart who thought him special enough to buy him a gift. He had his family, of course, but that wasn't the same.

She withdrew several coins from her reticule and placed them in the shopkeeper's hand.

When the transaction was finished and the matron had wrapped the item in paper, he was ready when the young woman turned and stepped toward the door.

"Which do you favor, miss? Peppermint, orange, or chocolate cream? I don't dare buy a mixture. Whichever one they end up with won't be to their liking."

Her lips curved up as she paused to take his measure. "They?"

"Yes, the cowhands that work on my ranch." Well, the Rim Rock was his ranch, as well as Pa's and Chaim's—and his ma and sisters. Heck, he couldn't say all that.

She came a little closer, perusing the candy in his hand. "I prefer plain chocolate. I'm sure you won't go wrong with that." She smiled up into his face.

Her voice was that of a songbird's. Dustin thought the angels had descended from heaven.

Reaching up, her hand quivered slightly as she angled the watch pinned to her bodice to check the time.

Another good sign.

"Thank you. I'll get the plain chocolate cream on your recommendation."

"Young man," the clerk screeched. "You can't stand there all day holding the merchandise. It'll melt! Either make your purchase, or put it back."

Dustin spun. His thoughts were still on the beauty he'd discovered in the store. "I will, ma'am. Right now. I'm buying two whole boxes. Just give me a moment to—"

At the sound of the door closing, he turned around to see the back of the woman's dress as she hurried away.

He wanted to run after her, get her name, but he had an appointment in a few minutes that he couldn't miss. A friend's life depended on it. He had just enough time to finish this purchase and take the confections back to the hotel. With a couple of days left in town, he'd find her. She didn't look like a local—too soft and clean.

Yes, he'd find out who she was before he left if it was the last thing he did, or his name wasn't Dustin McCutcheon.

Brushing a thin layer of dust from the armrest of his seat, Dustin ignored the stale air and the light sheen that slicked his forehead. The temperature had to be eighty degrees in the room.

Cowboys in need of a wash and Mexican laborers packed the medium-sized San Antonio courtroom, waiting for the afternoon session to begin. Chaim, his younger brother, sat sullenly at his side, his resigned expression painful. Sounds from the busy street drifted in through the open windows on the far wall. He glanced out to see a miniature dust devil swirling down the boardwalk.

Dustin leaned close. "Cheer up, Chaim. Emmeline won't be gone for long. Before you know it, you'll be asked to cart your carcass back here to San Antonio to meet her train. She's only leaving for a month."

Chaim stared straight ahead at the empty judge's bench, the rise and fall of his chest the only indication he hadn't yet died of a broken heart. He glanced over, his eyes filled with uncertainty.

"Thirty days is twenty-nine days too long. Especially with the wedding just around the corner. Her leaving now doesn't feel right."

Spotting his brother's uncertain gaze, Dustin couldn't think of any response except to shrug. He thought her departure was strange as well, but he wouldn't make matters worse by agreeing.

His brother turned toward the front. "And now I have to spend a good portion of my last twenty-four hours she's here, sitting in this sour-smelling hellhole."

"Stop stewing. Ed needs our help. You'd want him to testify for you if the tables were turned."

Chaim nodded. "I know, I know. Still, I don't have to like it."

The door next to the judge's bench opened, and a guard walked out. Following were three scruffy-looking individuals, the type who'd hang out in dark alleys and frighten women and small children. Their legs, shackled with heavy chains that scraped on the wood floor, moved in unison. Their arms were bound at the wrists.

Next in line shuffled a relatively clean-cut fellow who looked vaguely familiar. The young man scanned the crowd for a few seconds, his light ice-blue eyes visible all the way back to where he and Chaim sat. Presumably not finding the person he was looking for, he dropped his head, causing his thick corn-colored hair to flop in his face.

Lastly, their friend Ed Felton appeared. The cowhand had been accused of a murder here in San Antonio the same evening he'd been visiting their ranch in Rio Wells. Dustin and

Chaim were present to give testimony to that fact. Another guard brought up the rear, a shotgun cradled in his arms. The uniformed men lined the five prisoners against the side wall.

As Dustin watched the proceedings with interest, enjoying the diversion he'd been given from ranching, a disheveled man rushed through the double doors that led in from the street. He kept his gaze trained on the downward-slanted aisle as he hastened to the defendant's table. There he brushed away the dust on a chair, took a seat, and set a stack of rumpled papers before him.

"I'm certainly glad he's not defending me," Dustin whispered to Chaim. "Not with Butch Halford presiding. Something about him screams overworked. Yes, sir, I'm mighty thankful I'm not in any of their boots today."

He smiled and stretched back in his chair.

Ed Felton saw him from his place in the lineup, and a look of relief passed over his face.

Dustin gave him a nod, sure his friend was good and ready to get out of that sinkhole they called a jail. A few months ago, Dustin himself had spent a night there along with his cousin John, incarcerated for busting up a restaurant. He'd been angry over losing Lily to John, and had followed them to San Antonio for the wedding—not to cause trouble.

But then he'd downed a few too many whiskeys while drowning his sorrows. All he wanted was to have a little talk with his cousin and congratulate him, or at least that was what he'd told himself.

One word led to the next, and soon he and John were throwing punches in the restaurant. They were both hauled into jail for disturbing the peace. Brandon Crawford—the sheriff of Y Knot who'd followed his sweetheart, Dustin's cousin Charity, from Montana Territory to Texas—had bailed them both out in the morning, much to their relief.

Embarrassment filled Dustin at the memory. He'd let his anger over losing Lily get the best of him, which ruined her wedding night with John. Dustin had learned his lesson the hard way, and vowed to himself to be a more patient, civil person.

And I'm working on it. Yes, indeed, he was.

He rested back into his chair, mulling over what he'd do tonight while Chaim was out to dinner with Emmeline. Maybe find a good steak, play a little poker, and see what kind of female attention he might corral.

If only the young woman in the store hadn't hurried away so quickly when he'd been distracted. Now *that* was a woman! One worth getting to know . . .

A murmur at the door stirred the predominantly male crowd, and he glanced back.

It was her! The woman. Hope still existed.

Snapping straight in his seat, Dustin barely had time to take in her tall, picturesque beauty before he heard the bailiff call out, "All rise." As he stood, he remembered that bounty of fawn-colored hair piled high on her head all too well.

She hurried forward to an empty seat in the front, ignoring the interested looks from the gawkers. The prosecuting attorney appeared and claimed the table opposite the defendant's.

Judge Halford came through the side door. A commanding presence filled the room as the man strode to the bench, his black robe billowing around him, and sat. The judge banged his gavel several times, frowning at the crowd as they took their seats amid a murmur of voices. His brow arched when his gaze landed on him and Chaim.

"Order in the court!"

Standing, the bailiff held a piece of paper before his bespectacled eyes. "Case number eighty-five, the city of San Antonio charges Spiny Ford, Luck Drummond, and Jason Jarome with illegal entry and robbery."

The prosecuting attorney stood. "On Saturday night last week, the three defendants are accused of breaking into a home at 23 China Hill Road. The owner, Javier Smith, was not at home. Eight hundred dollars' worth of gold coins were stolen from beneath the floorboards of his bedroom. Gold coins of the exact amount, split three ways, were found at each of their residences. Gerald Black saw them at midnight, hurrying away the best they could from the crime scene, with several large sacks shaped like money bags."

"Are you calling the witness?" the judge asked the prosecutor.

"No, Your Honor, he can't be found." The counselor shot a disgusted look at the three in chains. "I won't be surprised if his body turns up floating down the Blanco River, or in a shallow grave."

Judge Halford looked at the defense attorney. "Mr. Wormer, how do your clients plead?"

"Not guilty, Your Honor?"

"That sounds like a question, Mr. Wormer. Are you asking me or telling me?"

The man grasped the edge of the table. "Telling you, Your Honor."

The three accused looked amongst themselves and snickered.

Dustin would be amused if the possibility of the missing witness didn't mean the man had most likely been murdered. He leaned over to say something to Chaim, but closed his mouth at the utter devastation he saw on his brother's face.

His lovesick sibling had been in a trance since his fiancée announced she was going home for a visit. Dustin liked Emmeline Jordan well enough, he did, but to his way of thinking, she'd jumped pretty darn quickly at a chance to go home to Boston when she received the letter from her mother about her father being ill.

Texas and Boston were worlds apart—at least, that's what his cousin John had told him. John had lived there several years while he received his doctor's training. It was also where he'd met Emmeline Jordan. She'd originally come to Rio Wells to marry John, only to meet and fall in love with Chaim. Her father was indeed sick, but with gout, a condition that was not life-threatening and surely treatable. She'd promised to be back in plenty of time before the wedding planned in a month.

Right. Dustin didn't want to be skeptical, but cynicism was part of his nature, albeit a part of his nature he wanted to change. At this point, he couldn't help himself.

Tomorrow, after Emmeline departed on the nine o'clock eastbound train, Chaim would need his support more than ever. And Dustin planned to be there for him. Hopefully, once she reached Boston and got a taste of her beloved home-sweet-home, she'd still want to return to Rio Wells and become Mrs. Chaim McCutcheon.

Women!

"They were all home in their beds," Mr. Wormer, the defense attorney, went on in a small voice. He took out a handkerchief and wiped his sweaty forehead. "None of the accused went out that evening at all."

One of the said suspects sneered and discreetly jabbed his elbow into the side of another.

"Do you have a witness to corroborate that?" Judge Halford asked.

Mr. Wormer swallowed. "No, sir."

Dustin actually felt a little sorry for the defense attorney. The skinny man looked so unsure of himself.

He leaned over and whispered close to Chaim's shoulder, "Do you recognize that kid in the lineup? Seems I've seen him somewhere before."

Chaim looked at the tall young man in chains. "Seems I do, but I don't know from where. He looks familiar, but his face isn't ringing any bells."

"Do you have any defense at all?" the judge barked. Seemed his anger intensified as the room grew warmer.

From his fifth-row seat, Dustin noticed the woman in the front straighten and look over to the same fellow he'd asked Chaim about. Was she here for him?

Dustin craned his neck, but all he could see was the back of her head and a small portion of her profile. The meager glimpse he'd had when she'd rushed forward hadn't been enough. This was the first woman since losing Lily that stirred his interest. He'd like to know more about her.

Much more.

The judge slammed down his gavel. "Given that these three men have been in my courtroom on almost a weekly basis on lesser charges for the past eight months, and given that you don't have any defense worth speaking of, Mr. Wormer, and given the evidence is pretty clear even if the witness isn't here to state it, I'm sentencing them to a year in the penitentiary—if for no other reason but to get them out of San Antonio. If, indeed, Gerald Black is found dead with circumstances pointing to these three, I'll hang 'em, no more questions asked. Maybe that'll wipe the stupid grins off their faces."

A ripple of whispers went through the gathering, and the three accused snapped their mouths closed.

"They finally get what's coming to 'em!" a man in the back of the room shouted. "Two months ago, they ruined a good portion of the inventory in my store and didn't care less. I've had to close my doors because of the varmints. Good riddance! I hope they hang!"

"Order!" the judge called out.

The bailiff stood, but before he could read the next case number, he spotted the judge waving him off.

"I know what's next." The judge looked pointedly at the prosecutor, who picked up on his cue without missing a beat.

"San Antonio charges Noah Calhoun of Santa Fe, New Mexico, with disorderly conduct, fighting, and property damage."

Dustin sat forward, shock pushing a sharp breath from his lungs.

"Noah Calhoun?" He looked at Chaim. "Did I hear that right? What's a Calhoun doing in Texas?"

Chapter Two

Chaim turned to Dustin, his eyes wide. "That's where we've seen him. The stockyards in Kansas City. He's a heck of a long way from home to be courtin' trouble."

Dustin shook his head. He turned and searched the courtroom for Noah's oldest brother, Jock Calhoun Jr., or the second in line, Patrick Calhoun. The family included several more brothers that he hadn't had personal dealings with at the stockyards, and he was sure he wouldn't recognize them, even if they stood in front of him.

Bad blood had simmered between the McCutcheons and the Calhouns for as long as Dustin could remember. At one time their fathers had been friends, but that was over twenty years ago.

As the story went, Jock Calhoun had been traveling to Fort Stockton to bid for the army contract to supply beef to the outposts. At that time, the only ranches in the area large enough to handle such a contract were the Calhoun ranch that used to be located in North Texas, and the McCutcheons' Rim Rock ranch in West Texas. The ranch that landed the contract would be set for as long as they held it.

On his way there, Jock Calhoun had been bushwhacked and left for dead, but he didn't die. He recovered to say that before he'd passed out, he'd seen the brand on the horse of his attacker. The RR of the Rim Rock. Claimed Winston McCutcheon had arranged the whole thing so his ranch would win the bid when Calhoun didn't show up.

When Dustin's pa had heard the claim, he went straightaway to Calhoun to assure him that wasn't the case. His pa had tried repeatedly over the years to convince Jock Calhoun that he had nothing to do with the ambush that left Jock a broken man, but to no avail. Since the Rim Rock had signed the deal and grew to be the most prosperous ranch in the territory, Jock Calhoun stayed firm in his convictions.

The situation remained Calhoun's word against his pa. The strain between the two clans had steadily grown worse with Jock spreading accusations his pa had no way to refute.

Judge Halford leaned forward. "State your case."

"Two weeks ago," the prosecuting attorney said, "Mr. Noah Calhoun and an unknown friend, who skedaddled before the sheriff could arrest him, banged up the Morning Star Saloon. One of 'em rode a horse halfway up the staircase, busting the thing to smithereens, while the other went several rounds with the locals."

Shaking his head sadly, he eyed the judge. "Sebastian Abano lost three of his five remaining teeth. Two front windows were smashed, as well as glassware, the chandelier, and the establishment's full stock of whiskey, to the tune of fifty-five dollars. The place was left in a shambles and has been closed ever since."

The judge nodded, encouraging him to continue.

"Calhoun was arrested but had inadequate funds to pay compensation. These men were present at the time of the fight, and all identify Noah Calhoun as the lawbreaker who started the trouble, as well as riding the horse up the staircase."

The attorney pointed to three men in the second row, and they dutifully raised their hands while nodding their heads.

The woman sitting in the front of the room leaned forward, elbows gripped to her sides. Her head turned back and forth, following the proceedings. She was taller than most, and had straight, broad shoulders, making her appear strong and resolute. Her neck was as graceful as a swan's. Her beauty touched Dustin somewhere down deep.

"Mr. Wormer?" The judge looked at the defense attorney.

"My client pleads not guilty, Your Honor. Claims he and his friend were minding their own business when the fight broke out. He admits he threw several punches in self-defense, but that was after the skirmish started. Unfortunately, I was only handed this case this morning and haven't had a chance to question anyone." He dug through the creased and rumbled papers in front of him.

The woman bolted to her feet. "What? How can you properly defend him if—"

Judge Halford pointed his gavel. "Take your seat, young lady," he said sternly, and her hands fisted before she lowered herself into her chair.

She sure was determined. Dustin liked that about her.

"Why is that, Mr. Wormer?" Judge Halford asked.

"My partner, the defendant's counsel, is indisposed."

"He's unwilling to represent?"

"No, sir. He's out cold from consuming too much whiskey." Mr. Wormer dropped his chin for a moment. "He can't represent."

Laughter rippled around the courtroom, and the judge banged his gavel several times.

The woman surged back to her feet. "This is a travesty!" she exclaimed loudly. "A kangaroo court! Noah's a responsible young man. He wouldn't do such a thing."

"One more outburst and you'll be escorted out," the judge barked. "Do I make myself clear?"

She remained silent for a moment.

What is she doing fighting for a Calhoun?

Dustin thought she might go on, but finally she nodded and sank into her seat.

"This is getting more interesting by the second," Dustin whispered to Chaim. "Why the heck is a Calhoun down here in San Antonio? I don't see any of his family present, but that young woman seems to be invested. Wonder if they're involved."

I hope not.

Judge Halford heaved a deep sigh. "Do you have any defense at all, Mr. Wormer?"

"I believe I have a character witness here, Your Honor. At least, that's what these notes say." He scanned down a piece of yellow paper. "And we'll hear the words of the defendant himself."

"Very well. Call your witness."

Mr. Wormer sifted through his papers once again before he snatched one up. "I call . . ." His finger traced along a line. "Sidney Calhoun to the stand."

Chaim elbowed Dustin in the side and looked over his shoulder. "I thought you said you didn't see any Calhouns here. McCutcheons and Calhouns can't be in the same room without getting into a fight."

Dustin raised an eyebrow while lifting a finger to his lips.

Seeing the woman stand, straighten her skirt, and approach the bench caused a burning chunk of coal to land in Dustin's gut.

A Calhoun? What were the chances?

She stopped and looked at the judge.

"And you're Sidney Calhoun," the judge said. "I should have known."

"That's correct, Your Honor. I'm Noah's older sister." She didn't wait for a response but looked around with wide eyes. "Aren't you going to have me put my hand on the Bible?"

"No, I'm not. Somebody stole the Good Book from my courtroom this morning. I can assure you that when he's found, he'll wish for deliverance. You're an upstanding young woman. One, I'm sure, who would never tell a lie."

She batted her lashes at the man old enough to be her father, and smiled. "Yes, Your Honor. That's correct. Thank you for noticing."

"Oh brother," Chaim huffed out under his breath.

Warmth spread through Dustin's chest. And the uncomfortable burn wasn't because he was observing the daughter of his father's worst nemesis. The reaction was because something about her moved him. Earlier, even at first glance, the feelings she'd stirred made him think perhaps she was the one he'd been waiting for his whole life. The conviction put everything into perspective. Gave him hope.

Surprised at himself, he jerked his thoughts into submission. That was stupid. Life didn't work that way. Not out here in Texas, anyway. And especially not between a McCutcheon and a Calhoun. Fostering any such daydream was unthinkable and unwise. The reality was impossible.

"I always thought Sidney Calhoun was the third son," Chaim whispered, putting Dustin back on solid ground. "Guess on our trips to the stockyards, I was seeing one brother and thinking he was the other. I'm starting to remember something about a little sister."

"Agreed," he said, concentrating on what Chaim was saying. "I know Jock Jr. better than I'd like to, and Patrick too—or their fists, I should say."

Even though he'd noticed more about Miss Sidney Calhoun than her upstanding ladyship, as the judge had said, he needed to keep square in his mind who she was. That said, the name alone sealed his fate.

He shook his head and said in a low voice, "I can't count how many times we've come to blows over the lie they spread. Jock Jr. especially. He knows how to get my goat."

"Order!" Judge Halford barked, narrowing his eyes at Dustin and Chaim.

Had the grouchy old lawman recognized them?

The defense attorney cleared his throat. "Miss Calhoun, why do you think your brother is innocent of the charges?"

"Because, Mr. Wormer, Noah is too kind to do any of those things you just mentioned." She took a moment to pause and smile at her brother standing in shackles against the wall. "From a very tender age, he's been overly sensitive. As a matter of fact, he sometimes faints at the sight of violence or blood. He abhors fighting."

Dustin couldn't stop the bark of laughter before it burst past his lips. A Calhoun sensitive? Maybe to whoever got in the first punch.

She looked up, her gaze scanning the crowd for who had laughed, but didn't see him.

Judge Halford did, though, and shot him another look.

"So you're saying that since he's not the vicious sort, your brother would not take part in a barroom brawl," Mr. Wormer asked, his tone confident as he pulled his shoulders back.

"That's exactly what I'm saying, sir. Fighting goes against everything he is. He likes to read, and invent things. He's smart. Even entered university much younger than most. I'm sure if trouble were in the air, he'd leave the establishment."

Mr. Wormer nodded. "Very good, Miss Calhoun. That is all."

Her look was all wide-eyed innocence.

The prosecuting attorney stood. "Miss Calhoun, are you living here in town with your brother then? Sharing a dwelling?"

She gazed at the man. "No."

"Why then are you in San Antonio? You live in Santa Fe, at least seven hundred miles away. Could reality be that your brother has made a habit of getting into trouble, forcing you to come bail him out each and every time?"

A crimson blush crept up Sidney Calhoun's face. "Like I said, he's in school, sir, St. John's. I have talked to him about those silly pranks of his, and he's promised not to do anything like that anymore. He has his studies to think about."

The prosecutor leveled a hard stare. "That may be true, but it doesn't change the fact that Noah has gotten into trouble several times these last few months. And this is the third time he's left the university without permission, the third time he's been charged with a crime where you have had to plead his case and get it dismissed. Granted, they were small compared to this charge, but a pattern has been established." He smiled and held up a telegram. "At least, that is what Thomas Fell, the president of the university, has written here."

Dustin felt a moment of compassion for Miss Calhoun as she struggled with the statement the prosecution had uttered.

She blinked several times and looked down at the floor. "Just because Noah did a few foolish things in the past doesn't mean he's a drunkard and fighter, a destroyer of other people's property."

"What will you do if this court dismisses his case? Return him to the university so he can repeat the pattern?"

When she raised her eyes this time, she drilled the prosecutor with a defiant stare.

Dustin leaned forward, holding his breath. Things were not going her way.

"Miss Calhoun?"

"He *won't*."

"So you say. And have most likely said each and every other time he's made trouble before. You do admit that you have traveled several times to speak on Noah Calhoun's behalf?"

She stared back at him, her chin raised in challenge.

"Miss Calhoun?"

She nodded.

"Please answer the question out loud so the court can hear."

"Yes, I have."

The prosecutor returned to his chair and lowered himself slowly. "I thought so. That is all, Miss Calhoun. Since you have nothing more of value to add to this case besides the fact that you've become your brother's keeper, I have no further questions." He looked over at Mr. Wormer.

"No further questions either."

With jerky motions, she gathered her skirt. She glanced at the judge, all the while smiling with a stiff face.

Judge Halford tapped his pencil on the top of his desk as she crossed the room to her chair.

Her brother's attorney sighed. "I call Noah Calhoun."

"Do you swear to tell the truth?" Judge Halford asked the tall, defiant-looking lad.

Calhoun nodded. "I do."

"Fine. You will give your testimony from where you stand."

Mr. Wormer brushed the front of his jacket. "Did you start the fight in the Morning Star Saloon, ride a horse up the staircase, busting it up, shoot down the chandelier, and knock out Sebastian Abano's teeth?"

"No, I did not."

Mr. Wormer gave a curt nod. "No further questions."

Miss Calhoun snorted. To her credit, she stayed in her chair.

Dustin had to hand it to Noah Calhoun. He stood straight without a hint of fear. His voice, when he'd spoken, was clear and firm. Maybe he didn't know Judge Halford's reputation for quick judgments and even harsher sentences. The boy could be going away for a good long time.

Glad I'm not in Calhoun's boots.

"Busting up a man's livelihood is a serious charge, Mr. Calhoun," Judge Halford began, piercing Noah with a squinty-eyed gaze. "Nothing annoys me more than bad behavior with someone else's property. I was a victim once, many years ago. That fella couldn't pay back then either. Set me back years." He stopped, his gaze moving to the window, his full cheeks darkening.

Sidney Calhoun held up her reticule. "I've brought the money to pay," she said in a clear voice. "As much as it takes."

Perhaps she could feel what was coming down the tracks.

"Young Calhoun will be responsible for his own debts, Miss Calhoun. He won't rely on you anymore." The judge shifted in his seat and glanced briefly toward Dustin and Chaim.

Dustin frowned. Why was old Judge Halford looking at them?

"But since your assigned attorney has let you down, and being your earlier infractions were not much more than pranks, and being you're only"—he glanced at the paper in his hands— "seventeen years old, I'm stepping out and making a rather unusual ruling. Be assured, you won't get off in my court. I'm sentencing you to work out at the Rim Rock Ranch in Rio Wells. You will not step a foot off that property until you've earned enough money to pay off your debt."

The woman bolted to her feet, as did Dustin and Chaim.

"At the McCutcheons'!" she spat out as if she'd just bitten into a chunk of rancid meat.

She glanced over to her brother. Seeing his gaze trained on someone in the crowd, she turned and gaped at the sight of Dustin and Chaim standing four rows away, witnessing her brother's shame. All color drained from her face as realization apparently dawned on her who he was.

The judge smiled. "Exactly."

"Your Honor," Dustin entreated from his spot in the middle of the crowd. "You know the history between our families. This is a terrible idea. I'd appreciate it kindly if you'd reconsider. Chaim and I still have some time in San Antonio before we pull out. Who knows what trouble Noah Calhoun can get into by then?"

"You're exactly correct; I *do* know your two families' histories all too well. Winston McCutcheon and I go way back, as do Jock Calhoun and I. I respect both men as much as I do Grover Cleveland, the twenty-second president of these grand United States. But that doesn't stop me from doing what needs to be done here."

Pounding a finger on his desk, he said, "Seeing *your* face in my courtroom today, Dustin McCutcheon, reminds me how you busted up my favorite restaurant here in San Antonio not all that long ago, and got off practically scot-free with only one night in jail—"

"I paid restitution, Your Honor!" he blurted, feeling a drop of sweat roll down his temple.

"Order!"

Halford rapped the gavel so hard, Dustin feared the wooden tool would snap in two.

"I don't cotton to such irresponsibility. Therefore, to teach both you boxers a lesson you'll not soon forget, Noah Calhoun will stay in jail until you pick him up before you ride out. I'm assigning you as his guardian. Any trouble that he finds will fall on *your* shoulders."

Once again, the judge slammed down his gavel. "Next case!"

Chapter Three

Gobsmacked, Sidney squelched a gasp. She was so stunned she couldn't move, and certainly she wouldn't as long as Noah stood there in chains. An imaginary bear trap snapped around her neck, but she resisted the urge to claw at the neckline of her dress.

The attractive cowboy in the mercantile had been Dustin McCutcheon? The one with the charming smile, impossibly wide shoulders, and arms fit to wrestle a bear. How? Why? She'd even admired his backside, for goodness' sake. Horror over her unladylike behavior was shameful enough, but knowing the object of her curiosity was a McCutcheon made her actions all the worse.

Dustin and Chaim McCutcheon! How many times had she heard those despised names? She struggled to calm her raging thoughts. Noah under Dustin's thumb? And living in Rio Wells?

Their families had been friends once until someone—a McCutcheon, or someone they'd hired—had beaten her father near to death. Her dear pa had been left broken, still suffering years later from the pain that never really healed. Even worse was the knowledge he'd been betrayed by a friend.

If only Jock Jr. were here. Her oldest brother would have talked his way around that judge with ease, and this whole

McCutcheon mess would have been avoided. Tomorrow, she and Noah would have boarded the train bound for Santa Fe, and been home in a few days. As things stood now, she didn't know what to expect.

She shot a heated glance in Noah's direction. She couldn't wait to box his ears for getting into this mess in the first place.

Why can't he just stay in the dormitory where he belongs?

Her youngest brother leaned against the wall with the rest of the prisoners. He wasn't like her other brothers—rough and sturdy, and happy riding the ranch. Noah was all quick energy and cleverness, and she hurt to see him in shackles. And now he was sentenced to penal servitude with the McCutcheons.

She hadn't seen either of the McCutcheon brothers since she was a skinny girl of ten, peeking out from under an oversized, droopy brown hat as she sat her horse in the dusty stockyards in Kansas City. Forbidden to ride in the yearly cattle drive by her father, and ordered to stay home with her two younger brothers and the hired help, she'd taken matters into her own hands. She'd hidden away behind a large sack of potatoes in the back of the chuck wagon, enduring the musky air of the cramped storage bin from sunup until they stopped the jarring ride to make camp. At night, she sneaked out to relieve herself and drink water.

Cook discovered her in the dawning of day three, hungry and needing to stretch her badly cramped legs. By then, they'd traveled too far to send her home.

Sucking in several lungfuls of cool, clean air, Sidney had known what was coming, and didn't flinch when her pa grasped her by the arm and marched her behind a stand of trees. He whacked her bottom with his belt more times than she cared to remember.

Her two older brothers, then thirteen and fourteen—who were plenty old enough to earn their keep, as her father was fond of saying—grudgingly brought her a horse and assigned her a shift. If she wanted to ride trail, then she'd pull her own weight.

When their outfit had arrived in Kansas City, Jock Jr. pointed out Dustin and Chaim. They were walking with their father, the man her pa couldn't abide. Dustin was a year older than Jock Jr. He'd looked stern, even when his younger brother was kidding him. Soon after, she'd been taken to the hotel by her pa and ordered to stay put. After a day and a half of waiting, she'd been collected by Patrick, who recounted a fight between Jock Jr. and Dustin at the corrals.

By the time Sidney lifted her thoughts from the past, she realized the next case in the courthouse was well under way.

The prosecutor laid out the details, and then the defending attorney that had been so useless for Noah called Dustin McCutcheon to the stand.

She tried not to watch as the oldest McCutcheon testified that the defendant, Edward Felton, was at their ranch in Rio Wells on the night the victim of this case was murdered behind a tavern in San Antonio.

Determined not to look at him, Sidney whisked her gaze past the broad-chested cowboy to the window side of the room. From there, she moved her attention to the floor in front of her. When she had exhausted everything to inspect on the filthy tiles, she averted her eyes to the water-stained ceiling, demanding her ears ignore the deepness of the voice speaking.

Minutes crept by as Mr. Wormer whined out his questions. Dustin McCutcheon answered each with the ease of a toe dancer twirling around the dance floor.

Well aware she'd certainly be thought a fool if she continued counting the cracks above her head for one more second, she dropped her gaze to the reticule in her lap—anything to avoid looking at *him*. She'd heard stories about Dustin from Jock Jr. and Patrick. He commanded attention with each word he spoke.

He answered a few more queries and was dismissed. Chaim, his younger brother, was called next and corroborated the alibi. With the good word of the McCutcheons behind him, Edward Felton was almost certain of being cleared of any wrongdoing.

She glanced at her brother, seven years younger, and compassion dimmed her anger. He'd been such a tiny baby, barely surviving after their mother died in childbirth. He owed his life to the wife of a ranch hand who'd birthed a little boy only eight days before.

Pa had offered the woman twenty dollars a month, a good amount for a wet nurse, to care for him as her own. She'd kept Noah until his first birthday. Sidney remembered how he cried the day she brought him to the big house to stay for good, separated from everything he knew. Inconsolable, he cried for two days straight, the sound battering Sidney's heart. At least she'd known their mama for seven years. Little Noah had never felt the softness of her hands or heard the gentleness in her voice.

At that time, his rearing fell to her and Carmen, their housekeeper. Sidney remembered giving him a bottle, bathing him, and rubbing bacon grease on his raw bottom. He'd been a bright baby, so curious and intelligent, and he'd grown into a smart young man. He was doing so well in his engineering studies—why couldn't he just stick to his schoolwork instead of going off on these wild sprees?

As much as she hated to admit the fact now, Noah *was* irresponsible. After this last escapade, Jock Jr. was certain to pull him out of St. John's. The last time this happened, he'd threatened to do it, but now he'd be sure to make good on the warning. Being the youngest, Noah had a way of bending their pa to his will and getting his way. But with Jock Jr. that wasn't so. She cringed thinking of the storm that would descend when the two faced off.

But before he had to face his older brother, Noah would have to get through the time he'd been sentenced to spend among those murderous McCutcheons. Sidney didn't trust that family any more than she would an advancing scorpion.

Judge Halford banged down his gavel, dismissing the case. The guards ushered Noah through the back door, along with the three hooligans who'd gotten a year. In a rumble of chains, Felton's leg constraints were removed. The free man hurried out of the courtroom, but not before tossing a thankful grin at the McCutcheons.

The time had come for her to leave as well, but if she turned now, she was sure to come face-to-face with the infamous brothers. How she dreaded that exchange. What should she say? Every night her pa went to sleep cursing the name of their father.

Taking up her reticule, she opened the hook and took several drawn-out moments to find her folded handkerchief. With her eyes downcast, she dabbed at her lips, praying the brothers would be gone by the time she left.

Where has my gumption gone? I need to straighten my spine and hold my head high. I'm a Calhoun, and proud of it.

Taking her own words to heart, she stood, brushed her hands down the front of her skirt, and turned. Thankfully,

Dustin and Chaim had already left, as well as the majority of the spectators.

Exiting the courthouse, she headed straight for the hotel, the name Dustin McCutcheon playing over and over in her mind like a mantra. She needed to get a hold of her feelings, and take out Jackson, her dog and traveling companion, to stretch his legs.

Should she go to the telegraph office and send the bad news home? Pa and Jock Jr. were sure to be furious. *No, I'll wait until I can sit and think of what to do next. When I figure out a plan, then I'll let them know.* No use ruffling everyone's feathers since they couldn't do anything to help now anyway.

Proceeding down the street, Sidney jerked to a stop when a black cat darted out from an alleyway and traversed the boardwalk in front of her. She watched the feline scamper to the top of a stack of crates and disappear. *I don't want to cross that path. I can't deal with any more bad luck.* Since the hotel was on the opposite side of the street, she'd cross now and avoid the cat problem altogether.

Glancing both ways, Sidney hurried to the other side, dodging a few riders and a wagon. Rounding the corner, she spotted Mission San José y San Miguel de Aguayo. Enormous plants with velvety-soft-looking leaves and bright pink and lavender blossoms colored the whitewashed walls.

She stopped for a moment to enjoy the beauty. The bells of the mission rang out three times. Feathery white clouds covering the sky made the creamy ivory of the structure stand out all the more.

Her soul stirred, longing for something she didn't recognize. A gust of warm wind caressed her face, bringing with it a sweet scent of jasmine and the sound of laughter from far away. She closed her eyes, the sensation transporting her away from her all-male family, the struggles of dealing with an angry, broken father, and the daily business of ranching.

Giggling brought her around. A woman with two small children, one in each arm, walked behind her. The little tykes—girls or boys, she couldn't tell—were dressed in rags. All three were rail thin.

Sidney couldn't abide an empty stomach on a child. In Santa Fe, she volunteered at the orphanage, organizing fundraisers and helping out in the kitchen.

"Excuse me, ma'am," Sidney said in a soft voice, bringing the woman out of her thoughts. "Are you from around here?"

Both children buried their heads in their mama's neck as she said, "Yes, ma'am, I am."

"I've gotten a bit turned around. I'm looking for the Omni La Mansion del Rio Hotel." She hoped the small fib wouldn't get her in trouble with God. "My slippers aren't really made for walking." She lifted her hem to display the flimsy shoes that went with her best dress. In truth, she'd be glad to get back into her boots.

A smile made the woman's eyes come alive. "Why, you're almost there, miss. Just keep going along this route." She pointed with her chin since both her arms were full. "Once you pass St. Mary's Church, turn left on Crockett Street. You can't miss it."

When Sidney lifted her reticule, she saw the woman quickly look away. Taking charity wasn't easy for anyone.

"I'd like to thank you for your kindness."

The woman dropped her gaze to the ground. "Thank you, miss. My boys haven't eaten yet today."

Sidney did a quick count of the money in her bag. If her travels after Noah had taught her one thing, it was to bring extra money for unexpected happenings. Even if she were generous today, she'd still have plenty of funds for whatever should come her way.

She stepped close and opened her palm to show the woman two ten-dollar gold coins. "Do you have a safe place where you can hide this? Twenty dollars should keep you and your little ones fed for quite some time."

"Yes, miss!" The woman's throat worked as she swallowed several times. "Once I eat and am strong again, I can get my old job back at the wash house." Her eyes glistened. "I promise I won't waste your money. Thank you so much."

"You're welcome. I'm glad we met."

And she was. To be able to lend a helping hand was a privilege, something Sidney enjoyed. Now she just had to figure out how to keep Noah from making his situation worse.

Chapter Four

Finally at the hotel, Sidney pulled open the door and almost bumped into Dustin McCutcheon on his way out.

Can my luck get any worse?

She felt duped. In the mercantile, the butterflies their brief conversation had created were like the first sunshine of spring after a long winter. She'd *liked* him. His gaze had pulled her in like a fish on the line.

Scowling at him, she said, "Why didn't you say who you were when I saw you in the store?"

He removed his hat and held it in his hands. His dark wavy hair needed a trim, and black stubble covered his strong square jaw.

"You didn't give me a chance. I was getting around to that when you hurried off like a scared little rabbit."

She stiffened. The whalebone of her corset tightened around her, and she wished she hadn't dressed in her snuggest and most proper Sunday gown to make a good impression on the judge. Fat lot of good that had done her.

"But now," he continued, "since we've not been *properly* introduced, I say we fix that."

"Properly introduced?" She couldn't stop an indignant huff from passing through her lips. "Why would we be? Our families hate each other."

She shouldn't be so snappish. He was Noah's guardian, after all.

His face darkened.

"Besides . . . ," she went on, unable to stem her growing enmity. "I'm sure you have no desire to meet a *scared little rabbit*."

She glanced around, wondering where Chaim—the friendlier-looking of the two—had gone. People milled around the lobby, but she was only aware of Dustin and his proximity.

Dustin's smile faded, his mouth pulling into a straight, hard line. "Hate each other? I wouldn't go that far, Miss Calhoun. Hard feelings exist, but they're mostly one-sided. McCutcheons don't hate Calhouns."

He held out his hand, pressing the point.

She wished she had a rotten fish to oblige. "Of course, *you* don't. *Your* father wasn't beaten to within an inch of his life and then left to die, now—"

Dustin's eyes narrowed. His July-hot gaze cut off her sentence and almost nailed her to the wall behind, but he kept his hand outstretched.

She swallowed the rest of the words she was about to dish out and placed her palm in his, ignoring the disturbing warmth that seeped through her glove.

"That's better," he said in a smooth, deep voice. "First things first. Miss Calhoun, I'm pleased to make your acquaintance."

Aggravated, she pulled back her hand, anxious to separate herself from his heat.

"Second, my pa had nothing to do with that age-old accusation. He's tried on numerous occasions to talk sense into your pa, but he won't listen. We're sorry that misfortune fell onto Jock Calhoun, but no McCutcheon was responsible."

He fiddled with his hat. "And with all due respect, I don't take kindly that you're throwing around your words now as if they're fact. They've been a constant burr under my pa's skin. I'd say he's handled the situation pretty well for how much your family has gone out of their way to keep the falsehood alive."

"Truths don't lie."

He gave an exaggerated sigh and his left eye twitched. "Only in the minds of the Calhouns. If anything your pa had claimed were true, then my father would have been arrested years ago. But he hasn't. And he won't be. Time you let the past go."

Anger flashed hot under Sidney's skin. How *dare* he stand there and tell her what to do? She struggled for a retort, but his dark gaze that reminded her of warm chocolate kept distracting her.

Finally, he shrugged. "I think it best we change the subject, don't you?" His expression softened. "I have to say you gave me quite the surprise in the courtroom today. I've been under the incorrect notion all these years that Sidney Calhoun was a man."

A cocky grin grew across his face. "I'd totally forgotten the family had any female Calhouns besides your mother. I've only had the *pleasure* of meeting the men," he said, relaying his message loud and clear. "And that still stings. Guess I was wrong."

She'd like to slap that smug grin right off his face. And she could too, if she weren't still trussed up in this air-constricting garment of torture.

"Guess you were," she replied as genteel as a debutante at her coming-out party. She curled her lips into a pleasant smile.

"I *am* the only female in my family. My mother passed on years ago."

Raw-edged hurt made her breath hitch. Even after all these years, she still missed her mother deeply.

Dustin's chuckle faded away. "I'm sorry. I didn't know. Let me offer my condolences."

She waved off his sympathies and squared her shoulders. "Not your concern, Mr. McCutcheon."

"Contrary to what I'm sure you've been told, I don't bite, so you can put away your claws."

She lifted her chin, thinking about her pa and the limited mobility that kept him homebound much of the time. How his head only turned partially to the right. How pain radiated through him when he mounted his horse. At times, she had to hide her tears, so not to bring him shame. His spirit was nearly as broken as his body.

"I don't really care if you do bite, Mr. McCutcheon. I can see you were enjoying my brother's misfortune inside the courthouse today more than you'd like to let on."

"There's not one shred of truth in that statement. I wish no ill will on Noah or any of your family, for that matter—not even your father."

Sidney ignored how soft his eyes had gone. He acted as if he believed what he was saying, but she knew better. The McCutcheons hadn't gotten where they were today without telling a few lies or walking on a few friends. Maybe Dustin was telling the truth; she didn't know. But they wouldn't dare try anything while she was around.

That was the answer! She would go to Rio Wells too and would protect Noah, if she could.

Squaring her shoulders, she said, "There's been way too much bad blood between our families for us to be anything but adversaries—we're like fire and ice. We certainly can't be friends. I'll get through this debacle the best I can, but I won't enjoy a minute of it. You'd best know that right off."

His smile vanished. "You? Get through what? Your brother is the one coming out to the Rim Rock. Judge didn't say a word about his sister."

"You don't think I'd send Noah into the enemy camp alone, do you? He's only seventeen years old. Just a baby. What kind of people are you McCutcheons, anyway? Did you really think I'd just go home, leaving his welfare to you—so you couldn't be held accountable if anything happened to him?"

Dustin straightened.

She thought him as tall as Jock Jr. and maybe even taller. His scowl almost made her turn and run.

"Well?" she persisted.

"The McCutcheons are good people, despite what you've been told. But I'll be patient and understand your concern since you're Noah's sister." He gave her a pointed look. Any trace of friendliness that had been in his tone was now gone. "Sounds like he makes a habit of getting into trouble. I don't want him causing problems with my men."

She glared at his slight to her brother, ignoring the rich timbre of his voice that almost made her shiver. She forgot her response.

He chuckled and dismissively shook his head. "I do question your intellect, though, by you calling him a baby. He's a man, and he should start acting like one. In turn, people will begin treating him accordingly, not traipse after him to fix his messes. He has two feet. Let him stand on them."

"He already does." *Sometimes. When he concentrates on what he should be doing.*

The tall, dark, and a bit intimidating McCutcheon just stared.

"Sounded different today. Like I told the judge," he went on, "Chaim and I have some time here in San Antonio before we head back to Rio Wells."

Dustin dragged a brief, indifferent gaze up and down her length. "The wagon we brought from the ranch has already returned to Rio Wells, along with the extra men. If you plan on riding with us, get yourself a horse and clothes. Get a mount for your brother as well. I'm not responsible for that. We won't be waiting for a wagon to keep up. We'll be traveling light and fast."

Frowning, he added, "If you're short on money, you can borrow what you need from me. I wouldn't want you running out because of an unexpected bump in the road."

Dustin took a tiny step back as the color of Sidney Calhoun's face deepened to a profound shade of pink, and her lashes blinked at what he'd said. Seemed she didn't like his offer.

Maybe he'd gone too far, but he wasn't ready to completely forget the accusations Jock Calhoun had leveled on the Rim Rock for all these years. For now, to keep the peace, and to make this easier for his own father when the time came, he'd play nice. Try to win her trust. With a tinderbox like her, though, he could tell the task wasn't going to be easy.

"Those are my exact intentions, as soon as I'm finished here. Outfit myself and acquire two horses." She laughed, but the expression didn't travel to her eyes. "A Calhoun taking money from a McCutcheon! *That* will never happen."

He resisted the urge to roll his eyes. "As a loan."

"As anything. I've plenty of money, thank you very much. I won't be a millstone around your neck, to be sure, and neither will my brother."

Millstone? No, she certainly wouldn't be that. A few other choice descriptions flashed through his mind as he took in her fiery blue eyes and those finely chiseled lips that seemed in desperate need of a kiss. Not that he'd noticed.

She's right. McCutcheons and Calhouns don't mix. Period!

He snapped away his gaze, pulled on his hat, and touched the brim with a forefinger.

"I'm glad to hear that, Miss Calhoun. If you're through berating me, I'll let you go about your business. You have a lot to accomplish in a short amount of time."

Six o'clock rolled around all too quickly. Chaim had left an hour ago, intending to walk the gardens in the center of town with Emmeline before they went to a private supper to say their good-byes. Seemed they'd been doing that for days now.

That left Dustin on his own. He had a meeting with a San Antonio rancher they often did business with in the saloon in ten minutes, so he pulled on his boots and headed out the hotel door.

He'd tossed around the idea of sending a note to Miss Calhoun's room. Invite her to supper. *Wouldn't that be interesting.* That had been his thought in the mercantile, before he'd known who she was.

But after seeing the way she'd acted, he was sure she'd turn him down.

His meeting wouldn't take but a few minutes, and then he'd be faced with another long, lonesome night, pretending to have a good time. Gambling and tossing back whiskey, oh joy. Tonight his twenty-nine years was feeling pretty damn old.

He started down the squeaky stairs, taking note of the men in the lobby. One couldn't be too complacent in San Antonio if you wanted to stay alive.

At the bottom, he stopped. Did he dare? Miss Calhoun had to eat. If he could win her over, even a little, the ride back to Rio Wells would be more pleasant. An invitation was worth a try, for everyone's sake.

He strode to the lobby counter and waited for Jim, the clerk, to notice him.

"Mr. McCutcheon, may I help you?" the little dandy said, hurrying over. He fingered his perfectly knotted bowtie and smiled. The room was warm, and the clerk's forehead had a sheen that looked almost uncomfortable.

"I hope so, Jim. I'd like to send a note to Miss Calhoun. Do you know if she's in?"

The fellow turned and took a quick accounting of the door keys in their corresponding slots as Dustin followed his gaze. Two keys present. Rooms one and five.

"She seems to still be out, Mr. McCutcheon, but you can leave a note in her niche, if you'd like. I'll be sure she gets it as soon as she returns."

Dustin pushed away his disappointment. Maybe she wasn't alone here in San Antonio. She'd never said one way or the other, but then, he hadn't asked. He was all for being friendly, but he didn't want to make a fool of himself either, especially with the history they already shared.

"Mr. McCutcheon?" Jim shifted his gaze to the clock on the wall and then back at him.

No one ever died of embarrassment. Jock Calhoun was the one keeping the animosity between the two ranches going. As much as he didn't like the allegations the rancher had made over the years, Dustin recognized that Sidney hadn't been the instigator. By the looks of her, she'd only been a small child when the trouble had started.

A man waiting behind Dustin cleared his throat, forcing Dustin to decide quickly.

"Yes, I'll leave a note."

The clerk presented a pencil and paper.

Dustin stepped aside, letting the impatient man come forward. He gazed at the blank sheet, his mind suddenly empty. One didn't rush note writing. If they did, they'd be sorry. This was important work.

Stemming his impulse to crumple the paper, he sighed.

What would his pa think of him attempting to make peace of sorts between the two bloodlines? Surely, he wouldn't be happy. As much aggravation as his father and the ranch had endured over the years from Jock Calhoun, his father had only shared the bare minimum with the family. Just common knowledge through the grapevine.

Not as if he had much of a choice. They were stuck with Noah. Being civil to his sister couldn't hurt, and in his way of thinking, might actually make things better. He wasn't inviting old man Calhoun to supper. And he wasn't being disloyal to his father or the McCutcheon name.

Placing the pencil to the sheet of paper, Dustin quickly began to write.

Dear Miss Calhoun,

I'm dining tonight at the Longhorn. I'll be there at seven o'clock. If you're free, you're welcome to join me. Perhaps we can discuss Noah and how we should go about his rehabilitation.

Your new friend,

Dustin McCutcheon

There. That wasn't so difficult. The part about Noah would surely get her attention. He folded the missive several times and motioned to Jim, who was waiting patiently at the other end of the counter, feather duster in hand.

The man's features brightened when Dustin held up his finished script.

"Very good, Mr. McCutcheon." He took the note and slipped it into slot number five. "The moment I see her, I shall give her your message. Will there be anything else?"

A glance at the clock said Dustin had half an hour to conclude his business in the saloon and get a table at the Longhorn. The thought pulled the corners of his mouth into a smile.

"No, Jim, that's all. Thanks for your help."

"Always my pleasure to assist whenever you're in town, Mr. McCutcheon. You have a good night."

"You do as well."

Dustin stepped out into the evening air and made for the Bone Yard Saloon.

Chapter Five

Rio Wells, Texas

Lily McCutcheon crossed the floor of her dress shop and pulled the front door wide, loving the soft sound of the bells hanging above. A cool morning breeze wafted through, encouraged by the kitchen window she'd opened moments before on the other side of the building.

The dry Texas air soothed her soul, so different from Boston, where the clingy-moist atmosphere made one's clothes stick to the body no matter the time of day. Here the hard-packed dirt seemed so foreign compared to the lush green lakes of her German homeland.

How she missed her *Tante* Harriett on days like this. Something was sad about the mourning dove's call from the church graveyard on the outskirts of town. Or maybe her melancholy stemmed from the fact her shop, Lily's Lace and More, had flourished in the short time since opening, but her aunt wasn't alive any longer to enjoy the fruits.

If patronage kept up at this pace, she'd have so many projects, she wouldn't be able to keep up. Only so many hours were in one day. The success was all due to Tante Harriett insisting on teaching Lily everything she knew. Opening the shop had been their dream—*together.*

Lily glanced up into the sky, seeing an endless blue slate. *Are you watching me, Tante? Are you proud of what we've accomplished?*

She sighed and turned. Anticipating her husband's morning visit, Lily fluffed the pillow in the guest chair by the window, then shook out the dressing room curtain to loosen the dust that had accumulated over the past day.

She and John had a standing date each morning at nine. Two hours ago, he'd left their tiny living quarters above her shop to prepare for his day at his medical office next door. Soon, he'd be back for a cup of coffee and a tasty treat she'd whipped up in her itsy-bitsy stove.

"And how are you this morning, Ingrid?" Lily addressed the tall dress form standing in the corner, opposite the dressing room and next to her spools of handmade lace. A gown she'd created as a show piece sample draped regally on the headless dummy.

Lily playfully tapped her chin as if listening to the make-believe woman's reply. John had surprised her with the large-as-life addition he'd received in trade for his services.

"That's wonderful to hear. I hope you find your new home agreeable. Let me know if there's anything I can do to make you more comfortable."

Feeling silly, she went to the cutting table and ran her hand down the five new bolts she'd add to the fabric shelf later today. After which, she'd get to work on the two gowns she was currently creating.

John stepped through the front door and smiled. As usual, the sight of him brought a rush of happiness.

"How are Doc Bixby and Tucker this morning?" she asked, going to the stove for the cinnamon rolls. She kept them in the cooled oven where any flies that might have sneaked in through an open door couldn't find them.

"Hopeful I'll bring back leftovers." He put his nose in the air and gave a good sniff. "Smells awfully good, honey."

"Of course I made enough for them. Not doing so would be mean."

With a knife, Lily traced around the crispy brown edges and then set the pastry on a plate. She drizzled a sugar glaze over the top, enough that white gooey stripes overflowed down the sides. Next, she poured a cup of coffee and brought both over to the table where John had seated himself, his chin in his fist as he stared out the window.

"Penny for your thoughts," she said, smiling when his eyes went wide at the pastry before him. "You're thinking about more than that cinnamon roll. Where are you this morning?"

"Here, with you."

"No, you're not. I know what those lines on your forehead mean. What are you worried about?" She took the chair beside him, always thankful that they'd found each other.

He chuckled and playfully touched the tip of her nose. "Aren't you having one?"

She smiled; he couldn't distract her that easily. "I tested one when they first came out of the oven. If I indulge myself with another, I might start to look like Patsy."

John leaned forward and found her lips. "Then there would only be more of you to love." He nuzzled her neck as a sound of appreciation escaped his throat. "Besides, everyone loves that chubby pony at Cradle's livery. She's very popular—proving my point nicely."

Lily laughed and pulled away. "You say that now, but . . ."

Focused back on the pastry, he took a bite and chewed.

"If I got pleasingly plump, then we wouldn't fit in our tiny apartment above the shop any longer. There's barely enough room for the both of us, plus the cat. Imagine if I was twice the size I am now." She gave an exasperated sigh as she shook her head.

John's eyes widened and he bolted to his feet, almost upsetting his chair. His smile went from ear to ear, and he was all but sputtering.

"A-are you trying to tell me we're expecting a baby, Lily? Because if that's true, I'm the happiest man in the world!"

A moment of disappointment tightened her throat. She hadn't expected him to jump to that conclusion, although now she realized that was exactly how her words sounded. She'd been thinking along those lines herself more often than not these days. They both anticipated the exciting news, when it arrived.

"No, I'm sorry. That's not what I meant at all."

He took his seat and plucked his napkin off the floor as she tried to explain.

"I thought maybe we should get ready for when that happy day comes. Between the two of us upstairs, things are tight. I can't imagine soothing a crying baby with no place to walk him or her, besides navigating the narrow staircase."

John stopped eating and gave her a long look. He picked up her hand and brought the tips of her fingers to his warm lips, his gaze searching hers.

"Are you unhappy upstairs, my love? Truly, be honest now. We promised never to keep secrets from each other."

She looked away, unable to stare into his emerald eyes a moment longer and not blurt her idea to him. She'd been dreaming about this ever since Tante Harriett passed away last

July. Her aunt had helped her come to America, and now she wanted to do the same for her sister.

"No, I'm not unhappy at all. I could never be unhappy when I'm with you." She laid her palm on his cheek for a moment, and then let it fall away. "I've been thinking about how cute the apartment is, much more suitable for a single girl—er, woman—than an old married couple like us."

John took another bite, but he lifted his eyebrows and laughed. "Now I really know you're up to something," he said while chewing. "We're hardly an old married couple, Lily. We're practically still on our honeymoon, so to speak."

Her face heated, and she had to glance away. No truer words were ever spoken.

"Go on, spit out your idea before the secret chokes you. What's going on in that head of yours?"

She looked down at his cinnamon roll.

"Lily?"

"I've been thinking that perhaps Giselle could come from Germany. She turned seventeen on her last birthday, and wants very much to live here in Rio Wells with us. Make Texas her home. Find her own Western cowboy husband."

John quickly lowered his fork to his plate, his eyes wide. The smile faded from his lips.

Lily hurried on. "You know the business in the shop has picked up considerably since opening. I'm actually working on two projects at the same time—one even from out of town, with another to start. And I finished a gown just last week. If any of my ladies had wanted a rush for a special occasion, I couldn't have delivered it. But if Giselle were here working alongside me, we could turn twice the profit."

She leaned forward, her hands clasped tightly together between them. "I've almost paid off my debt to Dr. Bixby.

Every time I make a payment, he goes on for an hour about why I no longer need to. Next month, our profits will be free and clear."

"Lily, I didn't know you've turned into such a businesswoman. Your head seems to be filled with numbers, accounting, profits and loss, as well as fabrics. I thought . . ." He cupped his chin.

"A woman's mind can only be occupied with sugar icing and Venetian Gros Point lace?" She smiled to soften her words.

He lifted a shoulder. "Never that. I just hadn't known you were dwelling along these lines—paying off the debt, expanding your business, sending for your little sister. I'm surprised, is all."

"Do you mind? I spend many hours in there." She glanced into the body of the shop. "Sometimes the days get a little lonely. If Giselle were here, that wouldn't be the case."

"I see." Finished eating, John pushed back his chair and stared. "We don't want you to be lonely now, do we?"

She shook her head, excited that he seemed open to her idea. "That's why I'd like to start looking for a larger home. Then Giselle could have the upstairs apartment. I really enjoyed the cozy rooms when I lived there with Tante Harriett."

His brows fell. "And you don't enjoy them with me?"

"Of course I do! But the thought of setting up a real household with you, somewhere else, feels even better. Several places here in town are for rent." She took his hands in hers. "But can we afford it?"

He finished his coffee, wiped his mouth with his napkin, and set the cloth beside his plate. "I see. You want to move."

"Yes. And send for Giselle. Is that possible, John?"

She pulled her sister's last letter from the pocket of her skirt and opened the page. She scanned down all the personal items to the place that had almost moved Lily to tears. She cleared her voice and began to read.

"Have you asked your husband yet about my joining you in Texas? I'm so hopeful he'll say yes. I've saved every penny I've earned for the past two years from mending and watching Victoria's twin boys. I have thirty-five marks for my passage fare, and I promise to work off the rest once I arrive. I'll do exactly as you ask concerning the shop, and will work hard every day. I'll even work on Sunday, if you need me."

Lily glanced up and laughed. "She knows I'd never allow her to work on Sunday. She's being theatrical—that's Giselle's way. But you can see how much she has her heart set on coming?"

John didn't look convinced. And why should he? The amount of the fare was as big as the stars in the sky. How could she expect him to incur such a debt? She wouldn't if not for Giselle's heartfelt pleas, and the fact Tante Harriett had done the same for her without ever asking her to repay a cent. That's what she really desired. She needed to be truthful from the beginning.

"I understand the fare is a huge burden. Her savings falls short about one hundred and seventy-nine marks, approximately one hundred dollars. I can't ask you to pay it, John, but I can from the profits of the shop, if you will lend me the money up front until I can save it. Tante Harriett paid my fare, and I wish to do the same for Giselle."

John sat quietly as he listened, and then finally said, "What about the ocean crossing? It's dangerous for a single woman, especially as young and beautiful as she must be if she looks anything like you."

Lily lifted a shoulder, hopeful he was seriously considering her request. "That's true, but I sailed safely from Germany to Boston. She'll be fine if she keeps to herself and stays in her cabin for most of the trip. I was lucky to have a small family in my third-class cabin that looked after my welfare. We can pray for that."

Her eyes brightened as she added, "And if we start looking for a new home now, we'll have time before she'd even arrive in Boston, plus another two weeks if she came by stage, or faster if she took the train all the way to San Antonio, although that would increase the cost. That's plenty of time to find a new place and get moved."

John scooted his chair closer and pulled her into his arms. "I'll have to think about it, Lily."

She'd never seen him look so serious. A knot formed in her stomach.

"Can you be patient?" he asked.

She nodded, disappointed he wasn't as enthusiastic as she.

"Don't look so unhappy," he said, the smile on his lips not traveling to his eyes. "If it's meant to be, it'll happen. But promise me you won't be too disappointed if this arrangement doesn't materialize as fast as you'd like." He pressed several warm kisses against her forehead.

Resigned, she nodded. She'd done all that she could.

John stood and stretched, looking at the kitchen area. "You said you'd put some pastry back for Jasper and Tucker? I'm sure they're about ready to charge through the door from all the good smells drifting over to the doctor's office. Do you have any fittings today?"

He seemed uneasy, eager to leave. She hoped she hadn't overstepped her place.

Getting up, Lily went to the sideboard, retrieved the plate, and quickly iced the rolls. "I do. Mrs. Tuttle is coming in to try her blue velvet gown." She handed John the plate.

"You've outdone yourself this time. Those two won't know what hit them when they bite into these." He leaned in and bussed her cheek. "If you need anything, you know where to find me."

Lily hadn't expected John to say yes right away, but then, his anxious expression had her worried. Was there something going on that she didn't know about?

Chapter Six

The walk to the doctor's office was ten medium steps. In the empty kitchen behind his examining room, John set the plate of cinnamon rolls in the center of the table, wondering where Jasper and Tucker had gone. He proceeded to the back window and gazed out on the alley to view the rear of the buildings that lined Main Street. The sheriff's office, the saloon, and the Union Hotel. He grasped the back of his neck, his thoughts troubled.

Growing up in Montana on a prosperous cattle ranch like the Heart of the Mountains had afforded him any opportunity he'd been inclined to chase. He'd lived in a big house with a cook, nice furnishings, and a large loving family. Being honest with himself, he'd have to say he'd grown up pretty rich. His goal in becoming a doctor hadn't been to make money, but to help those in need. Make a difference in someone's life.

Bob Mackey, the man John had accidently shot and killed when he was only nine, popped into his mind. The memory of the merchant's white face, devoid of any life-giving blood, still deeply disturbed him. That horrible event had been his inspiration to become a doctor, along with a desire to leave his hometown, where a cloud of unhappiness followed his footsteps because of his inability to forgive himself.

John insisted on helping his parents pay for his schooling in the East with the money he'd saved over his lifetime. Then he'd used most of the remainder to buy Jasper Bixby's medical practice. These last few months working in Rio Wells had been an eye-opener. He had taken on his profession, understanding fully that being a small-town doctor was not a way to get rich.

He glanced in the mirror that hung over the dining table. The red scar that ran the side of his temple was still a bit noticeable. He blinked, feeling down. In reality, he was a poor town doctor, without the means to save any money. Yes, he owned the building and equipment that went along with the practice since Bixby had handed over the reins, but that was about all.

What about Lily? The idea of bringing her little sister out from Germany had about knocked him off his chair. His salary in Rio Wells equaled that of a ranch hand, about twenty-five dollars a month—give or take a little. He received other payment in food, dinners, and the happiness his knowledge had helped his new friends and made their lives a little better, but that was about all.

On the other hand, Lily's shop had really begun to sprout wings and fly. He was very happy for her indeed. Still, he didn't want her to be the one to use her earnings for household needs, and especially the rent on a new "proper" home. He hadn't known she was unhappy upstairs. His heart lurched when he considered what else she might be keeping from him. And now this.

One hundred dollars!

He could easily write home, and his father would send the sum with no questions asked, but he hated to do that. They'd already spent more money on his education than on all the other brothers and Charity combined. He couldn't make the request.

The front door opened and then banged closed. He turned when Bixby and Tucker appeared in the kitchen, followed by Lily's white cat.

John took a deep breath. "Where've you two been?"

"Went over to the mercantile to see if the supplies we ordered had arrived," old Jas Bixby replied, his gaze scanning the kitchen.

"Well?" Agitation was still biting at John. "Were they in? We're pretty low on laudanum, as well as suture thread."

Tucker, having already spotted the cinnamon rolls, had one in his hand and took a large bite.

Bixby regarded him with thoughtful eyes. "They sure weren't. Said they're on back order. We might consider stocking up on a few things so we don't have to worry every time we run low."

Silence prevailed in the kitchen. Bixby helped himself to the sweets on the table.

"That's a good idea," John said, realizing he should have done that months ago. He shrugged off his agitation. "What do you do around here for fun?"

At John's question, Bixby turned and gazed at him. "That's an odd thing to ask from someone who's been here long enough to know most people. Things we do, as well as things we don't. Somethin' troubling you, boy?"

Suddenly, the room around John appeared all the more shabby. He saw the clean, but basic, four walls. A well-worn table with six chairs, a clock, the front waiting room with a few straight-back chairs and a bookcase.

Was this how Lily saw the place? Did she regret marrying him? Had she settled to become a thrift-bare doctor's wife when they fell in love? His cousin Dustin could have given her so much more.

At Bixby's interested gaze, as well now as Tucker's, John shrugged. This wasn't their fault. He shouldn't take out his uncertainties on them.

"I guess I'm bored. Might be nice to have someone to heal or stitch up."

At the petty way that sounded, John headed to the pump to get a cup of water.

Bixby followed his movements thoughtfully. "You'd rather have someone suffering just so you could stay busy? I don't like the sound of that. You might think different if influenza or diphtheria hit Rio Wells. I've seen it, and such a disease ain't pretty. Keeps you praising each boring day that passes that everyone you care about is smiling and well."

"That didn't come out right. Of course, I don't want anyone suffering or sick." He rapped his knuckles against the countertop. "Sometimes I feel useless, that's all. It's not a sentiment I like."

"You may as well get used to it." Bixby walked over to the stove and shook the coffeepot. "There's enough here for three small cups." He glanced between John and Tucker. Tuck shook his head, as did John.

"Suit yourself." He poured the thick, cold brew into a mug.

Feeling mulish, John went for his hat. He'd take Bo for a ride. Maybe go out to the ranch and ride herd with Uncle Winston since both Dustin and Chaim were off in San Antonio.

"If Lily asks, tell her I'm riding out to the Rim Rock."

Perhaps his horse under him and the wind in his face could dispel the growing anxiety in his gut. Maybe, and maybe not.

Later that day, John arrived at the Rim Rock Ranch more conflicted than ever. He didn't have any answers. Lily had married a poor town doctor, one who owned a practice that would never make him rich.

Now, if he lived in New York, that would be a different matter altogether. Or if he had stayed in Boston like several of his instructors had encouraged him to do. One had even offered a partnership in his practice. The doctor said he was looking to slow down; said he had enough business for the both of them and then some.

But five long years in the city had John yearning for wide-open spaces like the ones he remembered from his youth. Air without the taint of coal dust, streets filled with people who knew your name, a thick steak of gamy venison. The city didn't have those things. He'd understood that he'd never be rich if he returned to practice in Montana or any other less populated place. A country doctor was just that. He was as different from a city doctor as a country mile was from a city block.

With disturbed thoughts, he dismounted and tied his horse to the hitching rail. Now that he had Lily to think about, he felt different. She wanted a home to make her own and to bring her sister to America. Both were understandable desires. She wasn't asking for the moon, but he didn't have any answers.

He gazed around a moment, taking in his surroundings. The bunkhouse was quiet. The place felt deserted. He didn't see anyone, so he went to the front door of the ranch house and knocked.

Maria, the Mexican maid, answered the door. She smiled when she recognized him. "*Señor* John, please come in."

Footsteps in the hall, hurrying his way, sounded on the large flag tile that covered every floor in the house.

"John," his aunt Winnie said, her voice filled with enthusiasm. She was always after him and Lily to come and visit. "What a nice surprise. What brings you our way on this beautiful November day?" She gave him a hug.

He felt a bit uncomfortable. "Actually, I just needed to get out of town for a while and take a ride. Thought I'd come and say hello."

Her smile ebbed. "Of course you did. You and yours practically grew up on the back of a horse. Dustin and Chaim as well. Ask them to sit inside for more than twenty minutes, and I'll have a mutiny on my hands. I was hoping Lily was with you."

"Nope, not today. She has a customer coming for a fitting. Once she gets sewing, not much of anything will distract her until she has completed the project. She's a hard worker."

"John, I hope you won't think me indelicate, but I must comment on how well the wound on your face has healed. For such a nasty cut, I'm amazed that only a small line remains. And look." She pulled up her sleeve, showing him the burn she'd gotten two weeks ago while taking biscuits from the oven. "I've never seen anything like it. That salve you gave me has almost made this disappear. I've had burns before that took weeks to heal, and then months for the redness to fade away. Not so here."

Astonished at how well her injury looked, he said, "I certainly can't take credit. Jas has been perfecting his recipe over the years. It's pretty amazing."

"And to think the juice comes from a simple little cactus. I'm sure it's messy to extract."

John shrugged. "Not too bad, just takes time and patience."

"Well, please thank him for me again when you see him. I'd like to get another small bottle to have on hand for emergencies."

"I'll be sure to tell him, Aunt Winnie. And the next time I see one of the family in town, I'll stick a bottle in their pocket to bring home to you."

He glanced around. The large, quiet room reminded him of one of the libraries back at the university in Boston. Two generous sofas faced each other, separated by a square coffee table. On the side wall was a large window facing east with a view that was devoid of any barns, outbuildings, or fence. Two large wooden chairs sat in one corner with a three-foot tall trunk between them, draped with a decorative woven blanket of a multitude of bright colors. A large oval mirror, rimmed in dark timber, hung on the creamy white wall over the fireplace. The top of each door and doorway was softly arched.

"Is Uncle Winston here?"

"Actually, he's out with Manolito and the hands at the herd. Dustin and Chaim are still in San Antonio, but they will be returning tonight."

He nodded. "Yes, taking Emmeline to the train." Emmeline, his former fiancée, was going home to Boston because her father had taken ill. "I'm relieved it's not life threatening."

"Yes," she said. "But until she returns, Chaim won't know what to do with himself. They're like two peas in a pod."

That was certainly the case. He wished Emmeline a safe trip to Boston and then a speedy return. He'd been so thankful after he'd broken off their engagement, only to find she'd actually fallen in love with his cousin Chaim while she had been staying at the ranch. The revelation had been a surprise, and a weight lifted from his shoulders. Knowing she'd found someone else took the sting out of the breakup, and the burden off him.

John fingered his hat brim, anxious to get back outside and on his horse, but he didn't want to appear impolite. "Where're Madeline and Becky?" he asked, deliberately unrushed. "The place feels pretty quiet."

Aunt Winnie smiled. "They went out early to the arroyo with their paints and canvas. I expect them back anytime. The air is warming, and they rarely stay out for more than a couple of hours at a time. Would you like to wait for them?"

He shook his head. That was the last thing he wanted. "I think I'll ride out toward the herd and see if I can locate Uncle Winston. Give Bo a good workout. He's been stalled up for too long."

"Winston will be delighted you did. Check at the bunkhouse. They'll know where to send you."

She followed him to the door and patted him on the back when he pushed on his hat and pulled down the brim.

"Next time don't knock. This is your home as much as the one in Montana." She gave him a stern look. "I mean that, John. Come again for supper and bring Lily. That young woman warms my heart."

Yes, he knew about that. Since marrying Lily, his love for his wife grew every day. No one had warned him marriage would be like that. He hadn't known her well-being and happiness would be his most ardent desire. And right now, *her* most ardent desire was to bring her sister to Texas.

Writing home to ask for a loan again crossed his mind. John was certain his pa would send the funds, no questions asked, as would any of his brothers. He could ask, but he didn't want to. His McCutcheon pride said he should figure out this problem on his own.

Frustrated, John strode out, gathered Bo's reins, and headed for the bunkhouse, intent on finding someone to direct him. He wasn't that familiar with the Rim Rock's pastures, but if locating Uncle Winston took the entire day, he wouldn't mind at all.

He had some thinking to do.

Chapter Seven

Finished with his steak and potatoes, Dustin set his fork and knife on his plate, resigned to the fact Sidney Calhoun was not joining him for supper. After he'd been seated, he waited a good forty minutes before ordering and had eaten much more slowly than was his norm.

He was disappointed, but not surprised. She'd made her feelings crystal clear today. The less she saw of any McCutcheon, the better.

Glancing around at the candlelit tables occupied by happy couples filled Dustin's chest with melancholy. The soft sounds of the single violin being played in the corner of the room added to his discomfort. Not that he was thinking about Miss Calhoun, or even Lily. The fact was, he'd been alone for a long time. He'd be damned if he could recollect the last time he'd been in love. An eternity since he'd had someone special to think about, or know she was thinking about him.

Who? He searched his memory. Annalise Bergonise? Could that many years have passed? She was a schoolgirl, and he used to put twigs in her hair to get her attention. There was always Martha Brown, yes, good and steady Martha. Daniel's widow had been sweet on him for the past two years, and let him know her feelings too, but Dustin couldn't muster any real interest in her. He liked her well enough as a friend, and her daughter Candy, who was a cute little snippet. But marriage?

Dustin shook his head and downed the last of his beer. He was pitiful. He'd had wild times in San Antonio and other places, with women who'd given generously of themselves, but he'd never entertained the thought of marriage. That was, until Lily Anthony came to town on a bullet-riddled stagecoach. She'd snagged his attention and got him thinking. And dreaming.

A small smile tugged at his lips as he remembered the first time he'd seen her as she stepped off the stage with her elderly aunt. For a short span of time, he really believed she was the one for him. Too bad she'd felt differently. His cousin John was a lucky man.

The waiter approached. "How was your supper, sir? Was the steak to your liking?" His gaze meandered to Dustin's empty plate.

"Very good, thank you."

"Will there be anything else? Coffee? Dessert? Whiskey?"

"No, thanks," Dustin said, suddenly feeling tired—and a bit too old.

One more day, and they could start home. He'd be glad to be back on Rim Rock land, but what would his days be like watching over the hothead Noah Calhoun? Pa wouldn't like that one bit.

He pulled money from his clip, enough for his meal and a tip, and exited the Longhorn.

The balmy temperature made the air feel heavy. He walked leisurely down the street, wondering where Chaim and Emmeline had dined, wondered if they'd finished and were perhaps taking a stroll hand in hand to extend their last few moments together.

Dustin had said his good-byes earlier before they'd gone for supper, knowing they'd want to be alone tonight and tomorrow. Love was a fickle lady, to be sure. She had a way of ripping out your heart, even when you didn't have anyone to love.

Entering the almost empty hotel lobby, Dustin removed his hat. He glanced at the number five slot as he passed by the counter, curious to see if Miss Calhoun had gotten his message.

"I gave her your note as soon as she walked in the front door."

Dustin had hoped to get away unseen. He turned to find Jim standing in the office doorway. Discussing why the young woman had not accepted his invitation was the last thing he wanted to do.

"Thank you. I appreciate it."

Taking the stairs, he passed by Emmeline's room and then Chaim's, contemplating the anxiety his brother would be shouldering come nine o'clock tomorrow morning. Good thing they had plenty to keep them busy the rest of the day, with an early departure the next.

Good thing, indeed.

Early the next morning, Chaim knocked quietly on Emmeline's hotel room door and waited, his stomach knotted as tight as his heeling rope cinched down on some poor calf's hooves. He glanced at his watch. Ten minutes until eight. The day and hour had arrived.

The door opened, and Emmeline greeted him with a wobbly smile. Like always, her dark hair was perfectly styled and her dress immaculate. She'd never looked more beautiful. A pain sliced his heart.

She searched his eyes. "Good morning."

"Good morning to you," he replied, leaning forward to gently kiss her lips. "Did you sleep?"

She lifted a shoulder. "Not really." Her lips trembled and she glanced away. "I tossed and turned all night," she whispered as she stepped forward.

He closed his arms around her.

He kissed her then, a real kiss, a kiss that would tell her how much he loved her and how much she meant to him. He buried his face in the crook of her neck so she couldn't see his tortured eyes, and took in her light lavender scent.

"Don't go."

She leaned back and ran her hands up his chest. "I have to. Please try to understand."

Even though they'd talked the subject into the ground, he said, "For your father."

She nodded. "Yes, of course."

Three doors down, a man stepped out into the hall, and Chaim and Emmeline moved apart.

The fellow hardly glanced their way before proceeding down the passageway and was gone.

Emmeline straightened her skirt and looked back through the open door.

"We better get moving," Chaim said. An elephant-sized dose of regret sat on his chest.

He stepped into her room and hoisted her travel trunk into his arms, and she gathered her train case and cape. In the hallway, he followed her until they arrived at the stairway, where she let him go down first.

They stopped at the hotel counter.

"Good morning, Mr. McCutcheon," the attendant said. "Miss Jordan, did you want that taken to the station?"

Chaim nodded and withdrew a few coins from his pocket. "Yes."

The fellow smiled and glanced at Emmeline. "You have a safe trip home, Miss Jordan. It's been our pleasure to serve you."

"Thank you, Mr. Wainscot. I certainly will."

The short little man with the balding head beamed, charmed by his fiancée's smile and attention, which wasn't surprising. She had a way of rendering most men speechless.

"I'll be looking for your return."

She smiled and nodded.

A short time later, his fiancée looked like a dark-haired angel standing next to the waiting train. Her cape elegantly draped her slender shoulders as people scurried past to get aboard and settled for the nine o'clock departure. Every few moments, steam hissed from under the steel wheels, making Chaim want to scoop her into his arms and carry her away, rendering the parting impossible.

He memorized the way she looked, how her gaze lovingly touched his.

"You know your transfer in Concepción, then," he asked gruffly, knowing he'd asked her the same exact thing last night. "I want you to be careful. Don't talk to any strangers."

Emmeline lifted her hand and placed her palm gently on his cheek. "My dearest Chaim, I know exactly how to do this. I came out from Boston by myself, remember? I'll be fine. And if I do get mixed up, all I need is this."

She pulled a paper from the pocket of her cape. "I have everything right here, thanks to you." He'd written out her schedule and how to make the changes.

Her smile lit her face. That she almost seemed excited to board the eastbound train hurt.

"But I won't stop worrying over *you*, Chaim. You're breaking my heart with all your sad puppy-dog looks."

In her usual fashion, Emmeline was talking silly to try to cheer him up, but it didn't matter. Nothing could make him feel better at a time like this.

He didn't reply, but wrapped her in his arms again and breathed deeply, holding back his rumbling emotions.

"I love you, Emmeline," he said. "I love you with all my heart. I'll be thinking of you every moment until your return."

He felt her shiver. Leaning back and not caring who saw, he captured her lips at the same time the whistle sounded from the great steam engine. They didn't have much time. The kiss was long and passionate. Her touch was painfully teasing as she fingered the hair on the back of his neck. Her lips, warm and sweet, had the power to drive every thought from his head. He wanted to beg her not to go—but he wouldn't.

With an anguished cry, she gripped his shoulders tightly as if she'd never let him go.

"Oh, Chaim. I *do* love you too. I love you so much I feel as if my heart has been hacked from my chest with a dull knife. I'll never be the same."

She pulled back and gazed into his eyes. So much passed between them in that instant, the significance was difficult to discern.

"Time to board if you're coming with us, young lady," the middle-aged porter said, standing behind them. Everyone else who had been on the train platform earlier was now boarded.

"This is it, Emmeline. Have a good trip, say hello to your parents, and tell them I'm looking forward to meeting them."

She smiled up into his face. "I will, my love. I will."

He helped her up the steps, her hand held firmly in his. When she pulled away and glanced down the aisle inside the train car, Emmeline's smile brightened.

Chaim stilled, a stone landing in his gut. Her words suddenly felt hollow. Why did she say she'd never be the same? Was this the last time he'd ever see Emmeline Jordan?

Chapter Eight

Dustin and Chaim sat their horses as Noah Calhoun was led from the San Antonio jailhouse, escorted by a potbellied old deputy holding a black Stetson. The man handed Noah his hat.

Sidney's brother, whose rumpled clothes and stubble-covered jaw made him appear quite disreputable, lacked any type of weapon. For that, Dustin was grateful. He didn't know what kind of man Noah was, and he didn't aim to find out by getting shot in the back.

The deputy instructed Noah to wait a moment, and went back into the building.

The ride back would be long and hot, but they'd arrive in Rio Wells by evening. He hoped Miss Calhoun and Noah would keep pace.

Noah sent him a disdainful look and then walked over to his sister where she stood with two mounts, saddled and laden with two heavy packs. Seemed she'd hit about every store in San Antonio yesterday. She had a Winchester in her scabbard and a six-shooter on her hip. A medium-sized shaggy brown dog sat at her heels.

"This should be interesting," he said under his breath to Chaim.

Since returning from the train station, Chaim had been quiet, keeping pretty much to himself—exactly like Dustin had expected.

Chaim glanced at him. "I don't like it. Pa will hit the roof. You know what he thinks of Jock Calhoun and his ludicrous claim. This will rile him good."

"Well, he'll have to accept him, because we don't have a choice. I don't like being responsible for this ruffian one little bit."

Chaim chuckled, the first sound of humor Dustin had heard from his brother in days.

"I'd hardly call Noah a ruffian," Chaim replied. "He looks pretty harmless to me."

"Don't let him fool you."

Dustin tried not to look at Sidney dressed in pants, shirt, vest, and Stetson. She wore the clothes easily, and by the way she moved, he presumed that was more her normal attire than the frilly dress she wore for her performance in the courtroom. The thick ponytail that reached the middle of her back reminded him of butterscotch candy.

"I'll tell you one thing," he said. "Noah's not staying in the house. The bunkhouse will be plenty good enough. That way, we won't have to see him past working hours."

Chaim tilted his head. "What about her?"

"I haven't the faintest clue what she's planning. I was assigned Noah, not his sister."

The deputy sheriff returned and handed a slip of paper to Noah, and then strode over to Dustin and Chaim with another.

Dustin extended a hand. "What's this?"

"Paperwork on what's expected."

Dustin glanced down at three chicken-scratched lines. "I'm to keep Judge Halford informed. Keep Calhoun under control.

Make sure he earns enough to pay off the saloon keeper, plus a fifty-dollar fine."

He refrained from smirking, keeping in mind the new leaf he was working on. "Not asking for the moon, are you?" He struggled to keep the contempt out of his voice. "I'd think foisting Calhoun off on me would be unconstitutional. I'm a private citizen, and don't hold any type of law office. I don't wear a badge. I have work to do, and he'll hinder my every move."

"Don't matter a whit," the deputy said. "If you're ordered by Judge Halford ta babysit for a few days, weeks, months, *or years* . . . you'll babysit." His lips flattened. "That's just the way things are around here."

That last statement gave Dustin pause. Back in Rio Wells, Pete Miller had been promoted to acting sheriff after Sheriff Dane was murdered. The town was shorthanded until the position could be filled by a lawman who wanted it, so Dustin wouldn't find help there.

Dustin folded the note and put the directive in his front pocket. "Mount up," he called to the Calhouns. "Time to hit the trail."

The two did, but stayed where they sat.

They aren't going to make this easy.

Dustin swallowed a curse and closed the twenty feet between them to where Sidney and Noah sat their horses.

"We don't like this any more than you do," he said, "I can promise you that. But that doesn't mean we have to make the experience worse. Let's get to Rio Wells, then get the ordeal behind us." He looked between brother and sister, noting the resemblance in their eyes. "Is that asking too much?"

When neither of the Calhouns responded, he exchanged a look with Chaim, who'd followed, and then turned his attention back to Sidney and Noah. The early November sun felt ten degrees hotter than a moment before.

"Fine," he finally said. "I can see why my old man calls yours stubborn-headed. I guess I can't blame him. You two are mulish, bad-tempered, and—"

When Noah spurred his horse forward, presumably going for Dustin, Chaim caught Noah's horse's bridle and pulled him around.

"We'll have none of that," he barked into Noah's face, and then shot an angry look at Dustin as well. "The ride is hard, and we're only stopping once to rest and water the horses. Keep this up, and you won't have the energy to cross the badlands. You'll ride behind, but don't think you can make a run for it. With only Miss Calhoun's weapons, you'd be easy targets for the Comancheros. The local bands know the McCutcheons and pretty much leave us alone. Stay close."

Dustin turned his attention to Sidney and motioned to her guns. "Can I trust you with those? You won't try to bust him out of my guard?"

She pinned him with an icy stare but didn't respond.

"Guess that means yes. Can we trust *him*?"

"Of course you can. Calhouns aren't murderers," she replied, clenching her jaw. "If you get killed, it won't be by us."

The dog sitting at her horse's hooves growled and bared his fangs.

"Charming," Dustin said, turning his horse toward the way that led to Rio Wells. "Let's go."

Chapter Nine

By noon, Sidney was more than ready for a break, preferably in the shade if they could find any.

The Calhoun ranch was situated in the hills of Santa Fe. She was used to cool breezes that brought new life and energy. Each evening, temperatures dropped after the sun set. Too bad Rio Wells was so much farther south. She missed the tall white fur and blue spruce, and the shorter silver sage and chokecherry that made Santa Fe beautiful. West Texas was stark, brown, and hot. The sea of granite rocks before her made her wonder how the McCutcheon cattle subsisted at all.

Still at a ground-covering jog that would save their mounts' energy, she leaned forward in her stirrups, giving her back a rest. She'd stopped several miles back and hefted Jackson onto her horse in front of her saddle. He was her working dog, but rarely was he required to run all day. She'd brought him along, thinking he'd be company on the train and in her hotel room, and that she'd be back in Santa Fe in no time. Now she wished she'd left him at home.

Sidney removed her hat, ran her already dirty shirtsleeve over her forehead, and tried to wet her lips with her tongue, all the while standing in her stirrups at the trot. Her mouth felt as sandy as the ground below. Her lips chapped. She screwed her

Stetson tightly back on, thankful for the relief from the unrelenting sun directly overhead. The scent of the warm leather hatband drenched in sweat reached her. The hat was worth every penny of the ten dollars the San Antonio merchant had charged, robbery or not.

Her attention, riveted to the back of Dustin McCutcheon, felt as hot as the sun in the cloudless sky. She'd gotten his note last night, only a few minutes after he'd left the hotel, according to the clerk. *What nerve.* Did the man think she'd just roll over because Noah was in his charge for the next few weeks? He'd wanted to talk about her brother's rehabilitation? Ha! More like he wanted to rub their bad fortune in her face.

She stiffened, thinking about his casual words. She'd as soon dine with him—or any other McCutcheon—as with a six-foot-long rattlesnake.

Heat waves in the distance wiggled toward the sky. Far off, a building came into view. Maybe that was where they planned to stop. Directly in front of her, Dustin's broad back brought to mind the time she'd seen him in Kansas City all those years ago.

She'd thought him handsome, but that was before she understood how dirty his father had played with her pa. If not for Winston McCutcheon, her father wouldn't be the crippled man he was today. Yes, they'd lost the contract, but that didn't bother her as much as the way her father's so-called friend had double-crossed him.

When Dustin glanced back, she jerked her gaze toward the arroyo filled with rocks, one lonely tree, and the bleached rib cage of a large animal. From the corner of her eye, she could see the brothers had reined down to a walk. Soon she and Noah were by their sides.

Dustin gestured at the building up ahead. "We'll unsaddle and give the horses a breather for about an hour. Refill your canteens and eat what you brought," he directed, glancing at her saddlebags. "By the time we reach Rio Wells, we'll be greeting the evening, and we won't be stopping again."

At this closer range, she could now make out a corral around back, a small lean-to barn, and a windmill.

Dustin and his brother drew their guns and split up as they approached the shack. Dustin rode wide and when he was close, he dismounted and advanced on the windowless building.

Chaim sat his horse with his weapon trained on the door.

With his back to the wall, Dustin eased along the front of the building, then nudged open the door with the toe of his boot. Several seconds passed before he crouched down to look inside.

Intrigued, she realized that if someone were waiting to shoot him, they'd have their gun aimed at about five feet high.

Turning, he waved them over.

"You pack any food?" Noah asked as they slowly rode toward the man who was in control of Noah's life.

"Meat, bread, jerky, and a few other things."

Noah smiled his thanks, but she could see his uncertainty. Sweat ringed his arms. He glanced at her with his uncommonly light blue eyes that always reminded her of ice on a lake. He uncapped his canteen and chugged down water before dismounting.

Sidney couldn't help but worry over his impulsiveness. Despite being his sister and not his mother, she'd raised him and loved him almost like a son. She didn't want to see him come to a bad end.

At the corral fence, Sidney did her best to ignore the brothers to her left. Leaning over, she carefully dropped Jackson to the ground and dismounted, feeling hot and sticky. Her back muscles ached. The dog trotted off into the rock outcropping behind the small settlement and disappeared.

Tossing her reins over the top rail of the corral, she went to her gelding's side and unfastened the leather ties securing her saddlebags to the saddle. She was about to heft them off when a hand reached over her shoulder and grabbed the bags before she had the chance.

Startled, she whirled to find Dustin standing behind her, his tall frame blocking the sun. "I can do that," she threw out, more surprised than angry.

"I know you can. Just thought you'd get your saddle off more quickly if I took your bags to the porch." He glanced at the saddle behind her head. "You got that?"

"Of course. I've been ranching almost as long as you have."

"Fine, then."

That was a phrase she was coming to know Dustin said often. He sauntered away with her saddlebag, his, and another that must have been Chaim's, so he wasn't treating her any differently. *Good.*

Turning back to her horse, she tossed up the stirrup, worked the supple cinch, and watched her brother over the top of her horse do the same with his mount.

Chaim finished unsaddling first and led both his and Dustin's horse into the corral and turned them out. He went to the tank at the base of the windmill on the outside of the enclosure and dipped a couple of buckets, rationing the amount of water to give the hot animals.

Chaim's gelding drank and then dropped to the ground. He rolled until he had both sweaty sides covered in dirt before he stood and shook off in a cloud of dust.

She turned her horse into the corral, watered him, and went in search of food.

Up the steep incline, Jackson barked and then let out a yip of surprise.

Not another snake!

Sidney whistled and turned for the cabin, not waiting for his return. That dog was always into something.

Chapter Ten

Dustin found three workable chairs inside the shack and brought them out to the porch, where an almost unnoticeable breeze kept the area cooler than inside the stuffy room. He arranged them in a semicircle, and then strode over to the four-foot-high holding tank beside the windmill.

After removing his Stetson, he held his breath and dipped his head in the water all the way to his shoulders, and let the coolness ease over his tight nerves. He stayed that way for a good ten seconds. Straightening, he dried with the cloth he'd brought, enjoying how the air briskly nipped at his skin. He felt fresher than he had in hours. Halfway back to the shack, he met Chaim.

"That's a darn good idea," Chaim said, heading for the windmill himself. "I'm glad we refilled our canteens as soon as we dismounted."

Sidney paced back and forth on the porch as she worried her bottom lip with her teeth. A bit of grime smudged her cheek, and her face was covered with the shiny film of sweat.

That was a feeling he knew all too well. Why should she suffer when he felt as fresh as a spring rose? Her brother, finishing up at the corral gate, headed off with one of the water buckets in hand. Dustin couldn't stop a smile when she looked his way.

He held out his towel. "The water feels mighty nice. You might give it a go."

Without a reply, she reached into her saddlebags he'd hung over the back of one of the chairs, withdrew her own small towel, and headed off for the windmill.

As hungry as he was, even his food couldn't tempt him away from watching what she was about to do next. His sisters wouldn't be caught dead sticking their head in a water tank. Madeline and Becky were a rancher's daughters, but they still stuck to the norms of society. Modesty was their middle name.

Would Sidney actually do it?

Chaim, his hair soaking wet, turned and followed Dustin's gaze when he reached the porch. "Is she actually gonna—"

His words were cut short when Sidney, without missing a beat, swept off her hat and plunged her head into the tank up to her shoulders. She stayed like that for a good five seconds.

Amazed, Dustin elbowed Chaim in the side.

Noah chose that second to join them. He turned to see what they were looking at and was presented with the back side of his sister as she toweled off her head. A moment passed before he realized what she'd done.

"Quit gawking at my sister before I—"

He didn't finish his sentence, just launched himself at Dustin's throat.

Dustin caught his wrist before he had a chance to throw any punches, and he bent Noah's arm around his back, forcing his face toward the ground.

"You better think twice the next time you take me on, Calhoun, because I'll not be holding back on you again. I didn't ask for the privilege of watching your every move," Dustin growled, his attention now on the youth. "If your sister didn't want to put on a show, she didn't have to go sticking her head in the tank."

Sidney approached with a shiny clean face as she finger combed her long hair, now wet and free from its constraint. As soon as she saw his hold on Noah, she scowled and hurried her last few steps.

"What's this?"

When Dustin shoved Noah away, the young Calhoun stumbled forward, off the porch and into the dirt, producing a cloud of dust. Sidney rushed to his side, but he shook her off when she tried to help him stand.

Turning, she glared at Dustin. "I asked you a question!"

"They were staring at you!" Noah threw out. "Making a spectacle of yourself. You should be ashamed."

"Let 'em stare! Maybe the bumpkins have never seen a woman before." Her jaw worked angrily as if she were holding back. "I don't know. You can't blame a person for wanting to cool off."

Noah's face flushed, and Dustin laughed at her attempt to rile him.

"And just so you know," she went on, her hair dripping down over her soaked shoulders to her back and front, "I'm not ashamed of anything I do. I'm hot and filthy. I may strip down, dive in, and take a bath. That sure would feel good."

Lord Almighty! Sidney Calhoun was one hell of a woman! He was sure not just anyone could take her on and live to tell about it.

Noah glared at her but held his tongue. He tromped to his saddlebag, and then eyeing the three chairs, plopped onto the edge of the porch with his back to the rest of them, gazing across the arid lands in silence.

Sidney took her saddlebag off the back of one chair and sat, settling the cumbersome leather in her lap. She rummaged through one side until she brought out a hunk of meat and bread wrapped in a cloth.

Her dog appeared and whined for a handout as he sat eye to eye next to Noah on the side of the porch. Sidney tossed him several strips of jerky and the heel of her bread.

The meal passed in silence, except for the dog that had started pacing the porch after he'd been fed.

Finished, Dustin brushed off his fingers and dropped his leather bags to the ground. "So, what kind of a name is Sidney, anyway? I always thought you were a boy."

Chaim straightened and shot him a *walk softly* look.

Sidney's brow arched. "It can go either way," she said, totally unperturbed. "I'd rather sound like a boy than a dog or a broken-down old gelding."

"She's got you there, *Dustin*," Chaim said on the tail end of a chortle. He tipped back his chair on its rear legs and rested against the building, looking at him with drowsy eyes.

Too relaxed to take any offense, especially since he'd started it, Dustin felt a smile playing around the corners of his mouth. "How come you're not married, Miss Calhoun? Usually by your age, a woman has a passel of children."

She fumbled the last of the bread in her hands, but quickly recovered. "My age? How old do you think I am?" Her face was as stoic as an Indian's.

His marital question had started out as payment for her name-calling. Now, though, her cool demeanor challenged him further. She thought he couldn't get under her skin.

Dustin looked at her for a good ten seconds, as if taking stock, and color blossomed in her cheeks. "Past thirty."

Chaim held his tongue, not giving him away. They had plenty of practice teasing Madeline and Becky at home.

Her lips instantly flattened out, and her nostrils flared the tiniest bit. "What business is my age to you, McCutcheon?" she snapped.

She busied her hands inside her saddlebags, pulling out a withered apple that had seen better days. She took a healthy bite and glared out across the scenery as she chewed.

"Absolutely none," he replied lazily. "Just passing the time. Thought we could get a little better acquainted."

Noah spun, his mouth a hard, straight line. Looked as if the kid was ready to explode with want of defense of the sister he clearly loved.

"She'll be twenty-five on her next birthday," he gritted out. "Has had several offers by the richest men in Santa Fe. Just this July, Gibson Harp, owner of the hotel, mercantile, and livery, came asking for her hand. He's still waiting on her—"

"Noah!" Sidney glowered at her brother, swallowing down a large mouthful of apple before she could respond.

Her bloodless face was pinched tight. Dustin noted a few light-colored freckles he hadn't seen before scattered across the bridge of her nose.

"If you feel the need to run your mouth, then blather about yourself or any of the rest of the Calhouns, but not me! I'd think you knew better than that."

Thoroughly chastised, Noah returned to his previous position and rested his chin on his palm.

Amused, Dustin glanced at Chaim, but his brother already had his eyes closed, so he tipped his hat forward. Crossing his arms over his chest, he slouched down in the chair, intending to have a brief nap. As soon as he'd settled, the dog jumped to his feet and let out a fierce bark.

Instantly, everyone was wide-awake. Without standing to draw attention, Dustin took a quick survey of the surrounding landscape. Sidney grabbed Jackson's collar and pulled him to her side, keeping him from sounding any more alarms.

Seeing nothing, Dustin stood, signaling the others to stay put and keep acting like nothing had spooked them. He glanced toward the back of the building, past the corral and the rock outcroppings some fifty feet away. Close to the top, amid the craggy boulders, several riders sat on horses.

"We've got company," he said under his breath, not turning from the men he watched.

"Comancheros?" Chaim asked.

"Thought you said they leave you alone," Noah said.

"They do," Chaim replied. "Usually. Maybe they're just looking. Or maybe they're outcasts, the very worst kind. They don't hold by any rules, and certainly not their own."

"Don't look like Comancheros to me," Dustin said. "Too well fed and mounted. But they're outlaws of some sort."

Sidney stood and slowly made her way to Dustin's side, keeping a secure hold on her dog. She glanced up the rise. "Are they after our horses?"

"That would be my guess," Dustin replied. "And our money, and anything else of value we have."

He didn't mention they'd want her too, but that was a given. He wanted to push her back, keep her out of view, but he knew better than to try.

Noah climbed to his feet. "I feel naked without a gun. You can't leave me defenseless."

"You're right," Dustin agreed, turning to face him. "Only thing, Sidney's rifle is still in its scabbard on her saddle, as are ours." He gestured to the corral fence where all the rigs hung, baking in the sun.

Noah took a step. "I'll get it. I can be there and back in five seconds."

Dustin grasped the young man's shoulder as he was about to leave the building's protective overhang and go out to the corral. "Let's not do that quite yet."

Chaim stepped close. "What're ya thinking?"

"I say we go about our business of resting the animals. It's more prudent now than ever if we have to make a run for it. If they meant to attack before we mounted up, they would've by now without coming out into the open. They'd want to take us by surprise."

Sidney nodded. "Besides, there's not much else we can do. But we don't want to get trapped down here after dark. They'd have the advantage of height, and knowing the land."

He watched her gaze drift to her brother and soften, a protective light moving across her face. She probably felt about Noah as he did about Chaim. Chaim might be a man, but he was still his little brother. One set to be married in little over a month. Dustin was determined not to let anything happen to him, or either of the Calhouns.

Another look at Sidney's profile, as businesslike as any man's and yet beautiful and soft, made him reach for his canteen. She wouldn't like him thinking those thoughts about her, *any* thoughts, for that matter—and neither would his pa.

"Let's all just sit back down and finish our rest. Your dog will let us know if they come any closer. When it's time, we'll ride right out of here."

Chapter Eleven

The hour came and went faster than Sidney thought possible. Jackson slept at her feet, seeming unaware now of the danger. She unscrewed her canteen and wet her parched mouth, watching the men as they sat in silence.

It was time to saddle up and get moving, and she was glad. The waiting was killing her.

She wasn't embarrassed to admit she was scared as hell. Her father always said a man dumb enough not to recognize danger when it looked him in the face was one stupid enough to get you killed. If a fight broke out, she'd rather it happened on the run, where they had a chance, where they could split up if needed. Here they'd be trapped like rats in this hot box, easy enough to be slaughtered.

Glancing about, she took in the dry land that stretched as far as the eye could see. *If only Jock Jr. were here.*

Her oldest brother had stepped into her father's boots when the patriarch of the Calhoun clan seemed unable to lift the load any longer. Oh, he let Pa think he was making the decisions and such, but her brother was the one orchestrating things to his liking. Jock Jr. was smart and hard, and he could get them out of any situation. She trusted him implicitly.

She glanced at Dustin and then at Chaim, her doubt growing in leaps and bounds. Were they good shots? Expert horsemen? Would they know what to do in a sticky situation where the decision of each moment could mean life or death? In a matter of minutes, she'd find out.

Dustin stood, and Jackson climbed to his feet and wagged his tail.

She was worried about her dog, as well. He'd have a better chance on the ground, and not as a target as each of the riders would be. The forty-pound animal was too bulky to try to hold in front of her saddle at a dead run.

Bad choice of words.

She scratched him under his chin and stroked his head several times, smiling into his face. Jackson was smart and tough. If he couldn't keep up, he'd find his way by scent.

When Chaim stood and stretched his back, she and Noah followed suit, her brother's uncertain glance making her stomach sour. Time might have arrived, but she'd not leave her brother defenseless.

"Noah's good with a six-shooter." She lifted her gun from its holster and checked the chambers. "At a run, a handgun would be better than the rifle. Do either of you have an extra?"

Dustin strode to the side of the porch and scanned the hill where he'd first seen the Comancheros. His wide shoulders filled his tan shirt. The fabric stretched across his back. She jerked her gaze away to rest on the black hat he held in his hands.

The older McCutcheon nodded. "Yeah. I'd already intended on giving him the one in my saddlebag." He withdrew the gun and handed it to Noah. "Don't make me regret this," he said, his steely voice pitched low.

Noah checked the chambers and then stuck the Colt in his waistband. "Thanks."

His tone could have been nicer, but at least the attitude was a far cry from his petulance before trouble arrived. For that, Sidney was glad. Like it or not, she and Noah needed the McCutcheons now more than ever.

Chaim opened the left side of his saddlebag. "Let's divvy up this ammunition."

Sidney hadn't planned on more than a few days in Santa Fe, just long enough to get Noah out of jail and head back home. She'd brought her gun, as she always did, but only packed a handful of shells. After learning Noah's fate in San Antonio and that they'd be riding on to Rio Wells, she'd purchased a box at a local gun shop. Still, the amount wasn't near enough if they got into a shootout. Helping herself to several large handfuls, she dropped them into her bag. Noah did the same.

Dustin screwed his hat down tight. He pointed out across the arid land, filled with brown blowing grass and boulders. A few lone trees dotted the landscape, and a copse here and there broke up the horizon.

"See that slight rise, where the skyline looks like the curve of a hawk's beak leaning on its side?" he asked, never taking his gaze from the direction he was looking.

Several moments passed as she struggled to find the spot he intended.

"Under the only dark cloud in the sky," he bit out.

"Yeah," she replied, ignoring the pinching sensation in her gut.

Her father wouldn't bear it if his youngest son was killed. Noah was the only Calhoun that resembled their mother, having the same eyes and hair. Him dying now would finish off her pa, especially if his demise happened in the presence of a McCutcheon.

Noah nodded. "Yeah, I see the mark."

"Good. Beyond that's Draper Bottom, a small community, and beyond that is Rio Wells. If we get split up, head there and wait. At a gallop, the crossing will take about an hour. Between here and there are a few places to hide out, rocks, a copse or two, but not much more. Ride hard and make for that town."

He turned and gave them all a hard look. The muscle in his jaw worked several times before he added, "I don't believe the situation will come to that. If they were planning to make a play, they would've by now, or before we had our horses under us."

He sounded confident, but Sidney wasn't letting down her guard until they hit that town. She didn't need or want platitudes to make her feel better.

"Our horses aren't under us," Noah said. "They'll make their move when we're in the corral."

A look passed between Dustin and Chaim.

Noah was right. In the enclosure, whoever they were would have a clear shot from up in the rocks. No need to waste a bunch of hard-won bullets. Just wait until they had their quarry in one spot.

Chaim gave a nod. "Could be."

Dustin looked her up and down and then glanced at Noah.

Maybe he thought they'd slow them down. She and her brother could outride a McCutcheon on any given day, as long as the horseflesh was one they'd bred on their ranch. She had no idea what the horses she'd purchased in San Antonio could do.

"Don't worry. We'll keep up," she said, squinting her eyes right back at him.

"Good." He turned. "We'll all go at once. Saddle as fast as you can. The horses are rested and have had plenty to drink. They'll go a long way. Be as quiet as possible. The outlaws may be taking a little siesta themselves, and we can get a head start. We should mount up at the same time and ride out silently, unless, of course, shooting starts."

"I'm ready, brother," Chaim said. "Nothing's gonna happen. I intend to get married on the date that's planned, so I'm not getting killed now. To disappoint Emmeline like that is not in my makeup."

Dustin chuckled. "Good to know."

Sidney didn't miss how Dustin's gaze lingered lovingly on his younger brother.

Wedding? She hadn't heard a thing about Chaim and a fiancée. She hoped he hadn't gone and jinxed them all by saying that. Everyone was probably thinking the same thing. Why the heck did he have to voice the possibility and give it life?

Dustin hitched his head, and the four stepped out from under the lean-to shed roof and made for the corral in an eerie silence.

A grasshopper clacked from somewhere around Sidney's boots, but she kept her gaze trained on the hill. It didn't slip her notice that Dustin walked in her direct line of fire, as if shielding her from harm. The sun was warm in the cloudless sky. A trickle of sweat ran between her shoulder blades, making her shiver.

"When you shiver, mi florecilla, *someone is casting a shadow on your grave."*

Startled, Sidney pushed away the memory of Carmen's superstitious words. Their housekeeper, who had also functioned as a nanny for the early part of Sidney's life, ran the ranch house with great efficiency, even to this day.

At any other time, Sidney would have smiled, thinking of the sweet nickname Carmen had given her, meaning *my little flower*. The pleasantly plump woman was afraid of her own shadow, and she knew every superstition on the face of the earth. In this case, Sidney prayed the motherly woman was dead wrong.

Another bad choice of words.

With a pounding heart, Sidney plucked her bridle from her saddle horn and strode through the gate Dustin had opened. Without a word or a sound, they went to their horses, slid on the bridles, and hurried back for their rigs.

Noah's horse flipped his head and shied away every time her brother attempted to slip the leather crown piece over his ears.

I knew that horse would give us a problem!

The McCutcheons were almost finished. She dropped the cinch in her hands and let the equipment swing under her horse's belly, then ran over to Noah's horse.

Noah's face was beet red, and angry lines fanned out from his mouth. If they hadn't been under a threat, by now he'd be cussing a blue streak. She grabbed the tall bay's ear and pulled his blazed face down until they were eye to eye.

"Mulish broomtail," Noah mumbled, slipping on the bridle. "I hope he can run."

"Hurry up," she whispered. "The McCutcheons are waiting."

Dustin had finished the job she'd started with her horse, his hands swiftly pulling her cinch strap and lacing the end onto the front rigging dee. Completed, he secured the back cinch.

Noah went for his saddle and was back in a moment.

Jackson trotted between the horses, his serious gaze following her every move, but thankfully he kept quiet.

Chaim was already mounted. His horse danced with excitement from the strange way he had been hustled out of his rest. The younger McCutcheon watched the hill behind them, his gun drawn and ready to defend them if the need arose.

"Mount up," Dustin commanded quietly.

"Noah's not quite ready—"

"I said mount up."

She did, all the while feeling as if she'd lose the bread and jerky she'd eaten only a little while ago.

Dustin held Noah's skittish horse until her brother was finished. Just as Dustin's foot hit his stirrup to mount, a cry sounded from somewhere on the hill, followed by three rapid-fire shots.

Chaim returned several shots of his own.

Her horse reared when a bullet landed between his front hooves, causing her off-side foot to slip from the stirrup. Sidney grasped his thick mane, ready to ride as soon as his feet touched the earth.

Chapter Twelve

Dustin leaned forward, giving his horse full rein. Chaim and Noah had been first out of the gate and led the way. Sidney was directly in front of him, her left foot still searching for the stirrup as they galloped out into the open land.

He glanced back. A handful of outlaws, no more than five, descended the hill on horseback behind the shack, giving chase. As he'd thought, they must have been resting as well, counting on hearing them saddle up. Out of range for gunplay at this point, the only sounds were his horses' hooves in the dirt and the air rushing by his ears.

When Sidney reached down to touch her sidearm and then glanced back at him, he hoped she'd concentrate on riding and leave the shooting to the men.

Pushing his horse close to hers, he shouted, "Hold your fire unless they start shooting. I'd rather outrun 'em if we can." *And I don't want to get killed by you.*

She nodded, lying over her horse's neck, urging him faster with her arms. He let her pull away, putting himself between her and the outlaw's bullets.

Chaim and Noah, a good five horse lengths ahead, rode hard. Chaim glanced back at him and caught Dustin's eye, but he waved Chaim on.

He checked behind to see the outlaws had cut the distance between them. It wouldn't be long before they started shooting. He'd guess they had about fifty feet before they'd be in range. As much as he didn't like to think it, they might be in trouble.

Sidney's golden braid bounced as she rode like she'd been born on a horse's back. A surge of protectiveness surged through him as he kept his gaze anchored to her back, the whipping of her ponytail, and the dirt flying from her horse's hooves.

Good girl. You ride like a man. Can't say I'm surprised.

Pulling his revolver, he was about to yell forward for her to catch the others when her horse stumbled. To his horror, he watched her chestnut crumple to his knees and slide forward, his nose buried in the dirt. Dust billowed everywhere. Chaim and Noah galloped on, unaware that anything had happened.

No!

His heart thwacking painfully in his chest, Dustin instantly pulled up and holstered his gun. Unable to stop in time, he shot past her, but by the time he'd turned back, she'd somehow pulled herself out of the tangle of horseflesh and chased after her gelding. The horse had taken off at a gallop in the opposite direction and was already much too far away.

"Forget him!" Dustin yelled.

"My saddlebag!"

"No time!"

Dustin circled as dirt kicked up at her feet from an outlaw's badly placed shot. Clasping her forearm, he hefted her up and swung her behind. Good thing she was strong. She teetered precariously to one side for several strides, and he thought he'd lose her. Staying astride by some miracle, she locked her arms around his middle like a wet cinch dried in the sun, and shouted in his ear to get moving faster. They were already at a controlled gallop.

With her settled, he spurred his horse all out. Bullets whizzed past and peppered the ground.

The double weight meant his horse's strength could be gone in a short time. They'd be caught. The capture wouldn't be pretty for him, but much worse for her.

Galloping flat out, he drew his Colt and tried to swivel, but with her snug up against him, the action was difficult. He squeezed off two shots.

Sidney nudged his back. "I'll shoot! You keep riding!"

That was wise because the land they covered was dotted with scrub oaks, bushes, and rocks. Going down now would mean sure death.

He felt his mount dig deep for stamina. He'd lost sight of Chaim, but he was sure his brother would head straight back now that gunshots had been fired. Dustin hoped not. It would be hard enough on the family if he were killed; he didn't want Chaim to be killed too.

Or Noah and Sidney, he thought, feeling her heat through the back of his shirt.

The problems the families had shared in the past evaporated, and all he could think about was her. How she could make him smile or want to cuss. Her flashing eyes and what they did to his insides.

He remembered his first reaction to her in the mercantile. He was attracted to her, he grudgingly admitted to himself. Fine time to realize that now. He hoped this enlightenment was not just the last wish of a dead man.

She turned and shot a couple of rounds, and her shout of success said she'd hit her target.

Seconds later a bullet ripped by, tearing the sleeve of his shirt. He jerked back at the pain.

"You hit?" she hollered in his ear.

"Just grazed. Keep shooting!"

He hated that she rode behind, in essence acting as his shield.

"I'm out of bullets! I'm exchanging guns."

A dense stand of manzanita lined the left side of the trail only fifty feet ahead.

"Wait," he shouted. "Reload yours and take mine. When I say, give 'em both guns. We need to create a diversion so I can pull off the trail without being seen. Rebel's about spent. Won't be long before they catch us."

He felt her fumble around. She leaned over and reached under her leg to the saddlebag that held the ammunition as they galloped. She flinched when several more shots hissed past, making him think none of the outlaws were very good shots. Once she had her gun loaded, she drew his from the holster, gripping a weapon in each hand. They were almost to the spot he planned to turn.

"Ready?" he shouted.

He felt her nod.

"You're shooting to kill, aren't you, Calhoun?"

"Whatta ya think, McCutcheon!"

"Okay, we're almost there," he hollered over his shoulder. "When I say, open up and give 'em all you've got. Shoot fast, so they have to pull up and turn away. Ready. Now!"

Dustin glanced over his shoulder when she twisted. She'd crossed her arms in front of her torso, making turning easier. With a revolver in each hand, she alternated shots from side to side, which were coming fast. The only thing keeping her on the horse were her strong legs and incredible balance.

She whooped once, and he thought that must mean she'd hit her mark again. If that were true, that left three—a much more manageable number. When he started the turn with her guns still blazing, he reached back and grasped her thigh to help her stay seated.

In the cover of the brush, he immediately slowed and picked his way through the tight ironwood bushes, keeping his head down. Sharp barbs cut through the sleeves of his shirt, and he thought he heard her swallow a cry of pain. They reached an outcropping of rocks and he circled behind, giving them partial cover. He prayed the diversion was enough, and the riders would pass them being none the wiser.

Dustin let out a breath as the outlaws galloped by. "We don't have much time before they discover they've been tricked. Hand me your gun and slide off." He offered his arm, which Sidney grasped, slipping easily to the ground. She must have cut her face when her horse went down, because she had blood everywhere he hadn't seen before.

He quickly reloaded her gun and handed over the weapon. After doing the same with his own, he slipped the weapon into his holster.

Turning his horse, he headed out the way they came.

"What're you doing?" she demanded. "Wait up!"

"You hold tight." Dustin unwound his canteen and tossed it back. The container hit the ground at her feet with a thud. "If I don't return, stay out of sight overnight, and then before dawn make for the marker I showed you. Draper Bottom's not so far that you can't make it on foot."

"McCutcheon! Stop this instant!"

He made for the trail, wanting to be far from Sidney Calhoun when the outlaws returned.

"Why, you low-down, double-crossing, lily-livered . . ."

As dire as their situation was, Dustin couldn't help laughing at the fury in her voice. He was glad he was mounted and she couldn't catch him. He didn't know what would be worse—facing three bloodthirsty bandits, or a furious Sidney Calhoun after she'd been duped.

At the boundary of the brush line, he pulled up and listened. Hearing only silence, he took off at a gallop toward Chaim and Noah, and the unsuspecting outlaws.

Chapter Thirteen

Sidney was still giving him the silent treatment when the group ambled into Rio Wells an hour after midnight. She'd been angry as a cornered polecat when they'd returned to pick her up after subduing the outlaws.

The remaining three had galloped straight into Chaim and Noah on their way back, with Dustin quickly closing in from behind. One outlaw was killed, and the other two quickly threw down their guns.

Dustin noted the sleepy streets. Everything was quiet. Lanterns—in front of the hotel, the stage office, and the sheriff's office—gave a modicum of light, aided by the moon.

He glanced over at Chaim with Sidney behind his saddle. The three men had switched off carrying her. Her mutt padded quietly behind Chaim's horse, his head still surprisingly high after such a long journey.

Now, though, exhausted from hours on the trail, Sidney looked like a little girl worn out from a full day at school—but he knew better than to trust that perception. One of her hands hung loosely at her side, and she grasped the back of Chaim's saddle with the other.

He remembered his wild thoughts when they'd been outrunning the outlaws. Dangerous ones about him and Sidney . . .

Annoyed with himself, Dustin shook the crazy idea from his head. He'd better keep his distance unless he wanted to unleash a war within his own family. His pa would consider the turn in loyalty the ultimate betrayal if Dustin were to let himself befriend her, or even like her.

Besides, she was cantankerous. Liked to argue with every word out of his mouth. He needed someone like Lily, soft and compliant.

Reining up in front of the sheriff's office, Dustin dismounted. "Give me a minute, and then we'll be on our way out to the Rim Rock."

"The place is dark, Dustin," Chaim said. "Deputy Miller's not inside at this time of night."

Chaim looked almost as worn out as Sidney. "I intend to leave a note. The icehouse in Draper Bottom isn't much of a jail. Miller needs to get over there first thing and relieve Mr. Newson. We stressed the importance of not opening the door until Miller showed up, but Newson's forgetfulness has me worried."

"You tacked up several notes."

"I know, I know." Dustin shrugged and then massaged his tired neck. "Besides that, I was told to inform the law here of our arrangement with Noah Calhoun the moment we hit town. So that's exactly what I'm going to do."

Noah straightened in the saddle. "We almost done yammering?"

Dustin's gaze cut to the younger Calhoun. The impetuous Noah would be a burr under his saddle for as long as he was around.

"We'll quit yammering when I say we'll quit yammering. Got that? I'm already on Judge Halford's cranky side. I'm not making the situation worse by not following orders." He pointed. "I'm not *you*, Calhoun."

Cradle Hupton, the livery owner, came strolling down the boardwalk, black suspenders stretched over his beefy shoulders and an ample coffee mug in his hand.

"Boys, you're home!" he said, his pleasure at seeing them unmistakable by the large grin stretched across his face. "Did Miss Emmeline get off safely to Boston? I'll sure miss seeing her purty face around town, and her teasing nature. She liked to make me blush and did so often. I'll be happy when she's back—as Mrs. Chaim McCutcheon," he added quickly. His eyes went wide when he spotted the woman behind Chaim's saddle.

"She did," Chaim replied, offering nothing more.

He wasn't saying much, but Dustin knew bringing Chaim out of this funk over Emmeline would take a lot longer than a ride from San Antonio.

"Meet Miss Sidney Calhoun and her brother Noah." Dustin gestured to Sidney and then to Noah. He dismounted and dropped one rein of his tired mount.

Without any help, Sidney slipped off the back of Chaim's horse. A grimace crossed her face when her boots hit the dirt.

"Did I hear you right?" Cradle asked, his normally smiling mouth pulling down at the corners. "Did you say *Calhoun*?"

Sidney stretched both elbows behind her back and then raised one arm over her head, working out her sore muscles. She'd pitched her hat off her head when the sun had gone down, and now the headpiece dangled from a leather strap down her back over her long, messy ponytail.

Not that he'd noticed.

"You did," she said. "And to be perfectly clear, we're the same Calhouns from Santa Fe who've had a running feud with the McCutcheons for years. Does that make it seem odd that we'd show up in town after midnight, riding double?"

By cracky, this girl had spunk. Even being chased by bullet-slinging outlaws couldn't dampen her spirit. Dustin was thankful for the two horse lengths between them.

He smiled when she gave him the stink eye. "Miss Calhoun's a bit put out that I dropped her off when we had unfinished business with a few outlaws between San Antonio and Draper Bottom. She fancies herself one of the men. Noah, Sidney, this is Cradle Hupton, the livery owner and blacksmith. We passed his place on the way in, and you'll see it again on our way out to the ranch."

Cradle stood speechless. The livery owner, as well as the rest of the townsfolk of Rio Wells, had heard a thing or two about the Calhouns over the years. He took a long drink from his mug before answering.

"Pleased to make your acquaintance." His tone was a bit stiff as his gaze strayed back and forth between the two newcomers. Wasn't difficult to see he was figuring out how he should treat them.

His gaze came back to Dustin. "Would any of you like a cup of coffee? Just made a fresh pot back at my place." His gaze drifted back to Sidney and lingered admiringly.

Knowing Cradle, he'd want to get off the touchy subject as soon as possible, which was proven when he switched it up himself.

"A fellow ambled into town yestreen, claiming he'd brought the beans all the way up from South America. Poor ol' mule looked busted." He lifted the mug. "Tastes mighty good, if I do say so myself."

"Not me," Noah said, looking down with a bored expression from the back of his horse.

Dustin shook his head. The kid wouldn't try to make any points with the locals. He'd do his time in Rio Wells and be on his way.

Noah wrinkled his nose and glanced about. "I couldn't stomach anything with that horrible stench in the air. What's that stink, anyway?"

Cradle's shoulders pulled back. The youngish blacksmith watched over the town as if the developed plot of land was his child. His love for Rio Wells was evident in everything he did.

"The hot springs," Dustin said before Cradle had a chance to get mad. "You won't be badmouthing the smell quite so much after you spend a little time soaking your aching bones. But I won't bore you with the details tonight. You'll get used to it."

He'd had enough of the kid. All he wanted to do was fall into bed and sleep for a week. Unfortunately, that wouldn't happen for a while yet.

True, Noah had held up his end when capturing the outlaws, and Dustin hadn't felt in any danger when the youngest Calhoun had swung around the borrowed revolver with the ease of a marksman. Still, he'd not endure any lip or have him insult the good people of Rio Wells.

What would his pa think when they showed up with him at this time of the morning?

"That's right," Cradle added. "The hot springs, odious smells and all, have been a boon for the town. Folks have come all the way from Colorado and Nebraska to sit in the healing waters." He chuckled. "I'm used to the aroma myself."

Dustin disappeared into the jail. The place was cool and dank, and the memory of Sheriff Dane's body laid out on the cold stone floor still brought a jarring anger.

Over five months had passed since his senseless murder, but the dustup felt like yesterday. The lawman had been a fixture for fifteen years. Deputy Miller was doing the best he could, but he was a family man at heart. They needed a new sheriff in Rio Wells, and Miller would be the first one to say so. He'd be happy to hand over the badge to someone with more experience.

Dustin quickly scribbled a note. The last leg of the trip wouldn't take long. He'd be in bed in the next half hour if he had anything to do with it.

He returned to find Doc Bixby chatting with Sidney.

"Doesn't anyone in this town ever sleep?" he asked, giving the old doctor an affectionate rub on the back.

"There you are," Jas Bixby said, looking over the rim of the spectacles. "This little gal says you were grazed by a bullet. You want to step over to the office so I can take a look at it? No need to wake that cousin of yours."

"More like you're dying to get your hands on somebody and do a little doctoring, now that you're retired." Dustin felt Sidney studying him, and turned. "Did you search the doctor out on my behalf?"

One slender shoulder lifted. "Search out help for a McCutcheon? He happened to walk around the corner all by himself."

"Just following the yapping." The old doctor's gaze wandered the length of his form. "She mentioned you'd been hit. Where's the wound? I don't see anything."

"That's because there isn't one. The bullet only ripped my shirt. I need a tailor, not a doctor. Didn't even break the skin." He fingered the spot the outlaw's bullet traveled. "See?"

Doc Bixby took a moment finding the location in the dim light. "You were lucky, all right, yes, you were."

"Did she happen to tell you she got a nick on her forehead when her horse took a fall? I'll bet she didn't mention a thing about that."

Dustin pointed, drawing the doctor's attention from himself onto her. She'd washed her face in Draper Bottom, removing all the blood. Amazing how much a tiny head wound could bleed.

The doctor's eyes went wide.

"I'm fine," she said, pinning Dustin with her no-nonsense look.

Noah gave a hefty sigh from the back of his horse. "We gonna sit here all night?" he complained. "'Cause if the answer's yes, I'm gonna head down the street to that hotel."

Dustin felt like smiling when Sidney shot Noah a reproving look. *Good. She needs to wise up where her brother is concerned.*

Her gaze moved past Noah, past the saloon, to the dark windows of the hotel. "I wonder if they'll extend credit since all the money I had disappeared with my saddlebag, along with my music box and horse. Noah's funds disappeared out of his saddlebags when the deputy locked him up in San Antonio. We're pretty much destitute for now."

Her voice was a bit sad, surprising Dustin.

"What?" Bixby squawked. "Don't tell me with all the rooms you got out at that ranch of yours, Dustin and Chaim McCutcheon, you haven't offered this little lady a place to stay!"

To make her mad, Dustin arched his brow at the word *lady*. "Of course we have, Doc. That's been the argument all the way from Draper Bottom. You try to get her to say yes. I dare you."

He wasn't letting her stay just anywhere. His pa might not like seeing her out at the ranch, but his sisters would. They were always clamoring for news of other places, the styles the women were wearing and whatnot.

Even with Sidney in the house, he'd not waver about Noah lodging in the bunkhouse. He'd been arrested, and this was a punishment. Dustin wasn't rewarding him for bad behavior. Manolito would keep an eye on him and let Dustin know if he took a step out of line.

The doctor pulled back when he saw her straighten up for a fight. "Naw, I believe you if you say so."

Sidney looked back and forth between him and the doctor. "I don't see that I have much of a choice for tonight—or should I say, the rest of the morning. Tomorrow, though, I'll be back in town and register at the hotel."

Cradle's eyes went wide, a large smile blooming. "How long you two planning to stay in Rio Wells?"

"He's staying as long as needed to work off a debt he incurred in San Antonio," Dustin said, gathering his reins. "Don't know about Miss Calhoun. She's free to come and go as she pleases."

He mounted and then held out his arm to Sidney, strangely looking forward to having her behind his saddle once again.

Her gaze went hard. "How far out to the ranch? Can I walk? After all the hours I've spent on the sweaty back of a horse, walking sounds good." She looked around at the men. "Doing so will stretch my legs. Point me in the right direction, and I'll meet you there."

"No need to do that, Miss Calhoun," Cradle quickly offered, just as Dustin was about to laugh at her theatrics. "Won't take me but a minute to hook up the buggy. Chester hasn't been out in days. The crotchety ol' thing gets stiff if he don't get out now and then." Cradle's gaze filled with hope. "It's a nice night for a buggy ride. There's a full moon to light the way."

She turned to the blacksmith. "You'd do that for me? I *am* awfully tired of sitting on the horse's prickly hide."

Oh brother.

"Give me one minute, and I'll be ready."

Before Dustin could talk sense into either of them, he saw Cradle turn and hurry away.

"You really shouldn't play with the man's feelings like that. It's not nice."

Doc Bixby stood quietly, and Chaim looked asleep in his saddle. Noah's blank face held little clues to what he was thinking.

Sidney crossed her arms. "Who says I'm playing? He offered me a ride and I took it. Is that against the law?"

Dustin shook his head.

"Thought as much," she said. "Since this is your hometown, I'm pretty sure you won't shoot Noah in cold blood."

In the dim light, he almost missed her lifted eyebrow. "You have my word."

If that was how she was playing the situation, that was fine with him. Let Cradle coddle her; he was tired.

"Wake up, Chaim," he said. "We're leaving." Turning back to Sidney, he said, "When you get out to the ranch, knock on the door. I'll let Maria know you're on your way."

Chapter Fourteen

Cradle Hupton was back in twenty minutes, the buggy hitched and ready to go.

For the hundredth time, Sidney silently cursed her quick temper for letting Dustin ride off with her brother. If the situation were reversed, would her pa allow a McCutcheon on their land and in their house? She didn't think so. His bitterness was tragic, eating at him night and day. What if the man he hated, Winston McCutcheon, flew into a rage when he saw Noah, and pulled out a gun and killed him?

The buggy bounced in a deep rut, jarring her teeth—and her thoughts.

Mr. Hupton's glance was contrite. "Sorry, Miss Calhoun. Those potholes are a mite difficult to see in the moonlight. I'll try and be more careful."

She smiled. "No problem. I assure you I won't break. This seat is mighty comfortable."

The large eyes of the sturdy smithy made him look like an overgrown calf, complete with an abundance of dark lashes that would make any saloon girl jealous. He had a wholesome innocence about him that made her feel completely comfortable in his presence, even though they'd just met. Surely, Dustin wouldn't have let her ride off into the darkness with the man unless he was trustworthy. And neither would Doc Bixby. Sidney had liked the welcoming warmth in the old doctor's gaze from the moment he'd walked up.

"That's good to hear. I wouldn't want your brothers to come gunnin' for me."

Frowning, she glanced in his direction. She wasn't used to hearing her brothers referred to in a disparaging way.

"If you were to break, I mean," he added.

She laughed, trying for a little levity. "I can assure you that won't happen."

He shrugged and turned his shy gaze back to the road.

"I appreciate this ride. It's very kind of you, especially at this time of night." She glanced up at the full moon. "I suppose outlaws and Comancheros feel this is too close to Rio Wells for marauding?"

Ever since the attack today, after the McCutcheons had told her and Noah that the ride from San Antonio would be uneventful, she wasn't trusting anyone.

"Oh, absolutely, Miss Calhoun. You don't have to worry. Rio Wells has grown. We have ranches scattered out here among the rolling hills. You can't see 'em, but it's pretty civilized. We haven't had any trouble since four months back."

Again, she glanced at him, this time with a raised brow. "Four months, you say?" She still had her loaded Colt strapped to her thigh.

"That's right, last June. Can't count those murders, though. They were arranged by the town's skunk of a banker—but he's gone now, hung by a rope until dead. He'd hired a band of Comancheros to do his dirty work. They attacked a stage and killed a bunch of poor, unsuspecting folks. Later, he even had Dustin and Chaim's cousin kidnapped and left in a hot box to die."

"Cousin?"

"You bet. Charity McCutcheon. She's from the Montana clan of McCutcheons, and was here visiting." Cradle chuckled as he guided the buggy off the main road and onto a smaller one. "You're completely safe. As I said, since then and before, Rio Wells is a pretty dull place. Now, when you get out in the badlands or San Antonio, well, I can't promise you anything there."

The silhouette of a tall saguaro on the far horizon surrounded by stars snagged her attention. *That doesn't sound too promising.*

"Or the Rim Rock."

She glanced at his profile. "Why, Mr. Hupton? Because of Mr. McCutcheon? Winston?"

He shrugged. Seemed he didn't want to speak about his friends.

"Is that what you meant? I can't imagine it's anything different. I appreciate the heads-up."

"I don't like to say, being, well, I just don't. That said, everyone knows about the trouble between the McCutcheons and the Calhouns."

"I'm sure," she said, taking a hold of the handrail. "Why wouldn't he calumniate my family every chance he got? He had to do something to cover his dirty tracks."

Cradle straightened and snapped the reins over Chester's back with force. "I didn't say that. I've never heard Winston, or any other McCutcheon, say a bad word about the Calhouns." He reined Chester away from a deep rut before the wheel had a chance to hit. "Actually, I can't remember how I heard about the dispute, or what exactly was said. Word got around, but everyone knows Winston would never do anything dishonest."

Cradle's praise for Dustin's father stirred her anger, but she held her tongue. She'd said as much as she should, taking into consideration Cradle seemed to be a good friend of the family.

For the rest of the ride, she anchored her gaze out on the horizon, mentally preparing herself for the battle. These McCutcheons sure had pulled the wool over everyone's eyes. The situation was nauseating, to say the least.

"You're what?" Winston McCutcheon barked. Coffee sloshed over the rim of the mug completely forgotten in his hand. "Of all the stupid, idiotic things I've ever heard, this takes the prize. I won't allow it!"

His pa had been sitting in his office when he and Chaim arrived. Plagued by insomnia, his father usually killed several hours a night behind his desk. He'd heard their entry and met them as they came through the front door, a welcoming smile on his face that was now nowhere to be seen.

Straightening to his full height, Dustin met his father eye to eye. He didn't appreciate the fact his pa was accusing *him* of wrongdoing when the blame lay at the feet of good old Judge Halford. His father's long-time friend had a sick sense of humor.

"If I could change the situation, Pa, you know I would! Ol' man Halford was set. He was quite amused about it too." He glanced at Chaim for confirmation. "If you have a bone to pick, then go see him. I wouldn't bring this down on our heads—*your head*—if I could have avoided it."

"That's right, Pa," Chaim, the peacekeeper of the family, calmly agreed. He inched his way between Dustin and Winston. "It's not forever. The sentence will pass quickly."

"Sage words." Dustin shifted his weight.

If only Pa had been asleep. I wanted to save this confrontation until the morning, when we're all rested.

Chaim hooked a thumb over his shoulder. "Calhoun's tucked away in the bunkhouse with strict orders to Manolito to keep an eye on him. Nothin's gonna happen. Except we'll have a new hand for a short time."

"A rattlesnake nesting with my men," Winston hollered. "Now that thought makes me happy. How many times have the Calhoun boys gone to cuffs with you in Kansas?"

He glared at Dustin, and then at Chaim. "Too many times to count! And what about the window in his sleeping quarters? It's large enough for him to sneak out. I trust him as much as I trust his father. Which is not at all! How did this transpire, anyway? Why the Rim Rock?"

Chaim's face colored and Dustin swallowed a groan. "Halford picked us randomly out of the crowd."

"I heard all that! But I don't believe it. Halford knows how I feel about Jock Calhoun. Hell, *everybody* does." Unmindful of the others in the house, he shouted, his angry voice ricocheting off the walls like a gunshot in a canyon. "Jock Calhoun's sole purpose in life is to besmirch the McCutcheon name. I won't have any of his offspring on my land."

Dustin chanced a look at Chaim. They hadn't yet broken the news about Sidney—and her staying in the house. Before long, she'd knock on the door.

"You make them sound like cattle, Pa. Be reasonable."

"Reasonable?" Winston clapped down his mug on the entry table next to the wall, and then pushed an aggravated hand through his sleep-disheveled hair, his mouth a hard, straight line. "I've been nothing but reasonable *and charitable*, for so many years concerning Jock Calhoun that the whole thing has become a joke," he spat contemptuously. "And how am I repaid?"

His glowing red face looked as if he'd bitten into one of Maria's enchiladas filled with jalapeños. A sheen slicked his tall forehead.

"With more lies, more slander!" He turned to Dustin with the eyes of a hawk. "Wait a minute. Did you just say *them*?"

Now was *not* the best time to bring up Sidney. In his whole life, Dustin had never seen such an angry outburst from his father. The man needed to settle down before something really awful happened. His pa wasn't a spring rooster anymore.

Winston jumped into his next question, seeming to have forgotten his last. "What did you do, Dustin, to get this albatross hung around your neck? I know there's something! You're not innocent in all this. Why did Butch pick you out of all the people in the courtroom? A decision like that wasn't random; I know it." His father jabbed a finger in his direction. "Spit it out!"

Dustin held his temper in check. Escalating the situation wouldn't help with Sidney only a few minutes away. "Maybe you're right. Maybe I did have something to do with his decision."

Winston glared.

"If you remember, John and I busted up a restaurant in San Antonio on the night of his wedding. We both apologized and paid restitution. Halford did mention—"

"I *knew* it!" Winston shook his head vehemently. "So, this debacle does come down to *your* temper—again. You'll never learn, will you? And don't you dare lay any of that blame at John's door. It was his wedding night. I'm sure he wasn't out looking for a fight!"

His mother appeared from the hallway. "What in heavens is going on out here, Winston?" she asked, cinching the tie of her robe around her middle.

Her concerned gaze searched the room, and when she spotted him and Chaim, safely back from their trip to San Antonio, she smiled briefly before looking again at him. Her long hair fell freely around her shoulders, and thick socks covered her feet.

She hurried over to Chaim, pulled him down to kiss his cheek, and then did the same with him. Becky and Madeline shuffled into the room, their sleep-filled gazes wide with anxiety.

"Welcome home, boys," his mother added, her brows pulled together in worry. A look Dustin knew well passed over her face. "Well? Has something happened?"

Something had happened, all right. And she was about to knock on their ranch house door at any moment.

Chapter Fifteen

The buggy rounded a bend in the road and the Rim Rock Ranch came into view. The name of that ranch was burned into Sidney's heart. Even in the moonlight, the grandeur of the place was easy to see. So splendid, so rich—*so prosperous.* Several windows glowed from a light within.

Nerves tickled deep inside her stomach. Would Dustin be there? Would Mr. McCutcheon? Where was Noah, and was he safe? Could she dare hope they'd all gone to bed, and only the maid would be waiting, as Dustin had alluded to? Facing Winston McCutcheon tomorrow morning sounded so much better than facing him now.

"It's beautiful," she whispered under her breath, knowing the words she spoke came straight from the same angry heart that cursed the day Winston McCutcheon had been born.

The sprawling ranch house had white adobe walls, large glass windows, and an array of flowering potted plants she knew would be even more gorgeous in the light of day. Her stomach muscles bunched. Their ranch back in Santa Fe was beautiful in its own right, as well. But her home wasn't nearly as large, and the place didn't speak to the soul as this ranch seemed to be doing to hers.

She pushed away her envy. This wasn't about their success, but the way their riches were won at the expense of her father. Winston McCutcheon was to blame for her father's scars, inside and out. Jock Calhoun had been left with a limp, a twisted spine, and half an ear gone. And those were only the outside scars. Inside, he was much worse. He still functioned on the ranch, to a point. Not a second went by that Sidney didn't see the scorn he held for Dustin's father burning deep inside. She couldn't blame him one bit.

People around here might think Winston innocent, but she knew better. And so did Noah. As much as she was hardened to the McCutcheons, she prayed her younger brother wouldn't do anything foolish during his sentence here. Something that would really land him in trouble. She wondered where he was. In the house? Certainly not.

"Whoa, Chester," Cradle crooned softly to his gelding. "Here we are."

He hopped out of the buggy and hurried around to her side, offering her—a woman dressed in dust-covered pants, a shirt smelling like horse, and a sweat-stained cowboy hat—his hand.

Feeling very small in the shadow of the large home, Sidney had to clasp her fists tightly to keep Cradle from seeing them shake. Why hadn't she listened to Dustin and rode in with the men, with Noah? The confrontation would be over, and she would have had Dustin at her side. What if Winston was the only one awake? She'd go toe-to-toe with him, but she wouldn't like it. She had no other option but to knock on the front door and see who was there.

She glanced at Cradle, thankful for his presence and friendship.

"Don't be scared, Miss Calhoun. No one will bite your head off, despite what you may think. The McCutcheons are a fine family. If I know Winston and Winnie, which I do very well, they'll welcome you with open arms, despite your last name."

They walked up to the front door that must have been over nine feet tall. Cradle picked up the cactus-shaped iron knocker and gave it a gentle *rap-rap-rap*. He turned and smiled.

Sidney breathed in deeply, trying to fortify her nerves.

As if he'd been waiting by the door, an imposing man appeared at the instant the barrier opened. He was every bit as tall as Dustin, and looked every bit as strong. Gray streaks lightened his thick chestnut-colored hair. Lines born of hard work, responsibility, and heartache, she was sure, fanned out from his dark brown eyes. His firm expression held parts of Dustin and Chaim.

Winston McCutcheon in the flesh!

Too late! Too late to explain that Noah's older sister was traveling with him to make sure they treated her brother fairly.

Dustin stood behind his father, his nerves pinging from tension. Who knew Cradle would get out here so quickly?

After the first heated exchange with his pa where the news about Noah rattled him more than Dustin had ever seen, he'd hoped the livery owner would take his time arriving at the ranch. If he had, maybe his pa would have been in bed before Sidney came through the door.

Not so.

Several uncomfortable seconds dragged out. His pa stood there for a moment before glancing back at him, his eyes filled with questions. Sidney's back was so straight, they could have used her as a level. His pa was a smart man. He'd already put two and two together.

"Please, come in," Winston said, his deep, commanding voice filling the room. He looked from Sidney to Hupton. "Cradle. Miss Calhoun, isn't it? Don't stand out there on the doorstep."

A surprised murmur sounded from his sisters, and his mother joined Winston at the door.

Despite her bravado, Dustin knew Sidney must be frightened, facing down her father's adversary with nothing more than her tongue, sweat-covered clothes, and a pound of trail dust. She'd never say so, of course, but she didn't have to.

Dustin's conflicting emotions tied his tongue for a moment, but he felt Chaim's support at his shoulder. Could he himself handle this situation as gracefully as his father was doing, after all the years of heartache and anger Sidney's father had caused this family? Hearing her knock, Dustin had wanted to answer the door himself, but Pa had halted him in his tracks with only a look. Had Sidney heard the angry exchange only moments before?

The gun! He'd forgotten about her .45 Colt still strapped to her thigh. No crazy possibility existed that she'd use the weapon on his father, was there?

As Sidney stepped through the door as regal as a queen, Cradle waved a greeting to the family and stepped back.

"The hour's late. I best get back to town."

Quickly, Sidney turned. "Thank you so much, Mr. Hupton. I appreciate the ride a great deal. Your chivalry speaks volumes."

Several moments of silence encompassed the room after Cradle closed the door on his way out, and everyone digested the awkward turn of events.

"Dustin and Chaim have told me of your brother's situation in San Antonio. How he landed in jail," his pa said, going straight to the heart of the matter. "And how Judge Halford took liberties in designating Dustin as his guardian."

Even though the muscle in his father's jaw clenched several times, Dustin was amazed at his civil tone and stoic countenance. A gentleman through and through. Pride for the man who had raised him filled Dustin's chest.

"I can assure you," Sidney replied, looking Winston in the eye, and then toward the others, "Noah is innocent of the charges. He told me so himself. He didn't break up the Morning Star Saloon. The regulars just wanted someone to blame so they wouldn't have to pay for damages. He was in the wrong place at the wrong time. Nothing more." Her gaze traveled the room.

Despite her upward-tipped chin and the obstinate set to her mouth, Dustin knew she must be exhausted. It was late, already ten minutes past two. The memory of her clinging to his back behind his saddle as she peppered the outlaws with bullets, all without a moment of protest or fear, brought a squeezing to his throat. Who knew? Maybe he owed her his life.

"We're not any happier with this arrangement than you are," Sidney said. "Rio Wells is the last place we want to be. And especially on the Rim Rock Ranch."

Dustin wished she'd gentle her tone, at least a little. His father had done so for her.

Her gaze, although appearing arrogant, was shadowed with vulnerability as it skimmed over him once more, as if he were no more important than a cow patty left in the field to dry.

"If I hadn't lost my horse and saddlebags in a gunfight your sons assured me wouldn't happen, I'd still have the ability to stay in the hotel tonight. I'm sorry to impose." Her voice wobbled when her gaze touched his mother's face.

"Dustin!" his mother said, her tone rebuking him.

"I offered her money, Mother, but she wouldn't take it."

Please don't mention not accepting charity from a McCutcheon. Not tonight. Not now.

"Tomorrow, I'll send a telegram home," Sidney went on, thankfully skipping over that bone of contention. "My family will send funds."

Dustin didn't know how much more his father could take, although it seemed as if she were steering away from the topic of her father on purpose. He appreciated that, at least.

"Surely, the hotel will give me credit until then."

Her regard kept returning to his mother and sisters. Something there, in the back of her eyes, made Dustin's heart beat a little quicker. A defenselessness of sorts. Like a baby bunny searching for its mother in a den of wolves.

Winston tented a thick brow. "We'll make sure that happens. Dustin?"

"Absolutely."

"You really have no need to stay in the hotel, my dear," his mother said in her warm, gentle voice. "Housing two of Jock's children is the least we can do for an old friend. We have plenty of room and are happy to do it. Isn't that right, Winston?"

Several heartbeats passed before his pa nodded. "Indeed. The very least we can do."

If it were possible, Sidney's back straightened even further. "You and my father are not friends."

"So you say."

"Winston, Miss Calhoun is tired." His mother looked around for Maria, who had come into the room a few minutes earlier, rumpled from sleep with a lantern in her hands. "I'm sure the ride from San Antonio was long and dirty, as well as exhausting. Let Miss Calhoun go to bed, and the two of you can resume this conversation in the morning." She smiled, her eyes lighting in invitation. "If you choose to. You'll be fresher then and have something hot in your bellies."

Dustin nodded. "That's a good idea, Mother."

She turned to the maid. "Maria, will you see to the lavender room and make sure everything is in order? Turn down the coverlet, and warm a pot of water so Miss Calhoun can clean away the trail dust before slipping into bed. I'm sure she'll feel much better when she's bathed."

If I'd said that, Sidney would have my head on a platter.

The tightness of his pa's jaw was so imperceptible, Dustin was sure everyone had missed it except him.

"You're right, Winnie," Winston replied, slipping his arm around her back and pulling her close. "Whether Jock and I are friends is of no never mind to anyone at two o'clock in the morning. Good night, everyone." His tone put an end to the discussion. "Miss Calhoun."

Looking a bit confused, Sidney widened her eyes when his mother approached and gently took her arm.

"Come along, dear. There's a bed waiting just for you. And I'm sure between Madeline and Becky, we can find something for you to wear. In the morning, when you're rested, we'll all get better acquainted."

Sidney's gaze flicked over to Dustin with a look that was so quick, he wondered if he'd imagined it. He was sure he saw wonder in her eyes, as well as uncertainty. Thoughts of her behind his saddle, her arms gripped around his waist, made him swallow.

Good night, Sidney Calhoun, he thought as his mother and sister led her down the hall. *Rest well. Tomorrow should prove interesting.*

Chapter Sixteen

Somewhere a rooster crowed, and Noah opened his eyes. He hadn't been asleep but lying on his cot, listening to the cowhands already up and moving about in the large common area of the bunkhouse on the other side of his door. He'd lain awake the entire night, wondering what he should do about the cockamamie situation he'd landed himself in. Under Dustin McCutcheon's thumb, and living on the McCutcheon ranch.

The trip to San Antonio had sounded good at the time his friend Harry Brennon suggested it. Blow off a little steam before earnestly launching into his studies. Reading, comprehension, and retention were easy for Noah; he took half the time to do what others did all year. He didn't study for tests and still earned top marks.

Harry was the opposite of Noah. His bulky friend avoided his academics like the plague; he struggled with every subject. He also liked trouble. He'd been the one who insulted several rabble-rousers full of whiskey, starting the fight in San Antonio. Noah hadn't lied to the judge, but he'd just left out the part about Harry. Now he was the one made to work off months of recompense.

Noah wondered where his friend was now. He hadn't seen Harry since the saloon fight when the sheriff was slapping a pair of cuffs on Noah's wrists.

He locked his fingers behind his head and stared at a knothole in the ceiling. What was so all-fired important about him going to college anyway? No one in his family had gone before, and the reason certainly wasn't for the engineering degree he was working toward.

Jock Jr. had heard St. John's had adopted compulsory military training into their program. How convenient. His brother didn't think him tough enough, man enough, or gutsy enough to ranch with the rest of them. Even without asking Noah, the decision had been made.

So what? He'd comply. Then when he was finished, he'd make a life of his own, somewhere off the ranch.

Sidney was his main concern. He'd get through the days, do whatever McCutcheon wanted, even if eating crow was involved. Wouldn't make much never mind to him at all, but not so for his sister. She'd practically raised him, and her being here in Rio Wells hampered her chances of finding a suitable husband in Santa Fe.

Each time she traipsed after him, her reputation as a hellion grew. A few of the women in town had begun to give her the cold shoulder. Twenty-four and unmarried. That status didn't seem to bother her at all, but the rest of the family never seemed to forget. Pa especially wouldn't be happy with the news. And Jock Jr.? Noah didn't even want to think about his reaction.

With eyes gritty from the lack of sleep, Noah glanced at the tempting window above his head. He could be out and on his horse in five minutes, assuming he could find the animal without raising suspicions. He'd not steal a horse from the

McCutcheon ranch. They'd like nothing better than to hang him as a horse thief.

Besides, he couldn't leave Sidney.

From the other room, a resounding burst of laughter filled the bunkhouse plenty loud, even with his door closed. The clink of forks against plates mixed in with the aromas of bacon, butter, and coffee made his stomach rumbled. Breakfast was well under way.

Somebody rapped hard on his door. "If you want any eats, Calhoun, you'd better roll out of the sack. Lazybones go hungry."

He was at a disadvantage. They all knew him and knew his name. Certainly knew the history between the two ranches.

Annoyed, he stood, pulled his shirt over his sweat-stained undershirt, and opened the door before the man who'd called him lazy had a chance to move away.

"You callin' me names?" he asked as he buttoned his shirt.

The cowboy, surely a good ten years older, smirked. "Just calling a spade a spade. We're all finished, and you're—"

"Lay off, Paulson," a skinny fellow at the stove barked. He wiped his hands down the front of his apron, then took a large spoon and scooped something from a black cast-iron skillet onto a plate. "Remember what Dustin said. We're to give the kid a wide berth until he settles in."

The cook brought the plate, now heaped with food, to the table. "Here you go," he said not kindly and not unkindly.

While he listened to the cook, Noah took in the large square room. Ranch hands lazed around drinking coffee, already finished with their meal. Two continued to dress, three stared, some sauntered out the door. The ceiling, crisscrossed with sturdy beams, was used for hanging possessions—a heeling rope, a few hats, and several papers tacked from the top that moved when someone walked by.

Noah stepped over to the long bench and sat himself at the table. The plate of flapjacks, eggs, and bacon looked better than gold bars in the amber light of the lantern. A bowl full of chocolate bars sat in the center of the table that had seen better days. He forked in a mouthful, chewed, and swallowed.

The cook brought over a cup and gestured to the stove. "Help yourself to coffee, and also one of those, if you have a mind," he said, gesturing to the candy. "Boss brought 'em all the way from San Antonio. Says there's one for each man."

That doesn't mean me.

Wiping his mouth with the napkin next to his plate, Noah stood, stepped back over the bench, and went to the stove in the corner of the large room. He eyed the coffeepot's wire handle, knowing it would be hot.

Am I being set up?

Taking a rumpled dishcloth, he folded the checkered fabric several times and used it as a hot pad. The last of the dark brew trickled into his cup and stopped halfway to the brim.

"Guess you'll be up a little earlier next time," Paulson said from across the room. He chuckled, pulled on his hat, and headed for the door. "By the way, you're riding with me today," he said over his shoulder. "And I'm riding out in about," he glanced at the clock over the white enamel stove, "three minutes."

Hellfire! Living with a bunch of yahoos who'd like nothing better than for him to make a fool of himself, or worse, was going to be drudgery. Especially if he had to keep his temper in check the entire time.

He thought of Sidney. If not for her, he'd stir this beehive good. He still might.

Shame for bringing down the situation on the Calhoun name, especially with the McCutcheons, made him clench the fist that wasn't holding his coffee mug. But then a thought occurred to him.

Maybe I can turn this situation to my advantage. Make my pa proud.

He gulped down the little coffee in his cup at the same time he plunked himself back down on the bench, cut the tall stack of flapjacks with the side of his fork, and shoveled in a huge mouthful.

"You better get a move on, son," the cook mumbled. "Paulson meant what he said. Wolf that down and make tracks, if you know what's good for ya."

Feeling cranky with only two and a half hours of sleep, Dustin stood in front of the barn, speaking with Paulson while waiting for Noah. Manolito stood alongside, the reins of his horse in his hand.

"I don't want Calhoun to leave your company, Brick, is that understood?" Dustin said to his ranch hand. "If he gets into any trouble, doesn't matter what, I'll be held responsible. This isn't his first brush with the law, and by the way he acts, I'm sure it won't be his last."

Sighing, he added, "I have to go to town today, or else I'd break him in myself and show him the ropes. Work him as you would any other wrangler who'd hired on—without letting him out of your sight. Put him through his paces, and don't go too easy or be too tough. Don't let him trick you. He's sharp, and maybe a bit calculating. I'll be back before supper and check in to see how things go."

"He's a Calhoun!" Brick Paulson replied, jerking back his shoulders. "You expect me and the rest of the fellows to turn the other cheek after all the years of grief he's caused your pa? After everything he's said about this ranch? We're loyal to this brand, Dustin, you know that. We don't take kindly to slander, or that nonsense about how Winston paid to have Calhoun bushwhacked. Anyone that knows your father knows that's hogwash."

The ranch hand glanced away, the muscle in his jaw working double-time. "Now we're supposed to treat him like nothing has happened? It don't seem right."

"That's exactly what I'm asking."

"What about Winston and Chaim? They feel the same as you?"

Pa? Maybe not quite the same, but he knows how to put aside his own feelings.

"You're damn right they do. Now, don't make me angry. Calhoun won't be here that long."

Paulson glanced at Manolito and then back at him. "Any amount of time is too long to be bunking with a varmint like him, in my way of thinkin'. You best know, I don't like this situation at all, or what you're asking of the men. I can't promise you anythin'."

"You don't get paid to like it, Brick," Dustin snapped. This setup might be a rougher go for Noah than he'd first thought. "You do as I ask, and let me take care of the others. Understood? This is the Rim Rock. We treat everyone the same. Friend or foe makes no difference."

Noah rounded the corral fence and pulled up when he saw them waiting in the entry of the barn. He only paused for an instant before continuing toward them with stiff shoulders, and stopped a few feet away. The attitude Dustin had grown used to seeing on their ride from San Antonio was still evident.

"I'm riding into town today, Calhoun. Taking your sister to the telegraph office and then to the hotel, as well as tie up a few other errands. I'm trusting you to stay here with Paulson and behave. You don't need any more trouble dogging your heels."

Several hands stood around idly out of curiosity, waiting to see how the boss would handle Calhoun, and their heads whipped in his direction at the mention of a female Calhoun being on the property. He hadn't shared that part of the story yet with anyone outside the family, and the few who'd met Sidney in town early this morning.

"Manolito's our head man," Dustin explained to Noah. "Whatever chore you and Brick are assigned, you're to complete to his satisfaction. It's no less than I'd expect out of any man working this ranch."

"Sure, McCutcheon. You have me at a disadvantage, being my sister is beholden to you." Noah dropped his hands on his waist. "I'm ready to put in a full day of work for as long as it takes."

"I'm glad to hear that."

Dustin stepped away when he heard Noah call out, "Where's Sidney?"

"In the house. I haven't seen her this morning, but I'm sure she's up by now."

"The big house?"

Dustin glanced over his shoulder. "Well, she's not staying in the bunkhouse."

Noah's face turned red, and several men laughed as they mounted up and rode out. The kid wasn't making things any easier on himself by confirming what everyone already thought of him.

Without another word, Dustin walked away.

Chapter Seventeen

Later the same day, with her palms braced on the peeling paint of her hotel room's windowsill, Sidney glanced below at the inhabitants of Rio Wells.

I'm so far from home. Can't run back the way I've come.

Loneliness closed in around her. She'd been in other towns before as she chased after Noah and his ever-growing wanderlust, namely Roswell, Albuquerque, and Las Cruces, the city of crosses. He'd traveled all the way to Pueblo, Colorado Springs, Denver, and only two months ago, Fort Collins. The lawyer in San Antonio hadn't known the half of his transgressions.

But being here in Rio Wells was different. Her dismay wasn't caused by the extra miles or the new territory. This big, scary grip around her chest was related to the fact that Rio Wells was the home of the McCutcheons.

A woman in the postal station attached to the stage office lifted up the window and looked out onto the street, much like Sidney was doing right now. On the same block was a barbershop, a leather smith, and another building that wasn't marked. All three looked quiet.

She thought of the telegram she'd sent to be delivered to the ranch by Harold Carp. She shuddered. *Is Pa reading my plea now?*

In the telegraph office, Dustin had insisted on waiting. He'd remained by the door, giving her privacy but all the while staring a hole in the back of her borrowed blouse. He'd said he was waiting so he could escort her to the hotel when she was finished, and get her settled. But his motivations were clear.

He wanted to make sure I wasn't turned away. Who would extend credit to me, a total stranger in town?

Even though doing so galled her, she'd been forced to accept his loan for the price of the telegram, but that was as far as she'd go.

If the Union Hotel hadn't accepted her on credit until her father wired the money to the bank, she would have been in trouble. Dustin had remained a perfect gentleman the whole time, in spite of the history between them. Gentleman or not, that didn't matter. Her father would come through with money, and soon. That she could depend on.

She thought of Dustin now, and the slight look of disapproval he always wore when he addressed her. Well, not always. Not at the badlands shack when he'd been teasing her about her marital status. And not when he'd lifted her atop his horse, concern darkening his eyes as bullets sprayed around her feet.

She crossed the braided rug to the room's other window and looked out. She'd hated leaving Jackson at the ranch, tied to a post on the bunkhouse porch, but Madeline and Becky had assured her the dog would be fine. In no way could she have cared for him in the hotel and see properly to his needs. As much as she loved him, she knew he was sure to get into mischief, and she already had enough of that with Noah.

A knock sounded on her door.

"Yes?"

"Telegram, Miss Calhoun, the one you're waiting on." *The telegraph operator.* The one who couldn't stop smiling at her. "I was on my way to lunch, so I decided to drop by your missive. I hope you don't mind."

Sidney opened the door.

In his mid-thirties, the man stood hat in hand with the same amiable smile she'd already memorized. His dark blond hair receded an inch at the hairline, fell to the side of his tall forehead, and then was tucked behind his ears. He held a folded brown paper in his fingers.

"Thank you," she said. "Do I owe you something?"

"No. Sender paid the fee on their end. This is free of charge."

Thank goodness for small favors. I have less than a dollar left to my name.

"What about the delivery? That was very thoughtful. Do I owe you for that?"

He beamed. "No charge."

She glanced at the note he still clutched close to his chest.

"Oh!"

He extended his arm, and she carefully plucked the telegram from his fingers.

"Thank you again," she said, hoping he'd step away so she didn't have to close the door in his face.

He slowly inched back. "My name is Stanton Drake."

"I'm pleased to meet you, Mr. Drake," she said in her most businesslike voice.

He wasn't making this easy. He'd already learned her name when she sent the communication, and she had no intention of making friends in Rio Wells. The sooner she was out of here, the better.

Seeing his expression dim, she felt a bit uncharitable. He *had* gone out of his way for her, after all.

She gave him a wide smile. "And again, thank you ever so much for bringing this to me. The gesture was very thoughtful."

Mr. Drake drew up, smoothing the front of his shirt. "Can I interest you in a bite to eat?" he asked, seeming to rally. "I mean, you being new and all, I'm sure you don't know the eateries in town. My treat."

"Thank you, Mr. Drake, but I've just eaten." Her stomach pinched with emptiness, reminding her she'd turned down breakfast with the McCutcheons.

He shrugged. "Can't blame a fella for trying. Good day to you then, Miss Calhoun. I best be on my way if I want to open again on time." Seemed not everyone in Rio Wells was put off by the Calhoun name.

Sidney closed the door quietly and opened the paper.

COME HOME STOP THERE IS NOTHING YOU
CAN DO FOR NOAH STOP THAT BOY HAS
MADE HIS OWN BED STOP

Her hand shook. Did that mean her father wouldn't send any money for her living expenses? He wanted her to come home now? How did he expect her to do that without any funds? Besides, she'd not leave Noah here alone sentenced to time on the McCutcheon ranch.

Resentment ignited in her belly. How unkind! Couldn't he even ask how she was, or Noah?

Sidney crumpled the note, pushing back her angry tears. Surely her father would comply once he'd cooled off. This business with the McCutcheons had him seeing red. In a day or two, he'd soften and realize his mistake. He *would* soften, wouldn't he?

Turning, she gazed out the far window, her thoughts blinding her to the outside world. Of course he would. She was his only daughter, and he loved her. Before she knew it, funds would arrive at the bank, and all would be well.

She just had to bide her time and be patient.

Chapter Eighteen

Dustin left Sidney Calhoun in her hotel room and exited the building. He needed a bossy Calhoun she-cat with soft curves, a graceful neck, and lush lips about as much as he needed a hole in his temple. She was a Calhoun through and through, and he would be well advised to remember that whenever her airy scent captured his attention.

Just like her old man, she'd like nothing more than to see the McCutcheon brand wither and die. Her bitterness was her badge and she wore it well, in defense of her lying father. Dustin pitied the man who ended up hitched to such a bull-headed woman. She could have at least indulged his mother this morning by eating breakfast.

And now he had Noah Calhoun to keep straight with the law. Two Calhouns to think about was enough to give him a headache, but more, he intended to keep them both out of his pa's way as best he could. That family had caused his own family, and especially his pa, more heartache than ten years of drought, pestilence, and an avalanche of snowfall combined. A betrayed friendship was the worst hurt of all.

With saddlebags in hand, he strode down the boardwalk toward the bank. He'd pick up the payroll and get back to the ranch. He didn't like leaving Calhoun—even with Manolito and Paulson looking after him.

The memory of his pa's face when they'd broken the news pulled at him. His pa thought he was taking *their* side. Dustin didn't know how he could be any more loyal when he'd been ordered by a judge to oversee Noah. He hadn't asked for the job, and had tried his damnedest to get out of it.

Crossing Dry Street, he noticed his cousin John outside his doctor's office, washing the front window. Dustin turned and headed his way.

John's sleeves were rolled to the elbow, and a bucket of water sat at his feet. When John saw him approach, he dropped the large sponge he held into the bucket and reached for the towel draped over his shoulder.

"I see you have important business this morning, cousin," Dustin teased.

They had an on-again off-again running joke—of sorts. Ever since John had wooed Lily Anthony out from under his nose, perhaps it wasn't such a joke anymore, but they'd both gotten past the matter and were good friends, including Lily.

John laughed good-naturedly. "Someone has to do it, cousin." He gave his work a dubious stare. "Not leaving streaks behind is more difficult than you'd think."

Dustin lifted an eyebrow, astounded John didn't mind what he was doing, and actually looked to be enjoying the chore.

"Better you than me, I guess," he responded. "I suppose if I had a place here in town, I'd want to keep the condition up as well."

An unusual expression pulled at John's mouth. He toed at a nonexistent something on the boardwalk. "That may be the case, but you'd have the funds to hire someone to do the work for you."

What isn't John saying? "True enough."

"I'm surprised to see you in town today, Dustin. Didn't you only get back to the ranch last night?" The worry lines on John's forehead had disappeared and his demeanor was back to normal.

Dustin hoped there wasn't trouble brewing between the newlyweds.

"Picking up payroll at the bank."

"Today? Alone?" John glanced around and then back at Dustin.

Every other Wednesday was the usual pickup day for the Rim Rock, and funds doled out to the ranch hands on Friday.

"I'm not going it alone; I have a couple hands waiting at the bank. Colin Jorgensen, the new owner of the bank, is being quite obliging. I told him I wouldn't be in for payroll on Wednesday, like usual, since Chaim and I would still be in San Antonio, and he said that wasn't a problem. Any day was fine, he said, as long as he had notice. Quite a change from Shellston, who liked to control the air we breathe. I'm relieved to know that scoundrel got what was coming to him."

"My thoughts exactly. The way he treated Lily and Harriett when they first arrived in Rio Wells still sets my blood pumping."

"Well, Jorgensen wants to make a good impression on the town. Rebuild trust in the bank after the fiasco with Shellston. He's even had several families follow him south from Wisconsin. He purchased a bunch of deserted homesteads to resell at very competitive prices to bring new blood into Rio Wells. That's smart. And his plan is working. He also said a new merchant is opening a mercantile and dry goods store on Church Street." Dustin shook his head. "Jorgensen is a wealth of information. I learned more in an hour's talk with him than a month of Sundays."

"I've already met the new merchant," John said with a satisfied nod of the head. "Man, wife, and five daughters."

Dustin's eyes opened wide. "Five! My sisters and mother will be happy to hear that."

"As well as all the bachelors around town. Mr. Knutson will be very popular." John's face darkened. "Bixby told me about the Calhouns. Why're they in town?"

"I've been put in charge of Noah until he can pay off a fine he incurred in San Antonio. His sister followed, worried over our treatment of him."

John scoffed.

"Yeah. I feel the same. Anyway, it's a long, convoluted story. I'll retell the sorry account sometime over a—"

"Morning, Dustin, John," a female voice called.

Martha Brown stood with her young daughter, Candy, in front of Grady's Mercantile after exiting the store. They walked slowly toward the two men.

"Morning, Martha," John said. "Candy, how does that tummy feel today? Better?"

The child nodded.

"Mornin'," Dustin added, unable to miss the wide smile Martha shot his way.

She was nice enough, trim and pretty, but Daniel's widow couldn't understand he wasn't interested in *that* way. He didn't mind the attention she showered on him, just as long as she didn't read her desires into his actions.

He'd never want to hurt her feelings. Daniel had been a good friend, so Dustin watched out for Martha and Candy, as all the townsfolk did. But he couldn't marry her. She deserved a man who loved her for herself.

"Did Miss Emmeline get off on the train all right?" she asked.

She and Emmeline had formed a friendship in the few months his brother's intended had lived in Rio Wells.

"She did," he said. "And promises to be back before she's missed."

"Well, that's not possible because I miss her already. And I'm sure Chaim does as well. I wouldn't have had the nerve to take such a long trip with my wedding date so close."

My thought exactly.

"But then, Emmeline has proven she's brave after traveling alone to Texas in the first place," she went on. "Think of those train stops and strangers." Martha glanced down at Candy, who was playing a counting game on her fingers as she waited for her mother to finish her conversation and move on.

"She's a bold one, all right," John said, once again admiring his handiwork on the window. "And stubborn as well. I'm sure Chaim tried to talk her out of it, but once her mind is made up . . ."

Candy tugged on her mother's arm. "Mommy, can we go in the dress shop? I like looking at the pretend lady. Ingrid."

John laughed and nodded. "Go ahead. Lily's there. I'm sure she'd like the company."

Lily must have heard the conversation because she stepped out of her shop and smiled at them. "I thought I heard your voice, Martha. You too, Candy." She hurried over and wrapped the two females into her arms.

"Did you recognize my voice too?" Dustin asked, and then laughed at the way her lashes lowered to her soft-looking cheek. Lily McCutcheon was always such a delight to see. John was a lucky man.

"I did. But I didn't want to interrupt you and John."

"I can understand why. We had important window washing to discuss."

She was avoiding him, and that was fine. He understood. A day would come when hugging him felt as comfortable and natural to her as hugging Chaim was to her now. Dustin looked forward to that day, but also never wanted it to happen. Her cheeks had turned a dusty pink.

Martha spoke up. "As much as we'd like to come in, Lily, we can't." She looked down at her daughter and raised her brows. "My sister-in-law is expecting us at the post office. Louise wants our help in dressing up her work area since she spends so much time there. Today is our first meeting. We're sewing curtains."

She laughed, and then glanced at the watch penned to her bodice. "Why, we're late already. Come along, Candy. Another day, Lily, I promise."

Dustin watched them go, and Lily disappeared back into her shop. He needed to quit his lollygagging and get himself to the bank, and be on his way. Leaving Calhoun out at the ranch was playing with fire. He trusted Brick Paulson and Manolito with his life. Problem was, he had no idea how far Noah Calhoun would carry the grudge.

"Well, I'm off to the bank." Dustin saw that odd expression cross his cousin's face once more. He wished he had the time to learn what was on John's mind, but he had more pressing problems to worry about. "And then I'm headed back to the ranch. Duty calls."

Would Noah try to even the score with Winston, no matter how unfounded the stupid grudge might be? That was a question he couldn't answer.

Noah was a Calhoun, and he'd not trust him for a second.

Chapter Nineteen

When he was alone again, John hefted the water bucket, dumped the contents into the street, and headed toward the hot springs.

Mrs. Beck would arrive soon with Andrew, her six-year-old boy, for his biweekly treatments. The lad had patches of dry skin around his ankles that never completely disappeared. They itched something fierce, and the child was always scratching, making the problem worse.

After much reading on the healing effects of mineral water, John prescribed twice-weekly sessions for Andrew. Since the child was small, his mother didn't want him sitting in the hot springs for fear he'd somehow drown. Therefore, instead of that, John fetched water back to his office, where Andrew was inclined to stay soaking longer with the entertainment Tucker provided. When the sulfuric water cooled, they heated it, soaked some more, and then coated the boy's ankles in the aloe serum made by Bixby.

John's thoughts drifted to the problem that was never far from his mind. How could he earn more money?

He'd considered applying for the sheriff's job. Surely, he'd get that position with no problem. He bore the McCutcheon name, which everyone around here respected. Taking on outlaws didn't scare him, and he was a good shot.

Still, would sheriffing and doctoring mix? By his way of thinking, the duties were a contradiction. And what if an emergency occurred when the bank was being robbed? What if something happened when he wasn't around?

Sure, Bixby was always here. In all likelihood, the old coot would probably be around for a good long time, and John was glad for it. But the retired doctor was getting older by the day, and liked having turned the reins over to John. The doc had gone fishing three times last week.

No, he couldn't, and shouldn't, count on him. The two jobs didn't go hand in hand. As boring as Rio Wells was when nothing was happening, John needed to be in town in case something did.

Ranching was always a possibility. He was a proven hand at that vocation. A month's pay as sheriff earned about as much as riding for an outfit—twenty dollars a month. Maybe he could hire on at the Rim Rock, and ride for his uncle and cousins. Surely they'd welcome him with open arms.

But that solution didn't feel right either. If he was returning to ranching, he might as well pull up stakes and head back to Montana where he'd have a percentage in the ranch. Where he'd make real money. His pa had told him he was always welcome to come home anytime.

John knew one thing. He couldn't give up doctoring completely.

Nodding to a few women making their way past him on the boardwalk, he continued on, the bucket by his side, swinging from a rope handle. Bartending and clerking were options, but those jobs paid a pittance.

John rounded the corner of Dry Street and Spring.

Lily hadn't asked him about her sister since their last conversation. As a matter of fact, she'd steered clear of the subject altogether. Why? Had she spoken with someone? Had she discovered how little cash they actually had?

Having dealt with Jas Bixby for the last forty years, people of Rio Wells were not used to paying cash for services. Just yesterday morning, Martha had tried to leave him a fresh-baked pie after she brought Candy into his office complaining of a stomachache. A quick checkup and a few simple questions had revealed the little girl had eaten three unripe apples straight from their tree.

For those few moments he'd examined her daughter, John could hardly agree to take a whole pie, even though Martha had assured him that the pie had been made with perfectly ripe apples. On the other hand, he certainly could take his patients' money.

Bixby, a bachelor and in need of very little, had been fine with bartering. Being old and unmarried, he sometimes preferred the cooked and baked offerings over cash payments.

The townsfolk think bartering is the normal way to do business, and I don't have the heart to insist otherwise.

Sure enough, he was in a pickle.

Discouraged, John trudged down Spring Street. The sulfuric aroma grew stronger as he drew closer to the bridge. At the edge of the ten-foot wide steaming pond, he ignored the heat that touched his face and carefully picked his way down the bank, then dipped the bucket into the churning waters.

The hot steam brought to mind the image of Aunt Winnie's burn he'd recently seen. Bixby's salve had done an outstanding job healing that, and the same with the scar on his face. She'd even asked for more.

An idea struck him. He stood at the edge of the spring, staring at the bubbling hot water.

How many doctors did he know? The college had hundreds of students, most who went on to start practices of their own. Not only that, but he'd struck up a friendship with the dean, an older, retired physician who had all kinds of connections.

As far as he knew, aloe vera plants were nonexistent in cooler climates, which made procuring the restorative juice much more difficult. And who cared if they could anyway? Who had the time to go through the process of extraction? Wasn't ordering a case from a company in Texas easier?

John's heart raced as he thought through the possibilities. The concoction belonged to Bixby, but maybe he'd go fifty-fifty. John would do the work and make the contacts, and Bixby would provide the knowledge from his years spent tinkering with the formula. They'd have to take into account the cost of cooking up the salve, bottling, and shipping. Nothing of value was ever free or easy—at least, that was what his mother had always preached.

For the first time in several days, John's mood lightened.

Perhaps raising enough money to rent a real house in town wouldn't take long once production began. Then, if Lily wanted, she could use the profits from the shop to bring Giselle from Germany, and when his new business took off, he'd pay her back.

That was something he would insist on, and only if she didn't want to wait for him to save enough to do both. He was the breadwinner, and he aimed to stay the breadwinner. No wife of his would wear the pants.

He had work to do. First and foremost, he would speak with Bixby.

Chapter Twenty

The hour was well past three in the afternoon, and Sidney couldn't stay holed up in her room for one more minute. She pressed her hand to her middle, her empty stomach feeling as if it were filled with burning cinders.

How long before I keel over from lack of food? She ached for a strip of jerky. A small apple. Anything! *A piece of sweet cherry pie.* She closed her eyes and smiled, thinking of Carmen's favorite dish.

She hadn't had a morsel since leaving Draper Bottom yesterday. Perhaps gently refusing to take anything from the McCutcheons wasn't such a sound idea. The breakfast table had been covered with delicious-smelling fare, but she'd held firm. She'd not be beholden to the family that had tried to kill her father.

Dustin had tried his best to get her to accept a small loan so she could eat until her money showed up. Curse her foolish pride now. She'd eat her pride if she could, and enjoy every humiliating bite.

Her stomach gave a riotous rumble, as if agreeing. Several mouth-watering aromas had wafted through her open windows since she'd checked in, telling her someone, somewhere in Rio

Wells—and probably a McCutcheon, no less—was eating and enjoying the fare.

This morning spent at the ranch felt like a year ago. The two McCutcheon sisters had generously provided her with a skirt and blouse, since her spare had been lost along with her money in the saddlebags of her runaway horse.

She lifted the hem of the mulberry-colored skirt and gazed at her own black riding boots. They weren't the height of women's fashion, but no one would see them under the skirt. She dropped the hemline, straightened the crisp white blouse, and then looked at the matching mulberry bow tied around her neckline.

She'd brushed her hair to a sheen, thinking the golden mass that reached to the middle of her back blasé in comparison to Madeline's rich dark brown, or Becky's pale blond hair, lighter than Sidney's and much closer in color to Noah's.

She needed a job. Something to take her mind off her own troubles.

Renewed with purpose, if not sustenance, Sidney left her room and ventured downstairs. Peeping into the Lillian Russell Room, the restaurant located inside the hotel, she was surprised to see a multitude of paintings of scantily clad women, many shockingly so. She took a moment in the quiet dining room, now empty of patrons, thinking the artwork attractive in an enlightened sort of way, which filled her with the pluck to forge ahead. When she had money, she'd take supper here and enjoy every moment.

Back in the lobby, the man behind the counter didn't even glance up when she approached.

Should she ask him if he knew of anyone in town that was looking to hire? Where did a stranger go to find out? A church? The sheriff?

Remarkably, none of the people she'd met so far had flinched much when they heard her last name. They'd been surprisingly welcoming. She thought of Cradle giving her a ride to the Rim Rock, and Stanton Drake personally bringing her the telegram she'd been waiting on, and then inviting her out for a meal.

I should have accepted.

But mostly, the McCutcheons amazed her—all of them from Dustin to his siblings, and even his parents. She'd expected scorn, but they'd been hospitable. Would the McCutcheons fare in Santa Fe as well if the tables were turned?

No, she wouldn't ask the clerk about work. He might think her unable to pay and kick her to the street.

Sidney stepped out onto the boardwalk and walked with slow steps. From the post office across the street, she heard women's laughter, and even the high-pitched giggle of a child. The brick sheriff's office, the one they'd visited last night, was only two buildings over on her side of the street. She should start there.

She pulled open the door and looked inside. Vacant. Cool air rushed into her face.

Moving on, she continued toward the intersection where a black iron bench, two olive trees, an eye-level clock on a black pole, and a saguaro cactus dressed up the corner. A burly man dressed in farmer's clothes sat on the bench, studying the ground between his boots. The way he leaned dangerously to one side made alarm bells go off in her head.

His bleary red eyes opened wide, and a crooked smile appeared on his face when he noticed her approach. Clasping his hands together in a gesture of happiness caused his massive biceps to strain against the fabric of his well-worn shirt.

"Frrrancine?" he slurred, his voice filled with thankfulness and awe. He struggled to his feet. "I'm sooorry for lying to ya. Please forgive your Billy Willy." He grasped the clock pole to keep from falling. "I'll swear off the bottle if you'll let me come home. *Pleeeease,* Francine," he sobbed. "Nothin's the same without you. My life's gone straight ta hell."

Thunderous emotions stormed across his blotchy pink face. He held out a massive hand, and tears filled his eyes. Staying upright proved difficult, and he took an unsteady step in her direction.

A sudden urge to bolt punched Sidney in the gut. She glanced behind to see if indeed a woman named Francine had arrived to take *Billy Willy* home. No other woman in sight. As she'd presumed, he'd mistaken her for his beloved Francine.

In a split-second decision, she made for the first door she spotted, one that belonged to a cute little dress shop. Before *Billy Willy* was any the wiser, she dashed past him and slipped into the door, releasing a breathy sigh.

A young woman stood at the counter, speaking with an older lady. She was willowy with beautiful thick blond hair. The mass was piled loosely on her head, but the few tresses that had escaped streamed around her shoulders. A pencil stuck behind her ear looked out of place with her femininity.

The young woman glanced up and smiled. "I'll be with you in a moment," she said.

"Thank you, no rush," Sidney replied, liking her mellifluous German accent.

Relieved to get past the drunken sot without incident, she looked around slowly, admiring the pretty bolts of lace and the stunning garment on the dress form. Waves of maroon velvet billowed to the floor, trimmed with golden cord. An unusual piece of art on the wall had been made from fancy buttons, sequins, and other shiny objects used to decorate a gown.

A sandwich sign outside the window told her she was in Lily's Lace and More. Sidney assumed the pretty woman at the cutting counter must be Lily, for the name fit her to a tee.

"I'm so sorry to disappoint you, Mrs. Harbinger," said the young woman. "With Mrs. Tuttle's blue velvet gown to finish, and also the dress I've only just started for Miss Schad, I couldn't possibly take on another project to finish in thirty days. Not in good conscience, anyway. I couldn't deliver the garment on time."

The woman patted her shiny forehead with a folded handkerchief, and her nose wrinkled in annoyance. "But, Lily, I don't want any other designer. My gown *must* come from your shop. There has to be something you can do? Surely, a way must be found . . ."

Sidney straightened, her hand stilling in midair as she reached to feel a bolt of soft-looking velvet trim. She wasn't eavesdropping, but in the minuscule shop, she couldn't avoid hearing the conversation between the two ladies. She looked up and inched toward the counter. The poor girl looked wretched about having to turn away a prospective customer.

"Perhaps you can speak with Teddy Moore?" Lily offered. "As you know, he makes dresses, as well as—"

"I'll do no such thing!" Mrs. Harbinger cried, her nose lifting into the air. "I want something from a true dressmaker for my fiftieth anniversary celebration. Teddy is merely a tailor. If I can't have you, I don't know what I'll do." She pressed the hanky still clutched in her weathered-looking fingers to her lips. "Actually, Lily, I can't believe you're treating me in this manner. I've been your *best* customer since you've opened."

Now standing close to Mrs. Harbinger, Sidney softly cleared her throat, and both women looked over.

"Excuse me, but I couldn't help but hear about the dilemma you're in," she said, giving Lily a knowing look. "This woman needs a new gown, and you need help in your shop to make that happen. May I offer you my services?"

Lily's brow wrinkled into a frown, but a wide smile began on Mrs. Harbinger's face that would have had the portly woman committed.

Sidney's stomach pushed her on, imagining all the delicious foodstuffs she could afford once she'd put in a day's work. "I'm available right now."

"Hire her, Lily!" Mrs. Harbinger cried. "I need this gown, and you need the help."

Lily hadn't stopped staring at her throughout the conversation. She seemed to be taking her measure, calculating something in her mind.

"I don't know," she said slowly. "John and I usually talk over every decision. What experience have you had sewing clothes?"

Not much. But when Sidney imagined the feel of a hot roast beef and gravy dinner weighing her stomach, her mouth watered. She needed this job, but she wouldn't lie.

"Some. As a girl with my mother, and a little more with our housekeeper. I have several brothers, so I've darned more socks than I can count, and sewed on a multitude of buttons."

Lily's expression darkened. "So, really none at all with dressmaking?" The shopkeeper's voice said everything. She needed someone with experience.

"I won't disappoint you," Sidney said quickly. "I'm a good, hard worker and a fast learner. If nothing else, I can cut a straight line if you have me cut out the pattern. How hard can that be?"

Lily tapped her finger against her lips for several seconds. "You might be surprised."

"I'm sorry, that was a stupid thing to say. I'm sure you're right, and sewing a beautiful creation takes time and talent. Just give me a try with this one dress—or this one day, if that arrangement makes you feel better," she practically begged, looking at Mrs. Harbinger.

I'll get on my knees if I have to.

"Oh, I forgot to say, I'm not here permanently, only for a couple of months at the most. Still, I'm in desperate need of a job for the time being. I'll give you all I've got for the time I'm here, if you want me." Sidney clasped her hands at her waist. "I promise; you won't be sorry."

"Do it, Lily!" Mrs. Harbinger said sternly, her gaze bouncing between her and Lily. She reached out and nudged the shop owner just above the elbow. "Hire her so I can have my dress. If you don't, I just might cry!" The woman sucked in a deep breath, and her large bosom expanded.

Lily stuck out her hand. "How can I argue with that? You're hired."

Sidney inhaled as a huge wave of relief poured over her, as well as a good dose of uncertainty. Could she do as she'd just promised Lily?

Pushing away her doubts, she grasped Lily's hand firmly. "Thank you. My name is Sidney, and I'm staying at the hotel. Room sixteen." She glanced around. "What would you like me to do first?"

Chapter Twenty-One

Anxious to check on Noah, Dustin loped into the ranch yard a few strides ahead of the two riders he'd brought along as guards for the payroll, and then pulled his horse to a halt. Dismounting, he handed his reins over to the hired help, the twelve-year-old son of one of their ranch hands.

"Thanks," Dustin said, almost smiling at the seriousness of the lad intent on doing his job properly.

Seeing the boy turn to lead away his gelding, Dustin stopped him. "Hold up. I need to get my saddlebags." *And the men's two weeks' worth of wages.*

Dustin slung the bags over his shoulder, thanked his men for their help, and then headed inside. Walking into his father's office, he found Chaim comfortable in the chair by the unlit fireplace, and his father behind his large mahogany desk.

He plunked the money down.

"How'd it go?" Winston asked, his voice so neutral, his words sounded strange. The lines around his eyes had deepened, and he looked haggard. He wasn't letting on, but this situation with Noah and Sidney had him on edge.

"No problems. I like Jorgensen; he's a decent man. I think Rio Wells will see a lot of positive changes now that we're rid of that thief who used to run the bank."

Chaim looked up from the newspaper he was perusing.

Maria stepped into the room. *"Buenas tardes, Señor* Dustin. May I bring you the thing to eat?"

He smiled. Her English never improved, even after all the years working at the Rim Rock. He noticed the cups of coffee his father and brother were drinking.

"Gracias, Maria. A cup of coffee, if it's already brewed."

She hurried away.

"And what about the other business?" Winston asked. "The Calhoun girl? Is she holding true to her roots and causing trouble around town? I wouldn't expect any different."

Sidney was now *business?*

"Her name's Sidney, Pa, and she was only a girl when this whole fuss started. I don't think we can lay the blame at her door."

Dustin wasn't taking sides. *He wasn't!* But, damn it, Sidney wasn't responsible for her father's sins. As irksome as she could be at times, no logical person could hold her accountable.

"But to answer your question, yes, she's settled in the hotel, and they've given her credit until funds arrive from Santa Fe. She sent a telegram, but I didn't wait for the reply. She should have funds soon."

"Maybe," Winston grumbled. "What if her old man personally brings the money? I don't like the situation one bit. Dealing with that family in Kansas once a year is bad enough."

Chaim nodded. "He has a point."

"He wouldn't go to that trouble," Dustin countered. *But to spite Pa, he might.*

Winston took a healthy hit from his mug and clapped it atop his desk. "She could've taken a loan from us, but she's cut from the same cloth as her old man. Would rather make us worry about her than accept a little help. As they say, the apple doesn't fall far from the tree." He pointedly looked at Dustin, his lips crushed together in a straight line. "Don't let that pretty face fool you, Dustin."

"Me?" he barked out. "Why do you think that?"

"I just do."

"Well, don't. She wouldn't take any money outright, but I left an envelope in the safe at the hotel with instructions to deliver it later tonight. By then, she'll be good and hungry, and more than happy to accept."

Winston grunted, gazing at him over the rim of his cup. His bloodshot eyes attested to a lack of sleep.

Maria returned with a tray full of goodies. The slender, forty-something woman had a way of walking that always brought to Dustin's mind a ghost floating through a graveyard at midnight. Not because she was scary, but because her steps were totally silent, and her head moved along a perfectly straight plane as if her feet didn't touch the tile floor.

She set the tray on a table under the window and turned in his direction. "Here are you, *señor.*"

"*Gracias,*" Dustin said.

"Thank you, Maria," Chaim added.

She held up a finger, her eyes going wide. "You *niños* eat not too many. I prepare good supper." Her stern tone couldn't hide the amused twitching of her lips.

"What about me?" Winston asked playfully.

She just smiled and hurried away.

Dustin eyed the persimmon cookies with interest. Taking one, he put the whole thing in his mouth, the mild sweetness firing his taste buds. He chewed for a second, swallowed, and repeated the process.

"Have either of you seen Noah today? I paired him with Brick, and instructed Manolito not to let him out of his sight. You haven't heard of any trouble?"

"The day's been dead as a doornail," Chaim said with a shake of his head. "I keep expecting Emmeline will walk into the room any moment. Doesn't feel right around here at all."

Dustin picked up another cookie and turned. "I'm headed out to the bunkhouse to check on Noah." He glanced at Chaim. "Coming?"

"Naw." Chaim raised the newspaper and shook out the pages, sticking his nose inside. "I'm plannin' to sit right here until supper."

This is worse than I thought!

"That's a good four hours. Won't you get bored?" Dustin would climb the walls if someone asked him to sit inside for more than ten minutes.

"I'm bored already, and nothing's making me unbored until Emmeline returns. My life's nothin' without her."

Chapter Twenty-Two

Today was not only payday, but shower day for anyone who felt so inclined. Noah stood at the end of a line, waiting for his turn at the outdoor facility. He'd been told that bathing wasn't a requirement of a hand receiving his pay, but was highly encouraged. Made sense since most men he knew went straight into town as soon as they had money in their pockets, and blew their whole month's earnings on whiskey, women, and poker.

A warm breeze fluttered his hair across his forehead. He'd left his hat and shirt inside his small sleeping quarters, thinking the less he had to carry back, the better. With a towel under his arm, he'd followed Larry Linstrom, a relatively amicable cowhand, out the fifty feet behind the bunkhouse.

Two walled-in stalls, open at the top and bottom, stood under a large cistern. The tank was filled from a pipe leading from a rivulet on the top of the knoll. The siding was tall enough to cover a man's body and head, but his legs were visible from the knees down. A sturdy platform, constructed of wooden slats, kept the person showering above the dirt and mud. Beyond the stalls, the land sharply cut away.

Noah smelled strong, even to himself. He couldn't last another day in his present condition, since the jailers in San Antonio hadn't cared if their guests went their entire life without bathing. The memory made him suck in a lungful of clean air.

The white cotton towel hanging over the door of the first stall disappeared inside. A few moments later, the door opened and a middle-aged cowpoke came out, his towel wrapped around his sinewy middle and his wet hair finger combed back.

The next fella in line advanced. A couple of minutes after he closed the door, his clothes, wrapped into a ball, came flying out as if he'd given them a healthy pitch, and over the embankment they went.

Curious, Noah strode over to the drop-off to see a container twenty feet below heaped with dirty laundry. *Ah, someone must come along and do the wash. That's not so bad. I should have worn my shirt.* He was amazed that everyone's toss had hit the mark. *Years of practice.* He took mental note of the target.

Finally inside, Noah stripped down and let the cool water flow over his head. He'd given his pants and unmentionables a hefty toss, wondering how they kept the clothes straight once they were laundered. Oh well, wasn't his problem. He had extras in his saddlebag.

He closed his eyes. The water felt good.

A moment hadn't passed before his sister popped into his head. How was she? Guilt for the mess he'd created weighed his shoulders. Was he the only one at home who noticed her unhappiness? She might profess she loved ranching and her life, but he wholeheartedly doubted it. And now she was navigating strange waters among enemies, with no one to help.

Or maybe there was someone. McCutcheon. The man's interest in her was impossible to hide.

He lifted the small clump of soap from a shelf nailed in the corner, and rubbed the slimy mass over his chest, lathering up good.

I need to quit worrying. She's smart. A Calhoun. She can take care of herself. I didn't ask her to come trailing me like a mama cat following her kit.

Another stab of guilt.

Didn't I? She always follows. I'd be pretty damn stupid to think this time would be different.

What if she decided to go home? She wouldn't cross the badlands alone, would she?

Dang it. His body jerked. She might.

Agitated, he lathered his hair, his face, every appendage, and then stuck his face up in the stream, his eyes tightly closed.

A chuckle reached his ears from somewhere. He didn't give that a thought until he reached for the towel slung over the top of the door and discovered the rub gone.

With the good report from Manolito and another from Brick Paulson, Dustin let go the breath he'd been holding and relaxed his shoulder against the stones of the bunkhouse fireplace. He'd expected the worst. Noah running off, getting into a fight and hurting someone, or worse. This was certainly a welcome surprise.

The men who weren't out on watch at the moment were lounging around the bunkhouse main room or playing cards at the table. One fella sat in a chair with a small writing desk on his lap, pen and paper in hand. The serene, wholesome atmosphere actually made him proud. The McCutcheons provided in every way possible for the men who rode for their brand.

According to Switchback, the bunkhouse cook, Noah was at the showers and should be back anytime.

"Coffee, boss?" the cook asked, stirring a large pot of beans. A foot-high stack of tortillas sat on the side of the stove with a basket filled with corn on the cob.

"No, thanks. I'm waiting for Calhoun."

Right then the door banged open with a crack. Outlined in the evening light was Noah Calhoun, buck naked except for his boots. If the expression in his eyes was any indication of his mood, he was furious.

Laughter erupted.

Dustin glanced around the room. Wasn't difficult to see every man there had been waiting for the show.

A round of unruly glee reverberated around the bunkhouse and into Noah's head like a hive full of bees.

Dustin McCutcheon stood in the middle of the room. His eyes wide, he barked out a surprised chortle.

Unashamed, Noah stomped across the wooden planks, overtop the braided rug that divided the room, and into his sleeping quarters. Once inside, he slammed the door so hard, his hat fell from the small antler stub on the wall.

He counted to ten.

The laughter in the other room continued.

A McCutcheon had gotten the best of a Calhoun—*again*! He recognized Dustin's voice as he growled out an order for the men to shut up, but the laughter continued for almost another minute. After that, silence was restored to the room.

Someone rapped on his door. "Noah, I didn't know—"

"Bite it, McCutcheon! I wouldn't expect any different from hands at the Rim Rock."

Heated grumbles sounded through the door as Noah pulled on his extra pair of pants. He'd give them a taste of their own medicine as soon as he was decently covered. He threw a shirt angrily over his shoulders and pulled the garment into place.

"Nothin's sacred to you, is it?" he yelled. He clenched his jaw, grinding his teeth so tightly, he heard them squeak.

"Just a little good-natured hazing. No harm done," Dustin said through the door. The laughter in the man's voice was impossible to hide.

Again, a buzzing filled Noah's head. He yanked open the door and shoved Dustin back before the devil knew what hit him, throwing a punch into his face. Dustin was taller and outweighed him by a good twenty pounds, but still he stumbled back and caught the heel of his boot on a chair. He fell halfway to the floor before righting himself.

Several men jumped to their feet and dashed forward. Noah took a blow to his own face, but planted several punches he knew couldn't have felt good. In seconds, Dustin was back, pulling off his men as they jabbed a few punches of their own.

Horrendous clanging filled the small space.

Whirling, Noah saw Switchback with the dinner triangle held high, rounding it with lightning speed with the metal spoon in his hand. The sound painfully ripped through Noah's head.

The distraction gave Dustin an opportunity to get his men under control, shoving them back toward the other side of the room. He stood between them, hands on hips and gaze intense. Blood ran from the corner of his mouth, and he wiped it away with the back of his hand.

"No fighting in the bunkhouse!"

Unspent energy still coursed through Noah. His stare connected with Brick Paulson, the man he was sure was behind the childish stunt that had left him naked as a jaybird.

Outnumbered by a good ten or twelve, he had to be sensible. He couldn't take them all on. McCutcheon was the only one that mattered. All the others could go straight to the devil.

Chapter Twenty-Three

Early Saturday morning, Lily quietly made her way down the stairs, not wanting to awaken John. She avoided the fifth step, which squeaked loudly with anyone's weight, and continued into the kitchen.

John had stayed up late last night at his office, poring over books that didn't look like his normal medical journals. When she'd asked what he was doing, she'd watched him smile and shove them under the *Farmer's Almanac*, the periodical that Doc Bixby subscribed to.

Each time she moved close so she could tell him about the assistant she'd hired, she'd see a smile and receive his kiss—his best method for stopping her questions. She eventually gave up, returned to the shop, and pulled out her novel.

This morning, though, as soon as she'd served his first cup of coffee, she'd share her news.

Nervous, Lily swallowed down her uncertainty. Would he care that she'd made such a major decision without consulting him first? Surely he'd be happy, wouldn't he?

Without the promise of Sidney's help, she couldn't take on the gown Mrs. Harbinger commissioned yesterday. And now, if Sidney turned out to be helpful at all, Miss Schad's dress was sure to be completed on time, if not early, as would Mrs.

Tuttle's. The workload was a worry that had plagued Lily for the past two weeks. She was punctual and promoted herself as such.

Sidney. She was a lovely young woman. Pleasant and smart. Older than herself by a few years, she suspected. By the time Lily had made a pot of tea at four and brought out a plate of shortbread cookies, she noticed the young woman looked practically starved. She had tried to hide the fact, but her hand shook with intensity when she reached for a cookie.

Lily scooped coffee beans into the grinder and began turning the handle, knowing John wouldn't sleep long after she'd left the bed. She pumped water into the heavy coffeepot, but as she turned, she accidently caught her funny bone on the pump handle and let out a screech, clenching her eyes closed as pain rippled up and down her arm.

"Lily? Lily! Are you all right?" John bounded bare-chested down the stairs, his expression tight. His rumpled hair fell over his forehead and into his eyes. "You cried out, darlin'. What happened?"

The pain was still too great for her to utter a sound. She clenched her fist open and closed a few times, and then dashed away a rogue tear from her eye.

"I'm sorry to wake you," she pushed out through her tight throat. "I know how tired you were when you finally came to bed last night."

"I don't care about that! Are you hurt?"

"Just something silly. I hit my elbow when I turned."

His brows tented. "Caught your funny bone?"

She nodded.

He took her arm and rubbed her elbow in a soft circular motion. He increased the pressure until he was rubbing quite brusquely. "I'm sorry."

"Don't be. My clumsiness is the cause, nothing else. Next time, I'll look before I move."

"If this place weren't so darned small, there wouldn't be a problem. As it is, this kitchen with the table and chairs can hardly hold the two of us."

As if to prove his point, he took a small step and the table nudged into his back. Her back was to the door that led to the alley. The kitchen was so tight, they'd be in trouble if anyone else entered.

"See what I mean?" he said. "It's amazing we've lived here this long."

The discouragement in his voice tugged at Lily. She hadn't meant to bring the smallness of their living arrangements to his attention again, or the fact she'd like to move in the first place. They'd only been married such a short time. She shouldn't bother him with things that weren't a necessity. He hadn't mentioned her sister since they'd talked, and she didn't really know where he stood on the matter.

She pulled out a chair. "Now that you're up, sleepyhead, have a seat while I put the coffee on to boil. After we've eaten, I have something exciting I want to share."

At least, I hope Sidney is as exciting to you as she is to me. A plus was that Sidney didn't want a permanent position. Hopefully. Giselle would be here in a few months to take her place.

He rubbed his bare arms. "Oh?"

"Uh-huh, but have your coffee first. And something hot in your belly. Do you mind waiting?"

John chuckled, leaned down, and kissed her lips. "Am I that much of a bear that I need my coffee before you'll share your news? I'm becoming a little worried."

Heat prickled her cheeks as she shook her head.

He started up the stairs. "I'll grab a shirt in case someone stops by."

John couldn't imagine what Lily was being so mysterious about. Whatever the announcement was, it wouldn't top his news he'd have in a few days. He still needed to do final figuring and contact a handful of his acquaintances back east. They would take a few days to track down by telegram, and then get replies.

The whole idea was all still up in the air, but at least John had hope. Hope of providing a better life for Lily. Hard work didn't scare him, and actually, he welcomed the prospect. He'd grown up on the mountain, ranching from before the sun topped the mountains and until the orb sank low in the west. A great deal of the equation depended on Bixby, and whether or not he'd give his blessings to proceed. He'd have that answer later today.

John slipped his shirt over his shoulders. Turning, he caught his reflection in the mirror. He stepped closer to examine the line left by the knife attack. *Hardly noticeable.* This could earn a lot of money if he played his cards right.

"John, your eggs are on the table," Lily called.

"On my way." He exited the bedroom and practically skipped down the stairs, taking his spot at the table. "There, that didn't take me long."

She poured his coffee. "When you're finished eating, I wondered if you'd like to go with me to the cemetery to tend to Tante Harriett's grave. I've been in the shop so much this last week, I find myself longing to be outside. Take a walk."

"Sounds like a perfect Saturday morning." He glanced down at his breakfast, thankful he'd married a woman who was not only beautiful, but knew how to cook. "I'll make short order of this so we can get going."

Cutting his eggs with the side of his fork, John lifted a section into his mouth. He chewed and swallowed. As promised, he was finished in less than three minutes.

"Now, what's the big surprise?" He patted his stomach. "Catch me now when I'm fed and feeling fine."

Lily eased into the chair across from him. The way she nervously chewed on her bottom lip and avoided his gaze made him think this was a bigger deal than he'd previously thought.

"Lily?"

"You know I've been pretty busy in the shop."

"You're being a bit modest about your success, aren't you? You've been working steadily since the day you opened, and now things are picking up even more."

Smiling, she nodded. "That's true."

He wiped his mouth and set his napkin next to his plate. "Tell me, Lily. You're making me edgy. What's troubling you?"

Her eyes softened. "I'm sorry. I didn't mean to do that. I've taken on an assistant to help in the shop."

Surprised, he sat back.

"It's only temporary," she rushed on to say. "I would have talked this important decision over with you first, but the woman dropped into my lap when I needed the help. Mrs. Harbinger, almost giddy with joy, insisted that I hire her then and there so I could accept her next consignment."

Another gown. Lily is providing more than me. Much more. He pushed away a prickle of envy.

"Of course you needed to hire her when you had the chance. That was a good decision."

She blinked twice. "You're not angry?"

He picked up his cup, not wanting her to see his uncharitable feelings. "Angry? How can I be angry with your success? Every woman wants a gown designed by Lily McCutcheon. You're doing fantastic."

I wish I could say the same. I want to provide for you—so you won't have to work so much if you so choose.

Relief moved across Lily's face. "Thank goodness, my love," she said softly. "I was fearful somehow you'd think me aggressive or something, and that I'd planned the entire thing. My new assistant is very nice, and staying in the hotel for the time being. I think she really needs this job."

"I trust your judgment. She has experience then, making clothes?"

"Not much, but she can do the things I instruct, if I keep a close watch on her progress. The same way my aunt taught me."

"And did she tell you why she's in Rio Wells? What brought her here?"

"No, we never had a chance with Mrs. Harbinger standing there and listening to every word we said. But I liked her instantly, and she looked honest, and . . . and, I trust that."

All his good feelings, the hope, the excitement had left John in a whoosh. Lily would take care of their money problem singlehandedly, and enjoy doing it. A few more dresses a month, and she was there already.

"Fine then. I'm excited to meet her. She'll be here Monday morning?"

"Yes, bright and early."

John leaned in and kissed her cheek, marveling on its softness. "Then how can I argue with that?"

Chapter Twenty-Four

Sidney sat bolt upright in bed, the light blue counterpane slipping down to her hips and exposing her chemise. She blinked the sleep from her eyes as the brisk air that filled the room brought gooseflesh to her arms.

What had awakened her so abruptly? She looked around, remembering she was in the Union Hotel in Rio Wells—an eternity from Santa Fe. With a sigh, she slowly lowered herself back to the sheets, the mattress dipping with her weight, and tried to remember her disturbing dream.

Something had brought a surge of fear, and then a bolt of happiness. She struggled to remember. A fish? Yes. She'd fallen into a stream and come face-to-face with a fat spotted bass with shimmering scales.

Carmen had an interpretation for everything, especially dreams. She'd said that if you dreamed of a lizard, then you had an enemy; a turkey, you'd soon see a fool. But a fish? Sidney couldn't recall.

"Remember, mi pequeña florecilla, *when you dream of a* pescado, *someone you love is expecting a* bebé.*"*

A baby? Again, Sidney sat up, wondering who could be in the family way. She didn't know that many young women. A wife of one of their cowhands? No. Only two lived at the ranch, and both were well past child-bearing years.

She wasn't expected at work until ten this morning. Her stomach rumbled, objecting to its emptiness. Lily had promised to pay her thirty-cent salary daily, and had done so at closing time on Friday. She'd stretched the meager amount over the weekend, buying a cup of soup for five cents, and stale biscuits for a penny each, from the Lillian Russell Room. After today, she'd have enough for something substantial from the Cheddar Box Café.

The hotel clerk had offered her an envelope of cash left behind by Dustin, but she'd refused and told him to put it right back in his safe until Dustin returned.

Finished with her toilette, she stepped into the long mulberry skirt belonging to Madeline McCutcheon, pulled up the garment, and fastened the hooks. Slipping her arms into the borrowed white blouse, she did up the buttons, stopping at the top. Both of Dustin's sisters had treated her kindly, as had his mother, Winnie McCutcheon. They'd fussed over her like three mama hens over one chick.

A filmy memory of her own mother clouded her eyes. Sidney touched the first fastened button and went down the row saying, "Rich man, poor man, beggar man, thief." Her mother had taught her the rhyme when she was a tiny girl. The numbering would determine what kind of man she would marry. "Doctor, lawyer, Indian chief."

A girlish laugh slipped out from between her lips. *Imagine.* She was twenty-four years old. There was one button left. Dustin's face popped into her mind, and she moved her finger down,

"Rich man," she whispered, lost in her thoughts.

Realizing what she was doing, she jerked away her finger. Thoroughly disgusted with herself, she crossed the room and pushed the window down, closing out the chilly morning air. Had she no loyalty at all?

Back at the mirror, she assessed her rumpled reflection. She'd worn these garments nonstop for the last three days. She had nothing else except the pile of dusty clothes she'd arrived in at the Rim Rock.

Showing up to her first full day of work for a dressmaker clothed as a man in pants and a vest wouldn't do. She'd feel uncomfortable, and Lily wouldn't be pleased. Whether she liked accepting charity for a few more days until she could figure out how to get something else to wear made no difference. Again, she wished her saddlebags, money, and Carmen's music box hadn't been lost.

Sidney pinched her cheeks and waited for them to color. Back in Santa Fe and the daughter of a well-to-do rancher, she was sought after by most of the single men. Now she resembled a waif, a penniless stray alone in Rio Wells.

Well, that wasn't quite true. She knew her boss, Lily, and Mrs. Harbinger, the brusque customer in Lily's shop. Oh yes, and the telegraph clerk, Stanton Drake, with his tall, shiny forehead.

How was Noah? Had he stayed out of trouble for the last two days? He'd had plenty of time to skedaddle, if he had the notion.

She shook her head in irritation. If only he'd stayed in school and not run off in the first place.

Chapter Twenty-Five

With a stomach full of butterflies, Sidney stepped inside the small one-room shop at ten o'clock sharp. A cluster of bells over the door announced her arrival. Glancing up, she noticed a four-leaf clover pinned above the door frame, and smiled. *I'm not the only superstitious person in Rio Wells.*

The room, with the large picture window that framed Dry Street, was empty. The savory aroma of coffee lingered in the air.

"Sidney, is that you?" Lily called from the second floor.

"Yes."

"I'll be right down. Please make yourself comfortable."

"Thank you." Sidney took a moment to admire the finished sample on the dress form. Such fine craftsmanship! Lily truly was an artist.

A moment later, Lily hurried down the steps, greeting her with a wide smile.

"Happy Monday," she said. Her lemon-colored skirt hugged her trim waist and looked so nice with her light blond hair. The cheery yellow goldfinch, abundant in the winter trees in Santa Fe, came to mind.

Happiness Sidney hadn't felt for a long time filled her. Things would work out—*somehow.* She and Noah would get through this ordeal and go home. Then she'd never have to look at Dustin McCutcheon or *any* of his family ever again.

A small slice of her cheerfulness ebbed away, and the realization startled her. The warmth of Mrs. McCutcheon, as well as Dustin's sisters—and Chaim too. She'd thought they hadn't meant a thing to her. Now she wondered.

"I like your lucky charm." Sidney pointed to the dry green splotch above the door. "The elusive four-leaf clover. Every girl's dream."

"Isn't it cute? A gift from an old admirer—before I said yes to my husband's proposal." Her face softened when she glanced up at the inch-sized, alfalfa-colored leaf, one small corner turning black. "Now he's a very dear friend."

Sidney's brows popped up. "Oh?"

"Yes, on the day the shop opened, he brought the keepsake over and wished me luck. His hands actually trembled. It's carried many blessings, to be sure."

Lily pulled a bolt of deep cobalt fabric from the shelf and unrolled the expensive-looking cloth on the cutting table. Her hands moved quickly, nimbly.

"I've been thinking about you all weekend, Sidney. I'll have so much fun teaching you to be my assistant. After which, I'll get so much more accomplished." She paused and lifted a brow. "If you learn quickly," she said with a warm, cheerful smile.

Heat rushed into her cheeks. "I'll do my best, Lily. I hope I won't let you down."

"Of course you won't. I felt the same when I started working with my aunt in Boston. She was a master of her craft. Had been creating gowns, frocks, evening wear, and wedding dresses for many years, and for a few of the most significant women in Boston. Three governors' wives, the last being Mrs. George Robinson. I was honored to hem three of her ball gowns, as well as a few for her nineteen-year-old daughter, Annie."

Lily smiled brightly as she tenderly pressed out the wrinkles. "Also, the mayor's wife, and even the wife of the first Negro judge in America. Josephine Ruffin, whose maiden name was St. Pierre. I say that because she liked to share all sorts of stories about her family. A lovely, soft-spoken woman with the most beautiful eyes I've ever seen."

A small laugh slipped past Lily's lips. She shook her head in wonderment.

"She had an aversion to using the front door, and often tried to enter from the back. Tante Harriett put a stop to that. Those were wonderful times. Me newly arrived from Germany. Everything in America was like a dream." She gave Sidney a confident smile. "We'll take each task one day at a time. You'll be amazed at how fast you learn."

"I don't want you to go easy on me. I can take instruction, and criticism."

Lily's hands that had gone back to smoothing, stilled. She turned and looked at Sidney, narrowing her gaze.

"Are you hungry, Sidney? I made a pan of sweet rolls this morning. And there's coffee too—at least enough for one cup."

Sidney blinked and looked away. She'd never felt so humbled, but darn, she wanted that pastry.

"I'd love one," she heard herself say.

What would her pa think? And her brothers? A Calhoun taking charity hand over fist.

"Wonderful! And coffee?"

She nodded. "But I can wait until it's time for a break." *Do we get breaks?*

"Oh no. You must have one now. They're so much better when they're warm."

Embarrassed, she stood rooted to her spot by the cutting counter and listened as Lily moved around the small alcove of her kitchen.

"All right, it's ready."

Scooting into a seat at the table, Sidney gazed at the delicious-smelling pastry and the coffee that was calling to her in a lovesick voice. Aware of Lily at her side, she took a sip and let the hot beverage slip down her throat and plunge into her empty stomach.

"Take your time. I'll start pinning the pattern." Lily patted her arm.

She smiled, feeling overwhelmed with gratitude. "Thank you, Lily."

"No need for thanks. I'm glad to have you here."

Sidney made short work of the scrumptious goodness, as well as the coffee. She didn't think she'd ever tasted anything quite so flavorful. Her stomach felt warm, rich, and full. A moment of empathy for all the people in the world who didn't have enough to eat overcame her. She'd only been hungry for a couple of days, but what if this condition was her entire life—much like the woman she'd helped in San Antonio. And her sweet little boys.

Finished, Sidney wiped her mouth with her napkin and stood, taking her plate and cup to the sink. She set them in the empty dishpan, wondering if she should quickly wash them or get back to the pinning. Antsy, she washed the stickiness from her fingers and then hurried to Lily's side.

"Thank you again, that was delicious." She admired the fabric on the table. "What would you like me to do?"

"See how I'm arranging the pattern pieces to get the best possible cut with the least amount of waste?"

She nodded.

"This particular fabric is quite expensive, so we don't want any mistakes. At this stage, I go very slowly, methodically, I don't get—"

The bells chimed, and a young man stuck his head in the front door. "Morning, Lily!"

". . . distracted." Lily gave a patient smile. "Good morning, Tucker," she replied with great affection. "How're you?"

"Good. Thank you for the cinnamon rolls." He patted his flat stomach. "They were mighty fine indeed."

"I'm glad you liked them."

"I best get goin'. Doc has me on an errand, but I couldn't pass by without saying thanks."

"Wait, there's someone here I want you to—"

The door slammed closed.

"Oh well. Plenty of time later for introductions. Now, what was I saying?"

"That you're careful at this stage and don't let distractions hamper you."

"So much for good intentions. Anyway, you can begin pinning the paper to the fabric on the far end of the table. Keep in mind the pattern pieces will slip when you first stick the pins through. Be very careful that they don't. I want them just where they're placed. I will check everything before we begin to cut."

A moment of trepidation kept Sidney still.

"Go on, now," Lily said, encouraging her. "You can't make any awful mistakes—yet." She gave a little laugh. "Believe me; I've made my share of blunders, but you'll never learn if you don't begin."

Sidney worked steadily for a good thirty minutes without looking up. That wouldn't be bad except she'd stuck her finger three times, and now had to be extra careful not to spot the material with blood. She'd pressed her hanky to the tip until the bleeding stopped.

"Will you be all right if I run upstairs?" Lily asked.

"Of course."

Alone now, Sidney took a deep breath, letting the air out slowly. Very few people were as kind as her new boss. Lily had just about read her mind about being famished, and again about her jitters around the material.

Sidney glanced at her finger. No blood. She stretched her back. The posture of leaning over the table was tiring muscles she wasn't used to using.

The door opened and Dustin stuck his head inside. "Lily, is John here? He's not at his office." He was looking at a newspaper in his hand.

"I'll be right down, Dustin," Lily called. "Come in and make yourself comfortable."

As thankful as she was for her job and the food she'd just eaten, Sidney felt a flush warm her neck, knowing perfectly well that two pink splotches would soon appear on her cheeks. Chastened to the core, she wondered what Dustin would think when he found out she'd taken a job as a seamstress.

Dustin finally looked up and saw her leaning over the table. Their gazes met and held.

Chapter Twenty-Six

Dustin blinked. Sidney Calhoun! Standing at the cutting table in Lily's shop, a pincushion strapped to her wrist, and three pins protruding from her lips like a porcupine. For as out of her element as she seemed, she looked beautiful in the soft light drifting through the windowpane and reflecting a light green tint off his mother's old emerald curtains used on the dressing room.

Ducking her head, Sidney whisked the pins from her mouth and stuck them into the round pad on her arm.

Footsteps sounded as his cousin-in-law hurried down the stairs. "Dustin, good morning! I'm so happy you stopped by. I have fresh pastry, if you're interested."

He glanced at Noah waiting for him outside on his horse before he stepped inside and removed his hat. The kid had promised to mind his manners. After what had transpired with the showers, and the strained weekend since, he didn't dare leave him alone with the ranch hands again—at least, not for a while. At this point, no one was to be trusted—neither the cowhands nor Noah.

"No, thank you, Lily," he called, still staring at Sidney. "I'm looking for John. He around? I checked his office first, but no one's there."

Lily stopped short when she came into the room, glancing between him and Sidney. A tiny frown formed. "Do you two know each other? You look strange."

He nodded. "We do. As a matter of fact, her brother works at the ranch for the time being." He'd filled John in on the circumstances of the Calhouns, and was sure Lily would get the details sooner or later. He wouldn't go into it now in front of Sidney.

"That's wonderful! A family affair." She sidled over to Sidney and whispered something into her ear, causing Sidney to glance over his head at the four-leaf clover tacked over the door frame.

The ghost of a smile pulled at Sidney's lips.

"John ventured out around nine thirty to speak with Mr. Knutson," Lily went on. "Just a block over at the end of Church Street. The house with several large barns. You know the place?"

"I do," he responded nicely as if she hadn't just tattled on him about the clover. "It's been vacant for a good while. Needs work."

Dustin couldn't stop his gaze from wandering back to Sidney. She still wore Madeline's skirt and Becky's blouse. He realized that was all the clothing she had since the rest of her things had been lost with the horse.

What was she doing here in Lily's shop, pinning a pattern to a length of material?

"That's right." Lily smiled, picking up her scissors and turning them over in her hands. "John's being quite secretive about something." She resumed her position behind the cutting counter.

Dustin arched an eyebrow. "Secretive, huh? That doesn't sound like John." He couldn't think of anything else to say, and an uncomfortable sting of embarrassment prickled his cheeks.

Lily looked at Sidney and shrugged. "Yes, secretive. That's exactly what I said. Do you have any idea what it's about?"

He shook his head. "Sorry, I don't."

"And if you did, you wouldn't tell me." She tilted her head as she waited for his reply, not doing a very good job of hiding her amusement.

"Of course I would."

"I don't think so. You men stick together."

Dustin decided the time was ripe to change the subject. "So, Sidney." He gestured to the pins in her hands. Were they quivering? "You're working for Lily now? Lily McCutcheon?"

Sidney's head snapped up so fast, it was apparent she hadn't known that little fact.

At the strange reaction, Lily's eyes went wide. "Is that a problem?"

Guilt for dropping the surprise on Sidney stabbed him. He'd never do anything intentionally to hurt her. Maybe to open her eyes, but nothing more than that.

"N-not at all," Sidney sputtered.

The color of Sidney's face belied her words, which was not lost on Lily. His cousin-in-law had befriended her, and Sidney seemed to like Lily a lot. He could understand that since liking Lily was easy to do.

"Noah's outside," he said. "I'm sure he'd like to speak with you." A small gesture to smooth things over.

Sidney nodded and set the pincushion on the counter.

At the same moment, John walked through the door. He pulled up short at the crowded room.

"My, my, my, what do we have going on in here?" He continued over to Lily and kissed her cheek. "Dustin," he said with a wide smile. He extended his arm and they shook hands. "Are you pestering my wife?"

"Absolutely."

"Good." John noticed Sidney. "And who do we have here?"

For all the grief he'd received over the last few days he'd known her, Dustin couldn't help but feel compassion at the situation Sidney found herself. Surrounded by McCutcheons. The same McCutcheons she'd been taught to hate for as long as she could remember.

"This is Sidney, my new assistant." Lily waved an open hand. "And I just learned her brother is working out at the Rim Rock. Sidney, I'd like you to meet my husband, John McCutcheon."

"Mr. McCutcheon," she said, her face pulled tight with strain.

John nodded with a smile. "My pleasure."

Dustin was sure she'd like to box John's ears just for the name alone.

Lily looked between them. "Am I missing something here? Dustin, go bring in Sidney's brother. I'd like to meet him."

He sent Sidney a stern look. "He may not want to come in."

"Nonsense," Lily argued.

When had she gotten so bossy? She wasn't letting this go. "Why wouldn't he want to come inside and see his sister? Sidney, what do you think?"

"I'll go speak with him," she said, casting a glimpse at Dustin. She passed by John without a second look and was out the door.

John glanced his way. "Is she . . . ?"

Dustin nodded.

Lily came around the counter and peered out the window. "My gosh, you two have me intrigued. What in land's sake is going on? Oh, there he is. He's dismounting, and they're talking."

Noah practically fell out of the saddle when the door to the funny little dress shop Dustin had entered opened again and Sidney walked out. She was garbed in a rumpled maroon skirt and a white blouse he'd never seen before. But he knew that flushed face and frown all too well.

Shame filled him. *I've done this to her, brought on this whole worrisome mess. If I hadn't run off, she'd be home in Santa Fe, and possibly even married to Gibson Harp by now.* The man was rich and would make her a good husband. The courting had started, even if Sidney claimed she wasn't interested.

When she spotted Jackson sitting obediently by his horse, she smiled, and he dismounted as she approached. They hugged. Then she crouched and wrapped her arms around her dog. He heard her murmur to the animal and stroke his head.

"How are you holding up?" he asked. "Where're you staying?"

"At the hotel. They're extending credit until Pa sends money."

When she pulled back, a frown had replaced her smile. The frown turned to dismay when she noted the bruising on his face.

"What happened? Did you and Dustin get into a fight?" She reached up and touched his cheek, her eyes assessing the damage.

"Just a bit of a scuffle with a couple of cowhands. Nothing important," he replied. "Something was bound to happen sooner or later, so I opted for sooner."

"Noah, you promised to behave."

"I am."

"Are the McCutcheons treating you fairly?"

"Fair enough," he said, keeping the embarrassing shower ordeal to himself. "What're you doing here dressed like that? Where're your riding clothes?"

"I don't have time to answer all your questions right now. I'm working here. I just found out my boss is a McCutcheon." She shrugged and shook her head. "Seems they're everywhere. I'm to bring you inside."

"Working? Doing what? Sewing?"

"Yes. Jobs aren't a dime a dozen." She glanced up the street when several women stepped out of the mercantile on the far side of the doctor's office. "This one was the only thing I could find. I didn't want to take anything more from the McCutcheons. We're already indebted up to our eyeballs. Little did I know . . ." Her voice died away.

He glanced across the street to the bank kitty-corner to the shop where a handful of men went about business. One caught Noah's eye, but before Noah could get a good look, the bulky fellow pulled back into the alley out of sight. Noah wondered what had grabbed his attention.

"Stay," she said to Jackson, and then took Noah by the arm and propelled him toward the door.

There were still many things he wanted to ask. Had she sent a telegram home? What kind of a response had she received? This was the most trouble he'd brought down on himself, and now Sidney. He didn't feel good about what he'd done.

"Miss Calhoun? Noah?"

The doctor they'd met the night they arrived ambled out of the building next door. His well-worn sweater was haphazardly buttoned over his middle, leaving one end longer than the other. With his wrinkled face and bent shoulders, he looked about as ancient as the few craggy hilltops around this hellhole they called Rio Wells.

"I hope you both got settled."

Noah exchanged a quick glance with Sidney. If the timeworn codger only knew.

"Dr. Bixby," Sidney said. "Hello." Worry melted off her face and was replaced with a smile. "We've settled in, of sorts. As best we can, anyway." She gestured to the building. "And I'm working here for the time being."

His eyes lit up. "You and Lily? Working together? Why, that means I'll be seein' you from time to time." He chuckled and shook his head. "That brightens my day considerably."

"Yes. But right now we're needed inside," she said, taking a quick, uneasy glance at the door. "They want to meet Noah."

"Fine then. I'll just come along too, if you don't mind. Gets rather lonely sittin' in that doctor's office day in and day out."

Good. Reinforcements. The doctor stood on neutral ground.

The door to the doctor's office opened again and out came a young lad.

The old man smiled and waved him over. "Tucker, come meet my new friends, Sidney and Noah Calhoun."

The lad's stride faltered, and his face clouded over. Noah felt sure he'd heard the name Calhoun before, and that he was loyal to the McCutcheons.

The young man halted next to Bixby. His sleeves were rolled halfway to his elbow, and his left hand was missing.

"This is Tucker Noble, my young assist—" Bixby laughed again and put his arm around the newcomer's shoulders. He was as tall as the old man and wiry. He looked strong. "Actually, he *used* to be my assistant for many years. Now he works for that young whippersnapper doctor who took over my practice, John McCutcheon. I'm just here along for the ride, grateful to be livin' rent-free. Life's good, if I do say so myself."

John McCutcheon? I've never heard of him. A glance at his sister told him Sidney didn't seem surprised.

"Hogwash," Noble retorted. "You do as much doctoring as John does. He'd be hard-pressed without you."

Bixby coughed into his hand. "Chicken poo. But I thank you for saying it, Tucker boy. Now, let's get inside before they send out a search party."

Turning to the door, Noah reached for the handle.

So, more McCutcheons in Rio Wells beside the head honcho, Winston, and his sons, Dustin and Chaim. He'd heard about the sisters, but he'd paid them no mind.

John McCutcheon was a doctor? If he was young, he'd have gone to medical school to get a degree. That was interesting. Most places weren't grandfathering in self-taught men any longer. Used to be just about any old Tom, Dick, or Harry could claim they had healing knowledge.

In a spurt of inspiration, Noah found he was actually looking forward to meeting this particular McCutcheon.

Chapter Twenty-Seven

Inside the shop, Sidney glanced at Lily, unable to tell if the men had filled in her boss on the situation. Would Lily's attitude change? Why in heaven's name hadn't she asked for Lily's last name before she went begging for a job? And accepting meals? Heat rose to her cheeks for the third time that day.

"Well, what do you know," Doc Bixby said, his shrewd gaze traveling the faces. "Dustin's here too? I didn't expect to see him for a good long time, being he was just in town a few days ago." His gaze lingered on her a bit before moving on to Dustin and back again.

The old doctor apparently had his own ideas about why so many people were gathered here this morning.

"Bixby, Tucker," Dustin said. His gaze took in Noah and then slipped away. "Noah and I are riding over to Draper Bottom to make sure Deputy Miller has things under control. A Texas Ranger from San Antonio is supposed to arrive today to collect the two outlaws we left behind. I'll sleep better knowing that small, unprotected community is rid of those vermin. Come to find out, they're wanted in three states." One eyebrow tented. "I stopped in to say hello to John. I had no idea Sidney was here."

Her pride prickled.

Lily came forward. "You must be Sidney's brother," she said graciously, holding out her hand to Noah. "I see the resemblance."

Noah, always a flirt, took Lily's hand into his and smiled into her eyes, eliciting another small laugh from her boss. He actually went so far as kissing the back of her fingers. When he wanted to, her brother could charm the socks off a turtle.

"Welcome to Lily's Lace and M-more, Mr. Calhoun," Lily stuttered, her fair complexion showing a blush.

John cut his gaze to his wife's face, and Dustin glowered.

"Your sister is a great help to me."

"Pleased, Mrs. McCutcheon." He'd yet to release her hand. "Do I hear a hint of a Bavarian accent mixed with your German? It's lovely."

Lily blinked. "Why, y-yes, you do. You're the first person to pick up on that. How did you know?"

"Several of the engineering students at the university I attend are from Europe. One sounds much like you."

"*Used* to attend," Dustin threw in, which garnered a glance from Noah. "Some time will pass before you return to Santa Fe."

Sidney watched with interest as Noah remained unruffled. His calm demeanor was the true distinction between him and her other brothers. And he was a good actor.

"You're right. I haven't had a chance to give that much thought. I suppose I have to consider myself out of university for now, at least for this semester. I'll make up the time when I get back."

One of Dustin's brows arched. "I'd think you've had plenty of time to contemplate the ramifications of your actions. I know I have."

"Don't be such a grouch, Dustin," Lily said. "Mr. Calhoun isn't the first young man to be sidetracked by life, I'm sure." Addressing Noah, she said, "Your sister is wonderful. I can tell she will work out perfectly."

"I don't know about that," Sidney replied, humbled by Lily's words. "I've stuck my finger several times already. I feel like I'm all thumbs."

"That's because you've just started. But you've been company when I would normally only have Ingrid to speak with. And she is far too shy for her own good." She glanced at the dress form in the corner and laughed. "Work is so much more enjoyable with you around."

John McCutcheon reached out to Noah and grasped his hand. "I'm John McCutcheon. I hail from Montana, and the McCutcheons in Y Knot. You've probably heard about the Montana McCutcheons." He looked between her and her brother in question.

Sidney shook her head, thankful that up until now her family hadn't realized more McCutcheons existed than what they knew about here in Texas. "No, not a thing."

Doc Bixby puffed out his chest. "I had the distinct honor of meeting Miss Calhoun and Noah when they rode in the other night. I'm tickled she'll be working here. Means I'll get to see her more often than not."

"Only for a short time," Sidney felt compelled to say. "Until Noah works off the debt he owes in San Antonio. As soon as that happens, we'll be on our way back home."

Without being rude, she needed them to know a smile and a handshake wouldn't erase the years her pa had suffered. She kept that belief firm in her mind. But the Calhoun ranch was many miles away from Rio Wells, and the longer she stayed away and the more people she met, the harder holding on to the grievances became.

"You're a doctor then?" Noah said to Lily's husband.

Surprise shot through Sidney. Seemed Noah not only was trying to impress Lily, but the men as well. She wondered why.

"That's correct. I've been out of school for almost a year. Been here in Rio Wells since last May. The area is hot and dusty, but I like it." His gaze flicked over to his wife and he smiled. "I hear you're getting a degree in engineering."

Noah dipped his chin. "That's right."

He glanced at Sidney, and she saw something she'd never before seen in her brother's eyes. Regret? Pain?

"At this rate, though," he continued, "graduating might take me longer than I planned."

"I'd like to hear about your studies when you have free time," John replied. "Compare my experience with yours. I feel privileged to have had the opportunity of a higher education."

John seemed genuinely interested, and the look of admiration on Noah's face almost stole Sidney's breath. He was different from her other brothers. Where they were coarse, strong, and content with doing a day's work and nothing else, Noah was bright, clever, and inquisitive. He didn't really fit in with the rest of the family. And he made no effort to rectify that notion.

"What free time, John? For now, he's ranching with us," Dustin said. "He has plenty to do."

"That may be, but he can't work every day." John tented a brow. "Surely, he'll have a day off now and then."

Dustin grunted and gave a nod, his jaw stiff. Perhaps he hadn't intended for her brother to have any free time at all.

"When you do, Noah, stop by my office next door so we can talk."

"We best get moving," Dustin said, shifting his weight to the other leg, his hat still resting in his fingers.

Dustin and Noah were riding all the way back to Draper Bottom—alone? Sidney didn't like the sound of that. A great deal of lonely miles to tempt Noah to bolt.

When she felt a gaze on her face, she found Dustin watching her.

He lifted a shoulder. "Want to ride along, Sidney?"

I'd love to keep an eye on Noah! And you!

She waved toward the pattern. "Thank you, but I've work to do here."

"Just thought you'd like a little time with Noah, nothing more." Dustin secured his hat and headed for the door.

Chapter Twenty-Eight

Dustin mounted his horse, mentally reviewing every word Sidney had said and each look she'd tossed his way. Was she warming to him? He remembered their first meeting in the San Antonio mercantile before she'd known he was a McCutcheon.

Across the street at the telegraph office, Fred Billingsworth stepped outside. He'd been demoted from his position as mayor of Rio Wells after the Shellston affair a few months back. The spherical man reminded Dustin of a circus bear, with large sweat rings under his arms and his dark cotton trousers pulled tightly around his middle. He withdrew a folded handkerchief from the front pocket of his rumpled shirt and wiped his forehead, all the while grimacing up at the sun.

"Our old mayor," he said quietly to Noah. "Fred Billingsworth."

"Old mayor? He looks pretty young to me."

Dustin shot Noah a look of irritation. "Old as in demoted from his post. Now he's just a clerk until we have a new election. He answers to the head of the town council, Deputy Miller, and just about anyone who feels the need to boss him around." He chuckled. "Riles him good. Used to be he had his hand in just about everybody's business—and not in a good way. Not so now. He claims he had no idea what Norman

Shellston was up to, and we have no way to prove his claim one way or another."

"Shellston?"

"The former banker. Was involved in extortion, murder, and attempted murder. He was hung shortly after being arrested and tried."

"McCutcheon," the overweight man said when they ambled over.

"Billingsworth," Dustin replied.

One corner of the man's mouth pulled down in a frown. "This the Calhoun I've been hearing about?"

Annoyance shot through Dustin. Didn't take long for word to get around. "Yeah. Noah Calhoun, Fred Billingsworth."

"I hope you're keeping him on a tight rein, McCutcheon. Rio Wells doesn't need any trouble."

Dustin leaned his arm down on the saddle horn. "Not like the kind you and Shellston leveled last May?"

"I didn't have anything to do with that, and you know it!" the man replied, snapping back his shoulders.

"We just don't have any proof." Dustin tipped up his hat with a forefinger and shifted in the saddle. "Yet." He let a slow grin grow across his face. "But I'm still looking."

He'd never liked Billingsworth. The ex-mayor and Shellston were related, brothers-in-law, if he remembered correctly.

The pudgy man straightened and pierced them both with his best fussy look. "Good day." He turned on his heel and marched around the corner much like a rabbit running for its hole.

From a standstill, Dustin squeezed his horse into a lope, and Noah followed. This day had gotten away from him. They had things to do.

A ball shot out the open door of the Cheddar Box Café and bounced across the road. Candy, her skirts flying, bounded out the door and ran right in front of the path of their horses without looking.

"Candy!"

Martha Brown bolted out after her, just in time to witness him and Noah rein to a sliding stop only inches from her daughter. The little girl toppled to the ground in fright, doing a somersault before coming to an abrupt halt.

Her eyes round with fear, the child darted a look from them to her mother, and then back at the horse's front hooves prancing in in the dirt.

Dustin swung out of the saddle at the same time Candy scrambled to her feet. Louise Brown, Martha's sister-in-law, followed Martha into the street, weaving their way through the traffic of horse and riders to where Candy waited.

Dustin went down on one knee, taking Candy by her small, shaking shoulders. Tears filled her eyes.

"Are you all right, Candy?" he asked, pulling her into his arms. "Did you hurt yourself when you fell?"

Behind him, Dustin felt Noah's presence. He'd dismounted and come forward, holding both horses' reins.

Crouching by Dustin's side, Martha scooped Candy from his arms and hugged her to her chest. Several moments passed before she set the child back on her dust-covered boots.

"Are you hurt?" Martha asked in a strangled voice, brushing dust from Candy's dress. She picked a clump of something that suspiciously looked like horse manure from one long braid.

Seemed Martha had yet to gather her wits about her. Dustin was fearful she would cry too.

Candy shook her head. "I'm fine, Mama." The ground rumbled as a large wagon passed. "Just my dress needs a good washing."

Martha stood. "Explain yourself, young lady! How many times have we had this discussion?" She glanced up at Dustin who'd also stood, and then her gaze shifted to Noah before returning to Candy. "If Mr. McCutcheon and his friend had been in a wagon and unable to stop, instead of on horses, then you could have been killed."

Candy's gaze was anchored in the dirt at her mother's shoes.

Martha took a finger and gently lifted the child's face. "Do you understand?"

Candy nodded.

"I don't think you do. We've discussed this before, many times." More riders passed by in the opposite direction, giving the group plenty of room. "Yet the first time your ball gets away, you forget everything and dash after the toy like your head is filled with cotton. Consequences will occur, missy, for your open disobedience and thoughtlessness. You won't get away with a simple smile and an *I'm sorry.*" She shook her head. "You're too old. You know better."

When Candy's face crumpled, Dustin actually felt sorry for the girl. "Martha, maybe this talking-to is punishment enough. I'm sure if Candy had stopped to think—"

"Mr. McCutcheon!"

He blanched at her use of his surname. He'd hit a nerve.

"Are you butting into business that's none of your concern?" She straightened dramatically at his meddling, and a square of white linen fluttered from her dress pocket and into the dirt at their feet.

Noah bent quickly and picked the cloth up.

"Ma'am," he said, holding out the material. "Your kerchief dropped into the street."

She looked up into his face as if noticing him now for the first time. Blinking rapidly, she took a small step back and glanced over her shoulder at Louise still standing behind her.

"T-thank you," she finally sputtered, and rested a hand on Candy's shoulder.

Dustin's gaze cut between the two. Martha must be a good seven years older, but her face had colored up as if she'd been struck by lightning. Nothing good could come of Daniel's widow and Noah Calhoun.

"As long as Candy's not hurt, Mrs. Brown, we'll be on our way." He touched the brim of his Stetson and turned to mount, but not before he saw her eyes go wide.

"Won't you introduce us, Mr. McCutcheon, er . . . Dustin?" Her voice had dropped a good three notches in volume and was now soft as a daisy.

He didn't like the direction this morning was going. He should have stayed in his warm bed and let the day pass him by.

"No, I'm not. He's a hand who'll only be here for a short—"

"My name's Noah Calhoun, ma'am. And you are?"

Lord above, Dustin almost cursed under his breath. These Calhouns didn't know when to quit.

"I'm Martha Brown, and this is Candy, my daughter."

For the first time in a long time, Dustin didn't feel like a slice of cake when Martha looked his way.

"And this is my sister-in-law, Louise Brown."

Noah tipped his hat. "I'm pleased to meet you both. But I'm more delighted this little girl wasn't hurt."

"We best get moving," Dustin drawled, and turned to mount. "There's only so much light in one day, and we've burned a heck of a lot already."

Louise plopped her hands on her hips. "What's gotten into you, Dustin? You're about as sociable as a week-old bunion."

"Nothing's wrong with me. Just have a ranch to run."

"Are you here to stay, Mr. Calhoun?" Martha asked, directing her attention back to Noah.

Dustin was sure the man was loving every moment of the women's attention.

"That's difficult to say, ma'am. I have a debt to work off, so just depends on how fast I can get that done." He lifted one shoulder. "It's not a small amount."

She brightened. "Work? I have lots of things out at the ranch that I've let go. Why my back porch is almost ready to fall—"

Fall off? She was stretching the truth a mite. Dustin had been out there last month, and everything looked fine.

"He has plenty of work at the Rim Rock, Martha. More than enough to keep him busy until his responsibilities are taken care of. I can send out a hand to do your work, as we've done in the past. What needs doing—besides the porch, I mean?"

She gave him a dismissive wave. "Just things, Dustin. I don't like to depend on the Rim Rock for everything. I'm grateful for all your help throughout the years since Daniel passed, though."

Fine. "I'll send someone out tomorrow to see to your needs. Ladies."

Dustin mounted up. With a cluck of his tongue, he sent his horse down the road, soon to hear Noah following.

Chapter Twenty-Nine

The day had passed in a blur of activities. Sidney glanced at the watch-brooch pinned to her bodice. Fifteen minutes until five. Quitting time.

She straightened from the hem she stitched and stretched her shoulders. Flexing her fingers from the tedious work, she glanced outside from the cozy chair Lily had set in the front window where the light was best, facing the town that was becoming familiar.

She wondered about Noah, and how he fared today with Dustin. An image of Dustin inquiring about her preference to chocolate flavors eased through her mind.

Warmth crept into her face. She'd been attracted to him. She'd liked his build and face—but mostly the depth of his gaze. Even the timbre of his voice had sent chills racing down her back. The memory of his crooked smile brought one of her own.

However, that was before she'd known he was a McCutcheon. Why in heavens was the first man she'd been attracted to have to be from *that* family? Forbidden fruit. *Life is so unfair.*

With a sigh, she picked up the hem of Mrs. Tuttle's blue velvet gown and inspected her stitches. Her work had improved considerably. Her stitches were tighter, more perfectly spaced. Lily truly was an artist, she thought, noticing the delicately tapered sleeves, the minimal bustle dropped a bit lower than usual, and the two front pleats. Sidney hadn't seen such craftsmanship, even in Santa Fe.

Lily hummed as she went about her duties in the kitchen. After settling Sidney with Mrs. Tuttle's gown, showing her what she wanted done and how to do it, her boss had hurried away to put something on the stove for supper.

Sidney glanced around the interior of the shop filled with all sorts of interesting articles of textile and fabrics. Earlier, she'd asked Lily about the intriguing artwork fashioned from buttons, sequins, and sparkling doodads that hung on the wall that Lily herself had created.

Astonishment filled Sidney over all Lily had accomplished: she was an artist with a thriving business, as well as a loving wife who cared for her husband.

Savory smells drifted around the shop, making Sidney's stomach rumble. For lunch, she'd told Lily she had food back in her room, which wasn't the truth. In the hotel, she'd paid for a cup of tea and taken the brew upstairs, enjoying the moments of solitude before returning to the shop at one sharp.

Lily appeared, wiping her hands. "How's that going?"

"I'm three quarters of the way finished."

"Wonderful. Mrs. Tuttle will be in around noon tomorrow for her final fitting. You should be finished by then, don't you think?"

"Absolutely. If you like, I can stay past five. I don't mind working until it's done. Would you rather I complete it tonight?"

Lily came close to inspect the hem. "No need for that. Tomorrow morning is soon enough. I don't want to work you too hard. Then the job's no fun." She winked. "I've set you a place at the table. Eating will be tight with the three of us in my small kitchen. Do you like chicken and dumplings?"

Sidney jerked up her chin. "Lily, I couldn't!"

"Why not?" Lily asked, her eyes wide. "Don't you like my cooking?"

In honesty, she had enjoyed the cinnamon rolls she'd tasted and a few other treats Lily had brought out during the day. She'd love to stay for supper, especially for chicken and dumplings, but the thought of taking more charity than she already had left a heavy pit in her stomach.

"Of course I like your cooking." She didn't know what else to say.

"Then what is it? Me? Because I'm a McCutcheon?" Lily smiled and batted her eyes. "I've only married into the fold. Think of me as an Anthony. That was my maiden name."

Confused, Sidney looked away from the kind young woman who had befriended her. Given her a job, even though she had little sewing experience, and had offered her handouts right and left.

"You make my beliefs sound silly."

The smile faded from Lily's face. "Not silly, just unfounded. I can tell you're struggling. For now, why don't you let the past go? Just for supper tonight. I'll enjoy having you as a dinner guest. John will as well. He's only a Montana McCutcheon, so he doesn't count. What do you say?"

As much as Sidney wanted to stick to her principles, she acknowledged her tummy wouldn't let her. "I'd like that very much, Lily. Thank you. But only if you let me help. What can I do?"

"Everything is ready, and we're just waiting on John." She glanced at a small clock placed on the counter where she wrote up orders. "And he should be here any time."

Lily lifted the heavy garment from Sidney's lap and carried it to the dressing room where she hung projects that were near completion.

"If you'd like to wash up, you'll find a clean hand towel by the pump in the kitchen. Soap as well. I'm running upstairs to freshen up."

"Thank you. I will," Sidney replied as Lily dashed up the staircase to the apartment on the second level.

The door opened when Sidney was at the pump.

"Lily?" A moment passed. "Something sure smells delicious in here. I have a surprise for you. Something that'll make you happy."

The sound of footsteps brought Sidney face-to-face with the doctor. He pulled up as if he'd forgotten Lily had an employee. His face actually took on a deeper hue.

"Lily's upstairs," she said, feeling awkward as she dried with the towel.

He held a letter in his hand as his gaze took in the three place settings at the table.

"I'll be right there, John," Lily called from her bedroom. "Hungry?"

"You bet. Even more so now that I smell what's cooking." Taking a potholder, he removed the lid from the heavy pot on the stove. Replacing it, he winked at Sidney and smiled. "My wife's an excellent cook. Stems from her German heritage."

When Lily appeared in the doorway, John gave her a quick kiss on the lips and held up the letter.

Lily's eyes lit with pleasure. "From whom?"

"Charity. Or I should say, Mrs. Brandon Crawford."

She clapped her hands together. "They went and tied the knot! How wonderful. Did you read it without me?"

"No." He pointed at the envelope. "Just read the return address."

Lily's excitement fairly bubbled. "I'm glad they didn't wait once they arrived home. Those two should have been married years ago. They're meant for each other."

As self-conscious as Sidney felt, she still enjoyed being around such heart-felt emotions.

Lily laid the letter on the table. "Let me dish up the supper first, then we'll read the news while we eat. After that, I want to know what you were up to this morning. You intentionally sneaked out earlier today before I had a chance to ask."

They were just sitting down when the door to the shop opened again. "I know you're closed," a voice called out. "Do you mind if we come in?"

Dustin? Surely, Noah would be with him. Sidney watched as John hurried to the door, wishing she could go herself.

"Come in, cousin!" John said enthusiastically. "Have you eaten? We're just sitting down now."

Lily poked her head around the corner and waved them in. "Absolutely. I've made plenty. Do join us. That way, Sidney can catch up with her brother, and we can visit with you. I presume . Noah is with you, since he was this morning."

Dustin and Noah appeared at the entrance to the kitchen. The sight of Dustin standing there with his hat dangling from his fingers brought a rush of warmth to her face. He smiled, looking a bit windblown and dusty. Noah hung back, waiting for the others to make their decision.

"There's no room for us," Dustin said, his gaze grazing over her face before he took in the small table in the corner dressed with three place settings.

Lily turned and looked at her table. "You're right about that."

"Besides," he went on, "you've got everything ready. We're intruding."

Lily beckoned with her hand. "Of course you're not intruding. Family can't intrude. The table out back has ample room for five. I like to take coffee outside sometimes. The afternoon breeze is all but gone, and the evening is perfect for eating outside. What do you all say?"

"In the alley with a view of the back door of the jail?" John said, his mouth pulling down.

Lily turned on him. "Where's your sense of adventure, John? Not only is there a nice view of the jailhouse door and your medical building, but if you look across the open lots, you can see a small portion of the hot springs and the curve of the bridge."

His frown deepened. "If you say so. I'd rather you have a real yard for entertaining. Not a dusty old alley with horse manure."

"I sweep that away."

An unknown look passed between them, and Sidney wondered what it meant.

"Fine then," Lily said. "Give me one moment to run upstairs to grab my tablecloth, and we'll have the table set in a jiffy. The food is ready to be served, and the bread just out of the oven. I won't hear another word from you, Dustin McCutcheon, about why you can't stay."

"Thank you," Dustin mumbled, still clutching his hat. He smiled at Sidney as she came forward.

"How was your day?" she asked, enjoying this more amiable Dustin McCutcheon very much. "Did you get everything accomplished?"

Since this morning, the start of a dark stubble had shaded his square jaw, and his tired eyes regarded her with interest—or humor. Whatever the expression was, she liked it.

Her face heated, and she couldn't stop a small smile from pulling her lips.

Oh yes. If there wasn't bad blood between the families, she could fall in love with Dustin McCutcheon in the blink of an eye. Maybe she already had.

Chapter Thirty

Dustin was still surprised at himself for stopping in at Lily's shop on their way back to the ranch. They could have easily ridden through and been home in another twenty minutes. Then he could have taken supper with the family, and Noah would be in the bunkhouse.

"We did," he said, answering Sidney's question about whether he'd accomplished what he'd planned that day.

He liked the fact Sidney wasn't scowling any longer. She seemed pleased to see him. Had she spent the hours since he'd left reminiscing about the past few days as he had?

"Draper Bottom is once again safe," he went on. "The marshal hauled away our desperados to San Antonio. They won't be causing anyone else any trouble. Miller rode back with us and is over in his office."

She laced her fingers together in front of Madeline's skirt. "Miller?"

Dustin nodded. "Our deputy sheriff."

"That's right," Sidney said. "I remember now." She glanced toward the window. "And my dog?"

"Lying on the boardwalk in front," Noah answered.

She nodded. "Noah, are you doing everything Dustin asks?"

"Sure." He flashed a mischievous grin. "I'm getting paid to ride around and do nothing."

Lily was back with a blue-checkered tablecloth in her hands. She passed them by and went down the step.

"I need to help Lily," Sidney said, smiling at her brother. "You're exactly where Dustin wants you to be, so don't complain. If he wanted you doing something else, he'd tell you. He's not shy about that. In a few days, after receiving a tough assignment, you may be wishing you were just riding around again."

Sidney removed the place settings from the kitchen table and followed Lily through the back door. She'd been out here once today, when she opened the door for a mewing cat. A small shed roof gave enough shade to cover the table. Piano music from the saloon across the alley and two doors down livened up the mood.

"There," Lily said, smoothing down the cloth. "This will do nicely."

John stepped out of the shop with a lantern in his hands. "I've brought this out, Lily," he said, setting the lamp in the middle of the table. He took a moment to light the wick. "I know how much you like a centerpiece."

Sidney finished setting the table as Dustin pulled out the benches, and John, with two thick potholders, brought out the large pot of chicken and dumplings.

"The fare's not fancy," Lily said after making one more trip for the loaf of bread. "But it'll warm your insides and stick to your ribs. That's what counts. Earlier, I baked a cobbler for dessert. We won't go hungry."

They all took a seat, and John offered a brief blessing. Afterward, he ladled an ample serving into the middle of each plate as Dustin sliced the warm loaf, and then passed around the breadboard.

Somehow, Dustin ended up next to Sidney and across from Lily and John. Noah sat on the end with his back to the sheriff's office.

Dustin had never contemplated taking supper in an alley before, but he had to say he was enjoying himself immensely. He guessed things changed once a man got married. John's marital state didn't seem to hamper his actions, and his cousin was one of the happiest men he knew.

"Lily, this is mighty good," Dustin offered. "Thank you for having us."

"I second that, Mrs. McCutcheon," Noah added politely. "I can't ever remember such a rich flavor."

The young man surprised him at every turn. Dustin had expected a grumpy, taciturn companion during the ride today, but Noah had proven himself a pleasant chum.

"You're welcome, Dustin, and thank you, Noah. I like spur-of-the-moment parties. This is nice. Oh, we received a letter from Charity." Smiling, she glanced between Sidney and Noah. "That's John's baby sister and Dustin's cousin. Shall I read it? I can hardly wait."

"From Charity, you say?" Dustin had just swallowed a large forkful. "This should prove interesting."

Noah's brows shot up at the remark, making Dustin chuckle. "You'd understand if you knew her. Nice young woman, just has a knack for getting into mischief. A lot of mischief. Wouldn't you say, John?"

John seemed different this evening. He had a secret he was keeping; Dustin was sure. His cousin hadn't stopped smiling since he and Noah stepped through the front door.

"I would. Go on, darlin'." John motioned to Lily, who held the post in her hands. "Let's see what's happening at home in Y Knot."

Chapter Thirty-One

Lily pulled the two folded papers from the envelope, aware of the others' attention on her as they quietly went about finishing their supper.

She'd yet to meet the rest of her Montana in-laws; that was a trip she looked forward to making. Charity was a dear. Lily was so glad John's younger sister had secretly ventured to Rio Wells last May to check on her brother. Her forged friendship with Charity would last the test of time and distance.

"Give me a moment to quickly read this to be sure nothing's included I can't share with you all."

John nodded.

Lily felt the warmth of her husband's gaze on her face. She sucked in a breath at the message and continued. A sigh escaped her as she whipped the first page behind the other and began the second.

"You're being mean, sweetheart," John said. "Can you read for all of us? We're dying to hear."

"Yes, I can. You won't believe what's transpired." She cleared her throat.

"Dearest John and Lily," she read aloud. "First let me say I miss you both very much. Mother, Father, and the rest of us await your much-anticipated visit to Y Knot, and the Heart of the Mountains. Please come soon. Everyone here grows impatient to meet Lily and hug you both."

Lily smiled and looked up. "Besides Charity, I've yet to meet John's family."

Dustin cleared his throat, and she corrected herself.

"I mean the ones in Montana. I love his Texas family very much!"

Dustin smiled and nodded.

Lily couldn't miss the way Sidney watched his every move. If she wasn't mistaken, a romance was budding—or maybe had already blossomed.

"Go on," John prompted.

"On the evening we arrived in Y Knot, Brandon and I surprised the family with our intention to marry. Although I don't really think many were surprised, even though they acted like they were. Plans were made, but before the day could arrive, we had several events that almost postponed our nuptials for good."

John leaned forward. "What? I can't imagine what happened."

"It's big," Lily said, bringing a finger to her lips.

He gave her arm a gentle nudge. "Go on."

"If you aren't seated already, you might want to do so now before you read further. Luke has another sister. A Cheyenne sister. She appeared near death in the loft of Luke's barn on the night Brandon and I were to announce our engagement. Her name is—"

"Hold up, Lily," John said suddenly, his tone uncharacteristically sharp. His face had lost color, and his brows drew down, causing deep grooves in his brow. "This sounds personal. Maybe we should read the rest later."

What could be more important than finding you had more family? Lily didn't understand his reluctance.

"But it's good," she said softly. "Nothing is here that can't be shared with your Texas family and our new friends." Lily took in the faces intently watching her.

"Cheyenne?" Noah asked. "What's that mean?"

"Means I have a half-breed cousin," Dustin replied. "Luke McCutcheon. He's famous all the way down here in Texas."

Lily didn't like the way John's mouth went flat at Dustin's comment. The last thing she wanted was for trouble to start up between the two as in the past. Perhaps John was right, and this was a touchier subject than she realized.

She reached out and laid a hand on John's arm.

"My mother was abducted when she was a young woman," John explained, cutting a cold look at Dustin. "After my older brothers Matthew and Mark were born. By the time my father found her and brought her home, she was in the family way with Luke. He's a few years older than me, and is a part of our family just like the rest of us. We don't think of him as different." He glared at Dustin. "Or as a *half-breed*."

"Point taken, cousin. I'm sorry. I didn't mean any disrespect," Dustin offered, his shoulders slumping. "Facts are facts, though, and I was just answering Noah's question."

John jerked away his gaze from Dustin and looked at his empty plate. "The Cheyenne girl's presence must have been difficult for my father, dredging up the time my mother spent in captivity. I've been told he went half crazy when he couldn't find her. Months passed. All he did was eat, sleep, and search. Nothin' else mattered."

Lily ached at the sadness in her husband's voice. "I'd guess having her there must have been even more difficult for your mother. I can't imagine how she felt."

He nodded. "That's so. Mother said she wouldn't trade that time if it meant giving up Luke."

"Shall I go on?" Lily asked.

She hoped John would say yes. He was protective over Luke. Maybe more openness would take the sting out of his perception of the situation. The tension she felt building a few moments ago had dissipated, and Lily was relieved.

"John?"

He nodded.

"Her name is Fox Dancing. She's younger than me, and very beautiful. Her glossy hair reaches all the way to her posterior and shines like black obsidian. Her eyes miss nothing and could cut you like a knife if you were her enemy. But, of course, we're not. Not surprising to any of us because of Luke's temperament, she is a fierce warrior and can best most men. And yet, she has a charming smile that reminds me so much of Luke. Seeing it made me tear up on several occasions. As you can imagine, Mother and Father were shocked—as we all were. Especially Luke. A beautiful relationship has formed, one that will last forever."

Finished with the first page, Lily slipped the sheet behind the second and continued.

"The whole story is too long to write, and so you must come home to hear the details. However, I will say, after a frightening escape from several small-minded men in the area, she went home to her father and family. They've held out from relocating to a reservation by hiding, but she fears that a move onto the controlled land given by the whites will be the next step. She wants Luke to come meet the man who sired him, but at this point in time, Luke says he will look out for his growing family and not take the time—yet.

"In case you're wondering, our nuptials did take place, and Brandon and I are now man and wife. We couldn't be happier. That too had a scary moment where Brandon took off to Kansas to follow a dream. Yes, a dream he'd never voiced to me, which about tore the heart from my chest—and us apart as well. But again, you'll need to come back to Y Knot to hear about it. I wish the two of you could have been here for the small ceremony we had at the ranch. The nuptials were beautiful.

"Now, write back as soon as possible and tell me all your news there. How are my cousins, Dustin, Chaim, Madeline, and Becky? How are Uncle Winston and Auntie Winnie? Have Chaim and Emmeline married? They make such a darling couple. Is Lily expecting yet?"

At the last question, Lily's hand wobbled. Now *that* was quite a private matter to be blurting out for the world. She felt the blush creep up her face, and forced herself to go on.

"Are Theodore and Becky still an item? Is old Dr. Bixby still as cantankerous as ever? I miss all my friends in Rio Wells, and I can't wait to hear the news from Texas. Your devoted little sister, Charity Crawford."

Lily looked up for a second and smiled before continuing.

"Postscript: There is even more news about our beloved Roady, but I'm saving that for my next letter. If you want to hear, you'll have to return a letter to me. Just remember, John, your *not* writing last time was what compelled me to sneak away from Montana and visit you unannounced in Rio Wells. Keep that in mind, and write back soon! Love you all!"

Lily folded the two papers and slipped them back inside the envelope. She glanced at the faces.

"That's a lot of news," John said. "Makes me realize how long I've been away from home."

He reached for her hand, wrapped it in his warm one, and brought her fingers to his lips for a kiss. "We'll have to do that soon, Lily. My parents aren't getting any younger. And I haven't seen my brothers for years. Maybe we should plan a trip this spring. Bixby can cover for me for a month or so. All you have to do is plan your projects accordingly, so you can be free."

"Or have Giselle here to cover for me while we're away. To keep the shop open."

She waited for him to shake his head. His silence on the topic had her thinking he wasn't as happy about the idea as she was. Or about moving to a larger place.

John laughed, the sound rich and inviting. "Maybe you're right."

Lily's moment of contemplation was chased away by John's remark. Was he warming to her idea?

She stood, not wanting to ask him further where he'd have to explain everything in front of an audience. But he was in an incredibly good mood.

Her gaze slid to Sidney. "Or perhaps Sidney will decide to stay on. Who knows if she'll fall in love—with Rio Wells."

They had the attention of the whole table. The sun had gone down and a chill was in the air. John's lantern gave a nice golden glow around the tabletop.

A fella staggered out the back door of the saloon and looked their way. He squinted and almost tripped over his large feet before turning in the opposite direction and stumbling away.

"Billy Burger," Dustin said under his breath. "Heard his wife up and left him last month and returned to her mother. The man has a tendency of being rough when he's liquored up, but is as timid as a lamb when he's sober."

"I heard the same," Lily said with a glance over her shoulder. "For one, I'm relieved, as well as the rest of the women in town. We didn't want to see any harm done to her. When I first came to Rio Wells, I was almost accosted by Billy, but Dustin whisked me into his arms to keep me safe," she said to Sidney, and then looked to Dustin. "Remember?"

"How could I forget?" Dustin replied with a chuckle. "Billy ended up headfirst in a water trough."

"Let me clear away these plates and bring out the cobbler. Would anyone care for a cup of coffee?"

Dustin straightened. "I'd love one, Lily, if it's no trouble."

"No trouble at all. I put a pot on the back of the stove before we came out. I'm sure it's already brewed."

"In that case, I'll have one as well," Noah said, catching her eye.

He seemed much more at ease tonight than he'd been this morning. She liked Sidney's brother. All this McCutcheon-Calhoun feud nonsense that was being talked about lately was foolishness. Life was short. Time shouldn't be wasted nurturing a twenty-year-old grudge.

"John?"

"Yes, I'll have a cup, Lily," he replied, scooting forward in his chair to stand.

With a hand on his shoulder, she gently pushed him down. "We seldom have guests. You stay and entertain, and I'll get the dessert and coffee."

"And I'll help," Sidney said as she stood and gathered the dishes to take into the house.

Lily went inside and Sidney followed with the dishes. She set the stack into the sink, and went for another load as Lily took her smaller dessert plates off the shelf and set them by the dish of apple cobbler.

Lily only had three, which meant she needed to wash two of the dinner plates. She quickly worked the water pump as Sidney brought in the last of the utensils. Lily took the forks from her and set them in the water.

She smiled. "We don't have much," she said, indicating the lack of cutlery and eating ware, and even space. "But we're tremendously happy. I can't imagine my life without John."

"It's easily seen," Sidney softly replied. "Any woman would dream of having a husband like yours."

"He's a McCutcheon. You best not forget that." Lily teasingly raised her brows. "As well as another tall, dark, and devilishly handsome man sitting outside. I believe he's captured your attention quite well already."

When Sidney didn't respond, but just stood there with her eyes wide, Lily laughed.

"Come now. Don't tell me you haven't noticed how he looks at you. Surely, you're not blind. The two of you are sweet on each other. And actually, I can see why. You both complement each other's strengths and weaknesses. I haven't seen Dustin this happy for months. Well, actually, since I've known him."

"You mean since you broke his heart?"

Lily grinned as she hurriedly washed the items she needed. "Yes, I guess I do mean that. But now I see God had a plan of his own—as he always does."

A burst of laughter from the men outside widened Lily's smile. Did Sidney really think she could hide her feelings for Dustin so easily?

"Let's get this dessert outside to the men."

Lily gathered up the cobbler, and Sidney poured the coffee before she followed her out. Was there a way to hurry along this romance?

Chapter Thirty-Two

Seeing Sidney come out the back door with three coffee cups in her hands, Dustin stood and stepped out from the bench. He reached for the teetering cup in the middle of her grasp and placed the coffee in front of his cousin.

Sitting beside Sidney all night had tested his fortitude. He'd wanted to ask her a thousand questions, just so he could hear her respond. Watch her facial expressions and gauge her reactions.

No denying the fact now—she stirred his blood. Made him think dangerous thoughts. Made him want something that could destroy his father. Or maybe not destroy, but disappoint and hurt.

Dustin hadn't missed Noah's quiet but scrutinizing gaze. He'd like to know what Sidney's little brother was thinking. On the ride to Draper Bottom today, their frosty relationship had warmed. They'd had nothing but time and so had engaged in a discussion of politics, beef prices, and ranching. The boy knew a great deal.

Did he fully trust Noah yet? He wasn't sure. But he did feel a lot different since their first day out of San Antonio.

As Sidney made another trip into the kitchen and Lily served the cobbler, something good and homey took Dustin by the heart.

"Here you are," Sidney said, setting a cup of coffee in front of him. "Last, but not least."

"Thank you." The plates, heaped with apple cobbler, were passed around, and the men waited until the women were seated.

"This looks mighty good—again," John said, smiling into his wife's face. "Lily, you're an amazing woman, and I'm a very lucky man." He picked up his fork.

Everyone else followed suit. For the next few moments, just the clinking of utensils on the ceramic plates blended humorously with the tinny piano music from the saloon. The sunlight had dimmed even more, making the lantern's light all the brighter.

"So, I have good news myself," John began. He set his fork in his plate and all but stretched back as he looked around the table thoughtfully. "And I see no reason not to share my idea this evening with you all. See what you think."

When Lily sat forward, she had a look of awe and love on her face.

Dustin noticed it and swallowed. He wanted what they had. True meaning to one's life meant having someone to share with. To love. He sneaked a glance at Sidney, who watched John with curiosity.

"Go on, cousin," he said. "Don't keep us in suspense any longer."

John nodded. "Maybe only my wife knows this, but I've been a bit languid here in Rio Wells of late. The town is small, and there's not that much for me to do as a doctor." He glanced at Lily. "I'm not complaining that people are healthy. That's good. And my true goal. But I've decided to take on another venture—or at least see if it's possible." He picked up Lily's hand. "That is, if my wife likes the idea." His face grew serious. "I hope you'll forgive me for springing this on you in front of everyone."

"John!" She squeezed his hand. Her tone was filled with trepidation. "What is this about?" Her smile had faded as well, her eyes dark with worry. "I hope I wasn't the one that brought on your dissatisfaction when I said I wanted to move. You know I'm happy wherever we are. Just as long as we're together."

"Don't panic yet, Lily. Everything is still just in the planning stages."

She pressed a hand to the base of her throat. "Too late. I'm already panicked."

"Some of you know about the salve Doc Bixby makes, the one that healed my scar so well." He pointed to the small, almost invisible line on the side of his face.

Dustin nodded, intrigued. Did this have something to do with John's strange comment a few days ago when he was washing the office windows? Dustin had felt his cousin's frustration then. He'd also sensed his cousin had had more on his mind than he was saying. Seemed he'd been right.

"I've already spoken with Bixby," John went on. "He feels he's too old to begin a new venture, but he doesn't mind if I do. He's given me his blessing to bottle and sell his concoction. Ship the blend to doctors in Boston. Other places as well, as the demand grows. For years, Indians and Mexicans have used the juice of the aloe plant, but time is needed to strip the juice, and the plants are scarce."

He paused and looked around the faces. "The plants only grow in certain places. Doc's recipe contains a few other ingredients that may be behind the incredible healing properties

I've witnessed over the months. Anyway, I'm excited as all get-out. I'll be productive in a way that won't interfere with my doctoring."

Lily's back was as straight as a board. Dustin could practically see her mind whirling.

"If I'm not in my office when someone comes looking for me, I'll be in Knutson's barn, only a few minutes away, producing and bottling the new product."

Dustin frowned. Certainly John knew a business venture of this size took capital to start. His cousin had shared how he'd spent most of his money helping out with the cost of his education. He wasn't flush with cash.

"What do you know about running a business?" he asked. "Your roots are in cattle and ranching, just like mine."

John's eyes narrowed. "Surely, cousin," he said in a flat voice, "you understand ranching is a business just like any other. Profit and losses. A bottom line that must be respected. I'm no country hick, and know plenty. I have sufficient information, and I'm confident enough in the product to move forward."

Dustin shook his head. He wasn't asking to be rude; he had another idea on his mind. "True," he replied. "It'll take capital. Do you have that?"

The eating had stopped, and several moments passed in strained silence.

John scrubbed a hand across his face. "I haven't quite worked that through yet. I've penciled out numbers for the items I'll need to get started: product acquisition, glass bottles, crates, and the cost of shipment. My time will be in exchange for the recipe; that's only fair. One of the stipulations Bixby has is that I take in Tucker on the deal with me. He's to have Bixby's share, and we're to split the arrangement seventy-five/twenty-five, working with me side by side. My contacts and experience against his labor."

He shot a quick glance at Lily. "I thought I'd write home for the startup costs. See if my father is willing to throw in. Invest in something other than cattle. I'm pretty sure he'll like the idea."

Tucker? Good idea, Dustin thought. Bixby had practically raised the one-handed boy after the Comancheros mutilated his arm and left him for dead after killing his entire family. As John's assistant, he earned five dollars a month, and was growing up fast. If this idea actually took off, he could be a wealthy man someday.

"I've been looking for a place to invest some of my money," Dustin said. "Why not keep this in Rio Wells? Montana already has enough riches of its own without looking to Texas."

John's mouth opened and then closed. His eyes narrowing, he sagged back in his chair.

"I'd like to invest," Dustin explained. "Become a silent partner. Put up the cash to get you started, for a small percentage of the profits."

John stared at him for a long time.

"Cousin?"

"If profits *are* produced, Dustin. I have no guarantees how this will pan out. I have several friends I went to school with who started their practices back east, and I hope to get them interested. Also my instructors and anyone they can point me to. This is all speculation."

"Are you turning down my offer? Almost sounds as if you think this new venture of yours is doomed to fail. I'm surprised."

John looked at Lily. Sidney observed him with a contemplative expression, and Noah sat quietly taking in the discussion.

"Well?"

"You should know, I have no way of paying you back if we go bust." John leaned forward and rested his elbows on the tabletop.

As serious as his cousin's expression was, Dustin could see a great deal of excitement igniting behind his eyes.

"Is that so?" he asked.

John nodded. "I'm nothing more than a poor doctor."

Lily reached over and took his hand.

Excitement for the new venture burned inside Dustin, as well as happiness to see the spark of life glowing in John's eyes. They'd make a good team.

"I'll take that chance," he said.

With a bark of laughter, John stuck out his hand. "It's a deal, cousin! Welcome to the fold!"

Everyone began talking and laughing at once. John stood, and Lily jumped up and vaulted into his embrace. As they kissed, Dustin dragged away his gaze, laughing and smiling at Sidney.

Even Noah seemed pleased to have been in on such a private matter of the McCutcheons. Did wonders never end?

John picked up his coffee cup and raised it high. "To McCutcheon, Noble, and McCutcheon!"

"Hear, hear," Dustin called out in a loud voice.

Sidney's laughter made the whole deal sweeter. Dustin didn't care if he lost his investment. Taking the chance was worth the adoring expression on her face.

"On to bigger and better things," he boomed out, feeling almost giddy.

"Hooray," the women chorused.

Suddenly, the laughter and celebration died out. Dustin turned.

His pa stood stone-faced in the tapered space between the shop and the medical office, taking in the scene—Sidney's high color, Noah's face-splitting smile, John and Lily arm in arm, and his own happiness.

The look of devastation on his father's face made Dustin clamber to get from behind the bench. He scrambled out and then stood rooted to the spot.

"I saw your horse out front," his pa said. "Heard you around back."

"Uncle Winston," Lily said quickly. "Can I dish you a plate of chicken and dumplings? They're still warm."

"No, thank you, Lily. I had my supper at the ranch."

Dustin was well aware the question his tone was asking. *Why didn't you return for supper, Dustin?* The dark-eyed gaze he knew so well circled the table and landed on Sidney. It lingered on her several seconds before returning to him.

"Apple cobbler then?" she said, gesturing to the glass dish in the middle of the table. "There's plenty."

Winston shook his head, and Dustin felt his hurt, his betrayal.

"What brings you into town this late in the day, Pa?" he asked, wondering what he could do or say to make things better.

"Just felt the need to stretch my legs a bit. It's been a fortnight since I've been into Rio Wells." He half turned toward the direction he'd come. "Don't mind me. Good evening."

"Don't run off, Uncle!" John said, hurrying around the table to where Winston stood. "We'd love for you to join us."

"John, I appreciate the gesture, but I'm headed to the saloon where there's a drink with my name on it. Nothing wrong with that occasionally. Unless any of you would like to join me, I'll be bidding you good night."

Feeling lower than a snake, Dustin listened to the fall of his father's boots on the ground as he walked away.

As much as he'd like to think different, Sidney and Noah were Calhouns, the children of his father's worst enemy, a man who had been a bone of contention for years. And here Dustin was laughing up a storm with them as if they were long-lost buddies.

When he thought about it like that, the situation turned his own stomach. If he didn't have Noah to watch over, he'd go with his pa and have that drink. Spend the time with him he should have since he'd been back from San Antonio.

The Calhouns had rocked his father's inner peace, and yet Winston had treated them both with hospitality. Dustin should have sought him out, but he hadn't. Sure he'd been busy—heck, they both were—Dustin going one way and his pa the other.

But that didn't excuse him. Not by a long shot.

Chapter Thirty-Three

Tired after so many hours in the saddle, Dustin ambled toward the dark ranch house, glad the day was finally over. The moon had just topped the trees and gave a small measure of light. He knew this route by heart, and could walk the well-worn path with his eyes closed.

Feeling down, he sighed. He'd seen Noah back to the bunkhouse and made sure all the men understood exactly where Dustin was coming from. Another infraction like what happened at the showers might cost someone their job. He'd hate to see that happen so he'd advised everyone, especially Noah, to tread lightly. The situation was a tinderbox. Afterward, Noah had gone to bed without a word to anyone.

"Dustin."

He hadn't noticed his brother leaning against the corral fence in the dark.

"Why're you still up?" he asked, but he knew the answer. Chaim was missing his runaway bride.

Well, she wasn't actually runaway yet, but Dustin wasn't holding out too much hope. His gut told him they'd seen the last of the Boston beauty, which would be a real shame. He liked Emmeline. She fit in with his family. His mother would be crushed if the young woman didn't return, as well as both sisters. But most of all, he prayed to God she didn't break his younger brother's heart.

Chaim straightened as Dustin drew near. "Time's only eight o'clock."

At the ranch, they turned in early since they rose early to beat the heat. This time of year the temperature wasn't so bad, but the habit of rising at four thirty was difficult to break. That made falling into bed in the early evening easy.

"That's so. Did you see Pa tonight?" Dustin asked. "At supper?"

"Yeah, why?"

A horse ambled over to the corral fence and snuffled at Chaim's back.

"Just wondered. He showed up in town, said he was going to the saloon for a drink. I would've joined him if I didn't have Noah attached to my side. The more I can keep those two apart, the better."

Chaim grunted. "Now that you mention it, he was rather quiet. Madeline and Becky were prattling on about a festival, a museum attraction coming through Texas, or some such thing. I didn't pay much heed."

A wagonload of guilt pressed down on Dustin's chest. The expression in his father's eyes had been haunting.

Dustin hadn't chosen the Calhouns over his pa. He wouldn't do that. *Ever!*

His thoughts of Sidney made him keep his gaze far away from Chaim. The affair shouldn't be about choosing, he argued in his mind. She'd only been a small girl when the ambush had happened to her pa. Since then, she'd not had control over his pigheaded ways or the lies he'd spread.

A troubled memory of Sidney telling him Calhouns and McCutcheons were like fire and ice beleaguered him.

Was that the truth? She hadn't acted that way tonight.

He didn't need to add to his brother's problems. Come a few weeks from now, Chaim's plate would be full to overflowing with grief if his betrothed didn't return. They'd almost lost Chaim a few months back when he'd been shot by Harland Shellston. The bullet had come dangerously close to his heart, and his life had been touch and go for days. Dustin remembered how frightened he'd felt at the moment he understood that Chaim might actually die. He'd been damn angry he hadn't been able to help.

John had breathed life back into his lungs, or his brother would be a fresh mound in the family graveyard. If he was protective over his brother, he had every right to be. He glanced at him, and his heart swelled. He hoped Chaim wasn't in for heartbreak too.

Madeline was just coming out of her sorrow over the stranger who'd bought her box lunch at the Fourth of July celebration last July, wooed her, and would have married her as well if Dustin hadn't discovered he was more interested in being a part of one of wealthiest ranches in Texas. Once the scoundrel had learned they were on to him, he'd cut and run.

Love. Relationships. Dustin would have wondered if they were worth the time and effort at all if he didn't remember Sidney's warmth tonight as she sat at his side.

"Well, I guess I'll turn in," he mumbled, gazing at the house.

A deep loneliness crept into his bones. He'd never choose the Calhouns over his pa. That was hogwash.

But what about Sidney? His heart trembled at his answer. Could he break his father's heart, as well as his spirit? That's what would happen if he entertained any more of these whims he'd been having since running into her in San Antonio. He needed to get his head on straight. Prioritize his values.

"Something on your mind, Dustin? I know you're not just standing out here taking in the sight of the corral."

Dustin grasped his brother's shoulder. "Not much of anything important. Just checking on you."

Chaim chuckled. "Thanks, brother. I'm doing fine."

The huskiness of Chaim's voice said otherwise. Dustin would keep a close watch on him. Not get caught up in his own troubles and forget his brother was going through a really rough time.

He turned from the house and took several steps before Chaim said, "Where're you off to? The house is that way."

"Just thought of something I want to check on."

"Noah?"

"Nope."

"Need any help?"

"Sure don't. I'll catch you in the morning, brother. We have a day of cattle sorting to get finished."

Inspiration had hit Dustin like a windfall. Why hadn't he thought of this before? Because his pa was always playing down any talk of the lies Jock Calhoun spouted. The last five years had been pretty quiet, only catching glimpses of the Calhouns when they hit the stockyard. Since there was no fixing the problem, ignoring any talk was the best action to take. One man's word against another man's word was a special kind of hell.

Now that he had a definite purpose in mind, Dustin walked quickly in the moonlight, alongside the barn and then striding along the sandy wagon trail that passed the bunkhouse. The track meandered through a patch of ironwood and scrub oaks until it opened on this side of the main horse pasture, where a small cabin was nestled under a few loblolly pines. A light glowed in the window, and for that Dustin was thankful. Until he had a chance to flush out these ideas rolling around in his head, he'd not get any sleep.

Diaz Sanchez resided here alone, retired now, quietly living out his remaining days in solitude. The ancient Mexican seldom ventured up to the bunkhouse anymore where he'd lived since the ranch was first built. Maria cooked his meals, and another woman saw to the cleaning of his small cabin. Except for his failing eyesight, his bent old body was in darn good shape for his eighty-five years.

Dustin knocked on the door.

"*Hola?*" a scratchy voice called out. Sounded as if he'd been asleep.

"*Señor* Sanchez, it's Dustin McCutcheon. May I come in?"

"*Sí, sí,* Dustin. Come in, *por favor.*"

Dustin ducked under the low door frame. He stepped inside, taking in the neat room, the faint scents of rosemary and garlic still lingering on the air from the evening meal, and the wide smile on the man's face.

"Sit," Diaz said, gesturing to the chair to his left. "Get comfortable, *amigo.* Something important has brought you out late this evening. How can I help?"

Dustin shook his head in amazement as he lowered himself into the chair. "You know me pretty good, don't you, *amigo?* There're no secrets kept from Diaz Sanchez."

The old man beamed.

No one knew his full history except that when he'd signed on, he'd said he was the only remaining person in his family line. All had been slaughtered by renegades deep in southern Mexico.

After he'd hired on with Winston McCutcheon, he never quit the ranch, never took a wife, and never spoke of his past.

As a boy, Dustin had asked Diaz several times about his past, being an inquisitive kid, but the man had a way of talking around a question so long a young mind forgot where the conversation had started. A sly old fox wrapped in a lamb's coat, Dustin was sure.

"I'd like to talk to you about the early days. A few years after the ranch was established and was growing. Do you remember back then?"

Diaz's gnarled hands moved up and gripped the arms of his chair. "My mind is as good now as it was back then. I remember everything!"

Chapter Thirty-Four

Sidney tossed and turned, haunted by dark, probing eyes and a slash of chiseled lips, sometimes mocking, sometimes teasing, and all the time desirable. Every time they came close, and she thought they were about to kiss her, the face came into focus and transformed into that of her older brother Jock Jr.

In her dream, he scowled and pointed an accusing finger. *You've sold out to the enemy. You, a Calhoun, are in love with a McCutcheon!*

No! That's not true! I've done no such thing. I'm watching over Noah, making sure he doesn't make his problems worse.

She blinked and opened her eyes. The creamy haze of morning, brush-stroked with pinks and golds, filtered through her windowpane. The hotel was quiet, as was the town. The air felt cool on her skin.

Four days had passed since the dinner in the alley with Dustin. Four days to wonder about him as he hadn't made an appearance in the store since. Four days to dwell on her insecurities, going over each and every word of their conversation.

Such thoughts . . .

Sidney pulled the blanket around her neck and snuggled in, pushing away her troubled feelings. One by one, events from the past paraded through her mind. From Dustin yanking her off her feet from the sandy badlands desert floor and onto the back of his horse, then galloping away, to him smiling into her face, filling her with happiness. Dustin calling her old, and then waiting for her to take the bait. Dustin's voice making ripples of awareness move through her body.

Why couldn't Gibson Harp be swoon worthy like that? The thirty-five-year-old merchant in Santa Fe, the one who believed he was courting her, was nice looking and said all the right things. He went out of his way to make her feel special. She'd gladly say yes to his proposal if he could make her heart trip over itself with only a look, like Dustin could. Or sent a bevy of tingles racing through her body each time he happened to touch her arm.

Dustin McCutcheon. The devil in a cowboy hat. That man had cast his spell over her well and good. She'd not forget him anytime soon.

She rolled to her side, taking in the ever-lightening sky on the other side of the glass as she tucked her hands beneath her cheek. What awaited her back in Santa Fe? On the ranch, or even as a wife to Gibson Harp? After her time spent in Rio Wells, even living off of thirty-five cents a day, her prospects seemed bleak.

As a woman, she held no stock in the workings of the family ranch, not like the rest of her brothers. Her father had said her mother's jewelry belonged to her, but she'd not seen it. Other than that, she was more or less a hired hand around there. She had some money, but not enough to start a business of her own like Lily McCutcheon. The thought of her feisty employer brought a smile to her lips.

Lily. She had it all. A trade that brought her pleasure, gave her an outlet to be creative, and made money to boot. From her short time working in the shop, Sidney had ascertained her employer was well respected far and wide. The finished products set tongues wagging. She accomplished the feat with ease and humility, as if fashioning a gown of exquisite quality was as easy as baking bread. Her cowboy-doctor husband clearly worshiped the ground she walked on. Love in abundance existed between them, which seemed to multiply every time Sidney was around the two.

A sigh escaped her lips, and she realized she needed to get up and get moving. Today was a workday. She had three hours before she'd report to the shop, but that didn't mean she should lay about slovenly like a lazybones.

A knock on her door brought her wide awake.

"Sidney, are you in there?"

Lily.

Sidney jumped up, pulled the quilt off the bed, and wrapped it around her shoulders. "Coming."

She hurried to the door and pulled it open. There stood Lily, looking clean and fresh with a basket, and what looked to be two folded garments in her arms. She smiled warmly.

"Please, come in." Sidney swept her arm, gesturing her boss inside. "I apologize for not being dressed. I was just lying about, thinking."

"No worries. It's only seven o'clock. Much too early for a proper call."

Lily went to the small table next to the window and set down the basket. She extracted several cloth-covered plates from within and placed them on the tabletop next to the lantern and a copy of the newspaper.

"I hope you don't mind, but I brought you a little something." She flicked her hand at the veritable feast waiting to be consumed. She hadn't yet mention the clothes she'd nonchalantly placed on the bed as she'd crossed the room. "Go on. It's two poached eggs with toast and jam." She set the basket at her feet.

Heaven. Just hearing the names of the items made Sidney's stomach rumble. "Lily, you must stop spoiling me so. Thanks to you, I now have funds to feed myself until my father sends the money he's promised."

The money is coming, isn't it? He didn't really promise me anything. I must check at the bank today.

"You hush. Thirty-five cents a day is hardly enough to keep a snail alive. If I want to make sure you have energy to get through the workday, I will. Besides, I didn't set out to bring you breakfast. Dustin stopped by and left you a note. Instead of waiting for you to come in at ten, I thought you might like it now." She wiggled her eyebrows suggestively and laughed. "It's so much fun playing Cupid."

A note from Dustin? Dread washed through Sidney. *Please don't let it be bad news about Noah.*

"And we can also go downstairs and have a cup of peppermint tea in the restaurant. It's my treat." Lily held out a small piece of white paper folded in half. "Go on and read it, and then eat. I'll go see if we're too early to take a table downstairs."

Sidney nodded as she lifted the missive from Lily's fingers.

Lily lifted one of the garments on the bed and shook it out. "These are from my friend Martha Brown. She doesn't mind in the least lending them to you, so no fretting."

Sidney held the brown corduroy skirt up to her waist as Lily unfolded a nicely ironed yellow blouse. Yesterday, they'd discovered Lily's things were a bit too snug on her.

"They're lovely. Again, thank you for all your kindnesses."

Lily gestured to the armoire that held Madeline's skirt and Becky's blouse. "Be sure to bring in the garments you've been wearing, and we'll wash and iron them today. Then you'll have two outfits."

Wanting to die of shame, Sidney smiled her thanks. What could she do? She hated taking such charity, but she had no other choice. Now she knew how the poor mother in San Antonio felt. Thankful and humbled at the same time.

"Having something new to wear will be nice. Thank you so much, Lily."

"Eat the eggs before they're cold. I'll see you downstairs. I have another surprise I think you'll like once we have our tea, so hurry."

As soon as the door closed, Sidney opened the note.

Dear Sidney,

We've been sorting cattle the last few days, making getting to Rio Wells impossible.

First, let me say, Noah is fine. I know that's the first thing that would jump into your head when you saw this note. He's healthy, following orders, and keeping to himself.

That said, keeping Noah out of my father's sight is increasingly difficult. To make things easier, I kept Noah with me, and we camped out by the herd.

She heard what he wasn't saying. That staying out was unwarranted, just to keep Noah out of trouble, out of sight, and protect his father. Dustin's compassion for his father's feelings was noteworthy.

Leaving him for long in the bunkhouse is not a good idea. I don't want to see anyone else get hurt. I can't guarantee someone in our employ won't start a fight, even though they have been warned with termination.

Such distraction! And inconvenience! Dustin was undertaking a lot of trouble for the Calhouns. Even to the point of threatening his own ranch hands. Most men wouldn't give a whit if Noah didn't fare well at the hands of the help. Her heart shuddered.

For that reason, I've made a decision I hope I don't regret. I'm assigning him to John, to help him set up the barn for his new business. Noah swears he won't cause trouble. I'm trusting his word. I believe Noah respects and maybe even admires John. If you're reading this note, then you can be assured your brother is already in town and is in good hands.

Respectfully yours,

Dustin

Noah! Here in town! Here with Dustin's blessing and his trust, her brother would behave.

Sidney stared long and hard at the missive, unwarranted dread swirling around in her empty stomach. Noah wouldn't go and do something stupid, would he? *He's been running off at the drop of a hat, and you wonder that!* Ashamed for her faithless thoughts, she considered all that Dustin was doing to protect not only his father, but her brother as well. And if she were honest, for her.

Jerking the quilt from her shoulders, Sidney tossed the covering back on the bed. With shaky hands, she stepped into the skirt Lily had brought and shimmied the garment over her hips. As fast as she could go, she fastened the hook and eye behind her back and reached for the blouse.

Lily was waiting. Maybe the other surprise she'd alluded to was walking to where Noah worked with John. She felt frantic. Somewhere along the way, Dustin's opinion of her and her family had become important. Dustin, as well as the other McCutcheons. Lily, John . . . even Winston. They'd all been so kind.

Grasping a comb off the dresser, she ran the tool through her hair. Having no time for fussy styles, she quickly plaited her tresses down her back and let the braid swing. Using the same water she'd washed in last night, she splashed her face, briskly toweled dry, and brushed her teeth.

Taking a second to examine the results of her toilette, Sidney pinched both cheeks several times until they stung. She couldn't wait to get downstairs to see what Lily was talking about.

Chapter Thirty-Five

"**O**n the count of three . . ."

Dustin and Noah grasped the bulky wooden crate, lifted it, and walked the cumbersome piece out the barn door to the wagon that would move the trunk to Mr. Knutson's other barn. The new merchant had generously offered this barn to John for a dollar a month. The hard dirt floor was uneven under Dustin's boots, making the going slow.

"Gently, please," Mr. Knutson said, following while wringing his hands. "Right there. Next to the blue one."

The Wisconsinite pointed to the other six crates they'd already loaded in the wagon. Longish dark blond hair was still thick for his middle age.

"I don't quite remember what's inside, but I know it's important. Belongs to my missus." He scratched his head. "Or one of my girls. Anyway, it's traveled intact all the way from Milwaukee, and I wouldn't like to see anything be broken now."

John followed with a box hefted in his arms, his clothes already marred with dirt and sweat. Tucker was last with an armful of gardening tools.

Dustin had presented his dilemma about Noah to his cousin, and then offered him Noah's help. John had been overwhelmed with gratitude. Since Tucker only had one hand, lifting large objects was a difficult task. Noah's strength would be appreciated.

John clamped Dustin firmly on the shoulder. "You showed up just in time, cousin. I don't know how I can thank you for staying to help. Does a man good to have family nearby."

Dustin chuckled. "You're laying on the horse puckey mighty thick today, John. No need for that. I'm happy to help if I can." He nodded toward Noah. "Just make sure this fellow never leaves your sight. I mean it. I trust him, but also need to follow Judge Halford's orders. In my way of thinking, one McCutcheon is as good as another." He trained John with a meaningful look. "When I'm done in the late afternoon, I'll ride back in and collect him."

Noah listened to the discussion, his face a blank slate.

Figuring out Sidney's younger brother was a challenge. He seemed sincere about toeing the line. After the time spent with him camping under the stars, and the conversations they'd had, Dustin wanted to trust the fellow. But he had to remember Noah was a Calhoun. And that didn't bode well.

Maybe he's just waiting for me to let down my guard. No telling the havoc he could cause if he wanted to.

"That's a lot of extra riding," John said. "You sure you want to do that? Noah could take my old room upstairs at the doctor's office. It's vacant. Bixby and Tucker won't mind."

"No doing. Too risky."

Without saying a word, Noah shrugged and then ambled into the barn through the tall, propped-open doors. The four followed him in, and John commenced to show Dustin around.

A rapping sounded on the barn doorjamb. "Knock, knock," Lily's voice called out. "May we come in?"

Dustin turned to see Lily and Sidney, the latter going up on tiptoe to reach her brother's cheek with a kiss. Standing next to Noah, she looked quite small.

He wanted to talk to her, tell her the things he'd learned the other night from Diaz Sanchez, but he wasn't quite ready. He needed to do a little more digging first. Get more information.

"Lily!" John strutted forward. "I wasn't expecting to see you. Or you either, Miss Calhoun. Please come into my—" he looked back over his shoulder to Tucker and Dustin, "into *our* new office and manufacturing facility."

John's puffed-out chest reminded Dustin of a proud father. You'd think he'd just given birth to this barn.

Both women entered with smiles on their faces. Sidney was dressed in a different skirt and blouse, not new, which looked vaguely familiar. He tried not to stare, but days had passed since he'd seen her, and his eyes wouldn't obey.

"Mr. Knutson, I'd like you to meet my wife, Lily McCutcheon," John said, leading Lily over to the man. "She owns the most successful dress shop in Rio Wells."

Lily beamed. "The only dress shop in Rio Wells," she corrected.

"That too," John agreed. "Still, you can't deny it's very popular with all the women. You'll have to bring by your wife and daughters. Lily'll be happy to show them around town. This is her assistant, Miss Sidney Calhoun. She's sister to Noah here."

The man smiled and made a small bow. "I'm happy to make your acquaintance, Mrs. McCutcheon and Miss Calhoun. It's good to know other young women live in town for my daughters to befriend. They weren't eager to leave Wisconsin. Once the store opens and they get involved in town and meet people, I believe they'll cheer up. Now that I've met you, I have hope for the situation."

"Store? What kind?" Lily asked. She glanced at John and smiled.

"A general dry goods, as well as items that are popular with the ladies," he responded. "My wife and daughters help in that department, of course."

"That's wonderful. A few days ago, John shared that a new merchant with five daughters had moved to Rio Wells." She held out her basket. "I've brought you two jars of jam I put up last week. For you and your family."

"That is very kind of you. Thank you. Would you like to go to the house? Deliver the fruits of your labor yourself? I'd be happy to introduce you."

"Oh no," Lily responded. "The hour is much too early to show up unannounced." She shared a secretive glance with Sidney. "But I do hope I'll have the pleasure of meeting them soon." She handed him her basket.

"Of course you will," he replied, darting a glance out the barn door and to the large house beyond the garden. "Soon." The word was feeble. "Just not quite yet. They're still adjusting to the heat."

Dustin frowned. The weather was quite mild this year.

John put his arm around Lily's back. "When they're ready then."

Mr. Knutson nodded and smiled, fine lines fanning out from his eyes. "I will do that, Dr. McCutcheon. And you all must come and visit my new mercantile on Church Street. I don't know yet when we will open, but I will let you know." He pulled a watch from his pocket and flipped open the lid. "I must be on my way. I have an appointment at the bank, and I don't want to be late." He lifted the basket. "Thank you for your kindness."

They watched him walk away.

"A new mercantile," Lily said with pleasure. "I do wonder how Nel and Betty will feel about another store."

"Competition is good. Keeps prices down," John said.

Dustin closed the space between him and Sidney. "Can I talk with you for a moment? In private?"

This growing closeness he'd been nursing for the past four days was about to overflow. He needed to speak with her, to see if this crazy notion that he had of them actually being together and building a life was just wishful thinking. He had enough information from Diaz that he just might sway her.

Since Monday night, when a sliver of hope had been given, he'd spent every waking moment thinking about her—whether lying in his bed, stretched out on the cold, hard ground next to a campfire, or riding his horse. Sidney Calhoun had occupied his every thought.

Her glance bounced around the occupants of the barn. "Of course. Where?"

He took a gentle hold of her elbow, guided her outside, and then to the side of the barn, shaded by a thicket of pines. The location was private and they wouldn't be overheard by the others.

Still happy over her unexpected appearance, he had to tamp down his eagerness. "I've missed you."

She pulled up, her eyes wide. "What did you say?"

"I said, I've missed seeing you these last few days. I've grown accustomed to you scowling at me and calling me names."

Dustin realized he wasn't always the most congenial man, and was often scolded by Madeline and Becky to cheer up and smile, and not be so cynical. But he was working on that. He was serious by nature, which wasn't all *that* bad of a quality.

Especially when he thought of Billy Burger, who spent almost every living day in the saloon, getting snockered.

Several women had told Dustin he was handsome. He was tall and fit. Surely, Sidney found something in him attractive.

But your name's McCutcheon. That's all she needs to scorn you forever.

Sidney glanced away and then back into his face, her eyes troubled. Her fingers fiddled with an ivory button on the front of her blouse. "I don't know what you're talking about. I'm not *that* bad."

"You're not? That look on your face right now says you'd like to kick me, or do me other bodily harm if I let you. There's no other reason I can think of for your peevishness except our growing attraction to each other. I've felt the spark ever since our meeting in the store in San Antonio. I'll bet you have too."

She blinked at his directness. "You big oaf!"

"See what I mean? That's just another way of saying *I like you.* Because of our family history and your obvious dislike of anyone or anything McCutcheon, I didn't want to admit this to myself. Well, now I am." The hand he had pressed to a nearby tree trunk he let fall to his side. "I like you, Sidney. I like you a lot."

First, she looked at him as if he'd lost his mind. Judging from her expression, he thought maybe he had. When she whirled and was about to march off, he stopped her by grasping her arm.

"Wait," he said, and she threw cobalt daggers his way.

As if those will do anything to change my mind.

"It's understandable, Sidney. You're scared. Worried how your family will react. But I'm begging you, if you can't *think* anything nice about me or the rest of the McCutcheons, don't *think* anything at all."

Impatience and a bit of confusion marked her face. "You've bungled the saying. If you can't *say* anything—"

"No, not with you. I stick by my rendition. You don't say much, but I can see the wheels in your head turning so fast, I expect to see steam coming out of your ears. Still, you keep everything all bottled up inside. You may smile and make nice when you're with us, but I can hear your thoughts railing against the McCutcheon name."

Frustrated with the situation, he took a few steps away and then paced back. "Those beliefs are what you've been taught. You worry over your loyalty to your family, and that mixes you up. And hurts you. I wish, just for a little while, you could forget all that. Like you did Monday night in the alley. You forgot about the past and your father's anger. You sat at my side and enjoyed the evening. The night was about the best of my life. We could have so much more."

"That's not the way of it at all," she said, but it was. He could tell by how quietly she said the words.

"Judge us for who we are now, not on what you've been told over the years." That was the longest speech he'd ever given, but the look on her face said his words hadn't made a lick of difference. "If I weren't a McCutcheon, I know you'd like me well enough. Hell, you'd be in love with me. I can't fight a wall of lies that keep us apart."

"I think you're mad," she whispered, gazing into his face.

"Do you?"

Knowing she would pull away if he dared to take her in his arms, he stepped forward, and without touching any part of her body, leaned down and pressed his lips to hers.

A spark jumped between them. Desire surged.

He sucked in a breath before he leaned back just far enough to search her eyes. "I *am* mad. Mad for you. I admitted that shocking fact to myself yesterday. You've cast your Calhoun spell over me, Sidney, and I never want to be free."

Chapter Thirty-Six

Girlish laughter seeped into Sidney's shocked system as Dustin's proximity kept muddling her thoughts. She still felt his lips on hers, pressing, claiming, even though he'd drawn back.

She swung around to find three girls standing not five feet away, arm in arm, watching them as if she and Dustin were a super-secret science experiment.

"Oh!" Sidney said in surprise, heat springing into her face.

Dustin took a respectable two steps back. She didn't dare look at him just yet, fearful he'd see just how much his brief kiss had affected her.

"You must be the Knutson girls," she said, struggling for something to say.

She hoped she hadn't scandalized them too much with her and Dustin's behavior. They were sure to tell their mother. They looked young, perhaps somewhere between thirteen and sixteen. All three were tall and slender with the same honey-colored hair that hung down their backs in ringlets. Each had light blue eyes that were uncannily similar. Their dresses of varying shades of blue were each accented by a lovely crochet lace collar and cuffs. So close in appearance, the girls almost looked like triplets.

"My name is Miss Calhoun, and this is Dustin McCutcheon," she forced out through her lips. "I'll bet you're looking for your father. I believe he went into town."

They unhooked their arms. "No. We're not looking for Father," the tallest and apparent oldest said. Her gaze kept slipping back to Dustin's face. "My name is Breezy Knutson. This is my sister, Sunny Knutson, and our baby sister, Rainey Knutson. We're pleased to make your acquaintance." When she smiled and nodded, her golden curls bobbed up and down.

Dustin barked out a laugh. "Let me guess. The other two sisters are named Stormy and Snowflake."

His earnest glance caused a warm and wonderful sensation inside. When had she let him under her skin?

Dustin in love with her? Could that amazing thought be true? He'd been on her mind almost constantly since the dinner in the alley. Why was fate so cruel? The only man who set her world spinning was an impossibility.

The smallest girl laughed and then snorted. She playfully batted her eyes. "No. You're wrong, Mr. McCutcheon. Their names are Wendy and Misti. Misti is nineteen and Wendy, the old maid, is twenty-one. But don't tell her I said so."

"How unkind!" The second the words were out, Sidney wished she could call them back. "I didn't mean to say that. I just wonder how . . . how your parents keep you all straight," she said, unable to come up with an excuse for her surprised outburst. The young girl had seemed so innocent and sweet. "You look so much alike, and with the similar names, telling you apart must get confusing."

Breezy didn't look quite so curious anymore. Her lips puckered. "Sometimes."

Rainey glanced over her shoulder at their house and then wrinkled her petite, upturned nose, scanning the area. She turned back. "What're you two doing out here anyway? Alone and unchaperoned," she whispered conspiratorially. "Mama wouldn't be pleased if one of us was kissing in secret."

Sidney felt Dustin straighten beside her.

"Rainey!" Breezy said sternly, once again making her curls bounce. "That is *none* of your business!" She held out a placating hand. "Please forgive my little sister, Miss Calhoun. Mama said things out here in Texas were different than in Wisconsin. People are wild and uncouth. They don't hold to the norms of society. Nevertheless, we're bound to hold fast to our standards of upbringing and what we've been taught, even if we will appear different. That was thoughtless of Rainey to point out your immoral behavior."

Wonderful. My reputation has been ruined in one swoop of Dustin's lips.

She cut a censoring gaze to Dustin. "We're beside the barn," she said tersely, feeling about a foot tall in the midst of her growing agitation. "*Not* behind it. The gesture was nothing more than a friendly little peck."

Why she was explaining was beyond her. Except that she had come to love and respect Lily, and didn't want to bring any shame down on her in any way.

Sidney looked from face to face. Nothing she could say now would change their minds. She was a tainted, loose woman. Probably someone their mother would make them cross the street to avoid.

She let go a breath. "Shall we go back inside with the others? Would you like to meet Lily McCutcheon?"

Sunny, the middle girl who had been silent until now, finally spoke up. "Oh no. We're not even supposed to be outside without our nanny. We wanted to explore when we heard all the activity out at the barn, and sneaked out. Since Nanny's still napping and Mother is engrossed with accounting, no one will be the wiser to our investigation. But we better not stay out any longer."

At that, they smiled before they turned and hurried away.

The girls still have a nanny? Sneaked out? This will be interesting.

As they stepped back inside, Sidney was surprised to find Chaim in the middle of the fray. Lily gazed out a back window, and John was handing Tucker a shovel.

"With all the crates cleared away," he said, "we'll level out the dirt footing and begin laying a wooden floor by tomorrow. Things will stay much cleaner if we have a floor."

Dustin pulled her to a stop and whispered, "Sidney, I'm sorry the girls caught us kissing. I know you're probably upset about that."

"We weren't kissing; you were kissing me. Once. I had nothing to do with it." She hated to sound so peevish, but a romance with Dustin was bound to end in sorrow. Best to nip the desire in the bud first thing.

He looked at her for a long time, his lips pulling down at the corners. "Whatever you say." His voice was hard.

She hated hurting his feelings.

"What are you doing for money?" he asked. "Has your father sent the transfer yet?"

"I'm going to the bank this morning on my way to the shop. I'm sure more than I'll ever need will be waiting." *I hope the money is there. How nice to have some extra again.*

"I wish you would have used the money I left at the hotel. The clerk said you haven't touched a penny. Seriously, sometimes—"

"I've made it this far with no help except the cost of the first telegram. I'll be fine after today. But I do appreciate your concern," she said quickly in a low voice. Lily was on her way over and would be there in only a moment.

"What if I told you I might have evidence my pa is innocent of all the charges your pa holds against him? Would that change your mind toward me?"

Sidney's heart slammed against her breastbone. The feel of Dustin's lips on hers still had her rattled.

"Do you?"

"I'm working on it. I've been busy out at the ranch, but tomorrow—"

"Sidney, are you ready to leave?" Lily asked, touching her arm. "We still have a little time if you'd like to stay and enjoy the sunshine outside. Maybe the Knutsons wouldn't mind if we walked through their gardens."

"Actually, Lily, I need to go to the bank. See if the money transfer has arrived." She glanced over at John and Chaim in conversation. "When did Chaim arrive?"

"Just a few minutes ago. Said Winston was wondering about Dustin, and sent him into town to check on him. Seems strange to me, but who knows." Lily looked up at Dustin and shrugged.

Sidney couldn't miss the way Dustin straightened at the news. His pa most likely thought he was with her, which he was. She didn't want to cause strife within the family. The sooner she and Noah got out of Rio Wells, the better for everyone concerned.

"I better be going too," Dustin said, his mouth still set in an angry tilt. "We've moved all the heavy trunks. John, Noah, and Tucker should be able to handle the rest." He touched the brim of his hat in good-bye. "Lily."

Then he turned to her. "Sidney," he said, his eyes softening. "We'll finish this discussion this evening when I come back to collect your brother."

Chapter Thirty-Seven

"**I**'ll see you in a few minutes, Lily. This shouldn't take me long," Sidney said, holding open the door to the bank.

The squat building's bat-and-board siding looked newly painted, and the two small windows were sparkling clean. The structure might not be much to look at in terms of a bank—at least not like the one they had back in Santa Fe—but whoever owned the establishment was trying to do a nice job. She guessed the beauty of the bank didn't matter as long as the money inside was safe.

"Take all the time you need," Lily replied. "We still have almost an hour before the shop opens. You know where to find me."

Sidney stepped inside and glanced around.

"May I help you?" a young man asked from behind the counter. A straight part divided his slicked-down hair.

"Yes. I'm expecting a money wire sent to me here from my father in Santa Fe. My name is Sidney Calhoun, and his name is Jock Calhoun. Do you know if anything has arrived?"

Please, Lord, let the transfer be here.

He pursed his lips. "No. I don't recall any wires coming in. Let me go ask Mr. Jorgensen. But don't get your hopes up too high. I usually know everything that transpires, since I'm the only clerk besides the owner. We haven't had a transfer of funds for weeks." He smiled and nodded. "I'll be right back."

Sidney twisted her hands as she tried to hide her disappointment. "Thank you so much."

She was too keyed up to sit. First the kiss from Dustin unleashing a torrent of desire and love bursting in her heart, and now this. Something was up with her father. If the money hadn't arrived already, she felt almost certain nothing ever would. Why? She didn't understand his motivation. How did he expect her to live?

A bubble of anger pushed up her throat. How mean! She was his only daughter. What was he doing?

She was ashamed when she thought of the McCutcheons and how good, kind, and generous they'd been with her and Noah since their arrival. She could have as much money as she wanted, a comfortable room in their gorgeous home, and three square meals a day, if she only said the word.

A door opened and closed. Footsteps came her way.

"Sorry, Miss Calhoun. No wire transfers since the one I mentioned three weeks ago." He shrugged. "Is there anything else I can help you with?"

She kept her disquiet contained. "No, thank you. I'll check back in a day or two. Pa must have been delayed."

With as much aplomb as she could muster and her head held high, she went out the door.

Should she send another telegram? One to Patrick this time. See if her second oldest brother would step in and help since Jock Jr. and her father were cut from the same cloth.

She couldn't go on living on thirty-five cents a day. Her hotel bill was adding up. Everyone here would think her a fraud. *Think all the Calhouns a fraud.*

Was there more behind her father's silence? He wouldn't make the trip out to Rio Wells himself?

She pushed aside the outlandish thought as Dustin's money in the hotel's safe tempted her. Last Friday, she'd refused the envelope. Would she actually have to stoop so low? That thought fueled her anger, and she vowed that would never happen.

In a daze, she started for the shop, knowing the telegraph office was directly across the street. That would mean seeing Stanton Drake, who'd gone out of his way to hand deliver her telegram.

She stood facing the telegraph office, clutching her reticule. She had forty cents. The last time she used the services, the cost was fifty-five cents, which Dustin had paid.

She almost laughed, thinking how much she'd changed. She realized just how rich she'd been back in Santa Fe, spending a day's wages on a whim. Well, she wasn't home now, and she had things to do.

Sidney pulled open the telegraph office door.

Stanton Drake looked up. He recognized her, and a smile grew across his face. He stood, hurrying around the counter to meet her halfway across the room.

"Good *morning*, Miss Calhoun. I'm delighted to see you." He gestured outside to Lily's shop across the street. "On your way to work?"

"Yes, I am," she said with a forced smile.

This had been a mistake. She wished she could march back out the door

He reached out and took her elbow. "What can I help you with? Would you like to send another telegram?"

What should she do? Were the prices set, and the rules couldn't be broken?

"Yes, actually." She glanced away from his hopeful face. "But I only have forty cents with me now." *Actually, I only have forty cents to my name.* "I was wondering if that would be enough."

His smile fell. "I only work here, Miss Calhoun. If it were up to me, I'd say yes. Forty cents is the base amount, and the cost goes up by the penny from there." His expression begged for understanding. "I could lose my—"

"Oh no. Never mind! I don't know what I was—"

The intense smile was back. He blinked several times and stuck his hand into his pocket. "I'll give you the difference," he offered, holding out a handful of coins. "I'd be happy to help."

Embarrassed over the situation, she pushed aside her swirling emotions. "That's very kind, but I couldn't. I think you can understand. I'll be back when I can pay in full."

"There's no need to wait," he pleaded, and pushed his money-filled hand closer. "I insist."

"No, no. But thank you for your kindness." The last thing she wanted was to be beholden to another man.

Father, I don't understand you.

Feeling totally deserted by her family, she smiled brightly and turned for the door, but Stanton Drake beat her there.

"If you change your mind, Miss Calhoun, remember I'm right across the street, just waiting to do your bidding."

Emotion welled. She'd been keeping a strong countenance for days, counting on her father doing the right thing. Dustin's face flashed in her mind. And then the money in the hotel safe.

No, she'd not use any of that. No matter what. She'd get through this predicament one day at a time.

Chapter Thirty-Eight

Chaim followed Dustin into the house, more than ready for the noon meal. By habit, he hung his hat by the door, his steps moving slowly, as if weighted by sacks of rocks from the quarry.

Over a week had passed with no word from Emmeline. No letter, no telegram. Four days after he'd put her on the train, he sent a cable to her house, needing to know that she'd arrived safely, but he'd yet to get a reply. That didn't mean anything. No way of telling if the telegram had actually reached her.

With a heavyhearted sigh, he pulled out a chair next to Dustin in the dining room and relaxed back into his usual spot. His father followed suit. Savory aromas and voices floating in from the kitchen indicated the meal would soon be out.

Madeline and Becky hurried into the room. Becky went into the kitchen, and Madeline took her seat across from Chaim.

She glanced at her family. "What in the world is wrong with everyone? You look like you've lost your best friends."

The three just sat there.

"Well?"

"Nothin', darlin'," Winston said. "We're tired and hungry, that's all. After we eat, we'll have more energy. We've been ranching since early this morning."

She huffed. "It's more than that. Chaim, have you heard from Emmeline yet? I miss her. When is she coming back? Many decisions still remain for the wedding, and I don't feel capable to make them without her, even if I am standing up as a witness. It's a shame her family won't be able to make the journey."

Another point that had Chaim sinking in self-doubt. From the get-go, she'd flatly said the trip was impossible for her parents. He wondered why. They were well-to-do, from what he'd been told, and could easily afford two train tickets. They'd stay at the Rim Rock, so they didn't need to worry about the cost of a hotel.

"Haven't heard a thing," he replied, reaching for his glass of water. He took a drink and set it back on the tablecloth, cutting her a look that said *please stop with the questions*.

Maria glided out of the kitchen with a tray of plates filled to the brim with food. She set one in front of his pa, Dustin, and himself. Becky was next, with two sparsely laden dishes for her and Madeline. She took a seat.

Winston looked around. "Where's your mother?"

"She said to go on," Becky replied. "She ate late this morning."

Winston grunted, grumbled out a brief blessing, and put his napkin in his lap.

Chaim followed suit, trying to drudge up a bit of enthusiasm for what was on his plate. His appetite was nil. This morning at the corrals, his pa had questioned him on Dustin's absence, and then sent him into town to fetch him back. He hadn't said anything more about the Calhouns, but he hadn't smiled much since their arrival. More disturbingly, he'd visited the saloon twice, which was completely out of character. Dustin returned without Noah, but his pa hadn't asked any questions.

Whenever his sisters inquired about Sidney, his pa turned silent. Being a genius wasn't needed to see Dustin had an eye for her. Chaim hoped his brother would keep a level head. Dustin might not talk about Sidney, but his preoccupation was a tell. A match with her would certainly bring trouble.

"What about you, Becky, darlin'?" his pa said. "How's your day going? Tell us something nice."

Strange way to put it.

"Theodore is coming to supper tomorrow evening, so Maria has granted me permission to help her prepare the meal. Theo has his doubts about my cooking. I plan to dazzle his socks off."

Chaim just looked at his sister, and Dustin did too. To be young and in love again, unmindful of the pain that rips one's heart into wheat chaff to be blown away by the wind.

How fast you've given up on your own love. Emmeline would be disappointed, Chaim thought as he angrily forked in a large bite of beef. *Yeah, well, I'm disappointed too.*

"He's making sure he knows what he gets before he pops the question?" he asked bluntly.

"Chaim!" Becky stiffened, but she smiled so brightly into her plate, he was sure he was getting pretty close to the truth.

How would Madeline feel if her younger sister married before her? There wasn't anyone in Rio Wells that caught his older sister's fancy. Maybe she needed to take a trip and meet new people. She could only paint and do so many needlepoints before she went crazy. He knew the feeling.

He shoved in another large mouthful. *Life. Women. The world . . .*

"Sidney, would you mind going over to the mercantile to see if the thread I ordered two weeks ago has finally arrived? I'm almost out." Lily held up Mrs. Tuttle's blue velvet gown and gave the material a shake, examining her work. "I'm doubtful, though. I think Betty would have brought it over herself, but I want to be sure. Oh, and please turn the sign on your way out."

"Of course, I'll go right now."

Truly, Sidney looked forward to stretching her legs. All morning and afternoon she'd been bent over, stitching one long side seam of Mrs. Harbinger's new order. Fresh air sounded good.

Just as she was about to reach for the knob, the door opened. She quickly stepped back.

More Knutson girls! Actually, she wasn't quite sure about that yet, because these faces were a bit different, older. They didn't have on the similar blue dresses with the crochet points, but the hair, eyes, and build were the same.

"Hello," Lily said. "May I help you find something?"

"Our father mentioned you had invited us to visit your shop. I'm Misti Knutson, and this is my older sister, Wendy."

Sidney stifled the thought that popped into her head at the words, *older sister*, knowing that if the term spinster could be applied to this pretty twenty-one-year-old, the word most certainly applied to herself at twenty-four.

Lily came around her working counter. "I most certainly did! I wasn't expecting to see you so soon. Please come in and—"

In came the other three girls Sidney remembered, followed by an older, darker-skinned woman. *The nanny.*

"Welcome, everyone," Lily said, waving them all into the confined space. "This is a nice treat at the end of the day." She sent Sidney a meaningful look that said to forget about the thread. She'd need her help here.

"That's her," Rainey whispered behind her hand to the nanny.

The words were just loud enough for Sidney to hear. The little hoyden was even so bold as to send her a smile. The girl's inquisitive gaze traveled the walls, taking in everything in her path, landing on the beautiful piece of button art at the end of the cutting table.

"Hello again," Sidney said to Sunny and Breezy, reaching for a degree of politeness. She was still put off by the earlier encounter.

She nodded at Rainey, but before she could greet her as well, the door burst open, smacking loudly against the wall. The Knutson flock, including the nanny, screamed at the top of their lungs and rushed forward in an effort to get out of the way of the intruder, almost knocking Sidney over. Her back caught the corner of the cutting table and jabbed painfully. She gasped.

The giant of a man who'd been sitting inebriated on the black iron bench her first day in town—and the same man Dustin had pointed out coming out of the back door of the saloon—stood in the doorway, his eyes blazing like the hot sun.

After a stunned moment of silence, Lily straightened to her full height. "Billy Burger, get out of this shop this instant!" she commanded with a stiff finger pointing toward the door. "Turn around and march out! I won't stand for any of your shenanigans!"

"Francine," he said with a snarl, "I told ya I wasn't putting up with yer nonsense and highfalutin' ways any longer! You're my wife! What I say goes!"

Spittle sprayed and hit Lily in the face, which she quickly wiped away. Before anyone knew what he was about, he snatched up Mrs. Tuttle's blue velvet dress from the cutting counter, and tore out the long seam down one side.

"Now you'll learn a lesson you'll not soon forget! No woman crosses Billy Burger! Not even you, Francine!"

Rainey, along with two of her sisters and the wide-eyed nanny, crouched in the dressing room, crying uncontrollably. The two older Knutson girls, Wendy and Misti, had flattened themselves as best they could between the bolts of Lily's handmade lace, as if trying to disappear.

His powerful arms stretched apart again in a fast movement, splitting the fabric down the middle of the bodice. The drunkard was strong, and the garment was ruined.

The hours Sidney had spent carefully stitching that dress had her seeing red. She took a step toward him, drawing his attention for the first time.

Without a thought for her safety, she pulled back and punched Billy Burger in the side with everything she had. She was a rancher. She roped and branded. She could hogtie with the best of them. But to her disappointment, he hardly flinched.

"Get out!" she screamed in his face. "Get out of here before I *really* get mad."

He brought up his elbow and caught her shoulder. Pain vibrated through her body.

Until that moment, Lily had stood in shocked silence, staring at the ruined pieces of what used to be Mrs. Tuttle's beautiful gown. Sidney reeled back in shock and agony, and Lily's eyes went wide.

"I'm taking you home, Francine. You wounded me when you ran away. You can't best Billy Burger! *I do'* means until death do us part!"

Texas Lonesome 263

He reached for Lily with a huge pan-sized hand.

Lily screeched and shrank back, knocking Ingrid to the floor in a soft thud. The dress form rolled on its side. One of the dowels slid out of the sleeve, tripping Lily and causing all the girls to scream as she scrambled to stay on her feet. But Billy's tight hold kept her upright. Her eyes widened, as if she just now understood the danger of the situation they were in.

Sidney reached for her gun out of habit, but then realized she hadn't worn the weapon since arriving in Rio Wells. She felt helpless. Her punch to his side had been no more than a mosquito bite, a mere annoyance.

I need a gun! That's the only way to stop him before he hurts Lily!

With a powerful sweep of his bulky arm, he sent the bolts of lace over Wendy and Misti's heads across the room, bouncing off the opposite wall.

Sidney never could abide a bully. He was enjoying his tirade way too much as he destroyed the place. She ducked behind him, bolted into the kitchen, and pulled open the small drawer on the side counter where Lily kept her utensils. She'd seen the gun the day she'd set the table. John probably kept the weapon there in case Lily needed protection in a hurry.

Well, today she did! Surely, being a McCutcheon weapon, the chambers would be loaded.

She whipped out the Colt, loving its weighty feel in her hand. Turning, she ran back into the main room, aimed, and fired without a second thought, sending a bullet straight through Billy Burger's shiny black boot.

The giant howled in pain.

Firing again, she repeated the process to his other foot.

Baying like the animal he was, he released his grip on Lily, who he'd dragged halfway to the door. Dropping to one knee, he looked at his feet as he struggled to figure out what just happened.

Blood welled from the two perfectly round holes in the top of his boots, and then ran down the sides.

Chapter Thirty-Nine

Dustin rode quietly down Dry Street, wondering what he'd say to Sidney to break through her obstinacy. Just past the livery, he encountered John, Tucker, and Noah, dragging themselves up Spring Street in his direction, exhaustion etched on each face. Noah led his horse while Jackson, Sidney's dog, walked at his heels.

Dustin waited until they were close and pushed up his hat, surveying them from the back of his horse. "Looks like I'm not the only one who's put in a long day."

"Got the floor laid and workstations built," John offered. His clothes were covered in grime, and Noah and Tucker didn't look much better.

John removed his hat and swiped a forearm across his brow. "Tomorrow we'll give the place a good scrubbing, make sure everything is in order, and then begin gathering a supply of plants."

Dustin sat back and got comfortable. He'd walked his mount the whole way here from the ranch, deep in thought, thinking of Sidney and what Diaz Sanchez had shared.

"That's progress." *Why can't my problems be of the non-female kind?*

Suddenly a loud screech brought around all four heads. Two seconds later, a gunshot rang out, followed by another.

"What—?" Dustin bit out, gauging that the disturbance was happening in Lily's shop.

John took off at a run, followed by Noah and Tucker. A touch of spur had Dustin's mount galloping in the shop's direction. He passed the others and was down the block in an instant. After sliding to a stop, he vaulted from the saddle and ran inside, gun drawn.

Gunpowder burned his eyes as he took in the shambles that was once Lily's shop. Fabric was strewn about, and spools of lace were everywhere. A passel of females huddled in the open dressing room, clinging to each other as they sobbed and cried, tears streaming down their cheeks. Two others, who certainly fit the Knutson brand, stood ashen faced, staring at Billy Burger and the puddle of blood growing around his feet.

Gurgling gasps pushed through the drunkard's lips as he hunched forward on the floor, pressing both hands to the top of his boots.

Lily stood close by, shaking violently, and Sidney—standing tall like a warrior princess, head up and shoulders back—held a .45 Colt in her hand. The triumphant look in her eyes rendered Dustin speechless.

Their gazes met and held as John, Noah, and Tucker crashed through the door, followed by Bixby and Cradle Hupton. There wasn't room for one more body in the shop.

"Lily!" John shouted, a madman until he spotted her. He pulled her into his embrace, holding her firmly to his chest.

"Help me, Doc! I'm gonna bleed ta death if ya don't do somethin'!"

Sidney took a small step forward. "It would serve you right, you ugly horned lizard. Do you know how many hours I spent on that dress?" She pointed at Billy with the barrel of the gun. "He came busting in here and started destroying things," she told the men. "I didn't shoot him until he manhandled Lily. He's lucky I didn't blow his head clean off."

A clamoring sounded on the boardwalk. More people tried to push in the door.

A middle-aged woman gasped. "Girls! Oh, my girls. My perfect princesses could have been killed in this hot, heathen town. Devils everywhere!"

Billy looked up at her as she took a step back, her hand pressed to her throat.

"Francine?"

Chapter Forty

In the wee hours of the morning, Dustin lay on his back staring at the ceiling of his bedroom. The temperature was warm for a November night, and he couldn't sleep. Sounds of the night filtered in the open window across the room, and thoughts of the dustup with Billy Burger yesterday kept taunting him. Someone could have been killed.

He had decisions to make. Sitting up, he swung his legs over the side of the bed, the sheet falling down around his hips. He rubbed a hand across his chest.

Only one thing left to do. He'd been weighing the pros and cons for the past two hours. Lighting the candle on his bedside table, he pulled on a pair of pants, picked up the candle, and crossed quietly to the door on bare feet.

Being careful not to make any noise, he turned the doorknob and slowly pulled open the door. The deserted hall loomed back at him, as if he were doing something wrong. The clock in the entry chimed three times.

At his father's office, he entered and then quietly closed the double doors behind him, making sure they didn't click.

Indecision kept him rooted to the spot. He could be opening a can of worms he might be sorry for later. And yet, he had to try. The sight of Sidney in Lily's shop had removed all doubt. He had to do something to clear their family's name, at least in her mind. The answer might lay hidden here.

Going to the shelf on the back wall, Dustin held the candle close to the spines of the ledgers. The most recent was 1875 to current. He passed that by and reached for 1860–1875. He set the archive flat on the desk and quietly lowered himself into his father's chair.

Dustin opened to the middle pages. His best guess was the incident happened in 1866, twenty years ago. If the brothers Diaz had alluded to weren't mentioned here, then he'd have to search earlier. The first column held the names of the ranch hands who had worked for the Rim Rock then—Alex Peabody, Drag Bag, Lester Marshal, Oren Newell—not near as many as there were today.

January, February, and March were the same. But in April, Drag Bag was gone. None of the names rang any bells.

He flipped several pages back to January of 1865. Same names minus Oren Newell, plus Henry Baker.

Nothing.

He flipped several more pages back to 1864, his father's penmanship totally recognizable, and traced his finger slowly down the column. More of the same, but—

His heart tripped. Law Harris and Shorty Harris, the brothers Diaz had mentioned. The old man had a suspicion but no proof, nothing solid to go on. That was for Dustin to find— if he could locate the brothers. He flipped back three years, seeing their names.

The office door opened. His pa stood in the doorway, a lantern in his hand. Exactly what Dustin had feared.

"Dustin." His tone said he knew exactly what his oldest son was up to. "Find what you're looking for?"

Dustin closed the ledger and stood. He had no idea how to answer.

Had Law and Shorty Harris had something to do with the ambush of Jock Calhoun? Had his father buried the truth for all these years?

No! He'd never believe that. Another reason had to exist for the distrust he saw illuminated in his father's eyes by the lamp he held.

Turning, Dustin replaced the two books he'd taken down and started for the door.

"Couldn't sleep."

The lame words were out of his mouth before he could stop them. He wasn't ready to share with his father what he was doing. The man might misconstrue Dustin's intent. Best to keep quiet.

Chapter Forty-One

The day after her shop had been destroyed, dismay filled Lily's chest as she gazed around the room. The area was straightened and put to rights, but the lingering residue of gunpowder in the air kept her nerves on edge.

Boon . . . jail break . . . jewel. A shiver crawled up her spine.

"What's wrong, honey?" John came through the back door, carrying the trash can. "I saw you shiver."

She wrapped her arms around her waist. "The scent of gunpowder on the air reminds me of Lecter Boon. The night my aunt killed him."

"And it's a good thing she did." He placed his hands on her shoulders and massaged. "Don't think about that. We'll get through this, just like we did then."

When her gaze moved to the bloodstained floor just inside the front door, he squeezed her shoulder. "I'll get rid of that if I have to pry out the boards and add new."

The door opened and Dustin came inside, hat in hand. He looked around, his expression mirroring how they felt.

"I told Lily you'd help me remove the bloodstains, even if we have to replace the floor."

Dustin nodded. "Absolutely. Don't you worry about that, Lily. How's the patient?" he asked, directing his attention from the floor to John. "Still locked up?"

"You bet. He's stretched out on a cell cot, wallowing in his pain. One bullet went clean through the boot and his foot, and the other I had to dig out. A month will pass before he's putting on any boots. He was so inebriated I didn't have to sedate him, but now that he's sobering up, he's none too pleased. From time to time, we hear him hollering."

"Sorry about this, Lily," Dustin said, sweeping a hand toward the room. "I hate to see such damage come to your shop."

She lifted a shoulder, tamping back a desire to let her tears flow one more time. The thought of Mrs. Tuttle's beautiful velvet dress torn to shreds was nauseating her. The woman lived out of town and hadn't yet heard what had transpired.

"Thank you, Dustin," she said. "We appreciate your concern. Even though Billy Burger deserves whatever he gets—and thank God, Sidney knows how to use a gun—I do feel a little bad for him. He's such a nice man when he's sober. Mrs. Knutson is pressing charges for 'almost' hurting her daughters and scarring them emotionally."

He gazed around. "Need my help?"

"Thanks, but Sidney was here for the past two hours. Everything is pretty much done, except for the bloodstain on the floor. Martha is lending me a small rug until we decide what to do. As you can see, I'm closed for the day. One Saturday won't hurt."

At the mention of Sidney, Dustin had straightened. Lily had the feeling that perhaps he'd come looking for her, as well as checking on the shop. Yesterday, they'd hardly kept their gazes off each other, but in the uproar, nobody had noticed except herself.

"You can find her walking around town. I think she was going down by the school."

Dustin left his horse tied in front of Lily's and walked down to the schoolhouse, where Sidney sat on a log in the playground. Not much there besides two rope swings attached to the branch of an old oak tree, and the dusty diamond-shaped path in the barren field. Her back was to him as she gazed over the terrain, as well as the road that led to the Rim Rock.

Is she thinking about Noah? Is she missing me?

He wondered if she'd seen him ride into town ten minutes ago. She seemed to be mesmerized by a handful of small wild goats climbing around a rock formation out behind the schoolyard a hundred yards away.

The crunch of his boots on the dirt drew Sidney's attention. When she turned, he smiled.

"Did you see me ride in? I came right by here."

She nodded. "I did."

So she wasn't as eager to see him as he was to see her. He'd probably scared her off by his declaration alongside the Knutsons' barn. Not to mention the kiss. Disappointment pressed his shoulders.

"Noah's fine, in case you're wondering. I'm trusting him with Manolito today. Gave me his word he'd behave."

"And your men?"

"Most have come around. No one wants to lose the good job they have at the Rim Rock."

She heaved a sigh. "Poor Lily," she said. "I feel so bad about yesterday. For an instant, I feared that brute would kill her." She turned back to the goats.

He wondered what she would do if he picked up her hand and held it in his. Rejecting the idea, he sat beside her.

"I'm thankful you were there, Sidney. John, me . . . we all are." He shook his head as dread climbed up his spine. "Billy Burger could have easily killed Lily with one hand."

"I'm thankful as well."

She sounded strange, almost a bit angry. He couldn't fathom why.

"Lily isn't the only one I was relieved about."

She glanced into his face, a deep V drawing her brows together. Her eyes held a myriad of questions deep within.

"I'm awfully glad you weren't hurt either. Can't tell you how long that thought kept me awake last night."

She didn't respond to his statement.

Was he pushing her too hard? He couldn't help his feelings.

A handful of brown wrens caught her eye, and she followed their progress across the sky.

"Sidney, I learned something a few days ago. Went digging for information about the feud. Well, more pointedly, the attack."

She turned and held his gaze. Color came up in her face. "You think your pa was involved? Like I've been saying all along."

"No." He shook his head. "But I'd like to prove to you that he wasn't. You're loyal to your family, and I'd like—"

"And you're not?" she responded quickly.

Her tone wasn't angry, just tired. Beaten down.

When he placed a gentling hand on her arm, she didn't pull away. They were making progress.

"I am loyal to my family, of course. Just as strongly as you are to yours. That's why I'm doing what I'm doing. This wrongful accusation has gone on long enough. Ride with me over to Draper Bottom. The area is safe, and won't take but a couple of hours. I have a lead I'd like to check out."

She just stared at him, thinking.

"And then again, the clue might just be a dead end. A wild goose chase." He shrugged and smiled. "Don't know about you, but I could use a wild goose chase about now."

"Just you and me?"

He turned his body so he had a better view of her face. "I don't want what I'm doing to get back to my father. He already thinks . . ." *I'm a turncoat. Best to keep that thought to myself.* "That I'm spinning my wheels. I'd rather keep this between you and me. The fewer people who know, the better."

"Riding out together without a chaperone?" she said hesitantly. "Those Knutson girls are everywhere, and they spread gossip faster than bunnies multiply. I don't know."

"When did you ever worry about propriety?"

A ghost of a smile pulled her lips. "Pretty much never."

"That's what I thought. Still, best if we meet just past the split in the road where a large deserted barn sits. Again, the barn is close enough to be safe."

"That's what you said before the outlaws attacked."

He chuckled. "You got me there, Calhoun. I can watch your approach, keep you safe."

Her brows tented as she mulled that thought. "Where am I supposed to get a horse?"

"Don't you worry about that."

"I'm not riding behind you!"

He chuckled again, bumped up his hat, and rubbed his forehead. "Didn't say you were. I'll get you a mount from the livery."

"How'll you explain needing an extra horse?"

"Holy smokes, Calhoun, you ask a lot of questions." He smacked his hands down on his thighs. "I don't know. I'll think of something. Most people don't give me the third degree like you do."

She nodded. "Fine then. One last thing. Where'd you get this information? And why didn't anyone go looking before this?"

"An old ranch hand who's living out his days in a small cabin on the ranch. I trust him. He's a good man. And why not before? I don't really know. That's a very good question." *And one I hope doesn't come back to haunt me.*

She studied the goats scrabbling amongst the rocks.

"Will you be missed?" he asked.

With a sigh, she turned and searched his face. "By who?"

The bareness of her voice gave him pause. Was she sad? Hungry? Was she loved at all at home? He couldn't do anything about the last question yet, but the other two he'd take care of on the ride to Draper Bottom.

"All right. Give me time to change into my riding clothes," she said. "Say, half an hour?"

He smiled inwardly. "Make that forty-five minutes. I have a few details to attend to, and I want to be there first." He stood and reached for her hand, pulling her to her feet.

The next few hours would prove very interesting.

Chapter Forty-Two

Sidney wondered if she'd lost hold of her senses. Crossing the hotel lobby in her riding clothes, hat in hand and her gun strapped to her thigh, she caught a curious glace from the clerk, but he said nothing.

She wasn't quite so lucky with the restaurant cook she'd become quite friendly with over the past twelve days. The man stepped in the door as she was about to step out. His gray bushy brows shot up in question.

Should have used the back exit.

"Miss Calhoun?" he said as he warily eyed her weapon. His knowing look said he'd gotten an earful of how she'd shot bullets straight through Billy Burger's feet without hesitation.

The man's heart was as large as his belly. Once he realized she was a long-term guest subsisting on a few coins a day, he'd acted. Each night she found a napkin with leftover biscuits tied to her doorknob. Their being a little dry hadn't bothered her a bit.

"Don't worry, Bernard," she replied with a kind smile. "I don't shoot my friends."

Why not give Rio Wells more to talk about? They already thought the worst. Her name was Calhoun, she been caught by Miss Tattletale kissing Dustin *beside* the barn, and now this escapade didn't leave much room that she wasn't much of a lady. But what would her reputation matter once she returned to Santa Fe?

"I didn't think you would; you just surprised me is all. I've never seen you gussied up like . . ." He waved his hand around, indicating the picture she created.

"A cowboy?"

"Never that," he replied, shocked. "But I'd say a cow*girl*. You're not in any trouble, are you?"

Wanting to avoid a lie, she shook her head. "I've been cooped up inside for several days when I'm used to being outside."

"Ah," he said, nodding. "You be sure to stay close."

Well, she wouldn't be staying close, but she'd be with Dustin. She wondered which was more dangerous, considering how much she'd enjoyed the feel of his lips on hers.

Some minutes later, she approached the large barn Dustin had mentioned, and was fifty feet away when he walked out from behind the dilapidated building, leading two horses.

"I was getting worried."

"Just keeping you on your toes, McCutcheon," she replied playfully.

His chuckle brought a spurt of warmth to her face. She was playing with fire and she knew it, but her actions were impossible to stop. Dustin got her, understood her without her needing to explain a thing. His appeal was something she couldn't explain, and she admired him all the more. Her attraction to him was greater and more real than the expanse of blueness above her head.

He handed her the reins to a quiet palomino mare and didn't assist with her mounting, which she appreciated. She slid a foot into her stirrup, reached for a handful of the mare's golden mane, and swung aboard, the familiar feel of the saddle welcome. Once she was settled, she watched him mount his own horse, the one she recognized all too well from their ride from San Antonio.

"You sure about this?" he asked. "You're being awfully quiet. I don't want to coerce you into doing something you'd rather not."

If he only knew. After that short-but-sweet kiss, he could coerce her into most anything he wanted.

"Seems you don't like my quiet, and you don't like my questions."

He barked out a laugh. "Point taken, Calhoun. I'll try and refrain from evaluating your moods." He gave her the crooked smile she'd already begun to look for.

She turned her horse and headed down the road. "I appreciate that. I'd say you've become overly interested in my comings and goings."

"My pa thinks the same."

Sidney shot him a look. She'd been kidding, but she could see he was dead serious.

Never could she remember being so aware of a man in all her life. His eyes, his mouth, the way he held himself in the saddle. The reality of why almost made her gasp. She wasn't the only one wondering about family, and this growing attraction between them.

The midmorning sun felt pleasant on Dustin's shoulders as they walked along the well-worn wagon tracks in relative silence. They'd taken the right fork past the barn, the one that led first to Draper Bottom, and from there would continue over the long stretch of uninhabited prairie and finally arrive at San Antonio.

The small settlement where they were headed had sprouted up years ago, started by the Draper family, even before Rio Wells was founded. Draper—along with his wife, ten children, and a few hands—had been stranded when the wagon carrying their supplies broke an axle.

Well stocked, they just put up a few shacks and began living off the land, as well as mining in a medium-sized tributary off the Guadalupe River, the same waterway that cut through McCutcheon land and provided water for their cattle. Soon other settlers came along and joined them.

Heard tell, old man Draper was a hell of a salesman. He'd have to be to get others to stay on and help build the place on the very edge of the prairie, with roving bands of Comancheros and Indians. Sidney didn't know it, but they'd been traversing McCutcheon land for the last few miles. Most likely would rile her if she knew.

"'Bout the prettiest land God created," he said, gazing out across a sea of brown grass. Texas was in his blood. He'd never be happy anywhere else.

From the corner of his eye, he caught her nodding.

"Sure is. Much different from our place in Santa Fe. Our ranch is greener. Cooler." She glanced at the sun. "Higher in the mountains."

"You're a Texan."

She tossed him a look.

"Born here, weren't ya?"

She nodded.

"Well, that makes you a Texan, even if your family moved out. Can't change the facts. Once a Texan, always a Texan."

Now a good distance from Rio Wells, Dustin reached back in his saddlebag and pulled out the loaf of wrapped bread he'd procured from the Cheddar Box Café, as well as a wax-paper-wrapped package of thinly sliced beef.

Her eyes widened.

He felt guilty, softening her with food. "When we're finished with this, I have dessert." He lifted out a can of peaches he'd bought at the mercantile. He'd also brought two canteens, one filled with water and another with apple cider, all things he'd rounded up as Sidney had been changing her clothes.

The food went down easily as they rode, and much quicker than he'd expected. She wasn't shy. More than eating the food himself, he enjoyed watching her indulge. She'd relaxed, softened. Her laughter had a way of making him smile.

He handed over the canteen of water and she took several long pulls, wiping away a few drops from her chin with the back of her wrist. He liked that she wasn't all stuffy and caught up with being so proper that one had to walk on eggshells around her.

"McCutcheon?"

He'd caught sight of a deer, and watched it dart away before he looked over. She had the canteen held out to him. The sun brought a sheen to her face, and wisps of hair pulled free of the restraint that kept her hair pulled back on her neck.

"You keep it. I've another here." He uncapped the lid to the apple cider, took a drink, and smacked his lips.

Her gaze searched his. "Beer?"

He chuckled innocently. "No. But I like the way you think. Cider. Would you like a taste?"

She stared at him and then at the canteen.

He'd sipped first on purpose. Wanted her to consider the possibilities. Get her thinking in the right direction. *I should be ashamed, but I'm not.*

"Don't mind if I do."

Good girl.

He laughed, sat back in his saddle, and handed her the canteen. He'd steered the conversation to her childhood, but she'd artfully diverted the questions back onto him. He was sure she held many hurts inside. But the food had mellowed her mood and she was being generous with her smiles, and for now, that was all Dustin cared about.

When all the food was gone, he filled her in about Diaz Sanchez, and that the old Mexican remembered two brothers from the time around the attack on her father, but not their specific names. Diaz had always wondered why one of them quit when word got around about what happened to Calhoun.

The lead wasn't much to go on, but something was better than nothing. If Dustin was to have a future with Sidney, he needed to clear his family's name, one way or another.

Chapter Forty-Three

When they reached Draper Bottom, Dustin pulled his mount to a halt in front of a run-down box of a mercantile. They'd passed two saloons, the only places in town that were doing any type of business.

"I'll ask inside. See what they know. The settlement doesn't have a sheriff or a mayor, or just about anything." He flipped his reins over the hitching rail. "You coming?"

Sidney dismounted. "Of course."

An old man was slouched in a chair behind the counter.

Dustin picked up a package of tobacco. He wasn't a fan, but someone in the bunkhouse would be interested. Better to make friends by making a purchase before he asked for information. Sidney stood quietly at his side, the immensity of the moment written on her face. The good name of one of their fathers was on the line, and might be proven wrong or right. He was confident the outcome would go his way.

Dustin gently cleared his throat.

The old man snorted loudly and then sucked in a deep breath. A moment later, his eyes opened and his chin lifted. He focused.

"Well, howdy," he said, slowly coming to his feet. "Didn't 'hear ya come in, young man. What can I do ya for?" A gap-toothed grin was directed at Sidney. "And you, ma'am."

With a finger, Dustin pushed forward the pouch of tobacco.

"Oh, sure. That'll be a nickel."

"Thank you," Dustin replied. He pulled out the coin and placed the money on the counter.

"Say, don't I know you?" the old man asked as he narrowed his gaze.

"You might." Dustin chuckled. "The name's McCutcheon, over from Rio Wells. This is Sidney Calhoun."

"That's right," he replied slowly, still looking Dustin over. "I've seen you around here a time or two. Welcome to Draper Bottom. We're a quiet little place, nothin' like Rio Wells, I'd imagine. Ain't never been there myself."

Dustin lifted the tobacco and pushed it into his front pocket. Leaning on the counter, he looked around and said, "I was wondering if you might know a fella by the name of Law or Shorty Harris? Might be between forty and fifty years old. I'm not sure."

The clerk scratched his chin. After a few moments, he shook his head. "Can't say as I do. Neither of those names rings any bells. Sorry. There're a lot of bleached bones between here and San Antonio. Maybe those fellas ya named are some of 'em."

"Could be," Dustin replied. He turned and looked around the store. "But I hope not. Newson around?"

"Oh, sure." The man's scratchy voice perked up. "Just walk anywhere down the street, and you'll find him somewhere. And if that don't work, go around to his icehouse. He ain't hard ta find."

"We'll do that. Thanks"—he patted the pocket over his chest—"for the smokes."

Sidney turned and walked with him out onto the porch.

When she sighed, he said, "We've only just begun. I hope you're not giving up yet."

"Do you really think after twenty years someone will remember something, something that would either condemn or clear your father?"

He studied her downturned mouth. "Yes, I do."

"You're a better man than me, McCutcheon."

"I hope so, Calhoun. I seriously do." He nudged her with his shoulder and smiled. "Let's go find Newson."

After walking the streets, and no one admitting knowing the Harris brothers, Dustin and Sidney veered toward Newson's icehouse, the place that had recently held the outlaws captive until the marshal could arrive.

"McCutcheon, you back again so soon?"

He turned to see Newson hurrying their way.

"That's him," Dustin said under his breath. "I hope he can shed a little light."

After introductions and a few words of greeting, Dustin got down to business, but the man only shook his head. Refusing to be discouraged, Dustin thanked him and moved on.

"What now?" Sidney asked.

"We'll go see another acquaintance of mine. Alistair Fry. Owns the forge and livery." He pointed down a side street. "It's just down this way."

A sweaty-faced Alistair looked up when they walked into the small, exceptionally hot shed. "Dustin!

"I know, I know," Dustin said, grasping the man's beefy hand. "I just couldn't stay away."

"Guess not. Only been a few days since you were last here."
He took his time looking Sidney over until she raised her chin.
"You'll be happy to know I got good news."

Alistair grasped Dustin's arm and led him into the adjoining
stable. Dustin glanced at Sidney and shrugged.

Sidney stopped in her tracks. "My horse!"

"You betcha," he proudly said. "Came in looking for water
yesterday morn. Couldn't get to my trough in my back pasture,
so he stood at the fence just waiting for someone to see him."
He wagged his brows at Dustin. "Been on the lookout for him
since you mentioned it, Dustin. With the outlaws and
Comancheros, it's pretty amazing that he's here at all. And it's
especially astonishing your money and possessions are still
inside."

Sidney gasped. "I can't believe this."

Alistair unlocked a large wooden cabinet and swung the
door wide, hefting out Sidney's saddlebags, and then handed
them over.

Dustin thought she would cry. She hugged the leather to her
chest, and a grateful smile blossomed on her face.

"Thank you. Thank you so much!" At first, her words were
directed at Alistair, but soon her attention slipped over to
Dustin.

Her eyes softened as she reached out and touched his arm,
the first contact she'd ever willingly given him. His chest filled
with warmth.

"I didn't do anything."

"You did. You asked Mr. Fry to be on the lookout," she
added with a smile. "That was very thoughtful."

She knelt, set the bags on the ground, and pulled out a large
object from one side. "The music box for Carmen's birthday. I
thought I'd lost it." She pointed to a delicate outline of a bird

inlaid in the memento's lid. "She loves birds and music. I thought it the perfect gift."

Carmen? Another mystery. "Your purchase in the San Antonio mercantile?"

Her face colored with emotion, she nodded. This was a side of Sidney he'd never seen.

In one fluid movement, she stood and wrapped her arms around the livery owner, making him sputter in surprise.

"No need for this, young lady. I'm happy to do whatever I can for my good friend Dustin McCutcheon. He looks out for me as well."

Dustin was warmed by his friend's fine declaration.

"I was getting ready to ride over to Rio Wells and deliver the horse and rig myself. Now I don't have to." He gave a toothy grin. "It's a good day."

That it was. And maybe a good time to see what he knew, if anything, about the Harris brothers.

When Dustin put his arm over Sidney's shoulder, he noticed she didn't pull away. "Let's go back out into the sunshine so we can talk."

"Sure," Alistair said, stepping out the door and into the noontime light. "How long ya staying?" he asked, looking at him and then eyeing Sidney.

He's just realized we rode out here alone.

"Not long," Dustin replied. "We're looking for information—*old* information. As soon as we ask around, we'll be heading back."

"What are you waiting on? Spit it out."

Sidney was hanging on his every word, her saddlebags clutched in her arms. Her changed attitude struck him, and he couldn't even imagine her tough outer facade any longer. The softness was back in her eyes, and he wanted to wrap her in his arms and never let anything in the world hurt her.

"We're looking for two brothers with the last name of Harris. They worked at the ranch some twenty years ago."

Fry planted his hands on his hips. "You think they're here in Draper Bottom?"

"Don't know. It'd be a stretch, but I heard their family once lived somewhere around here. Law or Shorty. Either one."

"Law or Shorty Harris?" the blacksmith mumbled.

Someone called out from down the street and he waved, distracted for only a moment.

"Sorry, Dustin, but I've never heard of either one. You know I pretty much know everyone, down to the town drunk that lives out back of the saloons and steals whiskey whenever the opportunity presents itself." He shook his head.

Disappointment crashed down on Dustin's shoulders. Was uncovering the facts so old, so hurtful, even possible? He wanted to be the one to unearth the truth for his father's sake, as well as for him and Sidney. The only thing that kept his spirits buoyed was knowing they still had a couple of hours together on the ride home.

"We best be going. Don't want to get her back too late. First, though, I need to ask around in both the saloons. Maybe someone there knows something."

Alistair nodded. "I'll get Miss Calhoun's horse saddled up."

Sidney extracted several dollars from inside. "Please take this reward, Mr. Fry. I never thought I'd see my things again." She touched the side of the bag. "Or my dress."

"Put away your money." He gave her a stern look. "I insist."

"That's very kind. While you're in the saloons, I'll go up and down and ask in the shops," Sidney said, turning to Dustin.

"That won't take you long." With a large hand, Alistair shaded his eyes and shook his head sadly. "Aren't but two other businesses besides the mercantile and saloons. And one of 'em's mine."

"Fine," Dustin replied, holding in his frustration. "I'll meet you back here."

Somewhere, somehow, he needed a lead on the Harris brothers if he wanted to clear the way for him and Sidney. Problem was, there wasn't a lead to be found.

Chapter Forty-Four

On the trail back to Rio Wells, Sidney rode the palomino mare and led the gelding she'd never expected to see again.

"Isn't life curious?" she asked, thinking of the money that had been restored, her dress, and Carmen's birthday present. She felt as if circumstances were looking up, even if they hadn't found any new evidence.

"I ponder that every day, Calhoun."

In a crinkling of dry wings, a grasshopper landed on Dustin's left shoulder. He looked down at the caramel-colored insect, his crooked grin appearing.

"Hey, little fella. You comin' along for the ride?"

She sucked in a breath.

He looked her way. "What's wrong? I wouldn't expect you to be squeamish around bugs."

"I'm not. Carmen says if a grasshopper lands on your left shoulder, you can expect misfortune. Brush it *off*, Dustin!"

She couldn't keep her voice from shaking when she said his name. Misfortune? What more could happen to Dustin? He'd been saddled with her brother, and now her. The last thing she wanted was to make his life more dangerous than it already was.

"Are you superstitious?" he asked, his grin broadening. He still hadn't removed the creature from his shoulder, which he playfully lifted. "And who is Carmen anyway? You mentioned her earlier when your music box was recovered."

When the grasshopper turned and stared Sidney straight in the face, she raised her hand to block the look. She didn't care that humor now shone in Dustin's eyes.

"At first she was only our housekeeper, but when my mother passed away giving birth to Noah, she stepped in to help, being a surrogate to me and my brothers. She's been with us all these years."

"I'm sorry," he said quietly. "Losing your mama so young must have been very difficult for you, the only daughter."

His tone sent a bevy of pleasant shivers up her neck. "At times."

"What was she like?"

Sidney swallowed down a lump of sorrow and lowered her hand. "Affectionate." She glanced over to him, holding his gaze. "And supportive." *All the things Pa's not.* "I just wish I could have had her a little longer."

He nodded as if he understood her feelings, but she didn't think that possible. Not in the mood to talk about herself, she gestured to the "little fella" still riding along. She wished he'd bat the creepy bug off.

"Carmen's superstitious. Has a saying for almost every situation under the sun."

"Don't worry about him." Seemed the grasshopper was determined to ride all the way back to Rio Wells. "He's just looking for something green to eat. Doesn't want to cause any harm—or make bad luck."

Embarrassed for creating such a commotion over a belief that seemed silly to him, she said, "You gave Lily a four-leaf clover for good luck on her first day in the shop. What's that, if not a bit superstitious?"

His face actually colored up.

She laughed. "Ah, that's different, right? Got you on that one, McCutcheon. What's your explanation?"

"I just wanted to give her something to . . ." His sentence faded away.

"Remember you by? Every time the gift caught her eye, she'd think of you? Maybe recall the words you'd shared." She turned toward him in the saddle. "Let's talk about that for a while. Was there a war between cousins for her affections?"

He kept his gaze trained straight ahead.

She was glad she'd brought up Lily. In reality, she had wondered about the two.

"A war? No, I wouldn't say that. I'd say a very strenuous, semi-friendly competition. You see, when John first came to town, he was engaged to another woman, and so was off-limits. While traveling here, Lily had fallen in love with him, but she chose me by default because he was taken. I always felt her heart belonged to him, but I didn't want to believe such a travesty."

He laughed. "But when John and Emmeline broke off their engagement, John was free. Only a few days passed before the two got together."

Sidney gasped. "Emmeline? As in Chaim and Emmeline?"

He nodded. "That's another story altogether."

At that moment, the grasshopper took flight. The insect hopped toward Sidney, its crinkling tan wings clacking with a terrifying premonition.

She screeched and batted it away.

"Geez, Sidney, I thought you were kidding me about not liking the grasshopper."

"I wasn't." Feeling foolish, she wanted to change the subject as quick as possible. "When we get back today, I'd like to treat you to a fancy dinner in the Lillian Russell Room. The aromas have been taunting me since I checked into the hotel. Now that I have the funds, I'd like to take you as my guest. If you hadn't told Mr. Fry about my horse, and to be on the lookout, then I might never have had my money and belongings returned. I owe you."

She almost laughed at the stricken look on Dustin's face.

"I can't accept that! I would have taken you there myself days ago if I'd known you wanted to go. Hog-tied you if you refused, and then thrown you over my shoulder."

"I wouldn't have accepted, and you know it." She pulled back her shoulders and lifted her chin. "And I still won't, so you may as well save your breath. Taking your charity goes against everything I am, but that doesn't mean I can't treat *you*. Please, Dustin, it's the least I can do for all you've done for me, and Noah. Let me do this one little thing. If you don't, you'll force me to take supper by myself. Surely, one of the perfect Knutson girls would see me and have more to chatter about."

He edged his horse closer, reached over, and brushed a lock of hair out of her face.

"Nothin' doing. We go, and I pay. I won't hear another word. A McCutcheon would *never* allow a woman to pay the bill. As big as I am and as little as my mama is, she'd still have my hide."

So close, his moving lips caught her gaze, and she had to force herself to look away.

"I don't care," she said, a bit breathless. "If you can ruin my reputation by kissing me in front of three scaredy-cat Easterners—"

"Midwesterners, Sidney. Don't you know your geography? Wisconsin is practically—"

"Don't change the subject on me, *McCutcheon*. I know what you're up to."

He chuckled.

"Anyway—I was saying," she continued as if he hadn't interrupted, "since the kiss and the ruination of my character, you can at least allow me to invite you out and pay the bill. Shift a little of that shame over to you. Dustin McCutcheon being kept by a woman. Imagine that."

She laughed, enjoying the easy feel of the afternoon. "Women *are* getting some rights, you know. In Wyoming Territory, they've been voting since 1869. Someday New Mexico Territory and Texas will get the vote too. Women'll be just as equal as men."

"That'll be the day!"

The twinkle in his dark eyes brought more warm shivers, and a longing she wasn't able to ignore.

"Women have three places, and three places only. At least the woman I envision marrying someday . . ."

She reined her horse to a stop, and the gelding she was leading dutifully stumbled to a halt by her side. She sat there as Dustin continued on for a few more strides before stopping.

He looked back with his crooked smile.

"And *where* is that, pray tell? I can't imagine you brought up a topic like that unless you mean to tell me."

Without a word, he stepped off his horse in one fluid movement and stalked her way. His smile was gone, and the fire in his eyes set off a cascade of tingles everywhere.

In five strides, he was at her side. He circled her waist with both hands and lifted her from the saddle before lowering her to the ground, but kept her captured between him and her horse.

She'd never felt so small, so desired. One thing was on Dustin McCutcheon's mind, and she wished he'd hurry up and get to it. Heat rippled through her body, sending all kinds of longings that kindled a fire within.

His hands still on her waist, he drew her to him, never relinquishing her gaze.

"Do you really want to know, Calhoun? You may regret the answer I give." His question was almost lost on the breeze.

"I do." She swallowed, anticipating what was to come.

He gently removed her hat and set it on her saddle. "My wife's place will be ranching by my side, in my arms, and in my bed." He lowered his lips to hers, nudging her until her back was against the side of her horse.

The scent of warm hide mixed with Dustin's unique essence had her almost limp with want. Who knew his large hands could be so gentle? They circled behind her head and lightly slipped the band off her ponytail, releasing her hair. He tipped her head, gaining better access to her mouth as his fingers slid through her long mane.

"I've been dreaming of this for so long," he whispered against her mouth. "And this." He turned his head the other way, gathering her closer.

When she thought she might expire from the pleasure, she felt him kiss his way to her neck, as if staking his claim on her person. She strained upward, wanting more, causing her breath to gasp in an embarrassing gulp of air.

Tension crackled along her shoulders and down her back. Only one other man aside from her father and brothers had ever kissed her, and the act was nothing even remotely close to what she was doing now. Gibson Harp had stolen a kiss once in the back of his mercantile while he was showing her a new display of pans. His moist, plump lips had left her cold, and even a bit disgusted.

Dustin's firm, scratchy lips asked sweetly for more.

Unable to stop herself, she shamelessly pressed her body to his and slid her arms around his neck. At her encouragement, he pulled her closer still, until she was as near to his powerful body as she could get without divesting herself of her clothes. He left no doubt where his thoughts were headed.

"Dustin," she forced out through her heavy breathing. His hands were now trailing sensations up and down her sides in a dangerous seduction. "*Dustin*," she tried again. "This is crazy. We're playing with fire. We know this can't—"

"We know nothing!" he said, his tone cutting through her haze of desire. "It's our fathers' war, not ours."

Dustin took her face in both his hands, his forehead tipped against hers as he let his breathing slow. He gazed into her eyes so long, she felt light-headed.

"Sidney, I love you. God help me, I do. And if you'd let the past go for just one instant, you'd say the same to me. You're just scared. Frightened of your feelings and of your family, and what they'll think when you tell them you love Dustin McCutcheon. This is *our* life, Sidney, not theirs. That's what you have to remember."

As if not willing to stop just yet, he found her lips with his, silencing her words of caution.

He's right, she thought. *I don't want to live without Dustin. He's my heart and soul. My everything.*

"Say it, darlin'," he whispered. "Say it so I can hear your words. Say you love me too. Say you'll be mine forever."

Chapter Forty-Five

Standing at the edge of the watering pond in their northern pasture, Chaim gazed at the pool of water as the swirls of mud disappeared down the small set of rapids they'd just cleared. His pants were soaked up to his thighs.

"That didn't take as long as I expected," he said to Brick and Noah, who were already mounted and ready to head back to the ranch.

Chaim pulled on his jacket, his fingers moving over the buttons by rote, his thoughts lost in Boston. Emmeline. And the letter he'd yet to receive.

"He looks none too pleased," Brick said, gesturing to the far bank where a hefty beaver paced back and forth, distraught his home had been destroyed.

A pang of sympathy for the homely critter with the paddle-like tail ran through Chaim. Every few steps, the large beaver bared his long orange teeth in their direction—although he'd run off fast enough if one of the men stepped his way. The descending sun caused his wet, messy-looking fur to glisten temptingly. No wonder the animals had almost been hunted to extinction.

Chaim didn't have the volition to kill it, even though that was the only way to make sure he didn't rebuild.

"Couldn't be helped," he said mostly to himself, as if assuaging his own guilty conscience for the ruin of the dam and beaver hut that had dwindled the runoff to a trickle. "The water holes downstream should be back to normal in a few days. We'll have to keep an eye on him, though, to make sure he moves on and doesn't rebuild."

"Absolutely," Brick said. "Cattle don't take long to die of thirst."

With nothing left to do, Chaim walked to his horse and took his reins from Noah. If camping out could be accomplished without raising questions from his family, he'd pack up and spend time away. Facing another sleepless night within the four walls of his bedroom had him jittery. The space felt like a prison, a cell, not home, not a place where he was loved and where his destiny lay.

He couldn't do it. He'd have to think of a way to get out under the stars, where the fresh air could calm his racing heart. Where he wouldn't have Madeline and Becky asking about Emmeline every other minute, or his mother's gaze following him with concern. If not, he was sure his head would explode from the relentless dissecting of Emmeline's last few days on the ranch, and the facts she'd fed him before she'd walked out of his life for good.

You're jumping to conclusions! Just last month, Pa received a post that was over four months old. A letter may be on its way. Chaim hardened his heart against false hope. *She should have answered my telegram by now.*

"Ready, boss?"

Brick's quiet voice snapped Chaim out of his thoughts.

Embarrassed for mounting and then proceeding to sit there like a statue staring at the water, he reined around his horse.

"Sure," he said. "Let's get home."

Home. Would his home ever feel right again? He didn't think so, not unless his fears turned out to be just that, and Emmeline returned.

The sound of galloping hooves filtered into Dustin's awareness, but finally having Sidney in his arms, where she belonged, had his head light and mind spinning. He pulled her closer, loath to give up her sweet lips.

"I *do* love you, Dustin. As God as my witness, I tried not to. The harder I fought the feeling, the further I fell. My heart didn't believe a word I was saying."

He'd dreamed of this moment since the day he snatched her off the sandy loam of the badlands and she'd ridden so fiercely behind his saddle, shooting at the outlaws. They didn't come much braver than Sidney Calhoun. How could he convince her the hurdle their fathers had created was conquerable, if they stuck together? Alone, they couldn't do it, but together, anything was possible.

She stiffened in his arms. "Dustin!"

The alarm in her voice snapped him straight. Men's voices, horses snorting, and the sudden silence of their hoofbeats made him swing around and draw his gun, ready to kill anyone to defend his love.

"Don't shoot!" Chaim shouted from thirty feet away.

Brick Paulson rode beside him, but the look on Noah's face was stuck in Dustin's head. He holstered his gun, relieved Comancheros hadn't ventured too close to Rio Wells.

"What the hell!" Noah barked, riding forward. His angry gaze darted between him and his sister. "Is this how you look out for her, McCutcheon?" He glanced around. "You out here alone? What were your plans, to take her here right under the clear blue sky?"

For the most part, Noah had behaved, did what he was told, and kept his thoughts to himself. This was the most belligerent and nasty the lad had been since the scene at the showers.

Dustin stayed his impulse of pulling him off his horse, only because he knew Sidney's brother was partly right. He'd had an ulterior motive when he asked Sidney to ride out today.

Guilty as charged.

"Stop!" Sidney shouted. "Don't make trouble where there isn't any."

"Isn't any? I think Pa and the rest might argue *that* point a bit, don't you?" The angry question was thrown at her with vengeance.

She pulled her shoulders back and pointed at her brother. "I'm a grown woman. I can do as I please."

As much as Noah's commanding tone bothered him, Dustin didn't want to take this any further today. The prudent thing would be to mount up, and they'd all ride into town together. Address this when they were all cooler, and more willing to listen. The last thing he wanted was for Noah to sway Sidney away.

He took her elbow but she gently pulled away, her eyes sad.

Just a small setback, he told himself. *I won't let Noah derail my plans—our plans.*

They mounted and were in front of the hotel in a handful of minutes.

Dustin glanced at Chaim, who hadn't said a word since the initial *don't shoot*. "I'll walk Sidney up. You can ride on."

"I'm not leaving here without you, McCutcheon," Noah said in a low voice.

"Fine. Give me one minute."

Sidney dismounted, her movements slow.

"Don't worry about your horse," Dustin said calmly. "I'll take him by the livery when I return the mare."

He saw her nod, although she seemed to be lost in a thoughtful daze.

She looked once more at Noah, and then they quietly entered the hotel. Without a word, she got the key from the clerk, and they proceeded up the stairs.

She stopped in front of the door. "What happened was a—"

"Don't you dare say it was a mistake," Dustin warned, unwilling to let her backslide even a little.

With her hat in her hands, she leaned against the door.

Surely, she was mixed up. She still believed his pa had set up her father. He had to find a way to prove Winston's innocence.

"We'll get around this," he told her. "And the past."

She shook her head. "I don't see that happening, Dustin. As much as it hurts me to admit—"

"Would you stop, please. I'm not letting something small like a twenty-year feud stop me from marrying the woman I love."

Her eyes went wide. "My father's only alive by—"

"That's not true! You'll have to trust me until I can come up with proof. I know that's asking a lot, but will you at least try?"

She stood silent, her gaze on the floor.

"Sidney?"

When he saw her nod, he heaved a deep sigh.

"Thank you. Now," he whispered, wanting her complete attention, "we were a bit distracted back there before I got to the good part, so I'm going there now. You're the only woman for me, Sidney. The only one I want ranching at my side, in my arms, and in my—"

She stopped him with a palm over his heart.

He chuckled. "I *love* you. That's all that matters." He tipped her head, seeing everything he needed in her eyes, but he had to hear the words cross her lips again—so she'd have to come to terms with them herself. "I guess your feelings matter some too. Do you love me, Sidney? Would you consider being my wife?"

A sad look dulled her eyes. His admission apparently had her scared, plus his questions. He'd liked to have gone slower, courted her like the lady she was, but their situation didn't allow for that.

"Sidney?"

Had he read her wrong? Dreamed up the whole thing out of his wishful thinking?

"Yes, I love you. And the thought of becoming Mrs. Dustin McCutcheon is, well, the most wonderful thought in the world." She slowly shook her head. "But I can't see us working. Not even for a minute. Not with my pa and yours."

Relief flooded through him and he smiled. That was the only hurdle he couldn't have conquered—if she'd said no. For now, if he didn't head downstairs soon, he knew Noah would come looking. Still, he had things he needed to say before he left.

"I'm not scared," he said softly. "Not of your family, and not of mine. They'll just have to come to terms." He put his forehead to hers. "And I'm not afraid of you changing your mind. You're brave and strong. You know as well as I do that nothing worth having comes easy. There's a price to pay for everything on this earth."

Unable to resist, he pressed a kiss to her lips. "We'll weather this storm, and we'll come out all the stronger. You'll see. I'm telling my family tonight, if that's all right with you."

She just stared at him, a small smile playing at the corners of her mouth.

"Fine then, consider it done."

He took the key from her hand and unlocked her door, letting the barrier swing open. She stepped away and glanced back, and a lance of uncertainty sliced him through.

Would things really work out? He was not nearly as confident as the words he'd just proclaimed.

Chapter Forty-Six

Three hours later and dressed for supper, Dustin paced the length of the living room with a crystal tumbler in his hand, waiting for the rest of his family to arrive as he played over the events of the day. He'd break the news about the marriage and let them gentle into that thought.

He wouldn't say anything yet about searching for the Harris brothers. Or clearing the McCutcheon name. Those little gems he'd save for later, after his parents got used to the idea of having a Calhoun for a daughter-in-law.

"Dustin, you're here early," Winston said, striding into the room and moving to the sideboard where bottles of various brands of expensive bourbon and whiskey sat on a silver-plated tray. He poured himself a glass and took a swig. Being today was Saturday, his father had taken the extra time to comb his hair and change his workpants. On workdays, that didn't always happen.

Dustin swallowed. He'd had big words for Sidney earlier today, but now he dreaded the thought of breaking his father's heart.

A long-suffering sigh escaped Winston's lips as he set down the tumbler. "I'm gettin' old, Dustin," he said, stretching his back. "Little aches and pains never bothered me before. Now they're the only thing on my mind."

Winston smiled, totally unaware of the cannonball Dustin was about to drop on the family. "So, did you have a good day, son? What did you do? I saw you didn't ride out with Chaim and Manolito."

Dustin noted how he ignored the fact Noah had been in the group.

Saving him from answering, his mother breezed into the room, looking lovely. She went over to her husband and pulled him down so she could kiss his cheek.

"I don't know why, but I'm feeling very sentimental tonight." She smiled at Dustin. "I'm glad you're home for supper, Dustin. Dinners together seem fewer and fewer as my children grow up and take on lives of their own. I'll be sad when everyone is moved out into their own places."

That day may be sooner than you think.

"I hope they won't want to do that," Winston replied, grinning at his wife. "If everyone stayed right here on the Rim Rock and filled this house with grandbabies, I'd be a happy man. We can build on, add more square feet. I can see the picture now, boys chasing each other as they run through this room, whooping and hollering, and little Madelines and Beckies twirling like ballerinas as they vie for our attention."

He heaved a deep sigh. "In Montana, Flood and Claire are already up to their eyeballs in grandbabies. I'd like a few dozen of our own."

Winnie rubbed Winston's arm. "Amen to that, husband." She slid her gaze over to Dustin and smiled. "All in good time."

Can they read my thoughts? That smile on Pa's face will dissolve fast enough when he hears his grandchildren will be carrying Calhoun blood.

"Is something wrong, Dustin?" his mother asked. "You look a little flushed. How do you feel?"

Like I'm going to puke. "I'm fine, Mother."

Maria appeared in the doorway to the dining room. "Dinner is almost ready, *señora.*"

"Thank you, Maria. I'm sure Chaim and the girls will be here straight away."

With a curt nod, Maria hurried away.

Dustin went to the sideboard, poured himself another stiff whiskey, and took half the glass in one gulp. The liquor scorched a trail straight to his gut, where the strong liquid pooled and began a slow burn.

Where were Chaim and his sisters? He wished they'd hurry and get into the room. The longer he put off the announcement, the harder breaking the "happy" news would be.

When a knock sounded on the front door, Dustin was only too happy to distract himself with whoever was there. He'd take care of business and send them on their way.

Grasping the knob, he pulled open the door. "Theodore!"

"Don't look so perturbed, Dustin. Didn't Becky let the family know she'd invited me for supper?"

She most certainly had. Yesterday at lunch. Dustin had totally forgotten.

I told Sidney I'd speak with the family tonight. If she hears I didn't, she'll think I've lost my nerve. And that I won't do.

Dustin stepped back, making room for the young man who held a small gift in his hands. Most likely in place of flowers, which were pretty scarce in a Texas November.

"I'm not perturbed, Theo. What gave you that idea?"

"The scowl on your face."

Dustin grinned, clamping the wiry youth on the shoulder, liking him very much. *Young love.* How easy courtship would be for Theo and Becky. Smooth sailing all the way.

The two walked into the living room, where Becky and Madeline had just arrived. Chaim ambled into the room and gave a nod.

His younger sister hurried forward, her face blushing into a soft pink glow. "Theodore, you've arrived."

He held out the small box tied with a soft lavender ribbon. "For you."

Becky looked around the watching faces until she found her mother.

Winnie nodded and smiled. "Why, Theodore, how thoughtful," his mother said happily.

Dustin's heart sank. He wanted this situation for Sidney. This heartfelt goodness that everyone in the room was experiencing as they watched the young couple. Was he setting up Sidney for more hurt than his love could offset? He didn't want to think of the possibility, and yet he knew it might be true.

His father inched in his direction. "Does a heart good to see such innocence in full bloom," he whispered close to Dustin's shoulder.

A stone plunged to the bottom of his stomach.

"They're perfect for each other."

With trembling hands, Becky opened the gift as everyone watched. She withdrew a snowy-white handkerchief, delicately embroidered with her initials, RAM for Rebecca Anne McCutcheon. Of course, if things went as his sister hoped, she'd need another one soon with RAB, for Rebecca Anne Browning.

Theodore's face reddened as she oohed and aahed over the dainty gift, lifting the fabric to her face to feel its softness with her cheek.

When Dustin looked up to find his mother watching him closely, he lifted a shoulder and smiled.

"Supper," Maria called, her face serious. One didn't mess with her at dinnertime.

Fifteen minutes later when the meal was well under way, Dustin supposed now was as good a time as any. Then he considered waiting until the plates were cleared and Maria brought in the dessert.

Chaim sat stone-faced and quiet.

A couple of times, he'd found Chaim looking at him, but his brother hadn't brought up that he'd caught Dustin and Sidney together in a compromising position that afternoon. Dustin owed him for that.

"Chaim, any news? I can't imagine why Emmeline hasn't telegraphed. At least to let us know how her father is," Madeline complained. "He must be suffering horribly to keep her so busy."

"A letter is on the way," Becky replied, her tone very ladylike. "Stop making such an issue, Madeline." She glanced at Theo sitting at her side. She and Madeline usually had opposing opinions, which could get loud at times.

His mother straightened, cutting a look at her older daughter. "Becky is right. Please stop tormenting your brother with questions about Emmeline. She is busy. That's all. She'll return when she returns. You must have something of your own to occupy your thoughts. Leave him be."

"Mother! The wedding is just around the corner. Things remain that need doing." Madeline glanced from one face to the other. "A party of this size does not happen overnight." She sent a pointed look to Becky. "Take note, dear sister. I'm only looking out for Chaim. He doesn't want anything last-minute and makeshift."

Chaim pushed back abruptly and braced his hands on the chair arms. "If you'll excuse—"

Dustin caught his arm. "Hold up, Chaim. I have something to tell the family. I'd like you to hear as well."

The look his brother shot back implied he knew exactly what Dustin was about to say.

Now that he'd started, nothing could keep him from speaking the news. *Quickly.*

His heart thwacked painfully against his ribs, and the suspicion he saw creeping into his father's eyes almost made him lose his nerve. But not quite. He'd battle for Sidney every inch of the way.

"Sidney Calhoun and I are courting. We plan to be married soon."

His father's palms crashed to the maple wood table, rattling all the dishware. His sisters' eyes grew round, and his mother went as white as a ghost.

"What did you just say?" his father asked, his face hardened into a grim mask. "I don't think I heard you correctly."

What people said about spitting it out fast was true. That hardest part was done.

"I said," he repeated in a firm voice. "Sidney and I are in love. Nothing you do or say will sway us."

"Over my dead body! Mesmerized right from the start. I warned you to stay away . . ." His pa's words slowed, and he turned away.

Theodore looked back and forth between Dustin and Winston, his confusion apparent.

"Dustin," his mother began, "How did this—"

His father stood, took a step away, and then stopped. "He's been spending every free moment with her," he said over his shoulder. "What did we expect?"

Chapter Forty-Seven

Sidney stood quietly at Lily's side, offering her friend and employer moral support.

"I can't tell you how sorry I am about your gown, Mrs. Tuttle," Lily said, her face an ashy gray-white. The remains of Mrs. Tuttle's blue velvet dress lay atop the cutting counter, impossible to repair.

Sidney hoped her friend wasn't coming down with an illness. She'd seemed a bit down the last three days, trying to reestablish her business since the Billy Burger incident, but she'd faltered somewhat each morning. Sidney no longer needed her job, but enjoyed spending time with Lily and liked the atmosphere of the shop.

Mrs. Tuttle dabbed the hankie to the corner of her eye with a trembling hand. "I don't know what I'll do."

The despair in the middle-aged woman's voice tugged at Sidney's heart.

"My husband expects me to make a showing in San Antonio. The event is very important to him and his investors. No time remains to order a new one."

Seeing Lily's face cloud over, Sidney knew she had to do something to help.

"All is not lost, Lily, Mrs. Tuttle," Sidney said as she moved a few steps to her left and swept her arm in front of Ingrid. "Look at this beautiful maroon velvet sample gown. The gold cording is lovely. The dress is stunning, to say the least. With a few alterations, I'm sure Lily could have it fitting you like a glove." She peeked toward Mrs. Tuttle to see what effect her words were having.

Both women stood in stunned silence. Their expressions said that neither had thought of the possibility.

"It's not blue," Sidney continued, "but I think the maroon . . . no, the hue is closer to a deep claret, would be spectacular with your rich, dark hair."

A small smile played around Lily's lips as Sidney asked, "What do you think, Lily? Can you alter this gown in time to meet Mrs. Tuttle's deadline?"

Lily clapped her hands together, a smile bursting onto her face. "I most certainly can! That is, if you want me to, Mrs. Tuttle. Sidney is absolutely correct. This gown looks as if it were designed just for you."

As the two jabbered away in happiness over the solution that had been right under their noses, Sidney backed away. She went to the window and gazed out at the town, asking herself if she'd be happy living here in Rio Wells.

Dustin hadn't come into town, but he had sent a message. He'd broken the news to his family. He'd written they were happy about the match, but she knew better. Ranching was taking up his time, but he loved her, couldn't wait to see her, and he'd be sending a buggy on Wednesday, which tomorrow, so she could have supper at the ranch. To really meet the family.

A buggy? Has he forgotten I have my horse stabled here in town? Of course not. But he'd prefer her to show up in a dress rather than her riding clothes. Be a proper lady.

She glanced over her shoulder at Lily, a *true* proper lady. Then she glanced up at the four-leaf clover over the door.

What had she gotten herself into? Yes, she loved Dustin. That would never change. Those few passionate moments in his arms had made her think she could overcome any impediment, no matter how great. Had she been a silly fool to think so?

Noah walked through the door and halted as he looked around. Certainly seeing her wrapped in Dustin's arms had him fretting for the last few days. He was worried, and she could understand that.

Their gazes locked. He hadn't softened in the least. When he lifted his chin her way, she went to his side.

"Any word from home?" he asked. He showed no sign that he was happy to see her.

"Hello, Noah," she said just above a whisper. "You're working in town today?"

He nodded.

"I'm sorry for the trouble I've—"

"*I'm* the one who caused you to get mixed up with McCutcheon. *I'll* take the blame from Pa. Just wondered if he'd returned your telegram yet."

"I haven't heard a word."

"Are you sending another?"

"Now that I have the funds, I could. But why should I? He didn't send any money when I needed it. I know that sounds childish, but I don't know what to think." She tried to hold his gaze, but he kept looking away. "I'm hurt."

"You should know by now that's just Pa. He doesn't have an ounce of care in him for anyone. Not even you. He's never loved any of us, just that age-old grudge he likes to nurse night and day."

"Don't say that."

Noah had been through the worst. Living away his first year, and never knowing his real ma. Sidney had tried to nurture him, love him, but now she could see his pain went much deeper than even she'd thought. He was different from her other brothers, and that alone sometimes brought out their father's scorn.

"Why not? It's true. The sooner you learn, the better you'll be." He touched the soft dressing room curtain, a trace of whimsy flitting through his eyes. "I just stopped in to see how you were. What's happening with you and McCutcheon? Things at the ranch seem awfully strained."

"We're planning to be married." She held her breath, praying he at least would have a good reaction to the news.

He whistled and wagged his head back and forth, his gaze anchored on the ceiling.

John McCutcheon stuck his head in the door and smiled. "You coming, Noah? I'm about ready to head back out to the barn with these barrels."

"Yep, I'll be right there."

Hearing the door close, she said, "Thank you for behaving. I keep expecting to wake up to the news you've burned down something or . . ." At his wounded expression, she clamped her mouth closed. "I'm sorry. I didn't mean that."

"I've grown up a lot, Sidney. Even if no one in *my* family sees the change."

She grasped his arm. "I see it, Noah! I do. That was a stupid remark that I didn't mean."

He nodded and turned. "I need to get to work." He shot her one last look. "You take care of yourself."

Chapter Forty-Eight

Heady scents of roasted chicken and garlic swirled around Dustin as he made his way up the steep stairway of the Union Hotel, heading for Sidney's room. She'd be home from Lily's by now and plenty hungry, he suspected—or hoped.

He'd come to surprise her. The days they'd been apart had been the longest of his life, and he was longing for a few more kisses. They had been on his mind since riding away and leaving her in Rio Wells.

He knocked on her door, a million thoughts running through his head.

"Yes?"

"It's Dustin."

The door flew open, and in a rustle of petticoats, she vaulted into his arms.

"Hey, what's this?" he asked, startled at her immediate reaction.

"I'm just happy to see you," she said, holding him tight, her soft cheek pressed close to his. "Nothing has seemed real since you left here on Saturday. I can't believe we spoke of marriage, and you actually braved telling your family. Your father."

He stepped back so he could see into her face. "Just like you'll be brave enough when the time comes."

He studied the tight expression that had him a bit worried. This commitment was not set in stone. Cold feet could change her mind at any time.

"Right?" His heart thumped in his chest. "Sidney?"

"Of course. You know I will."

He knew nothing of the sort. He knew what she wanted. He knew what she *thought* she would do once she was face-to-face with Jock Calhoun—but he couldn't be sure.

"Good." Nothing could be done about the situation with her father now, so he planned to enjoy this evening. She wore a new blouse with Madeline's skirt. "That's exactly what I wanted to hear. Now, gather up your shawl, because I'm taking you out to supper."

"I thought that was tomorrow night, out at the ranch?" Her eyes narrowed a fraction. "Your father doesn't want to see me."

"Not true in the least." *Pa didn't say those words exactly. He'll soften to the idea by tomorrow. He's stern, but he's not heartless.* "I just couldn't wait another night."

Turning, he glanced around to be sure the hall was still vacant and then kissed her soundly, taking his time to show her just how much he'd missed her. After more than a few moments that would brand the kiss proper, he pulled back just far enough to see into her eyes.

"Are you complaining, Calhoun?"

A smile so beautiful blossomed onto her face that the sight almost stole his breath.

"Not in the least, McCutcheon," she whispered against his lips. "I'm not ready. It wasn't all that long ago that I returned from the shop. I'm a mess."

His bride-to-be was the most stunning creature he'd ever set eyes on. "I didn't know you were such a fibber. You look absolutely beautiful. I hope you haven't already eaten. Are you hungry?"

"Actually, I'm starved."

He knew that feeling all too well. Her gaze stilled on his face, and he had to stop himself from backing her into the room and closing the door.

"Good." He corralled his thoughts back to where they belonged. "While we're at supper, we're discussing you moving to the ranch, where I can see you all the time, and I know you're safe."

Shaking her head, she placed a hand on his chest. "They aren't ready to see me every minute of every day—not quite yet, Dustin. We need to warm into this."

He hadn't thought this would be easy. If she could trust that his family liked her and wasn't against her, she'd soften her feelings about his father. He'd win her over, and she'd realize Winston wasn't the type to bushwhack anyone, let alone a friend, no matter how much money was involved.

With his hands on her shoulders, he turned her and encouraged her forward. "There's a pit in my belly that won't let me think squarely. Get your things, and I'll persuade you how wrong you are over a hot plate of food."

She hurried into the room that was perfectly picked up. The indentation on the bed's counterpane was the only indication she'd been relaxing.

"How's Billy Burger?" he asked. "I've been so busy I haven't had a chance to catch up on that issue at all. He healing?"

She'd gone to her dresser and was smoothing her hair with a comb and now pinching her cheeks, as he'd seen his sisters do on occasion. Such an intimate scene. A week ago, he never would have thought how much his life would change.

With her reticule and shawl, she turned toward him. "John says some time yet will pass before he walks without a limp. He's grouchy, and has moved back to his own place." She glanced into his eyes. "As bad as I feel about shooting him, I'd do it again if he touched Lily, or anyone else." She passed into the hall, and Dustin pulled the door closed. "Where're we going?"

"Can't you guess?" If Dustin hadn't already been walking on air from her passionate greeting, the excitement on her face would have put him there now.

"Lillian Russell Room?"

He nodded. "Our table awaits."

Sidney picked up her glass of wine and took a tiny sip. She wasn't accustomed to drinking, but Dustin had already ordered a fine bottle in celebration, and she'd not dash his good intentions.

The waitress had already taken their orders, so they sat in quiet conversation in a corner table in the cozy dining room. The soft light, made by a candle in the center of every table, almost brought the alluring paintings to life.

"Should I be jealous?" she asked softly, gazing up at a dark-haired beauty in a bed of burgundy silks that had momentarily caught his attention. The young woman in the artist's rendition held a small cluster of green grapes in her left hand, and her right hand was placed behind her head. Her smile was sweet, not seductive.

"Never, my love. You've captured my heart and soul."

His gaze was so intense, she had to lower her lashes. How had this happened? Her world changed in a heartbeat. She'd been thrust into this enchanted fairy tale where a handsome prince was captured by her love. The circumstance didn't seem possible. She feared she'd soon awaken to find herself back in her New Mexico bedroom, rising to gather cattle. Was that what would happen when the time arrived for Noah to go home?

He reached over and stroked her cheek. "You look unhappy."

"Not unhappy, just . . ."

"Worried? Don't be. Tonight is supposed to be a celebration. I've cleared the way for things on my end. I'll help you do the same with your family."

The waitress arrived, pushing a small tea cart. She uncovered their dishes of basil-roasted chicken, mashed potatoes drizzled in mushroom sauce, and creamed peas.

Sidney hadn't dreamed of eating something so decadent and delicious in this small rugged town.

A moment later, the waitress came back and refilled their water.

Dustin smiled at Sidney, and her breath hitched. She'd marry this man. She didn't know when, but she hoped the ceremony would be soon. She wouldn't miss Santa Fe, or her father, but she would miss her brothers and Carmen.

They gazed into each other's eyes as the food disappeared from their plates. Other diners were beyond her realm of consciousness. Her man was the most intoxicating human being on this earth.

He finished first, setting his knife and fork across his plate. "I can't remember when I've enjoyed a meal as much as I have this one," he said, stretching back. He reached for the bottle of wine and leaned to pour into her glass.

She smiled and shook her head.

He nodded, filling his own halfway.

"I agree. Chef Bernard has truly lived up to his reputation. Now I don't have to just imagine the foods that make those aromas drifting into my room. I've experienced them."

"Are you full? Did you get enough?" he asked when she placed her utensils across her plate.

"I couldn't eat another bite. Everything was absolutely wonderful. Thank you, my love." Embarrassed when the endearment slipped passed her lips as naturally as if she'd been saying them every day for ten years, Sidney jerked away her gaze.

"No, don't look away."

His voice was a soft plea, and she complied.

"I've been pining away for you in my heart, even before we met. Almost in despair that I'd never find you. Now that I have, I'm parched for your love."

"Dustin." That was all she could say. Living with her surly father and her brothers who were men of few words, she never dreamed she'd hear such endearments from a man—let alone one who was as rough, hardened, and competent as Dustin McCutcheon.

He leaned toward her, his forearms on the table. "Yes? It's all true. And there's more, but I struggle to find the words to bring them to life. They're more a feelin' in my heart. It's so full, it's almost painful."

She looked into his eyes. "I know what you mean."

The waitress cleared her throat, and they both gazed up.

"Would either of you care for dessert? We have dry apple pie or persimmon crumb cake."

Dustin gestured toward her. "Sidney? It's up to you."

"I couldn't, although they both sound delicious. Will you please give Chef Bernard our compliments? Everything was beyond my expectations." She would tell him herself sometime tomorrow when she saw him as well.

"Yes, Miss Calhoun, I'll be happy to."

"How about a walk around the town?" Dustin asked. "I need to stretch my legs and let all this food settle. Maybe a stroll down to the hot springs is in order."

She nodded, taken again by what a handsome devil Dustin was. She recalled her first impression in San Antonio that had captured her interest, and she'd toe-tapped out a little nervous beat in time with her heart. Then they'd spoken face-to-face in the hotel after the courthouse meeting, and his audacity had her gritting her teeth.

"What's so funny?" he asked as he pulled out her chair. "You're smiling."

"I'm just thinking about when we met. How self-assured you were, and how angry you made me."

He placed his hand on the small of her back and they proceeded toward the door into the hotel lobby.

Enjoying his closeness, she pulled her shawl around her shoulders.

"I'm still self-assured," he said. "If I see what I want, I go after it."

She glanced up into a satisfied smile. "Yes. I think I know that now all too well."

Tonight felt like a fairy tale, but she had to remember she still had her family's reaction to contend with. Her father was stubborn, but so was Dustin.

She thought back on the grasshopper. She didn't want anything to happen to Dustin because of her. Was she putting him in danger?

Chapter Forty-Nine

Buster Drier, the lamplighter, was just making his rounds when Dustin and Sidney stepped out of the hotel. Tucking Sidney's hand into the bend in his arm, Dustin smiled at the paper-thin bachelor as he lowered his torch. Reaching over his head, the man closed the glass door, hooked the latch, and started for the last street lamp in front of the stage office.

The dry evening air reminded Dustin how much they needed a good rain to tamp down all the dust. Soon, he thought, the weather would change, and winter would be upon them. He stopped and pointed to the moon. The glowing orb appeared to sit on the tip of the small church steeple, a block and a half away.

"It's beautiful," she gushed. Her firm hold on his arm felt like gold.

"Let's take the long way around to the hot springs. First, we'll go down Church Street and see how Knutson's new mercantile is coming along. Have you had a chance to venture over that way?"

"Just the one time to the barn last week. I'd love to get a better feel for Rio Wells . . ."

"Since you'll be living here soon?" Maybe he should stop pushing so hard, but he couldn't help himself. He needed to hear her firm commitment as much as possible. "Should we talk about when we're taking the big leap?"

She pulled his arm playfully. "You make marrying me sound like a prison sentence. Maybe you're getting cold feet."

"Nothing of the sort!"

As they approached the corner, he saw Doc Bixby relaxing on the iron bench as he smoked a pipe. Lily's white cat was curled in his lap.

"Evenin'," the old doctor said, the smile in his voice evident to Dustin. "Out for a stroll?"

Dustin nodded. "That's exactly right."

"It's a pretty night." He gestured toward the church. "I'm just watching the moon rise."

As they continued down the street, Dustin wondered if Sidney would object if he stole another kiss once they were alone. They turned on Church Street and headed toward the new mercantile. A half a block past the mercantile was the Knutson home, and the barn John was remodeling for his new business venture—*their* new business venture.

A large buggy pulled out from the Knutson house and headed in their direction. As the conveyance got closer, Dustin recognized Mr. Knutson driving and his wife at his side. The passel of girls, as well as the nanny, were lined up on the two bench seats behind.

As they pulled alongside, he felt Sidney stiffen. He touched the brim of his hat, and Mr. Knutson smiled. The wife was a dour-faced woman who looked as if a smile was as foreign to her as it was to a prisoner at the hanging tree. As luck would have it, Rainey, the youngest—and as precocious as they came—was seated on their side of the buggy.

"Mr. McCutcheon," she called out in a childish voice as the buggy went by slowly at a walk. "It's almost dark out here."

Knowing she was baiting Sidney, Dustin chuckled and smiled. What he wouldn't give to tweak her cheek!

"Good evening, Mr. and Mrs. Knutson," he called, ignoring the pesky child's taunt. "Beautiful night for a drive."

"Absolutely, Mr. McCutcheon," Mr. Knutson replied. "We're enjoying our new home immensely." He dipped his chin as he flipped the long reins.

As they pulled away, Sidney whispered, "I can tell by all the long faces. I wonder where they're going?"

"I really don't care as long as they take that little one far away." He shook his head. "She gives me the chills."

Sidney's relaxed laughter brought a swell of pride to his chest. Things had happened quickly. They still knew so very little about each other, but he anticipated the learning.

They stopped in front of the mercantile, and looked through the window into the dark. The shelves were half full, and other merchandise sat around in no apparent order.

"Still a lot of work to do," he said.

Sidney had become quiet, and he wondered why. Was she thinking of the uphill battle they had to climb?

Backtracking their steps, they turned onto Spring Street and headed for the hot springs, the twinkle of the street lamps creating a very fetching scene. He'd never beheld his hometown through eyes filled with love. He rather liked the view.

Now and then, a rider trotted by, or they'd catch a shout from someone celebrating a little too much at the Black Silk Garter. Life felt awfully good.

"Dustin, Miss Calhoun?" Cradle Hupton approached with his usual cup of coffee present. Dustin didn't miss his look of disappointment at Sidney's tight hold of his arm. "Good to see ya both," he said.

"And you, Cradle. What's new at the livery?"

The man shrugged, and then let out an ironic chuckle. "Not much happens there, Dustin. You know that." His longing gaze traveled over to Sidney. "Patsy, my pony, somehow worked open the latch on my feed room and made a mess. I'm keepin' an eye on her to be sure she don't colic." He shrugged and looked around. "Your gelding has settled in fine, Miss Calhoun."

"Thank you. You've been so helpful since our first meeting. I appreciate that greatly."

Jealousy stabbed Dustin.

"My pleasure." Cradle started forward. "I won't keep you two any longer. Good evenin'."

The three started off in opposite directions. They wouldn't have time to stroll all the way to the hot springs, and be in before dark. As much as he hated to start back for the hotel, he knew they should.

Soon, he thought. Soon, we won't have to go our separate ways—ever.

"Sidney Mayell Calhoun!" an angry voice rang out. "I'm ashamed!"

Sidney whirled before he could stop her.

In the dusky light, two horsemen approached, one hunched over with his left arm hanging at his side.

Chapter Fifty

"**P**a." The faint word was said on a gush of fear.

Dustin recognized the man riding next to her father as Jock Calhoun Jr. from the run-ins he'd had with Sidney's brother at the stockyards over the years.

Sidney tried to pull away but he held her hand tight in the crook of his elbow, unwilling to let her pretend things that weren't. Better to get the shock over as soon as possible.

The fact he was taking his girl out for supper in his hometown where he had nothing to fear meant Dustin hadn't worn his gun. Seeing the two armed men approach, Dustin felt as naked as a newborn babe.

"McCutcheon." The word was something dirty in the younger Calhoun's mouth. His father's narrow-eyed glare had Sidney trembling.

"Gentlemen," Dustin said, angry at the way they'd already dismissed Sidney. She'd been through hell, and they couldn't care less. These two men would be his in-laws. The fact he missed his .45 Colt while addressing them hit a humorous pinched-tight nerve, and he actually smiled.

"Something funny?" Jock Jr. asked. His face hadn't lost its scowl.

The streets were quiet, most everyone having gone inside for the night. Stanton Drake, the telegraph operator, heading in the direction of the saloon, watched from the other side of the street.

"Thought that was you, Sidney," Jock Calhoun said. "But when I recognized McCutcheon, I imagined I was seeing things."

"Pa, why didn't you let me know you were coming?" she asked, her free hand reaching out toward him. "How are you? Does your side hurt?"

Sidney's voice held a breathless quality he'd not heard before. He didn't like to think she was frightened of anything. Her concern for her father was evident.

"Maybe I wanted to see what my only daughter was up to. Now I know."

"She told you what she was doing here in Rio Wells," Dustin stated flatly before Sidney could answer. "I was right there when she sent the telegram. She's watching out for Noah. Keeping him in line."

Sidney's brother chuckled mirthlessly. "Is *that* what you call *this*?" He gestured to her hand held firmly under Dustin's. "I might say different."

Again, Sidney tried to pull her arm away, but Dustin wouldn't let her. He just stared back into the Calhouns' heated faces.

Damn. He didn't want to get into a fight, but Jock Jr. really set his teeth on edge. All the years of fistfights came rushing back. For Sidney's sake, he needed to work this out with words. Just like Winston had tried for years—but failed.

Stanton Drake still watched from across the street, probably having picked up on the tone.

"Where's Noah?" Sidney's pa asked, stretching up in his saddle the best he could as he looked down the street.

"At the Rim Rock," Dustin replied. "Where he's been ordered to stay by a judge. We don't have any say over that." He forced a smile—for Sidney. "You must be hungry. Why don't you stable your horses at the livery, and I'll buy you supper in the hotel restaurant." He squeezed Sidney's hand. "If you hurry, we'll make it before the dining room closes."

Jock Jr. laughed. "We'd rather go hungry than eat with vermin like you. We're loyal to our own." He pinned Sidney with a stare. "At least, some of us are."

"You have no call to speak to Dustin like that!" Sidney retorted, and Dustin felt the change in her body when anger replaced her fear. "I won't have you calling names and being ugly. The McCutcheons have been kind and charitable—all of them."

"Arguing won't get us anywhere," Dustin said. "Just so you know, Sidney and I are getting married on Saturday." Taking the bull by the horns felt great. "You've shown up at an opportune time . . ." *May as well drive the fact home.* ". . . to give your daughter away."

Sidney gasped and cut her gaze to his face.

Both men sat straighter, angrily looking between themselves. "That ain't going to—"

"It is!" Dustin said abruptly, cutting him off. He glanced down at Sidney, hoping he wouldn't see censure in her eyes for assuming Saturday would be fine with her. "Sidney, you and I are collecting your things at the hotel so I can take you out to the ranch. Tonight."

He hoped she wouldn't refuse. He trusted these two as much as he did the Comancheros who had abducted his cousin

Charity months ago. He didn't want to wake up and find Sidney gone.

She gently squeezed the crook of his arm. "I'll be fine here in Rio Wells, Dustin. Especially now that my father has arrived. I need to see them both settled and talk this out."

"I'm not leaving you."

"Please, go home. The situation will be easier that way. Don't worry; I'm not going anywhere without you. You think they could take me against my will?"

Her tone was stiff. He didn't dare push too hard and have everything backfire. *Sure they could, sweetheart, if they really wanted to.*

"I'll see you tomorrow night for supper," she said. "Just like we planned. And if you still want me then, I'll bring my belongings along as well."

He looked at the men. "You two staying at the hotel?"

"Where else?"

Chapter Fifty-One

The time was almost five o'clock in the morning when Dustin finally dragged himself back to the ranch. After he'd seen Sidney to her room and stayed around while her father and brother checked in, he'd collected his horse from Cradle. But he remained across the street, out of sight in the alley, making sure his in-laws-to-be didn't try something underhanded.

Once back home, he bedded down his animal himself, still too keyed up to sleep. He avoided the early-morning activity in the bunkhouse and entered the house quietly. A lamp burned in his father's office. Before he had a chance to move in that direction, he spotted his father coming out to meet him.

"Thought I heard you coming in."

Dustin only nodded. He could see the conjecture in his father's eyes. Thought he'd been with Sidney all night, and that bothered him.

"Have a minute to talk?" his pa asked.

Talk was the last thing he felt like, but he and his father were walking a thin line. Dustin didn't want to make matters worse.

"Sure. I'm not getting any sleep now."

In the office, Dustin dropped onto the sofa and scrubbed a hand across his whiskered chin. A nagging in his gut said he shouldn't have left town. As soon as he bathed, shaved, and grabbed a bite to eat, he'd head straight back.

His father watched him get comfortable before asking, "Things going all right?"

"They were until Jock and Sidney's oldest brother showed up in Rio Wells last night."

Winston lowered the coffee mug he'd just picked up without taking a drink. "Just what I feared. Backed into a corner, there's no telling what those two will do. Did you speak with them?"

He nodded.

"Tell them your plans with Miss Calhoun?"

He nodded again. "Her name's Sidney."

A few moments passed before his pa spoke. Something strange was behind his eyes, a look Dustin had never seen before.

"Maybe it's for the best they show up now, Dustin. A union between you and Sidney would only bring her heartbreak. Have you thought about that? They're a proud family, much like us. If you gave her up now, she could find someone else. She's beautiful. And smart. A woman like her wouldn't have any trouble in the least."

Even though Dustin had expected as much, he stilled, his father's words cutting him to the core. Had he been wrong? Would his family never accept her?

"I can't believe you just said that. Sidney and I are getting married on Saturday. I hope you'll stomach the idea long enough to come and give us your blessing."

His father stared back, unmoved. "Think long and hard. Some obstacles are too wide to jump, son. You're taking on more than you can handle."

Unable to listen another moment, Dustin surged to his feet, intent on leaving before he said something he'd regret. He loved his father and respected him. He couldn't understand why the man wouldn't soften on this issue.

A clamoring at the front door brought them around, and Switchback burst into the room.

"Fire in Rio Wells!" he shouted. "At the Knutsons'." That was all he said before the cook rushed out the door.

"Where's Noah Calhoun?" his pa called out.

"Don't know, boss," came the man's reply.

Dustin bolted past Switchback, saddled up, and galloped away, not waiting for anyone.

When Dustin arrived in town, Knutson's barn was engulfed in flames—along with John's good efforts.

A line of men passed buckets from several water pumps along the street. Halfway down the block, Billy Burger leaned on a crutch as he worked the iron handle with his massive arms, sending water gushing from a spigot. Bucket-toting men crowded around.

Spotting John at the forefront, Dustin pushed through the throng of men. Blistering heat licked his face as the orange-yellow flames crackled and popped. He grasped John's shoulder.

"Have you seen Sidney?" he yelled.

"No," John yelled back.

"What about Lily?"

"She's home, where I told her to stay and keep watch from the second-story window! I don't want her to be caught unprepared in case the fire spreads."

Cradle ran forward and pitched a bucket of water onto the fire, the action followed by a loud hiss. The man next to John hefted him a full bucket, and John did the same. Half the structure was gone, and Dustin figured they were trying to keep the flames contained. Joining together, the men worked endlessly until the fuel had been consumed and the last flame burned out.

The exhausted men stared motionless at the enormous black pile of rubble on the ground that an hour earlier had been Mr. Knutson's barn and the McCutcheon, Noble, McCutcheon venture. Chaim was shoulder to shoulder with Stanton Drake, Doc Bixby, Colin Jorgensen, and even the disgraced ex-mayor Fred Billingsworth. Their clothes were blackened and wet. All the ranch hands from the Rim Rock were there, as well as most of the men Dustin knew.

Winston stood with a group of ranchers, black soot covering his pinched face. He caught Dustin's gaze and started his way. When he neared, he gave his son an angry jerk of his head, and Dustin followed him to the outer shadows where they wouldn't be overheard. Dustin couldn't ever remember seeing him so angry.

"Was this Noah Calhoun's doing?"

Noah's absence in the bunkhouse had been going through Dustin's head the whole time he'd been pitching the water buckets. Had he stopped being vigilant because of Calhoun's cooperation, only to be duped?

"What about Sidney's father and brother?"

Anger and frustration made him want to cuss. "Don't know."

"Well, you *better* know. Rio Wells could have burned to the ground. Innocent folks could have died!"

His chin jerked up. "They didn't."

"And *thank God* for that!" Winston barked, his furious tone scorching Dustin. "You better find out where Noah is! Let's not forget, if he's done this, the blame is on *your* head! Not by my account, but Judge Halford. I don't like this one bit."

"I'm headed to the sheriff's office now," Dustin replied. "I don't see Miller anywhere here."

"I'll go with you."

They left the large crowd behind. When they turned onto a nearly deserted Spring Street, the quickest route to the sheriff's office on Main, Dustin saw Sidney running in his direction, her face a storm of confusion. Everyone else was at the site of the fire.

"You're safe!" she cried, the first thing out of her lips.

She was still in Rio Wells!

Dustin tried to embrace her, thankful his fears hadn't been fulfilled, but she pulled away. A few feet behind came her father and brother.

His gut tightened. Dustin glanced at his pa, dreading the trouble he felt coming. Surely, all the old hate-filled accusations would start flying once again.

Instead, his father strode right up to Jock Calhoun and threw a punch, sending the man to the ground. Shock reverberated through Dustin as Sidney screeched and ran to her father's side.

Jock Jr. rushed Dustin, but Dustin stepped away and shoved him to the ground.

"We're not fighting today," he said through clenched teeth as Sidney's brother picked himself up and slunk to his father's other side. Something told Dustin this would be about his father and Sidney's pa.

"I warned you!" Winston barked at Jock, both hands fisted at his sides. "If you ever set foot in my town, there would be hell to pay. I've put up with your lies and deceits everywhere else, but I won't here. Not for one second!"

"He's crippled," Sidney cried, helping her father to his feet.

The man wobbled as he wiped a trickle of blood oozing from the side of his mouth.

"How can you hit a defenseless man?" she cried, holding tight to her father's arm.

"Defenseless?" Winston choked out. "Ha! Crippled? That might be, but I'm sure not as bad as he wants you to think." He paced back and forth like a caged mountain lion.

All the years melted away until Dustin saw his father as a young man, the man he remembered when the ambush had happened. Dustin had been eight or nine. He recalled certain parts of that disturbing time in their history.

Winston glanced at him and then looked long and hard at Sidney, standing guard at her father's side. Hatless, he raked his hand through sweat-soaked hair, turned to the older Calhoun, and glared.

"I've come to a decision, you sorry son of a—" He shook his head. "Don't know if it's the right one or not, but at this point after all these years, I'm not sure if I care anymore. All I know is I don't want *my* son blaming me for his unhappiness! I've carried your secret for as long as I intend to. Jock Calhoun, bare your soul to your children. If you don't, then I will!"

Sidney's father practically shrank before Dustin's eyes. This was not the bully he remembered.

"I don't know what you're talking about, McCutcheon. Probably more of your—"

Winston took a menacing step toward Jock, and he straightened.

"What's he yammerin' about now, Pa?" Jock Jr. asked. "Don't let him push you around. I can take 'em both."

Dustin didn't care what Jock Jr. said. Sidney was all he could see. He understood why she'd looked so confused and sad when she'd run up to him; her dear father had been filling her head full of lies, uncertainties, and guilt all night long. Poor thing looked exhausted.

She avoided his gaze and kept hers on Winston, looking young and scared.

Winston glared at Jock. "It's amazing how the lines between truth and lies wavered as the years pass, eh, Jock? One thing you can always count on. Truth will always come out. It bides its time, waiting for the precise moment to set things right." He jabbed a finger in Jock's direction. "Now's the time, Jock. Start talking."

Scowling, Jock just stared.

A few people going home on Spring Street stopped to see what the problem was.

"Move along, folks," Winston told them. "This is personal."

Jock stumbled a few steps back.

"Fine. Don't say you weren't warned." Winston looked at Dustin, then Jock Jr. and finally at Sidney. "All those years ago, your father paid to have me bushwhacked. Things went sour somehow. I don't know. It's ironic, in a way."

"What?" Dustin couldn't believe his ears. If his father had known all along, why had he let Calhoun sully the McCutcheon name? That didn't make any sense. His face grew hot at all the fights and slander he'd endured. "Why didn't you say anything before?"

"Why, you ask?" Winston said, now staring at the ground. Seemed all the anger and hate seeped out of his pa right before his eyes.

Morning was here, and the sun was just now peeking over the rooftops. The soft light silhouetted his father, making his face hard to read.

"Why?" he said again, as if asking himself the question. "Because of her"—he pointed to Sidney—"and her brothers. Winnie and I knew Jock and Sidney's mother. We didn't see them often, because their ranch was a ways from ours." A ghost of a smile played across his face as he stared at Sidney. "She was just a little ragamuffin of a thing running after her brothers. Cute as a bug's ear. Did I want to see her lose her pa? Did I want to be the one to break her heart? No!"

Winston stopped talking for a moment and stared at the ground. "Once I saw what was brewing between the two of you these past few days, I knew the truth was fated to come out. But if I could stop the devastation, if I could keep you two apart, I would try—for her. I did try. I did. But destiny won't be cheated."

He sucked in a lungful of air. "And I kept silent because of him," he said, pointing at Jock Jr. "He's a handsome lad. Reminds me of my own sons."

He thumped his chest with his fist, and his face twisted in agony. "Did I want to be the one to tell him his father is a liar and a cheat? Possibly a murderer as well, if his intentions had been carried out? No! I knew I could handle a few verbal attacks. And I figured my sons, with their wide, strong shoulders, could do the same. As long as what they were saying wasn't true, no one could hurt my family. People who know us would never believe such a thing about the McCutcheon name."

"I never meant to kill you," Jock wheezed. "I was perfectly clear, I only wanted you detained until you'd be too late to make the bid for the cattle contract. But that was all. Your ranch was already twice the size of mine. I was wrong . . ."

Both Sidney and Jock Jr. pulled away, their eyes wide.

Winston shook his head, his mouth twisted. "I figured his physical scars, as well as the guilt he had to carry, were punishment enough, so I never turned him in. He got what he deserved by his own hand."

"How did you figure out the truth?" Dustin asked, amazed at this turn of events. He wanted to comfort Sidney, to take her into his arms, but he felt she might be uncomfortable with her father right there. He'd wait until they were alone.

"Jock had been throwing out to anyone who would listen that a Rim Rock brand was on the horse of his attacker. That was all a lie, to put suspicion on me, but I didn't know that. I began questioning my men, to make sure none were involved in any way. I hadn't orchestrated the ambush, but that didn't mean someone from the ranch hadn't had a hand in it. I interviewed the men separately."

With hands on hips, Winston began to pace. "There was one man, Shorty Harris, who said he had a friend who worked for the Calhouns. Said if he heard anything, he'd let me know. Well, about a year later, he came into my office with a farfetched story, one I had no real proof was true until today. Jock Calhoun wanted the army contract so badly, he'd hired a gunman to make sure I never arrived at the fort. Shorty's friend at the Calhoun ranch had gone out with Jock early one morning with a saddlebag full of cash. Jock had him wait at the end of a canyon while he rode in alone. When the day was well spent, the ranch hand went looking. Found Calhoun near beat to death."

"Who said that?" Jock Jr. barked.

Winston stopped his pacing and shrugged. "Don't know; Shorty wouldn't say." He looked at Sidney's pa. "I guess you're the only one who can fill in the blanks, Jock. I think we're entitled."

"Pa?" Sidney asked, her voice low. Every limb shook badly.

Her principles be damned, she needs someone at her side. Dustin crossed the imaginary line separating the McCutcheons from the Calhouns and wrapped her in his arms.

She turned so she could see her father. "Is that true? What Mr. McCutcheon said? Was it you all along?"

Jock Calhoun just stood there, looking broken and old.

"Best to come clean, Jock," Winston said. "If you do, you may have time left to repair the damage you've done to your family."

Jock nodded. "Most of it."

Winston's face resembled a hard slab of granite. "I've kept your dirty little secret for all these years. I deserve to know." He glanced at Dustin. "Dustin too. The truth is the least you owe us."

"After the bushwhack, I was delirious for days, almost died. I must have spoken the McCutcheon name, because before I knew what had happened, word got out that a McCutcheon brand was on the attacker's horse. I didn't start the rumor."

Anger clenched Dustin's chest for all his father had endured. "But you could have stopped it!"

Jock nodded, his face tight. "The gunman I hired changed up the plan. Decided to take his payoff and skedaddle without doing the job, after he beat me to death, of course. My hate festered. Winning the contract meant you'd become the most powerful ranch in the territory. Every time I thought about coming clean, I couldn't keep my anger and disgust for myself from growing. I was filled with hate, for myself and for your success."

Sighing, Jock added, "As the years passed, I accepted that version as truth. Believed the lie with my whole heart. When my wife died during childbirth, to me, the tragedy was your fault,

McCutcheon. And every other disappointing thing that's happened to me since."

Dustin turned to his father. "Why didn't you tell me and Chaim?" he asked, still unable to understand that.

Winston shook his head. "I planned to when you were adults, but whenever I tried, the enormity of the betrayal stopped my words in my throat. I'm sorry."

With a sob, Sidney pulled from Dustin's arms and dashed down the street. Dustin started after her, but his father grabbed his arm.

"Give her a little time to absorb everything. We have other matters at hand that need attention. Like finding Noah Calhoun to see if he was the culprit who torched Knutson's barn."

Chapter Fifty-Two

Sidney paced across the rug in her room, sorting out everything she'd just heard. Her head ached with all the hurtful information rolling around inside, which came on top of last night, when her father and brother had relentlessly demanded she give up her disgraceful idea of marrying Dustin. *The enemy.* The son of the most hated double-crosser in Texas.

What a farce! And what a fool she'd been! How would she ever face Dustin after all the things she'd said about his father? Shame scalded her face.

And now Knutson's barn had been burned to the ground. Had Noah finally had enough and extracted his revenge?

Tears born of embarrassment and shame leaked from her eyes. Her father—a liar! Willing to defame a man's good name to cover his own misdeeds. How would she ever hold up her head again?

A soft knock sounded on her door.

Dustin?

She turned to stare at the barrier. Over an hour had passed since she'd learned the ugly truth.

Again, the knock. "Sidney, open the door."

Dustin.

"Go away." She couldn't face him now . . . or ever. Had he just chuckled? There was absolutely nothing funny about today.

"I'm not going away, sweetheart. Please open up. I don't think they'll take kindly when I kick in this really nice door."

He'll do it too. She crossed the room and then just stood, looking at the doorknob.

"Come on, darlin', I have a hankerin' to feel you in my arms."

God help her, she couldn't stop herself from needing that warm, languid voice. She pulled open the door. The moment she saw his face, everything gushed out of her in one earth-shattering cyclone of hurt.

Dustin scooped her up in his arms. He kicked the door closed with his boot, but she didn't care. Let Rainey Knutson talk. Let all the Knutsons talk. Heck, why stop there? Let all of Rio Wells talk. All she cared about was the warmth of Dustin's chest, the strength of his arms, and the love she felt seeping from his heart to hers.

"Shh," he crooned. His hand ran down her hair that hung free. "Shh. Everything will be all right. Now, if you were leaving with your pa and brother and going back to Santa Fe, then I'd say you had something to cry over. But you're not. And you don't. Come Saturday, we're getting married. I won't take no for an answer."

Dustin eyed the bed, pondering how much more comfortable laying her down would be, but worried she might think him forward. Closing the door was scandalous enough. Instead, he rocked her back and forth, and let her exorcise her grief so the past couldn't hinder their relationship once he set things into motion.

"That's only three days, honey. Three days, and you'll be Mrs. Dustin McCutcheon." He whistled. "I like the sound of that."

"I can't do it, Dustin," she cried against the front of his shirt. "I can't face your father, or your mother. Or Chaim, Madeline, and Becky. The ugly truth is all too hideous."

"What your pa did has nothing to do with you. I won't have you talking that way. Didn't you hear what your future father-in-law said? He'd kept the information to himself to protect you. If that's not love, I don't know what is."

She looked up into his face, her eyes a watery mess. "What about Noah? I can't bear any more bad news."

"Well, good. Because I don't have any. Noah didn't do a thing. He actually went out to stop trouble before it struck."

She wiped her eyes on his sleeve, making him smile. Having a wife of his own was going to be pretty darn nice. He was looking forward to it.

Somewhat mollified, Sidney pushed out of his embrace and stood facing him, her expression no-nonsense. "What do you mean?"

She looked so beautiful, he'd rather kiss her than talk, but he knew until this was put to bed, there'd be no sugar for him.

"Does the name Harry Brennon ring any bells?"

"Noah's school friend?"

Dustin nodded.

"The one who started the trouble in San Antonio?"

"The one and the same. Seems that troublemaker followed Noah to Rio Wells. Thought he'd extract his own revenge on the hateful McCutcheons. Couple of days ago, Brennon sent a note to Noah when he was working with John, telling him to meet him in town last night in the Black Silk Garter. He had an idea. Fearful Brennon would do some horrible deed before he could stop him, Noah sneaked out of the bunkhouse and took a horse. Rode into Rio Wells alone. He found Harry Brennon in the saloon, all right, as drunk as a skunk and passed out on the floor."

Dustin pulled her closer, enjoying the feel of her against him. "Brick, our ranch hand, was in the back of the barn when Noah went for a horse. Knowing I gave explicit orders that Calhoun wasn't allowed out alone, Brick followed. He hoped to catch Noah breaking the law. Instead, he followed him into the saloon, where he found Noah reviving his friend with black coffee. All this happened before the fire. Brick and Noah actually buried the hatchet, got to sharing stories and drinking whiskey to commemorate the moment. They slept through the fire completely."

He broke into a wide grin. "How's that for good news?"

"The barn, Dustin! Who set the fire?"

He enjoyed how she was hanging on his every word, and how he had her complete attention. Did she have any idea what tonight meant? The truth had cleared the way for their love. She was hurt now, but he'd make sure she got past that, and soon.

"Dustin!"

"Little Rainey Knutson. Whatever made that hoyden sneak out of the house with a lantern at the crack of dawn has her parents mystified. She went into John's barn, and a good-sized spider dropped onto her head from the loft. Terrified, she threw down the kerosene lantern, causing the place to burst into flames. She's damn lucky to be alive. Let that be a lesson to her."

"You found this all out in the few minutes we've been apart?"

"Few minutes? Almost an hour has passed, honey. That's fifty minutes too long. When I know my girl's hurting, I don't mess around."

She gazed up into his face. "I'll remember that next time I'm feeling neglected." She smiled, and a bolt of lightning scorched him all the way down to his boots.

"I'm waitin'."

After bestowing a shy smile, she went up on tiptoe and pressed her lips to his.

Chapter Fifty-Three

Saturday Evening

"**W**ell, Mother, I guess you got what you were wishing for," Dustin said, his arm possessively placed around the back of his gorgeous wife, keeping her clamped next to his side. They stood together in the Lillian Russell Room, where every table was occupied with wedding guests, drinking wine and eating cake.

Sidney wore a lemon-yellow gown borrowed from someone that fit her figure in a most enticing way. Her hair was piled seductively on top of her head, just begging for him to extract a few pins so the weighty mass could fall down around her shoulders. Dustin's thoughts kept straying upstairs to the room they'd share tonight.

"Sidney and I will be living at the ranch for the time being until we decide what we want to do. I hope you're happy."

"Your father and I are delighted beyond measure," his mother replied. The huge smile that had begun with the first note of the piano when Sidney came down the aisle to meet him was still in place. No tears for this mother. She was thrilled her oldest would finally begin propagating. "The more in the house, the merrier, I like to say. And now I have three daughters. What could be better?"

She smiled at Sidney, who was conspicuously quiet. Dinner had ended over an hour ago, and the quartet now played. They'd danced and talked with friends until time to make the toasts, which Chaim had accomplished with great aplomb.

Dustin glanced at his brother, who'd received word from Emmeline yesterday. He still hadn't had a chance to have a good heart-to-heart with Chaim, but he'd learned Emmeline wasn't returning to Rio Wells.

When the music started up again, Winston came over and extended a hand to his new daughter-in-law. "May I have this dance, Sidney?"

She blushed and stepped toward him. "Of course."

For a few minutes, Dustin watched them, marveling how fate had come full circle. He glanced over to the table where her kin sat. They'd been subdued since the truth had been exposed, pretty much staying in their hotel room most of the time.

Dustin was glad they had stuck around. With everything that had happened, their presence meant a lot to Sidney, even if many things needed to be worked through. She even asked her father to walk her down the aisle. Other than that, not much contact had happened between them.

Noah sat with Martha and Louise Brown, and Candy as well. The four looked to be having a time to remember.

"Will you please excuse me, Mother?"

"Of course, Dustin." She rubbed his arm, the tells of her sentimentality blossoming on her face. Wobbly lips, crunched forehead, watery eyes. "I'm so proud and happy for you. Sidney is the perfect match for you, and will keep you in line. I couldn't love her any more than I already do."

Dustin kissed her cheek and headed for Chaim, who relaxed against the back wall, watching the dancers. They stood together a few moments in silence and just enjoyed the view of Sidney waltzing in their father's arms.

"So, how ya doing?" Dustin asked. Even though Chaim tried to hide his pain, the reality was the devastation was written all over him, for all to see.

"Congratulations, brother," he replied. "She's a beautiful bride. You're a lucky man."

"That I am, but that's not what I asked. You received word from Emmeline yesterday. What're your plans?"

He rubbed a hand across his face and let go a long sigh. "Plans?"

"I know you, Chaim, so stop with the riddles. I'm feeling your pain, and I see a faraway look in your eyes."

He nodded. "You do. I'm leaving for a spell. Tonight, as a matter of fact. When this shindig is over."

Dustin sucked in a breath. He hadn't thought Chaim would do something so drastic. "You can't leave. We need you at the ranch."

"You have plenty of help with the new hand." He shook his head. "I won't be missed. Not really."

"Noah won't be here forever."

Chaim turned and looked Dustin square in the eye. "I'm not talking about *him*." He motioned across the expanse of tables to Sidney and their father on the dance floor.

The laugh that came from his mouth eased a little of the pain left in Dustin's heart. Chaim might have lost Emmeline, but not his sense of humor.

"And it's not like I'm going for good," Chaim added. "I'll be back sooner or later. Maybe I'll head up to Montana. See Y Knot for myself."

All the way to Montana? Dustin bit out a curse. "Don't do this, Chaim!"

"I lost her, Dustin," he whispered. "Tell me you'd just sit around here doing business as usual if Sidney had gone back to Santa Fe. Somehow, I don't see that happening."

Chaim had a point. A good one. But so soon? Tonight? Dustin wasn't ready to lose his little brother. Protectiveness welled up inside him.

"What was her reasoning?"

"Does it matter?"

Not really.

He shook his head. "Guess not. But I'll go with you. Sidney and I both will," he quickly amended when he realized how silly that sounded.

"Your destiny is here, making Ma and Pa happy with all the little ones you'll have. They've been waiting mighty long for grandbabies. You can't be following me over hill and dale."

No swaying his brother, but Dustin totally understood. "Have you told 'em yet?"

"No. Didn't want to spoil their time."

A heavy stone landed in the pit of Dustin's stomach. He didn't want Chaim to go. Without warning, he pulled his brother into an embrace.

"You be careful." He almost choked on his words as a burning heat stung the back of his eyes. "Don't get yourself hurt, or worse."

When he noted John and Lily on their way over to where he and Chaim stood, he pulled away and wiped his eyes. He was going to miss Chaim; he certainly would.

Chapter Fifty-Four

Three and a Half Weeks Later

Bundled in sheepskin coats, Sidney rode with Dustin into Rio Wells, both sets of saddlebags near bursting with gifts for their friends.

Christmas Eve was only ten days away. John and Lily were hosting a small gathering at the shop, just for a few close friends, to celebrate the coming holiday. The crisp air that turned Dustin's nose red had yet to fall below freezing. Even with a cranberry-colored beak, he was still the handsomest man she'd ever seen.

Sidney glanced down at Jackson trotting at their heels. "He looks tired," she said, unable to stop a rush of affection for the friend she'd had for many years. "Guess he's getting old."

Dustin looked her way, down at the animal, and then back up at her. He was relaxed back in the saddle, and for the last few days had let his beard grow in. She liked the look immensely.

"You worried about him?" He lifted a shoulder. "Looks fine to me."

"No, not worried. Just feeling emotional, I guess."

He smiled and shook his head. "Can't figure you out."

Rio Wells looked beautiful. Wreaths hung on doors and windows, and candles flickering in windowsills added to the ambience of the kerosene lights. As they passed by the livery, she saw Cradle in his upstairs window, combing his hair. He waved and smiled, getting ready for the same party they were headed to.

After reining up in front of the dress shop, she spotted Dustin, already dismounted, at the side of her horse. She arched a brow.

"Be nice. I like helping you down."

She hid her smile and put out her hand. Once on the ground, she barely had room between him and her gelding.

"See what I mean?" He leaned in and captured her lips. When he pulled away, he chuckled. "Gives me the advantage. Sometimes, a man's got to do what a man's got to do."

The door to the shop opened. "Stop your kissing and get in here, you two lovebirds," John called. "The air's quite nippy out there."

From inside, she could hear Dr. Bixby's voice as well as Tucker's as they talked about something. A giggle she didn't recognize melded with their laughter.

"Be right in," she called, working the knots holding her saddlebags.

Finished with his, Dustin aptly did her other side and hoisted both burdens over his shoulder.

Lily met them at the door. "You haven't been to town for two weeks," she scolded. "I've been impatiently waiting to see you."

John took their coats, and the women hugged.

Lily looked her over. "You appear wonderfully happy. I can't imagine why."

Sidney's cheeks warmed. The fact that everyone in the world knew what activities she and Dustin had been up to was a bit disconcerting.

She pushed away her embarrassment. "How're you faring in the shop without me? I feel terrible about leaving you shorthanded."

"Nonsense," Lily replied. "Business is a bit slower now, but with John's excitement over the new business, he thinks we may send for Giselle by this summer. Until then, he agrees I should look for another helper." Lily's face lit up. "Did you hear the good news? Mr. Knutson is paying for the bottles, barrels, and such that were destroyed in the fire. John's venture is moving right along. Now, no more worries. This is a party." She put her arm through Sidney's and pulled her toward the kitchen alcove.

"Merry Christmas!" old Doc Bixby hollered, a cup of punch in his hand. His bright red shirt was for once buttoned properly and tucked neatly into his dungarees.

Tucker stood hand in hand with a young woman Sidney didn't know. Her pixie face was wreathed in a warm smile.

"Come meet our girl, Maisy!" Bixby added, unable to hide his affection. "Actually, she's Tucker's girl, but she's like the daughter I never had." He winked at her. "We'll keep her."

The cinnamon-scented room filled with guests while Sidney sipped eggnog, nibbled on Christmas cookies, and watched the festivities going on around her. Her heart, near to bursting with love, shuddered as she watched Dustin, John, Cradle, and Noah in some kind of manly discussion. Madeline and Becky had stayed home, just getting over a sour stomach.

Noah still had a few more months before he'd earned enough to pay off his debt. She wondered what he would do when time came for him to go back to Santa Fe.

"Have you heard from Chaim?" Lily asked softly, appearing at her side. "I'm still so shocked at his sudden departure. Every morning and night, I pray that God will hold him close."

"I know what you mean. Everyone's worried. But we did have a telegram from him yesterday. He arrived safely in Galveston, and he and Brick are seeing the sights."

"Galveston! Why there?"

"Dustin couldn't figure that out either. Guess he wants to taste the boom of a large city. Who knows where he'll go next? We were all very relieved when Brick Paulson threw in with him. Dustin says he's a real good man. Good with a gun and straight in the head. Winston and Winnie were thrilled. Gave him their blessing to go along and promised he'd have a job, with a promotion, the moment they returned."

"That's all good news. And your sisters-in-law? How're they feeling? Better?"

"I believe so. Becky had the worst of it. I think they're both on the mend."

Lily winced and discreetly rubbed her stomach. "I pray I'm not coming down with anything. I don't want to miss Christmas. Every time I think I am, the feeling goes away. Strange."

Before Sidney could respond, the door opened again. Lily had said they weren't expecting anyone else. The shop was filled to its capacity already. In strode the Knutson girls, dressed to the hilt. When Lily saw them, she raised a hand to her mouth, her eyes wide.

At the strained moment, Misti—Sidney thought, she was never quite sure yet which girl was which—took a tentative step forward, followed by her four sisters. The nanny brought up the rear and lingered in the doorway.

Misti extended a tray of goodies to Lily. "Thank you for the kind invitation, Mrs. McCutcheon. Rainey was over the moon to bring us the news yesterday. I hope we're not too late."

As if just now realizing the mistake by the surprise on everyone's faces and the deadly quiet room, the young woman lowered her brows and her smile ebbed away. She cut a not-so-nice-glance to her little sister, who stood twisting back and forth with a mischievous grin on her face.

Lily quickly stepped forward, her signature smile drawing the attention of everyone in the room. Without missing a beat, she graciously took the dish of goodies from Misti Knutson's hands.

"We're so pleased you could make it, Miss Knutson." Lily's welcoming glance extended to the other four sisters, and then the nanny. "Please come in and warm up."

Dustin ambled over to Sidney's side. His fingers found hers and he gave a squeeze, drawing her attention up to his smiling gaze. She marveled again at the turn of events in her life, her magnificent husband, and her wonderful friends.

"Things around here sure have picked up since I went to San Antonio," he said. His gaze dropped to her lips and became a bit wicked. "I'm thinking I just might send Judge Halford a little note. Thank him on his sound decision-making. Think he'd like that, darlin'?"

His molasses-warm voice next to her ear made her shiver with want. She could barely eke the words past her lips. He knew very well the power he had over her. She was putty in his hands.

"He'd think you'd lost your mind."

Dustin laughed. "You're right. He would think that. And because he will, I'm writing that correspondence tomorrow morning first thing. Right after we—"

Sidney slapped her hand over his mouth, halting his words. The room was very crowded. Surely, someone would overhear the daring talk he so loved to use to color her cheeks.

He covered her hand with his, pulled her close, and kissed her palm.

"Dustin." She tensed, wishing to pull away, but he wouldn't let her.

"Yes, Mrs. McCutcheon?" He searched her eyes. "Do you have something to say? Are you complaining about my affections?"

Sidney smiled back and shook her head. Overwhelming wonder filled her heart as she gazed at Dustin McCutcheon, her husband, a man larger than the whole West combined.

"Never in this lifetime, Mr. McCutcheon. I love you."

Acknowledgements

Heartfelt gratitude goes out to so many special people for their help in creating *Texas Lonesome*, book eight of the McCutcheon Family series.

My fabulous editors, Pam Berehulke of Bulletproof Editing, and Linda Carroll-Bradd of Lustre Editing, for their wonderful suggestions, sharp eyes, and deep and thoughtful guidance to round this story out to its fullest.

To Sandy Loyd, Lisa Cooke, and Saralee Etter, my author friends and first readers who spotted the missing opportunities of the story that I'd never want to miss. You gals rock!

To Kelli Ann Morgan for the new cover designs of my whole series, and especially for *Lonesome*. I finally have my little Western town. If you look very closely, I even have riders moving along the dusty roads of Rio Wells.

To my formatter, Bob Houston, for never scolding me for all the re-dos I ask him to make.

To the Pioneer Hearts Facebook Group of authors and readers, for making me smile every single day.

To my husband, Michael, for taking up all the slack so I can get my two thousand words a day. Thank you so much!

My awesome family—Matthew, Rachel, Adam, Misti, and baby Evelyn—you all set the moon and stars.

My four older sisters who always have my back—Shelly (in heaven), Sherry, Jenny, and Mary. No youngest sister could ever have such a wonderful family. I love you all.

To the most awesome readers in the universe—I can't tell you what your love and enthusiasm means to me. It's everything!

And to our Awesome God for making all this possible in the first place!

About The Author

Caroline Fyffe was born in Waco, Texas, the first of many towns she would call home during her father's career with the US Air Force. A horse aficionado from an early age, she earned a Bachelor of Arts in communications from California State University-Chico before launching what would become a twenty-year career as an equine photographer. She began writing fiction to pass the time during long days in the show arena, channeling her love of horses and the Old West into a series of Western historicals. Her debut novel, *Where the Wind Blows*, won the Romance Writers of America's prestigious Golden Heart Award as well as the Wisconsin RWA's Write Touch Readers' Award. She and her husband have two grown sons and live in the Pacific Northwest.

Want news on releases, giveaways, and bonus reads? Sign up for
Caroline's newsletter at: www.carolinefyffe.com
See her Equine Photography: www.carolinefyffephoto.com
LIKE her FaceBook Author Page:
Facebook.com/CarolineFyffe
Twitter: @carolinefyffe
Write to her at: caroline@carolinefyffe.com

61677106R20216

Made in the USA
Lexington, KY
17 March 2017